KT-441-963

Go Down, Moses

WILLIAM FAULKNER

Go Down,
MOSES

VINTAGE BOOKS
A Division of Random House
New York

Cover photo by Robert Wenkam

Vintage Books Edition, April 1973

Copyright 1940, 1941, 1942 by William Faulkner

Copyright renewed 1968, 1969, 1970 by Estelle Faulkner
and Jill Faulkner Summers

All rights reserved under International and Pan-American
Copyright Conventions. Published in the United States
by Random House, Inc., New York. and simultaneously
in Canada by Random House of Canada Limited, Toronto.
Originally published by Random House, Inc., in 1942.

Some of these stories first appeared in *The Atlantic
Monthly, Harper's Magazine, Collier's, The Saturday
Evening Post* and *Story Magazine.*

Library of Congress Cataloging in Publication Data

Faulkner, William, 1897-1962.
  Go down, Moses.

  I. Title.
[PZ3.F272Go8] [PS3511.A86]   813'.5'2   72-8062
ISBN 0-394-71884-4

Manufactured in the United States of America

To Mammy

CAROLINE BARR
Mississippi
[1840–1940]

Who was born in slavery and who
gave to my family a fidelity without
stint or calculation of recompense
and to my childhood an immeasurable devotion and love

1S595:J7

CONTENTS

Was

1.

Isaac McCaslin, 'Uncle Ike', past seventy and nearer eighty than he ever corroborated any more, a widower now and uncle to half a county and father to no one

this was not something participated in or even seen by himself, but by his elder cousin, McCaslin Edmonds, grandson of Isaac's father's sister and so descended by the distaff, yet notwithstanding the inheritor, and in his time the bequestor, of that which some had thought then and some still thought should have been Isaac's, since his was the name in which the title to the land had first been granted from the Indian patent and which some of the descendants of his father's slaves still bore in the land. But Isaac was not one of these:—a widower these twenty years, who in all his life had owned but one object more than he could wear and carry in his pockets and his hands at one time, and this was the narrow iron cot and the stained lean mattress which he used camping in the woods for deer and bear or for fishing or simply because he loved the woods; who owned no property and never desired to since the earth was no man's but all men's, as light and air and weather were; who lived still in the cheap frame bungalow in Jefferson which his wife's father gave them

on their marriage and which his wife had willed to him at
her death and which he had pretended to accept, acquiesce
to, to humor her, ease her going but which was not his,
will or not, chancery dying wishes mortmain possession or
whatever, himself merely holding it for his wife's sister and
her children who had lived in it with him since his wife's
death, holding himself welcome to live in one room of it
as he had during his wife's time or she during her time
or the sister-in-law and her children during the rest of
his and after

    not something he had participated in or even remem-
bered except from the hearing, the listening, come to him
through and from his cousin McCaslin born in 1850 and
sixteen years his senior and hence, his own father being
near seventy when Isaac, an only child, was born, rather
his brother than cousin and rather his father than either,
out of the old time, the old days

2.

When he and Uncle Buck ran back to the house from
discovering that Tomey's Turl had run again, they heard
Uncle Buddy cursing and bellowing in the kitchen, then
the fox and the dogs came out of the kitchen and crossed
the hall into the dogs' room and they heard them run
through the dogs' room into his and Uncle Buck's room
then they saw them cross the hall again into Uncle Buddy's
room and heard them run through Uncle Buddy's room
into the kitchen again and this time it sounded like the
whole kitchen chimney had come down and Uncle Buddy
bellowing like a steamboat blowing and this time the fox
and the dogs and five or six sticks of firewood all came out

of the kitchen together with Uncle Buddy in the middle of them hitting at everything in sight with another stick. It was a good race.

When he and Uncle Buck ran into their room to get Uncle Buck's necktie, the fox had treed behind the clock on the mantel. Uncle Buck got the necktie from the drawer and kicked the dogs off and lifted the fox down by the scruff of the neck and shoved it back into the crate under the bed and they went to the kitchen, where Uncle Buddy was picking the breakfast up out of the ashes and wiping it off with his apron. "What in damn's hell do you mean," he said, "turning that damn fox out with the dogs all loose in the house?"

"Damn the fox," Uncle Buck said. "Tomey's Turl has broke out again. Give me and Cass some breakfast quick. We might just barely catch him before he gets there."

Because they knew exactly where Tomey's Turl had gone, he went there every time he could slip off, which was about twice a year. He was heading for Mr Hubert Beauchamp's place just over the edge of the next county, that Mr Hubert's sister, Miss Sophonsiba (Mr Hubert was a bachelor too, like Uncle Buck and Uncle Buddy) was still trying to make people call Warwick after the place in England that she said Mr Hubert was probably the true earl of only he never even had enough pride, not to mention energy, to take the trouble to establish his just rights. Tomey's Turl would go there to hang around Mr Hubert's girl, Tennie, until somebody came and got him. They couldn't keep him at home by buying Tennie from Mr Hubert because Uncle Buck said he and Uncle Buddy had so many niggers already that they could hardly walk around on their own land for them, and they couldn't sell Tomey's Turl to Mr Hubert because Mr Hubert said he not only wouldn't buy Tomey's Turl, he wouldn't have that damn white half-McCaslin on his place even as a free gift, not even if Uncle Buck and Uncle Buddy were to pay board and keep for him. And if somebody didn't go and get Tomey's Turl right away, Mr Hubert would fetch him back himself, bringing Miss Sophonsiba, and they would stay for a week or longer, Miss Sophonsiba living in Uncle Buddy's room and Uncle Buddy moved clean out of the house, sleeping in one of the cabins in the quarters where the niggers used to live in his great-grandfather's time until his great-grandfather died and Uncle Buck and Uncle Buddy moved all the niggers into the big house which his great-grandfather had not had time to finish, and not even doing the cooking while they were there and not even coming to the house any more except to sit on the front gallery after supper, sitting in the darkness between Mr Hubert and Uncle Buck until after a while even Mr Hubert would give up telling how many more head of niggers and acres of land he would add to what he would give Miss Sophonsiba when she married, and go to bed. And one midnight last summer Uncle Buddy just happened by accident to be awake and hear Mr Hubert drive out of the lot and by the time he waked them and they got Miss Sophonsiba up and dressed and the team put to the wagon and caught Mr Hubert, it was almost daylight. So it was always he and Uncle Buck who went to fetch Tomey's Turl because Uncle Buddy never went anywhere, not even to town and not even to fetch Tomey's Turl from Mr Hubert's, even though they all knew that Uncle Buddy could have risked it ten times as much as Uncle Buck could have dared.

They ate breakfast fast. Uncle Buck put on his necktie while they were running toward the lot to catch the horses. The only time he wore the necktie was on Tomey's Turl's account and he hadn't even had it out of the drawer since that night last summer when Uncle Buddy had waked them in the dark and said, "Get up out of that bed and damn quick." Uncle Buddy didn't own a necktie at all; Uncle Buck said Uncle Buddy wouldn't take that chance even in a section like theirs, where ladies were so damn seldom thank God that a man could ride for days in a straight line without having to dodge a single one. His grandmother (she was Uncle Buck's and Uncle Buddy's sister; she had raised him following his mother's death. That was where he had got his christian name: McCaslin, Carothers McCaslin Edmonds) said that Uncle Buck and Uncle Buddy both used the necktie just as another way of daring people to say they looked like twins, because even at sixty they would still fight anyone who claimed he could not tell them apart; whereupon his father had answered that any man who ever played poker once with Uncle Buddy would never mistake him again for Uncle Buck or anybody else.

Jonas had the two horses saddled and waiting. Uncle Buck didn't mount a horse like he was any sixty years old either, lean and active as a cat, with his round, close-cropped white head and his hard little gray eyes and his white-stubbled jaw, his foot in the iron and the horse already moving, already running at the open gate when Uncle Buck came into the seat. He scrabbled up too, onto the shorter pony, before Jonas could boost him up, clapping the pony with his heels into its own stiff, short-coupled canter, out the gate after Uncle Buck, when

Uncle Buddy (he hadn't even noticed him) stepped out from the gate and caught the bit. "Watch him," Uncle Buddy said. "Watch Theophilus. The minute anything begins to look wrong, you ride to hell back here and get me. You hear?"

"Yes, sir," he said. "Lemme go now. I wont even ketch Uncle Buck, let alone Tomey's Turl——"

Uncle Buck was riding Black John, because if they could just catch sight of Tomey's Turl at least one mile from Mr Hubert's gate, Black John would ride him down in two minutes. So when they came out on the long flat about three miles from Mr Hubert's, sure enough, there was Tomey's Turl on the Jake mule about a mile ahead. Uncle Buck flung his arm out and back, reining in, crouched on the big horse, his little round head and his gnarled neck thrust forward like a cooter's. "Stole away!" he whispered. "You stay back where he wont see you and flush. I'll circle him through the woods and we will bay him at the creek ford."

He waited until Uncle Buck had vanished into the woods. Then he went on. But Tomey's Turl saw him. He closed in too fast; maybe he was afraid he wouldn't be there in time to see him when he treed. It was the best race he had ever seen. He had never seen old Jake go that fast, and nobody had ever known Tomey's Turl to go faster than his natural walk, even riding a mule. Uncle Buck whooped once from the woods, running on sight, then Black John came out of the trees, driving, soupled out flat and level as a hawk, with Uncle Buck right up behind his ears now and yelling so that they looked exactly like a big black hawk with a sparrow riding it, across the field and over the ditch and across the next field, and he was running too; the mare went out before he even knew she was ready, and he was yelling too. Because, being a nigger, Tomey's Turl should have jumped down and run for it afoot as soon as he saw them. But he didn't; maybe Tomey's Turl had been running off from Uncle Buck for so long that he had even got used to running away like a white man would do it. And it was like he and old Jake had added Tomey's Turl's natural walking speed to the best that old Jake had ever done in his life, and it was just exactly enough to beat Uncle Buck to the ford. Because when he and the pony arrived, Black John was blown and lathered and Uncle Buck was down, leading him around in a circle to slow him down, and they could already hear Mr Hubert's dinner horn a mile away.

Only, for a while Tomey's Turl didn't seem to be at Mr Hubert's either. The boy was still sitting on the gatepost, blowing the horn—there was no gate there; just two posts and a nigger boy about his size sitting on one of them, blowing a fox-horn; this was what Miss Sophonsiba was still reminding people was named Warwick even when they had already known for a long time that's what she aimed to have it called, until when they wouldn't call it Warwick she wouldn't even seem to know what they were talking about and it would sound as if she and Mr Hubert owned two separate plantations covering the same area of ground, one on top of the other. Mr Hubert was sitting in the spring-house with his boots off and his feet in the water, drinking a toddy. But nobody there had seen Tomey's Turl; for a time it looked like Mr Hubert couldn't even place who Uncle Buck was talking about. "Oh, that nigger," he said at last. "We'll find him after dinner."

Only it didn't seem as if they were going to eat either.

Mr Hubert and Uncle Buck had a toddy, then Mr Hubert finally sent to tell the boy on the gate post he could quit blowing, and he and Uncle Buck had another toddy and Uncle Buck still saying, "I just want my nigger. Then we got to get on back toward home."

"After dinner," Mr Hubert said. "If we dont start him somewhere around the kitchen, we'll put the dogs on him. They'll find him if it's in the power of mortal Walker dogs to do it."

But at last a hand began waving a handkerchief or something white through the broken place in an upstairs shutter. They went to the house, crossing the back gallery, Mr Hubert warning them again, as he always did, to watch out for the rotted floor-board he hadn't got around to having fixed yet. Then they stood in the hall, until presently there was a jangling and swishing noise and they began to smell the perfume, and Miss Sophonsiba came down the stairs. Her hair was roached under a lace cap; she had on her Sunday dress and beads and a red ribbon around her throat and a little nigger girl carrying her fan and he stood quietly a little behind Uncle Buck, watching her lips until they opened and he could see the roan tooth. He had never known anyone before with a roan tooth and he remembered how one time his grandmother and his father were talking about Uncle Buddy and Uncle Buck and his grandmother said that Miss Sophonsiba had matured into a fine-looking woman once. Maybe she had. He didn't know. He wasn't but nine.

"Why, Mister Theophilus," she said. "And McCaslin," she said. She had never looked at him and she wasn't talking to him and he knew it, although he was prepared and balanced to drag his foot when Uncle Buck did. "Welcome to Warwick."

He and Uncle Buck dragged their foot. "I just come to get my nigger," Uncle Buck said. "Then we got to get on back home."

Then Miss Sophonsiba said something about a bumble-bee, but he couldn't remember that. It was too fast and there was too much of it, the earrings and beads clashing and jingling like little trace chains on a toy mule trotting and the perfume stronger too, like the earrings and beads sprayed it out each time they moved and he watched the roan-colored tooth flick and glint between her lips; something about Uncle Buck was a bee sipping from flower to flower and not staying long anywhere and all that stored sweetness to be wasted on Uncle Buddy's desert air, calling Uncle Buddy Mister Amodeus like she called Uncle Buck Mister Theophilus, or maybe the honey was being stored up against the advent of a queen and who was the lucky queen and when? "Ma'am?" Uncle Buck said. Then Mr Hubert said:

"Hah. A buck bee. I reckon that nigger's going to think he's a buck hornet, once he lays hands on him. But I reckon what Buck's thinking about sipping right now is some meat gravy and biscuit and a cup of coffee. And so am I."

They went into the dining room and ate and Miss Sophonsiba said how seriously now neighbors just a half day's ride apart ought not to go so long as Uncle Buck did, and Uncle Buck said Yessum, and Miss Sophonsiba said Uncle Buck was just a confirmed roving bachelor from the cradle born and this time Uncle Buck even quit chewing and looked and said, Yes, ma'am, he sure was, and born too late at it to ever change now but at least he could thank God no lady would ever have to suffer the misery of living with him and Uncle Buddy, and Miss Sophonsiba said ah, that maybe Uncle Buck just aint met the woman yet who would not only accept what Uncle Buck was pleased to call misery, but who would make Uncle Buck consider even his freedom a small price to pay, and Uncle Buck said, "Nome. Not yet."

Then he and Mr. Hubert and Uncle Buck went out to the front gallery and sat down. Mr Hubert hadn't even got done taking his shoes off again and inviting Uncle Buck to take his off, when Miss Sophonsiba came out the door carrying a tray with another toddy on it. "Damnit, Sibbey," Mr Hubert said. "He's just et. He dont want to drink that now." But Miss Sophonsiba didn't seem to hear him at all. She stood there, the roan tooth not flicking now but fixed because she wasn't talking now, handing the toddy to Uncle Buck until after a while she said how her papa always said nothing sweetened a Missippi toddy like the hand of a Missippi lady and would Uncle Buck like to see how she use to sweeten her papa's toddy for him? She lifted the toddy and took a sip of it and handed it again to Uncle Buck and this time Uncle Buck took it. He dragged his foot again and drank the toddy and said if Mr Hubert was going to lay down, he would lay down a while too, since from the way things looked Tomey's Turl was fixing to give them a long hard race unless Mr Hubert's dogs were a considerable better than they used to be.

Mr Hubert and Uncle Buck went into the house. After a while he got up too and went around to the back yard to wait for them. The first thing he saw was

Tomey's Turl's head slipping along above the lane fence. But when he cut across the yard to turn him, Tomey's Turl wasn't even running. He was squatting behind a bush, watching the house, peering around the bush at the back door and the upstairs windows, not whispering exactly but not talking loud either: "Whut they doing now?"

"They're taking a nap now," he said. "But never mind that; they're going to put the dogs on you when they get up."

"Hah," Tomey's Turl said. "And nem you mind that neither. I got protection now. All I needs to do is to keep Old Buck from ketching me unto I gets the word."

"What word?" he said. "Word from who? Is Mr Hubert going to buy you from Uncle Buck?"

"Huh," Tomey's Turl said again. "I got more protection than whut Mr Hubert got even." He rose to his feet. "I gonter tell you something to remember: anytime you wants to git something done, from hoeing out a crop to getting married, just get the womenfolks to working at it. Then all you needs to do is set down and wait. You member that."

Then Tomey's Turl was gone. And after a while he went back to the house. But there wasn't anything but the snoring coming out of the room where Uncle Buck and Mr Hubert were, and some more light-sounding snoring coming from upstairs. He went to the spring-house and sat with his feet in the water as Mr Hubert had been doing, because soon now it would be cool enough for a race. And sure enough, after a while Mr Hubert and Uncle Buck came out onto the back gallery, with Miss Sophonsiba right behind them with the toddy tray only this time Uncle Buck drank his before Miss Sophonsiba had time to sweeten it, and Miss Sophonsiba told them to get back early, that all Uncle Buck knew of Warwick was just dogs and niggers and now that she had him, she wanted to show him her garden that Mr Hubert and nobody else had any sayso in. "Yessum," Uncle Buck said. "I just want to catch my nigger. Then we got to get on back home."

Four or five niggers brought up the three horses. They could already hear the dogs waiting still coupled in the lane, and they mounted and went on down the lane, toward the quarters, with Uncle Buck already out in front of even the dogs. So he never did know just when and where they jumped Tomey's Turl, whether he flushed out of one of the cabins or not. Uncle Buck was away out in front on Black John and they hadn't even cast the dogs yet when Uncle Buck roared, "Gone away! I godfrey, he broke cover then!" and Black John's feet clapped four times like pistol shots while he was gathering to go out, then he and Uncle Buck vanished over the hill like they had run at the blank edge of the world itself. Mr Hubert was roaring too: "Gone away! Cast them!" and they all piled over the crest of the hill just in time to see Tomey's Turl away out across the flat, almost to the woods, and the dogs streaking down the hill and out onto the flat. They just tongued once and when they came boiling up around Tomey's Turl it looked like they were trying to jump up and lick him in the face until even Tomey's Turl slowed down and he and the dogs all went into the woods together, walking, like they were going home from a rabbit hunt. And when they caught up with Uncle Buck in the woods, there was no Tomey's Turl and no dogs either, nothing but old Jake about a half an hour later, hitched in a clump of bushes with Tomey's Turl's coat tied on him for a saddle and near a half bushel of Mr Hubert's oats scattered around on the ground that old Jake never even had enough appetite left to nuzzle up and spit back out again. It wasn't any race at all.

"We'll get him tonight though," Mr Hubert said. "We'll bait for him. We'll throw a picquet of niggers and dogs around Tennie's house about midnight, and we'll get him."

"Tonight, hell," Uncle Buck said. "Me and Cass and that nigger all three are going to be half way home by dark. Aint one of your niggers got a fyce or something that will trail them hounds?"

"And fool around here in the woods for half the night too?" Mr Hubert said. "When I'll bet you five hundred dollars that all you got to do to catch that nigger is to walk up to Tennie's cabin after dark and call him?"

"Five hundred dollars?" Uncle Buck said. "Done! Because me and him neither one are going to be anywhere near Tennie's house by dark. Five hundred dollars!" He and Mr Hubert glared at one another.

"Done!" Mr Hubert said.

So they waited while Mr Hubert sent one of the niggers back to the house on old Jake and in about a half an hour the nigger came back with a little bob-tailed black fyce and a new bottle of whisky. Then he rode up to Uncle Buck and held something out to him wrapped in a piece of paper. "What?" Uncle Buck said.

"It's for you," the nigger said. Then Uncle Buck took it and unwrapped it. It was the piece of red ribbon that had been on Miss Sophonsiba's neck and Uncle Buck sat there on Black John, holding the ribbon like it was a little water moccasin only he wasn't going to let anybody see he was afraid of it, batting his eyes fast at the nigger. Then he stopped batting his eyes.

"What for?" he said.

"She just sont hit to you," the nigger said. "She say to tell you 'success'."

"She said what?" Uncle Buck said.

"I dont know, sir," the nigger said. "She just say 'success'."

"Oh," Uncle Buck said. And the fyce found the hounds. They heard them first, from a considerable distance. It was just before sundown and they were not trailing, they were making the noise dogs make when they want to get out of something. They found what that was too. It was a ten-foot-square cotton-house in a field about two miles from Mr Hubert's house and all eleven of the dogs were inside it and the door wedged with a chunk of wood. They watched the dogs come boiling out when the nigger opened the door, Mr Hubert sitting his horse and looking at the back of Uncle Buck's neck.

"Well, well," Mr Hubert said. "That's something, anyway. You can use them again now. They dont seem to have no more trouble with your nigger than he seems to have with them."

"Not enough," Uncle Buck said. "That means both of them. I'll stick to the fyce."

"All right," Mr Hubert said. Then he said, "Hell, 'Filus, come on. Let's go eat supper. I tell you, all you got to do to catch that nigger is——"

"Five hundred dollars," Uncle Buck said.

"What?" Mr Hubert said. He and Uncle Buck looked at each other. They were not glaring now. They were not joking each other either. They sat there in the beginning of twilight, looking at each other, just blinking a little. "What five hundred dollars?" Mr Hubert said. "That you wont catch that nigger in Tennie's cabin at midnight tonight?"

"That me or that nigger neither aint going to be near nobody's house but mine at midnight tonight." Now they did glare at each other.

"Five hundred dollars," Mr Hubert said. "Done."

"Done," Uncle Buck said.

"Done," Mr Hubert said.

"Done," Uncle Buck said

So Mr Hubert took the dogs and some of the niggers and went back to the house. Then he and Uncle Buck and the nigger with the fyce went on, the nigger leading old Jake with one hand and holding the fyce's leash (it was a piece of gnawed plowline) with the other. Now Uncle Buck let the fyce smell Tomey's Turl's coat; it was like for the first time now the fyce found out what they were after and they would have let him off the leash and kept up with him on the horses, only about that time the nigger boy began blowing the fox-horn for supper at the house and they didn't dare risk it.

Then it was full dark. And then—he didn't know how much later nor where they were, how far from the house, except that it was a good piece and it had been dark for good while and they were still going on, with Uncle Buck leaning down from time to time to let the fyce have another smell of Tomey's Turl's coat while Uncle Buck took another drink from the whisky bottle—they found that Tomey's Turl had doubled and was making a long swing back toward the house. "I godfrey, we've got him," Uncle

Buck said. "He's going to earth. We'll cut back to the house and head him before he can den." So they left the nigger to cast the fyce and follow him on old Jake, and he and Uncle Buck rode for Mr Hubert's, stopping on the hills to blow the horses and listen to the fyce down in the creek bottom where Tomey's Turl was still making his swing.

But they never caught him. They reached the dark quarters; they could see lights still burning in Mr Hubert's house and somebody was blowing the fox-horn again and it wasn't any boy and he had never heard a fox-horn sound mad before either, and he and Uncle Buck scattered out on the slope below Tennie's cabin. Then they heard the fyce, not trailing now but yapping, about a mile away, then the nigger whooped and they knew the fyce had faulted. It was at the creek. They hunted the banks both ways for more than an hour, but they couldn't straighten Tomey's Turl out. At last even Uncle Buck gave up and they started back toward the house, the fyce riding too now, in front of the nigger on the mule. They were just coming up the lane to the quarters; they could see on along the ridge to where Mr Hubert's house was all dark now, when all of a sudden the fyce gave a yelp and jumped down from old Jake and hit the ground running and yelling every jump, and Uncle Buck was down too and had snatched him off the pony almost before he could clear his feet from the irons, and they ran too, on past the dark cabins toward the one where the fyce had treed. "We got him!" Uncle Buck said. "Run around to the back. Dont holler; just grab up a stick and knock on the back door, loud."

Afterward, Uncle Buck admitted that it was his own

mistake, that he had forgotten when even a little child should have known: not ever to stand right in front of or right behind a nigger when you scare him; but always to stand to one side of him. Uncle Buck forgot that. He was standing facing the front door and right in front of it, with the fyce right in front of him yelling fire and murder every time it could draw a new breath; he said the first he knew was when the fyce gave a shriek and whirled and Tomey's Turl was right behind it. Uncle Buck said he never even saw the door open; that the fyce just screamed once and ran between his legs and then Tomey's Turl ran right clean over him. He never even bobbled; he knocked Uncle Buck down and then caught him before he fell without even stopping, snatched him up under one arm, still running, and carried him along for about ten feet, saying, "Look out of here, old Buck. Look out of here, old Buck," before he threw him away and went on. By that time they couldn't even hear the fyce any more at all.

Uncle Buck wasn't hurt; it was only the wind knocked out of him where Tomey's Turl had thrown him down on his back. But he had been carrying the whisky bottle in his back pocket, saving the last drink until Tomey's Turl was captured, and he refused to move until he knew for certain if it was just whisky and not blood. So Uncle Buck laid over on his side easy, and he knelt behind him and raked the broken glass out of his pocket. Then they went on to the house. They walked. The nigger came up with the horses, but nobody said anything to Uncle Buck about riding again. They couldn't hear the fyce at all now. "He was going fast, all right," Uncle Buck said.

"But I dont believe that even he will catch that fyce, I godfrey, what a night."

"We'll catch him tomorrow," he said.

"Tomorrow, hell," Uncle Buck said. "We'll be at home tomorrow. And the first time Hubert Beauchamp or that nigger either one set·foot on my land, I'm going to have them arrested for trespass and vagrancy."

The house was dark. They could hear Mr Hubert snoring good now, as if he had settled down to road-gaiting at it. But they couldn't hear anything from upstairs, even when they were inside the dark hall, at the foot of the stairs. "Likely hers will be at the back," Uncle Buck said. "Where she can holler down to the kitchen without having to get up. Besides, an unmarried lady will sholy have her door locked with strangers in the house." So Uncle Buck eased himself down onto the bottom step, and he knelt and drew Uncle Buck's boots off. Then he removed his own and set them against the wall, and he and Uncle Buck mounted the stairs, feeling their way up and into the upper hall. It was dark too, and still there was no sound anywhere except Mr Hubert snoring below, so they felt their way along the hall toward the front of the house, until they felt a door. They could hear nothing beyond the door, and when Uncle Buck tried the knob, it opened. "All right," Uncle Buck whispered. "Be quiet." They could see a little now, enough to see the shape of the bed and the mosquito-bar. Uncle Buck threw down his suspenders and unbuttoned his trousers and went to the bed and eased himself carefully down onto the edge of it, and he knelt again and drew Uncle Buck's trousers off and he was just removing his own when Uncle Buck lifted the mosquito-bar and raised his feet and rolled into the bed.

That was when Miss Sophonsiba sat up on the other side of Uncle Buck and gave the first scream.

3.

When he reached home just before dinner time the next day, he was just about worn out. He was too tired to eat, even if Uncle Buddy had waited to eat dinner first; he couldn't have stayed on the pony another mile without going to sleep. In fact, he must have gone to sleep while he was telling Uncle Buddy, because the next thing he knew it was late afternoon and he was lying on some hay in the jolting wagon-bed, with Uncle Buddy sitting on the seat above him exactly the same way he sat a horse or sat in his rocking chair before the kitchen hearth while he was cooking, holding the whip exactly as he held the spoon or fork he stirred and tasted with. Uncle Buddy had some cold bread and meat and a jug of buttermilk wrapped in damp towsacks waiting when he waked up. He ate, sitting in the wagon in almost the last of the afternoon. They must have come fast, because they were not more than two miles from Mr Hubert's. Uncle Buddy waited for him to eat. Then he said, "Tell me again," and he told it again: how he and Uncle Buck finally found a room without anybody in it, and Uncle Buck sitting on the side of the bed saying, "O godfrey, Cass. O godfrey, Cass," and then they heard Mr Hubert's feet on the stairs and watched the light come down the hall and Mr Hubert came in, in his nightshirt, and walked over and set the candle on the table and stood looking at Uncle Buck.

"Well, 'Filus," he said. "She's got you at last."

"It was an accident," Uncle Buck said. "I swear to god-frey——"

"Hah," Mr Hubert said. "Dont tell me. Tell her that."

"I did," Uncle Buck said. "I did tell her. I swear to god——"

"Sholy," Mr Hubert said. "And just listen." They listened a minute. He had been hearing her all the time. She was nowhere near as loud as at first; she was just steady. "Dont you want to go back in there and tell her again it was an accident, that you never meant nothing and to just excuse you and forget about it? All right."

"All right what?" Uncle Buck said.

"Go back in there and tell her again," Mr Hubert said. Uncle Buck looked at Mr Hubert for a minute. He batted his eyes fast.

"Then what will I come back and tell you?" he said

"To me?" Mr Hubert said. "I would call that a horse of another color. Wouldn't you?"

Uncle Buck looked at Mr Hubert. He batted his eyes fast again. Then he stopped again. "Wait," he said. "Be reasonable. Say I did walk into a lady's bedroom, even Miss Sophonsiba's; say, just for the sake of the argument, there wasn't no other lady in the world but her and so I walked into hers and tried to get in bed with her, would I have took a nine-year-old boy with me?"

"Reasonable is just what I'm being," Mr Hubert said. "You come into bear-country of your own free will and ac-cord. All right; you were a grown man and you knew it was bear-country and you knew the way back out like you knew the way in and you had your chance to take it. But no. You had to crawl into the den and lay down by the bear. And whether you did or didn't know the bear was in it dont make any difference. So if you got back out of that den without even a claw-mark on you, I would not only be unreasonable, I'd be a damned fool. After all, I'd like a little peace and quiet and freedom myself, now I got a chance for it. Yes, sir. She's got you, 'Filus, and you know it. You run a hard race and you run a good one, but you skun the hen-house one time too many."

"Yes," Uncle Buck said. He drew his breath in and let it out again, slow and not loud. But you could hear it. "Well," he said. "So I reckon I'll have to take the chance then."

"You already took it," Mr Hubert said. "You did that when you cam back here." Then he stopped too. Then he batted his eyes, but only about six times. Then he stopped and looked at Uncle Buck for more than a minute. "What chance?" he said.

"That five hundred dollars," Uncle Buck said.

"What five hundred dollars?" Mr Hubert said. He and Uncle Buck looked at one another. Now it was Mr Hubert that batted his eyes again and then stopped again. "I thought you said you found him in Tennie's cabin."

"I did," Uncle Buck said. "What you bet me was I would catch him there. If there had been ten of me standing in front of that door, we wouldn't have caught him." Mr Hubert blinked at Uncle Buck, slow and steady.

"So you aim to hold me to that fool bet," he said.

"You took your chance too," Uncle Buck said. Mr. Hubert blinked at Uncle Buck. Then he stopped. Then he went and took the candle from the table and went out. They sat on the edge of the bed and watched the light go down the hall and heard Mr Hubert's feet on the stairs. After a while they began to see the light again and they heard Mr Hubert's feet coming back up the stairs. Then Mr Hubert entered and went to the table and set the candle down and laid a deck of cards by it.

"One hand," he said. "Draw. You shuffle, I cut, this boy deals. Five hundred dollars against Sibbey. And we'll settle this nigger business once and for all too. If you win, you buy Tennie; if I win, I buy that boy of yours. The price will be the same for each one: three hundred dollars."

"Win?" Uncle Buck said. "The one that wins buys the niggers?"

"Wins Sibbey, damn it!" Mr Hubert said. "Wins Sibbey! What the hell else are we setting up till midnight arguing about? The lowest hand wins Sibbey and buys the niggers."

"All right," Uncle Buck said. "I'll buy the damn girl then and we'll call the rest of this foolishness off."

"Hah," Mr Hubert said again. "This is the most serious foolishness you ever took part in in your life. No. You said you wanted your chance, and now you've got it. Here it is, right here on this table, waiting on you."

So Uncle Buck shuffled the cards and Mr Hubert cut them. Then he took up the deck and dealt in turn until Uncle Buck and Mr Hubert had five. And Uncle Buck looked at his hand a long time and then said two cards and he gave them to him, and Mr Hubert looked at his hand quick and said one card and he gave it to him and Mr Hubert flipped his discard onto the two which Uncle Buck had discarded and slid the new card into his hand and opened it out and looked at it quick again and closed it and looked at Uncle Buck and said, "Well? Did you help them threes?"

"No," Uncle Buck said.

"Well I did," Mr Hubert said. He shot his hand across the table so that the cards fell face-up in front of Uncle Buck and they were three kings and two fives, and said, "By God, Buck McCaslin, you have met your match at last."

"And that was all?" Uncle Buddy said. It was late then, near sunset; they would be at Mr Hubert's in another fifteen minutes.

"Yes, sir," he said, telling that too: how Uncle Buck waked him at daylight and he climbed out a window and got the pony and left, and how Uncle Buck said that if they pushed him too close in the meantime, he would climb down the gutter too and hide in the woods until Uncle Buddy arrived.

"Hah," Uncle Buddy said. "Was Tomey's Turl there?"

"Yes, sir," he said. "He was waiting in the stable when I got the pony. He said, 'Aint they settled it yet?'"

"And what did you say?" Uncle Buddy said.

"I said, 'Uncle Buck looks like he's settled. But Uncle Buddy aint got here yet.'"

"Hah," Uncle Buddy said.

And that was about all. They reached the house. Maybe Uncle Buck was watching them, but if he was, he never showed himself, never came out of the woods. Miss Sophonsiba was nowhere in sight either, so at least Uncle Buck hadn't quite given up; at least he hadn't asked her yet. And he and Uncle Buddy and Mr Hubert ate supper and they came in from the kitchen and cleared the table, leaving only the lamp on it and the deck of cards. Then it was just like last night, except that Uncle Buddy had no necktie and Mr Hubert wore clothes now instead of a nightshirt and it was a shaded lamp on the table instead of a candle, and Mr Hubert sitting at his end of the table with the deck in his hands, riffling the edges with his thumb and looking at Uncle Buddy. Then he tapped the edges even and set the deck out in the middle of the table, under the lamp, and folded his arms on the edge of the table and leaned forward a little on the table, looking at Uncle Buddy, who was sitting at his end of the table with his hands in his lap, all one gray color, like an old gray rock or a stump with gray moss on it, that still, with his round white head like Uncle Buck's but he didn't blink like Uncle Buck and he was a little thicker than Uncle Buck, as if from sitting down so much watching food cook, as if the things he cooked had made him a little thicker than he would have been and the things he cooked with, the flour and such, had made him all one same quiet color.

"Little toddy before we start?" Mr Hubert said.

"I dont drink," Uncle Buddy said.

"That's right," Mr Hubert said. "I knew there was some-thing else besides just being woman-weak that makes 'Filus seem human. But no matter." He batted his eyes twice at Uncle Buddy. "Buck McCaslin against the land and nig-gers you have heard me promise as Sophonsiba's dowry on the day she marries. If I beat you, 'Filus marries Sibbey without any dowry. If you beat me, you get 'Filus. But I still get the three hundred dollars 'Filus owes me for Tennie. Is that correct?"

"That's correct," Uncle Buddy said.

"Stud," Mr Hubert said. "One hand. You to shuffle, me to cut, this boy to deal."

"No," Uncle Buddy said. "Not Cass. He's too young. I dont want him mixed up in any gambling."

"Hah," Mr Hubert said. "It's said that a man playing

cards with Amodeus McCaslin aint gambling. But no matter." But he was still looking at Uncle Buddy; he never even turned his head when he spoke: "Go to the back door and holler. Bring the first creature that answers, animal mule or human, that can deal ten cards."

So he went to the back door. But he didn't have to call because Tomey's Turl was squatting against the wall just outside the door, and they returned to the dining-room where Mr Hubert still sat with his arms folded on his side of the table and Uncle Buddy sat with his hands in his lap on his side and the deck of cards face-down under the lamp between them. Neither of them even looked up when he and Tomey's Turl entered. "Shuffle," Mr Hubert said. Uncle Buddy shuffled and set the cards back under the lamp and put his hands back into his lap and Mr Hubert cut the deck and folded his arms back onto the table-edge. "Deal," he said. Still neither he nor Uncle Buddy looked up. They just sat there while Tomey's Turl's saddle-colored hands came into the light and took up the deck and dealt, one card face-down to Mr Hubert and one face-down to Uncle Buddy, and one face-up to Mr Hubert and it was a king, and one face-up to Uncle Buddy and it was a six.

"Buck McCaslin against Sibbey's dowry," Mr Hubert said. "Deal." And the hand dealt Mr Hubert a card and it was a three, and Uncle Buddy a card and it was a two. Mr Hubert looked at Uncle Buddy. Uncle Buddy rapped once with his knuckles on the table.

"Deal," Mr Hubert said. And the hand dealt Mr Hubert a card and it was another three, and Uncle Buddy a card and it was a four. Mr Hubert looked at Uncle Buddy's cards. Then he looked at Uncle Buddy and Uncle Buddy rapped on the table again with his knuckles.

"Deal," Mr Hubert said, and the hand dealt him an ace and Uncle Buddy a five and now Mr Hubert just sat still. He didn't look at anything or move for a whole minute; he just sat there and watched Uncle Buddy put one hand onto the table for the first time since he shuffled and pinch up one corner of his face-down card and look at it and then put his hand back into his lap. "Check," Mr Hubert said.

"I'll bet you them two niggers," Uncle Buddy said. He didn't move either. He sat there just like he sat in the wagon or on a horse or in the rocking chair he cooked from.

"Against what?" Mr Hubert said.

"Against the three hundred dollars Theophilus owes you for Tennie, and the three hundred you and Theophilus agreed on for Tomey's Turl," Uncle Buddy said.

"Hah," Mr Hubert said, only it wasn't loud at all this time, nor even short. Then he said "Hah. Hah. Hah" and not loud either. Then he said, "Well." Then he said, "Well, well." Then he said: "We'll check up for a minute. If I win, you take Sibbey without dowry and the two niggers, and I dont owe 'Filus anything. If you win——"

"—Theophilus is free. And you owe him the three hundred dollars for Tomey's Turl," Uncle Buddy said.

"That's just if I call you," Mr Hubert said. "If I dont call you, 'Filus wont owe me nothing and I wont owe 'Filus nothing, unless I take that nigger which I have been trying to explain to you and him both for years that I wont have on my place. We will be right back where all this foolishness started from, except for that. So what it comes down to is, I either got to give a nigger away, or risk buying one that you done already admitted you cant keep at home." Then he stopped talking. For about a minute it was like he and Uncle Buddy had both gone to sleep. Then Mr

Hubert picked up his face-down card and turned it over. It was another three, and Mr Hubert sat there without looking at anything at all, his fingers beating a tattoo, slow and steady and not very loud, on the table. "H'm," he said. "And you need a trey and there aint but four of them and I already got three. And you just shuffled. And I cut afterward. And if I call you, I will have to buy that nigger. Who dealt these cards, Amodeus?" Only he didn't wait to be answered. He reached out and tilted the lamp-shade, the light moving up Tomey's Turl's arms that were supposed to be black but were not quite white, up his Sunday shirt that was supposed to be white but wasn't quite either, that he put on every time he ran away just as Uncle Buck put on the necktie each time he went to bring him back, and on to his face; and Mr Hubert sat there, holding the lamp-shade and looking at Tomey's Turl. Then he tilted the shade back down and took up his cards and turned them face-down and pushed them toward the middle of the table. "I pass, Amodeus," he said.

4.

He was still too worn out for sleep to sit on a horse, so this time he and Uncle Buddy and Tennie all three rode in the wagon, while Tomey's Turl led the pony from old Jake. And when they got home just after daylight, this time Uncle Buddy never even had time to get breakfast started and the fox never even got out of the crate, because the dogs were right there in the room. Old Moses went right into the crate with the fox, so that both of them went right on through the back end of it. That is, the fox went through, because when Uncle Buddy opened the door to come in, old Moses was still wearing most of the crate around his neck until Uncle Buddy kicked it off of him. Sothey just made one run, across the front gallery and around the house and they could hear the fox's claws when he went scrabbling up the lean-pole, onto the roof—a fine race while it lasted, but the tree was too quick.

"What in damn's hell do you mean," Uncle Buddy said, "casting that damn thing with all the dogs right in the same room?"

"Damn the fox," Uncle Buck said. "Go on and start breakfast. It seems to me I've been away from home a whole damn month."

The Fire and the Hearth

Chapter One

FIRST, in order to take care of George Wilkins once and for all, he had to hide his own still. And not only that, he had to do it singlehanded—dismantle it in the dark and transport it without help to some place far enough away and secret enough to escape the subsequent uproar and excitement and there conceal it. It was the prospect of this which had enraged him, compounding in advance the physical weariness and exhaustion which would be the night's aftermath. It was not the temporary interruption of business; the business had been interfered with once before about five years ago and he had dealt with that crisis as promptly and efficiently as he was dealing with this present one—and since which time that other competitor, whose example George Wilkins might quite possibly follow provided Carothers Edmonds were as correctly informed about his intentions as he professed to be about his bank account, had been plowing and chopping and picking cotton which was not his on the State penal farm at Parchman.

And it was not the loss of revenue which the interruption entailed. He was sixty-seven years old; he already had more money in the bank now than he would ever spend, more than Carothers Edmonds himself, provided a man be-

lieved Carothers Edmonds when he tried to draw anything
extra in the way of cash or supplies from the commissary.
It was the fact that he must do it all himself, singlehanded;
had to come up from the field after a long day in the dead
middle of planting time and stable and feed Edmonds'
mules and eat his own supper and then put his own mare
to the single wagon and drive three miles to the still and
dismantle it by touch in the dark and carry it another mile
to the best place he could think of where it would be
reasonably safe after the excitement started, probably getting back home with hardly enough of the night left to
make it worth while going to bed before time to return to
the field until the time would be ripe to speak the one word
to Edmonds;—all this alone and unassisted because the
two people from whom he might reasonably and logically
have not only expected but demanded help were completely
interdict: his wife who was too old and frail for such, even
if he could have trusted not her fidelity but her discretion;
and as for his daughter, to let her get any inkling of what
he was about, he might just as well have asked George
Wilkins himself to help him hide the still. It was not that
he had anything against George personally, despite the
mental exasperation and the physical travail he was having
to undergo when he should have been at home in bed
asleep. If George had just stuck to farming the land which
Edmonds had allotted him he would just as soon Nat married George as anyone else, sooner than most of the nigger
bucks he knew. But he was not going to let George Wilkins
or anyone else move not only into the section where he had
lived for going on seventy years but onto the very place
he had been born on and set up competition in a business
which he had established and nursed carefully and dis-

creetly for twenty of them, ever since he had fired up for
his first fun not a mile from Zack Edmonds' kitchen door;
—secretly indeed, for no man needed to tell him what Zack
Edmonds or his son, Carothers (or Old Cass Edmonds
either, for that matter), would do about it if they ever found
it out. He wasn't afraid that George would cut into his
established trade, his old regular clientele, with the hog
swill which George had begun to turn out two months ago
and call whisky. But George Wilkins was a fool innocent
of discretion, who sooner or later would be caught, whereupon for the next ten years every bush on the Edmonds
place would have a deputy sheriff squatting behind it from
sundown to sunup every night. And he not only didn't
want a fool for a son-in-law, he didn't intend to have a fool
living on the same place he lived on. If George had to go to
jail to alleviate that condition, that was between George
and Roth Edmonds.

But it was about over now. Another hour or so and he
would be back home, getting whatever little of sleep there
might be left of the night before time to return to the field
to pass the day until the right moment to speak to Edmonds. Probably the outrage would be gone by then, and
he would have only the weariness to contend with. But it
was his own field, though he neither owned it nor wanted
to nor even needed to. He had been cultivating it for
forty-five years, since before Carothers Edmonds was born
even, plowing and planting and working it when and how
he saw fit (or maybe not even doing that, maybe sitting
through a whole morning on his front gallery, looking at
it and thinking if that's what he felt like doing), with
Edmonds riding up on his mare maybe three times a week
to look at the field, and maybe once during the season stop-

ping long enough to give him advice about it which he
completely ignored, ignoring not only the advice but the
very voice which gave it, as though the other had not
spoken even, whereupon Edmonds would ride on and he
would continue with whatever he had been doing, the
incident already forgotten condoned and forgiven, the
necessity and the time having been served. So the day
would pass at last. Then he would approach Edmonds and
speak his word and it would be like dropping the nickel
into the slot machine and pulling the lever: all he would
have to do then would be just to watch it.

He knew exactly where he intended to go, even in the
darkness. He had been born on this land, twenty-five years
before the Edmonds who now owned it. He had worked
on it ever since he got big enough to hold a plow straight;
he had hunted over every foot of it during his childhood
and youth and his manhood too, up to the time when he
stopped hunting, not because he could no longer walk a
day's or a night's hunt, but because he felt that the pursuit
of rabbits and 'possums for meat was no longer commen-
surate with his status as not only the oldest man but the
oldest living person on the Edmonds plantation, the oldest
McCaslin descendant even though in the world's eye he
descended not from McCaslins but from McCaslin slaves,
almost as old as old Isaac McCaslin who lived in town, supported by what Roth Edmonds chose to give him, who
would own the land and all on it if his just rights were only
known, if people just knew how old Cass Edmonds, this
one's grandfather, had beat him out of his patrimony;
almost as old as old Isaac, almost, as old Isaac was, coeval
with old Buck and Buddy McCaslin who had been alive
when their father, Carothers McCaslin, got the land from

the Indians back in the old time when men black and white were men.

He was in the creek bottom now. Curiously enough, visibility seemed to have increased, as if the rank sunless jungle of cypress and willow and brier, instead of increasing obscurity, had solidified it into the concrete components of trunk and branch, leaving the air, space, free of it and in comparison lighter, penetrable to vision, to the mare's sight anyway, enabling her to see-saw back and forth among the trunks and the impassable thickets. Then he saw the place he sought—a squat, flat-topped, almost symmetrical mound rising without reason from the floor-like flatness of the valley. The white people called it an Indian mound. One day five or six years ago a group of white men, including two women, most of them wearing spectacles and all wearing khaki clothes which had patently lain folded on a store shelf twenty-four hours ago, came with picks and shovels and jars and phials of insect repellant and spent a day digging about it while most of the people, men women and children, came at some time during the day and looked quietly on; later—within the next two or three days, in fact—he was to remember with almost horrified amazement the cold and contemptuous curiosity with which he himself had watched them.

But that would come later. Now he was merely busy. He could not see his watch-face, but he knew it was almost midnight. He stopped the wagon beside the mound and unloaded the still—the copper-lined kettle which had cost him more than he still liked to think about despite his ingrained lifelong scorn of inferior tools—and the worm and his pick and shovel. The spot he sought was a slight overhang on one face of the mound; in a sense one side of his excavation was already dug for him, needing only to be enlarged a little, the earth working easily under the invisible pick, whispering easily and steadily to the invisible shovel until the orifice was deep enough for the worm and kettle to fit into it, when—and it was probably only a sigh but it sounded to him louder than an avalanche, as though the whole mound had stooped roaring down at him—the entire overhang sloughed. It drummed on the hollow kettle, covering it and the worm, and boiled about his feet and, as he leaped backward and tripped and fell, about his body too, hurling clods and dirt at him, striking him a final blow squarely in the face with something larger than a clod— a blow not vicious so much as merely heavy-handed, a sort of final admonitory pat from the spirit of darkness and solitude, the old earth, perhaps the old ancestors themselves. Because, sitting up, getting his breath again at last, gasping and blinking at the apparently unchanged shape of the mound which seemed to loom poised above him in a long roaring wave of silence like a burst of jeering and prolonged laughter, his hand found the object which had struck him and learned it in the blind dark—a fragment of an earthenware vessel which, intact, must have been as big as a churn and which even as he lifted it crumbled again and deposited in his palm, as though it had been handed to him, a single coin.

He could not have said how he knew it was gold. But he didn't even need to strike a match. He dared risk no light at all as, his brain boiling with all the images of buried money he had ever listened to or heard of, for the next five hours he crawled on hands and knees among the loose earth, hunting through the collapsed and now quiet dirt almost grain by grain, pausing from time to time to gauge by the stars how much remained of the rapid and shortening spring night, then probing again in the dry insensate dust which had yawned for an instant and vouchsafed him one blinding glimpse of the absolute and then closed.

When the east began to pale he stopped and straightened up, kneeling, stretching his cramped and painful muscles into something approximating erectness for the first time since midnight. He had found nothing more. He had not even found any other fragments of the churn or crock. That meant that the rest of it might be scattered anywhere beneath the cave-in. He would have to dig for it, coin by coin, with pick and shovel. That meant time, but more than that, solitude. Obviously there must no longer be even the remotest possibility of sheriffs and law men prying about the place hunting whisky stills. So George Wilkins was reprieved without knowing his luck just as he had been in jeopardy without knowing his danger. For an instant, remembering the tremendous power which three hours ago had hurled him onto his back without even actually touching him, he even thought of taking George into partnership on a minor share basis to do the actual digging; indeed, not only to do the actual work but as a sort of justice, balance, libation to Chance and Fortune, since if it had not been for George, he would not have found the single coin. But he dismissed that before it even had time to become an idea. He, Lucas Beauchamp, the oldest living McCaslin descendant still living on the hereditary land, who actually remembered old Buck and Buddy in the living flesh, older than Zack Edmonds even if Zack were still alive, almost as old as old Isaac who in a sense, say what a man would, had turned apostate to his name and

lineage by weakly relinquishing the land which was rightfully his to live in town on the charity of his great-nephew;
—he, to share one jot, one penny of the money which old
Buck and Buddy had buried almost a hundred years ago,
with an interloper without forbears and sprung from nowhere and whose very name was unknown in the country
twenty-five years ago—a jimber-jawed clown who could
not even learn how to make whisky, who had not only attempted to interfere with and jeopardise his business and
disrupt his family, but had given him a week of alternating
raging anxiety and exasperated outrage culminating in tonight—or last night now—and not even finished yet, since
he still had the worm and kettle to conceal. Never. Let
George take for his recompense the fact that he would not
have to go to the penitentiary to which Roth Edmonds
would probably have sent him even if the Law did not.

The light had increased; he could see now. The slide
had covered the still. All necessary would be a few branches
piled against it so that the recent earth would not be too
apparent to a chance passer. He rose to his feet. But he
still could not straighten up completely. With one hand
pressed to his back and still bent over a little he began to
walk stiffly and painfully toward a clump of sapling cot-
tonwoods about fifty feet away, when something crashed
into flight within or beyond it and rushed on, the sound
fading and already beginning to curve away toward the
edge of the jungle while he stood for perhaps ten seconds,
slackjawed with amazed and incredulous comprehension,
his head turning to pace the invisible running. Then he
whirled and leaped, not toward the sound but running
parallel with it, leaping with incredible agility and speed

among the trees and undergrowth, breaking out of the
jungle in time to see, in the wan light of the accelerating
dawn, the quarry fleeing like a deer across a field and into
the still night-bound woods beyond.

He knew who it was, even before he returned to the
thicket where it had flushed, to stand looking down at the
print of his daughter's naked feet where she had squatted
in the mud, knowing that print as he would have known
those of his mare or his dog, standing over it for a while
and looking down at it but no longer seeing it at all. So
that was that. In a way, it even simplified things. Even
if there had been time (another hour and every field along
the creek would have a negro and a mule in it), even if he
could hope to obliterate all trace and sign of disturbed
earth about the mound, it would do no good to move his
still to another hiding-place. Because when they came to
the mound to dig they must not only find something, they
must find it quick and at once and something the discovery
and exhumation of which would cause them to desist and
go away—say, only partly buried, and with just enough
brush in front of it that they couldn't help but find it even
before they got the brush dragged off. Because it was a
matter open to, admitting, no controversy, not even dis-
cussion. George Wilkins must go. He must be on his way
before another night had passed.

2.

He shoved his chair back from the supper table and
stood up. He gave his daughter's lowered, secret face a
single look, not grim but cold. But he addressed neither
her nor his wife directly. He might have been speaking to

either of them or both or to neither: "Going down the road."

"Where you going this time of night?" his wife said. "Messing around up yonder in the bottom all last night! Getting back home just in time to hitch up and get to the field a good hour after sunup! You needs to be in bed if you going to get that creek piece broke like Mister Roth——"

Then he was out of the house and didn't need to hear her any longer. It was night again. The dirt lane ran pale and dim beneath the moonless sky of corn-planting time. Presently it ran along beside the very field which he was getting ready to plant his cotton in when the whippoorwills began. If it had not been for George Wilkins, he would have had it all broken and bedded and ready now. But that was about over now. Another ten minutes and it would be like dropping the nickel into the slot machine, not ringing down a golden shower about him, he didn't ask that, need that; he would attend to the jackpot himself, but giving him peace and solitude in which to do so. That, the labor even at night and without help, even if he had to move half the mound, did not bother him. He was only sixty-seven, a better man still than some men half his age; ten years younger and he could still have done both, the night-work and the day. But now he wouldn't try it. In a way, he was a little sorry to give up farming. He had liked it; he approved of his fields and liked to work them, taking a solid pride in having good tools to use and using them well, scorning both inferior equipment and shoddy work just as he had bought the best kettle he could find when he set up his still —that copper-lined kettle the cost of which he liked less than ever to remember now that he was not only about to lose it but was himself deliberately giving it away. He had even planned the very phrases, dialogue, in which, after the first matter was attended to, he would inform Edmonds that he had decided to quit farming, was old enough to retire, and for Edmonds to allot his land to someone else to finish the crop. "All right," Edmonds would say. "But you cant expect me to furnish a house and wood and water to a family that aint working any land." And he would say, if it really came to that—and it probably would, since he, Lucas, would affirm to his death that Zack Edmonds had been as much better a man than his son as old Cass Edmonds had been than both of them together: "All right. I'll rent the house from you. Name your price and I will pay you every Saturday night as long as I decide to stay here."

But that would take care of itself. The other matter was first and prime. At first, on his return home this morning, his plan had been to notify the sheriff himself, so that there would be absolutely no slip-up, lest Edmonds should be content with merely destroying George's still and cache and just running George off the place. In that case, George would continue to hang around the place, merely keeping out of Edmonds' sight; whereupon, without even any farm work, let alone the still, to keep him occupied, he would be idle all day and therefore up and out all night long and would constitute more of a menace than ever. The report would have to come from Edmonds, the white man, because to the sheriff Lucas was just another nigger and both the sheriff and Lucas knew it, although only one of them knew that to Lucas the sheriff was a redneck without any reason for pride in his forbears nor hope for it in his descendants. And if Edmonds should decide to handle the matter privately, without recourse to the law, there would be someone in Jefferson whom Lucas could inform that not only he and George Wilkins knew of a still on Carothers Edmonds' place, but Carothers Edmonds knew it too. .

He entered the wide carriage gate from which the drive curved mounting to the oak and cedar knoll where he could already see, brighter than any kerosene, the gleam of electricity in the house where the better men than this one had been content with lamps or even candles. There was a tractor under the mule-shed which Zack Edmonds would not have allowed on the place too, and an automobile in a house built especially for it which old Cass would not even have put his foot in. But they were the old days, the old time, and better men than these; Lucas himself made one, himself and old Cass coevals in more than spirit even, the analogy only the closer for its paradox:—old Cass a McCaslin only on his mother's side and so bearing his father's name though he possessed the land and its benefits and responsibilities; Lucas a McCaslin on his father's side though bearing his mother's name and possessing the use and benefit of the land with none of the responsibilities. Better men:—old Cass, a McCaslin only by the distaff yet having enough of old Carothers McCaslin in his veins to take the land from the true heir simply because he wanted it and knew he could use it better and was strong enough, ruthless enough, old Carothers McCaslin enough; even Zack, who was not the man his father had been but whom Lucas, the man McCaslin, had accepted as his peer to the extent of intending to kill him, right up to the point when, his affairs all set in order like those of a man preparing for death, he stood over the sleeping white man that morning forty-three years ago with the naked razor in his hand.

He approached the house—the two log wings which

Carothers McCaslin had built and which had sufficed old
Buck and Buddy, connected by the open hallway which,
as his pride's monument and epitaph, old Cass Edmonds
had enclosed and superposed with a second storey of white
clapboards and faced with a portico. He didn't go around
to the back, the kitchen door. He had done that only one
time since the present Edmonds was born; he would never
do it again as long as he lived. Neither did he mount the
steps. Instead he stopped in the darkness beside the gallery
and rapped with his knuckles on the edge of it until the
white man came up the hall and peered out the front door.
"Well?" Edmonds said. "What is it?"

"It's me," Lucas said.

"Well, come in," the other said. "What are you standing
out there for?"

"You come out here," Lucas said. "For all you or me
either know, George may be laying out yonder right now,
listening."

"George?" Edmonds said. "George Wilkins?" He came
out onto the gallery—a young man still, a bachelor, forty-
three years old last March. Lucas did not need to remember that. He would never forget it—that night of early
spring following ten days of such rain that even the old
people remembered nothing to compare it with, and the
white man's wife's time upon her and the creek out of
banks until the whole valley rose, bled a river choked with
down timber and drowned livestock until not even a horse
could have crossed it in the darkness to reach a telephone
and fetch the doctor back. And Molly, a young woman
then and nursing their own first child, wakened at midnight by the white man himself and they followed then
the white man through the streaming darkness to his house

and Lucas waited in the kitchen, keeping the fire going in the stove, and Molly delivered the white child with none to help but Edmonds and then they knew that the doctor had to be fetched. So even before daylight he was in the water and crossed it, how he never knew, and was back by dark with the doctor, emerging from that death (At one time he had believed himself gone, done for, both himself and the mule soon to be two more white-eyed and slack-jawed pieces of flotsam, to be located by the circling of buzzards, swollen and no longer identifiable, a month hence when the water went down.) which he had entered not for his own sake but for that of old Carothers McCaslin who had sired him and Zack Edmonds both, to find the white man's wife dead and his own wife already established in the white man's house. It was as though on that louring and driving day he had crossed and then recrossed a kind of Lethe, emerging, being permitted to escape, buying as the price of life a world outwardly the same yet subtly and irrevocably altered.

It was as though the white woman had not only never quitted the house, she had never existed—the object which they buried in the orchard two days later (they still could not cross the valley to reach the churchyard) a thing of no moment, unsanctified, nothing; his own wife, the black woman, now living alone in the house which old Cass had built for them when they married, keeping alive on the hearth the fire he had lit there on their wedding day and which had burned ever since though there was little enough cooking done on it now;—thus, until almost half a year had passed and one day he went to Zack Edmonds and said, "I wants my wife. I needs her at home." Then—and he hadn't intended to say this. But there had been that half-year almost and himself alone keeping alive the fire which was to burn on the hearth until neither he nor Molly were left to feed it, himself sitting before it night after night through that spring and summer until one night he caught himself standing over it, furious, bursting, blind, the cedar water bucket already poised until he caught himself and set the bucket back on the shelf, still shaking, unable to remember taking the bucket up even—then he said: "I reckon you thought I wouldn't take her back, didn't you?"

The white man was sitting down. In age he and Lucas could have been brothers, almost twins too. He leaned slowly back in the chair, looking at Lucas. "Well, by God," he said quietly. "So that's what you think. What kind of a man do you think I am? What kind of a man do you call yourself?"

"I'm a nigger," Lucas said. "But I'm a man too. I'm more than just a man. The same thing made my pappy that made your grandmaw. I'm going to take her back."

"By God," Edmonds said, "I never thought to ever pass my oath to a nigger. But I will swear—" Lucas had turned, already walking away. He whirled. The other was standing now. They faced one another, though for the instant Lucas couldn't even see him.

"Not to me!" Lucas said. "I wants her in my house tonight. You understand?" He went back to the field, to the plow standing in midfurrow where he had left it when he discovered suddenly that he was going now, this moment, to the commissary or the house or wherever the white man would be, into his bedroom if necessary, and confront him. He had tied the mule under a tree, the gear still on it. He put the mule back to the plow and plowed again. When he turned at the end of each furrow he could have seen his house. But he never looked toward it, not even when he knew that she was in it again, home again, not even when fresh woodsmoke began to rise from the chimney as it had not risen in the middle of the morning in almost half a year; not even when at noon she came along the fence, carrying a pail and a covered pan and stood looking at him for a moment before she set the pail and pan down and went back. Then the plantation bell rang for noon, the flat, musical, deliberate clangs. He took the mule out and watered and fed it and only then went to the fence-corner and there it was—the pan of still-warm biscuit, the lard pail half full of milk, the tin worn and polished with scouring and long use until it had a patina like old silver—just as it had used to be.

Then the afternoon was done too. He stabled and fed Edmonds' mule and hung the gear on its appointed peg against tomorrow. Then in the lane, in the green middle-dusk of summer while the fireflies winked and drifted and the whippoorwills choired back and forth and the frogs thumped and grunted along the creek, he looked at his house for the first time, at the thin plume of supper smoke windless above the chimney, his breathing harder and harder and deeper and deeper until his faded shirt strained at the buttons on his chest. Maybe when he got old he would become resigned to it. But he knew he would never, not even if he got to be a hundred and forgot her face and name and the white man's and his too. *I will have to kill him,* he thought, *or I will have to take her and go away.* For an instant he thought of going to the white man and telling him they were leaving, now, tonight, at once. *Only if I were to see him again right now, I might kill him,* he thought. *I think I have decided which I am going to do, but if I was to see him, meet him now, my mind might change.—And that's a man!* he thought. *He keeps her in the house with him six months and I dont do nothing: he sends her back to me and I kills him. It would be like I had done said aloud to the whole world that he never sent her back because I told him to but he give her back to me because he was tired of her.*

He entered the gate in the paling fence which he had built himself when old Cass gave them the house, as he had hauled and laid the field stone path across the grassless yard which his wife used to sweep every morning with a broom of bound willow twigs, sweeping the clean dust into curving intricate patterns among the flower-beds outlined with broken brick and bottles and shards of china and colored glass. She had returned from time to time during the spring to work the flower-beds so that they bloomed as usual—the hardy, blatant blooms loved of her and his race: prince's feather and sunflower, canna and hollyhock —but until today the paths among them had not been swept since last year. *Yes*, he thought. *I got to kill him or I got to leave here.*

He entered the hall, then the room where he had lit the fire two years ago which was to have outlasted both of them. He could not always remember afterward what he had said but he never forgot the amazed and incredulous rage with which he thought, *Why she aint even knowed unto right now that I ever even suspected.* She was sitting before the hearth where the supper was cooking, holding the child, shielding its face from the light and heat with her hand—a small woman even then, years before her flesh, her very bones apparently, had begun to wither and shrink inward upon themselves, and he standing over her, looking down not at his own child but at the face of the white one nuzzling into the dark swell of her breast—not Edmonds' wife but his own who had been lost; not his son but the white man's who had been restored to him, his voice loud, his clawed hand darting toward the child as her hand sprang and caught his wrist.

"Whar's ourn?" he cried. "Whar's mine?"

"Right yonder on the bed, sleeping!" she said. "Go and look at him!" He didn't move, standing over her, locked hand and wrist with her. "I couldn't leave him! You know I couldn't! I had to bring him!"

"Dont lie to me!" he said. "Dont tell me Zack Edmonds know where he is."

"He does know! I told him!" He broke his wrist free, flinging her hand and arm back; he heard the faint click of her teeth when the back of her hand struck her chin and he watched her start to raise her hand to her mouth, then let it fall again.

"That's right," he said. "It aint none of your blood that's trying to break out and run!"

"You fool!" she cried. "Oh God," she said. "Oh God. All right. I'll take him back. I aimed to anyway. Aunt Thisbe can fix him a sugar-tit——"

"Not you," he said. "And not me even. Do you think Zack Edmonds is going to stay in that house yonder when he gets back and finds out he is gone? No!" he said. "I went to Zack Edmonds' house and asked him for my wife. Let him come to my house and ask me for his son!"

He waited on the gallery. He could see, across the valley, the gleam of light in the other house. *He just aint got home yet,* he thought. He breathed slow and steady. *It aint no hurry. He will do something and then I will do something and it will be all over. It will be all right.* Then the light disappeared. He began to say quietly, aloud: "Now. Now. He will have to have time to walk over here." He continued to say it long after he knew the other had had time to walk back and forth between the two houses ten times over. It seemed to him then that he had known all the time the other was not coming, as if he were in the house where the white man waited, watching his, Lucas', house in his turn. Then he knew that the other was not even waiting, and it was as if he stood already in the bedroom itself, above the slow respirations of sleep, the undefended and oblivious throat, the naked razor already in his hand.

He re-entered the house, the room where his wife and the two children were asleep on the bed. The supper which had been cooking on the hearth when he entered at dusk had not even been taken up, what was left of it long since charred and simmered away and probably almost cool now among the fading embers. He set the skillet and coffee pot aside and with a stick of wood he raked the ashes from one corner of the fireplace, exposing the bricks, and touched one of them with his wet finger. It was hot, not scorching, searing, but possessing a slow, deep solidity of heat, a condensation of the two years during which the fire had burned constantly above it, a condensation not of fire but of time, as though not the fire's dying and not even water would cool it but only time would. He prised the brick up with his knife blade and scraped away the warm dirt under it and lifted out a small metal dispatch box which his white grandfather, Carothers McCaslin himself, had owned almost a hundred years ago, and took from it the knotted

rag tight and solid with the coins, some of which dated
back almost to Carothers McCaslin's time, which he had
begun to save before he was ten years old. His wife had
removed only her shoes (he recognised them too. They
had belonged to the white woman who had not died, who
had not even ever existed.) before lying down. He put the
knotted rag into one of them and went to the walnut
bureau which Isaac McCaslin had given him for a wedding
present and took his razor from the drawer.

He was waiting for daylight. He could not have said
why. He squatted against a tree halfway between the carriage gate and the white man's house, motionless as the
windless obscurity itself while the constellations wheeled
and the whippoorwills choired faster and faster and ceased
and the first cocks crowed and the false dawn came and
faded and the birds began and the night was over. In the
first of light he mounted the white man's front steps and
entered the unlocked front door and traversed the silent
hall and entered the bedroom which it seemed to him he
had already entered and that only an instant before, standing with the open razor above the breathing, the undefended and defenseless throat, facing again the act which it
seemed to him he had already performed. Then he found
the eyes of the face on the pillow looking quietly up at
him and he knew then why he had had to wait until daylight. "Because you are a McCaslin too," he said. "Even if
you was woman-made to it. Maybe that's the reason. Maybe
that's why you done it: because what you and your pa got
from old Carothers had to come to you through a woman—
a critter not responsible like men are responsible, not to be
held like men are held. So maybe I have even already forgive you, except I cant forgive you because you can forgive

only them that injure you; even the Book itself dont ask a man to forgive them he is fixing to harm because even Jesus found out at last that was too much to ask a man."

"Put the razor down and I will talk to you," Edmonds said.

"You knowed I wasn't afraid, because you knowed I was a McCaslin too and a man-made one. And you never thought that, because I am a McCaslin too, I wouldn't. You never even thought that, because I am a nigger too, I wouldn't dare. No. You thought that because I am a nigger I wouldn't even mind. I never figured on the razor neither. But I gave you your chance. Maybe I didn't know what I might have done when you walked in my door, but I knowed what I wanted to do, what I believed I was going to do, what Carothers McCaslin would have wanted me to do. But you didn't come. You never even gave me the chance to do what old Carothers would have told me to do. You tried to beat me. And you wont never, not even when I am hanging dead from the limb this time tomorrow with the coal oil still burning, you wont never."

"Put down the razor, Lucas," Edmonds said.

"What razor?" Lucas said. He raised his hand and looked at the razor as if he did not know he had it, had never seen it before, and in the same motion flung it toward the open window, the naked blade whirling almost blood-colored into the first copper ray of the sun before it vanished. "I dont need no razor. My nekkid hands will do. Now get the pistol under your pillow."

Still the other didn't move, not even to draw his hands from under the sheet. "It's not under the pillow. It's in that drawer yonder where it always is and you know it. Go and look. I'm not going to run. I couldn't."

"I know you aint," Lucas said. "And you know you aint. Because you know that's all I needs, all I wants, is for you to try to run, to turn your back on me and run. I know you aint going to. Because all you got to beat is me. I got to beat old Carothers. Get your pistol."

"No," the other said. "Go home. Get out of here. To-night I will come to your house ——"

"After this?" Lucas said. "Me and you, in the same coun-try, breathing the same air even? No matter what you could say, what you could even prove so I would have to believe it, after this? Get the pistol."

The other drew his hands out from under the sheet and placed them on top of it. "All right," he said. "Stand over there against the wall until I get it."

"Hah," Lucas said. "Hah."

The other put his hands back under the sheet. "Then go and get your razor," he said.

Lucas began to pant, to indraw short breaths without expiration between. The white man could see his fore-shortened chest, the worn faded shirt straining across it. "When you just watched me throw it away?" Lucas said. "When you know that if I left this room now, I wouldn't come back?" He went to the wall and stood with his back against it, still facing the bed. "Because I done already beat you," he said. "It's old Carothers. Get your pistol, white man." He stood panting in the rapid inhalations until it seemed that his lungs could not possibly hold more of it. He watched the other rise from the bed and grasp the foot of it and swing it out from the wall until it could be ap-proached from either side; he watched the white man cross to the bureau and take the pistol from the drawer. Still Lucas didn't move. He stood pressed against the wall and watched the white man cross to the door and close it and turn the key and return to the bed and toss the pistol onto it and only then look toward him. Lucas began to tremble. "No," he said.

"You on one side, me on the other," the white man said. "We'll kneel down and grip hands. We wont need to count."

"No!" Lucas said in a strangling voice. "For the last time. Take your pistol. I'm coming."

"Come on then. Do you think I'm any less a McCaslin just because I was what you call woman-made to it? Or maybe you aint even a woman-made McCaslin but just a nigger that's got out of hand?"

Then Lucas was beside the bed. He didn't remember moving at all. He was kneeling, their hands gripped, facing across the bed and the pistol the man whom he had known from infancy, with whom he had lived until they were both grown almost as brothers lived. They had fished and hunted together, they had learned to swim in the same water, they had eaten at the same table in the white boy's kitchen and in the cabin of the negro's mother; they had slept under the same blanket before a fire in the woods.

"For the last time," Lucas said. "I tell you ——" Then he cried, and not to the white man and the white man knew it; he saw the whites of the negro's eyes rush suddenly with red like the eyes of a bayed animal—a bear, a fox: "I tell you! Dont ask too much of me!" *I was wrong,* the white man thought. *I have gone too far.* But it was too late. Even as he tried to snatch his hand free Lucas' hand closed on it. He darted his left hand toward the pistol but Lucas caught that wrist too. Then they did not move save their forearms, their gripped hands turning gradually

until the white man's hand was pressed back-downward on
the pistol. Motionless, locked, incapable of moving, the
white man stared at the spent and frantic face opposite his.
"I give you your chance," Lucas said. "Then you laid here
asleep with your door unlocked and give me mine. Then
I throwed the razor away and give it back. And then you
throwed it back at me. That's right, aint it?"

"Yes," the white man said.

"Hah!" Lucas said. He flung the white man's left hand
and arm away, striking the other backward from the bed
as his own right hand wrenched free; he had the pistol in
the same motion, springing up and back as the white man
rose too, the bed between them. He broke the pistol's
breech and glanced quickly at the cylinder and turned it
until the empty chamber under the hammer was at the
bottom, so that a live cartridge would come beneath the
hammer regardless of which direction the cylinder rotated.
"Because I'll need two of them," he said. He snapped the
breech shut and faced the white man. Again the white man
saw his eyes rush until there was neither cornea nor iris.
This is it, the white man thought, with that rapid and even
unamazed clarity, gathering himself as much as he dared.
Lucas didn't seem to notice. *He cant even see me right now*,
the white man thought. But that was too late too. Lucas
was looking at him now. "You thought I wouldn't, didn't
you?" Lucas said. "You knowed I could beat you, so you
thought to beat me with old Carothers, like Cass Edmonds
done Isaac: used old Carothers to make Isaac give up the
land that was his because Cass Edmonds was the woman-
made McCaslin, the woman-branch, the sister, and old
Carothers would have told Isaac to give in to the woman-
kin that couldn't fend for herself. And you thought I'd do

that too, didn't you? You thought I'd do it quick, quicker than Isaac since it aint any land I would give up. I aint got any fine big McCaslin farm to give up. All I got to give up is McCaslin blood that rightfully aint even mine or at least aint worth much since old Carothers never seemed to miss much what he give to Tomey that night that made my father. And if this is what that McCaslin blood has brought me, I dont want it neither. And if the running of it into my black blood never hurt him any more than the running of it out is going to hurt me, it wont even be old Carothers that had the most pleasure.—Or no," he cried. *He cant see me again*, the white man thought. *Now.* "No! Lucas cried; "say I dont even use this first bullet at all, say I just uses the last one and beat you and old Carothers both, leave you something to think about now and then when you aint too busy to try to think up what to tell old Carothers when you get where he's done already gone, tomorrow and the one after that and the one after that as long as tomorrow—" The white man sprang, hurling himself across the bed, grasping at the pistol and the hand which held it. Lucas sprang too; they met over the center of the bed where Lucas clasped the other with his left arm almost like an embrace and jammed the pistol against the white man's side and pulled the trigger and flung the white man from him all in one motion, hearing as he did so the light, dry, incredibly loud click of the miss-fire.

That had been a good year, though late in beginning after the rains and flood: the year of the long summer. He would make more this year than he had made in a long time, even though and in August some of his corn had not had its last plowing. He was doing that now, following the single mule between the rows of strong, waist-high

stalks and the rich, dark, flashing blades, pausing at the
end of each row to back the plow out and swing it and the
yawing mule around into the next one, until at last the
dinner smoke stood weightless in the bright air above his
chimney and then at the old time she came along the fence
with the covered pan and the pail. He did not look at her.
He plowed on until the plantation bell rang for noon. He
watered and fed the mule and himself ate—the milk, the
still-warm biscuit—and rested in the shade until the bell
rang again. Then, not rising yet, he took the cartridge
from his pocket and looked at it again, musing—the live
cartridge, not even stained, not corroded, the mark of the
firing-pin dented sharp and deep into the unexploded cap
—the dull little brass cylinder less long than a match, not
much larger than a pencil, not much heavier, yet large
enough to contain two lives. Have contained, that is. *Because I wouldn't have used the second one,* he thought.
*I would have paid. I would have waited for the rope, even
the coal oil. I would have paid. So I reckon I aint got old
Carothers' blood for nothing, after all. Old Carothers,* he
thought. *I needed him and he come and spoke for me.* He
plowed again. Presently she came back along the fence and
got the pan and pail herself instead of letting him bring
them home when he came. But she would be busy today;
and it seemed to him still early in the afternoon when he
saw the supper smoke—the supper which she would leave
on the hearth for him when she went back to the big house
with the children. When he reached home in the dusk, she
was just departing. But she didn't wear the white woman's
shoes now and her dress was the same shapeless faded
calico she had worn in the morning. "Your supper's ready,"
she said. "I aint had time to milk yet. You'll have to."

"If I can wait on that milk, I reckon the cow can too," he said. "Can you tote them both all right?"

"I reckon I can. I been taking care of both of them a good while now without no man-help." She didn't look back. "I'll come back out when I gets them to sleep."

"I reckon you better put your time on them," he said gruffly. "Since that's what you started out to do." She went on, neither answering nor looking back, impervious, tranquil, somehow serene. Nor was he any longer watching her. He breathed slow and quiet. *Women,* he thought. *Women. I wont never know. I dont want to. I ruther never to know than to find out later I have been fooled.* He turned toward the room where the fire was, where his supper waited. This time he spoke aloud: "How to God," he said, "can a black man ask a white man to please not lay down with his black wife? And even if he could ask it, how to God can the white man promise he wont?"

3.

"George Wilkins?" Edmonds said. He came to the edge of the gallery—a young man still, yet possessing already something of that almost choleric shortness of temper which Lucas remembered in old Cass Edmonds but which had skipped Zack. In age he could have been Lucas' son, but actually was the lesser man for more reason than that, since it was not Lucas who paid taxes insurance and interest or owned anything which had to be kept ditched drained fenced and fertilised or gambled anything save his sweat, and that only as he saw fit, against God for his yearly sustenance. "What in hell has George Wilkins——"

Without changing the inflection of his voice and apparently without effort or even design Lucas became not Negro but nigger, not secret so much as impenetrable, not servile and not effacing, but enveloping himself in an aura of timeless and stupid impassivity almost like a smell. "He's running a kettle in that gully behind the Old West field. If you want the whisky too, look under his kitchen floor."

"A still?" Edmonds said. "On my land?" He began to roar. "Haven't I told and told every man woman and child on this place what I would do the first drop of white mule whisky I found on my land?"

"You didn't need to tell me," Lucas said. "I've lived on this place since I was born, since before your pa was. And you or him or old Cass either aint never heard of me having truck with any kind of whisky except that bottle of town whisky you and him give Molly Christmas."

"I know it," Edmonds said. "And I would have thought George Wilkins—" He ceased. He said, "Hah. Have I or haven't I heard something about George wanting to marry that girl of yours?"

For just an instant Lucas didn't answer. Then he said, "That's right."

"Hah," Edmonds said again. "And so you thought that by telling me on George before he got caught himself, I would be satisfied to make him chop up his kettle and pour out his whisky and then forget about it."

"I didn't know," Lucas said.

"Well, you know now," Edmonds said. "And George will too when the sheriff—" he went back into the house. Lucas listened to the hard, rapid, angry clapping of his heels on the floor, then to the prolonged violent grinding of the telephone crank. Then he stopped listening, standing motionless in the half-darkness, blinking a little. He thought,

All that worrying. I never even thought of that. Edmonds returned. "All right," he said. "You can go on home now. Go to bed. I know it wont do a damn bit of good to mention it, but I would like to see your south creek piece planted by tomorrow night. You doped around in it today like you hadn't been to bed for a week. I dont know what you do at night, but you are too old to be tomcatting around the country whether you think so or not."

He went back home. Now that it was all over, done, he realised how tired he actually was. It was as if the alternating waves of alarm and outrage and anger and fear of the past ten days, culminating in last night's frantic activity and the past thirty-six hours during which he had not even taken off his clothes, had narcotised him, deadened the very weariness itself. But it was all right now. If a little physical exhaustion, even another ten days or two weeks of it, was all required of him in return for that moment last night, he would not complain. Then he remembered that he had not told Edmonds of his decision to quit farming, for Edmonds to arrange to rent the land he had been working to someone else to finish his crop. But perhaps that was just as well too; perhaps even a single night would suffice to find the rest of the money which a churn that size must have contained, and he would keep the land, the crop, from old habit, for something to occupy him.— *Provided I dont need to keep it for a better reason still,* he thought grimly. *Since I probably aint even made a scratch yet on the kind of luck that can wait unto I am sixty-seven years old, almost too old to even want it, to make me rich.*

The house was dark except for a faint glow from the hearth in his and his wife's room. The room across the hallway where his daughter slept was dark too. It would be empty too. He had expected that. *I reckon George Wilkins is entitled to one more night of female company,* he thought. *From what I have heard, he wont find none of it where he's going tomorrow.*

When he got into bed his wife said without waking, "Whar you been? Walking the roads all last night. Walking the roads all tonight, with the ground crying to get planted. You just wait unto Mister Roth—" and then stopped talking without waking either. Sometime later, he waked. It was after midnight. He lay beneath the quilt on the shuck mattress. It would be happening about now. He knew how they did it—the white sheriff and revenue officers and deputies creeping and crawling among the bushes with drawn pistols, surrounding the kettle, sniffing and whiffing like hunting dogs at every stump and disfiguration of earth until every jug and keg was found and carried back to where the car waited; maybe they would even take a sup or two to ward off the night's chill before returning to the still to squat until George walked innocently in. He was neither triumphant nor vindictive. He even felt something personal toward George now. *He is young yet,* he thought. *They wont keep him down there forever.* In fact, as far as he, Lucas, was concerned, two weeks would be enough. *He can afford to give a year or two at it. And maybe when they lets him out it will be a lesson to him about whose daughter to fool with next time.*

Then his wife was leaning over the bed, shaking him and screaming. It was just after dawn. In his shirt and drawers he ran behind her, out onto the back gallery. Sitting on the ground before it was George Wilkins' patched and battered still; on the gallery itself was an assortment of fruit jars and stoneware jugs and a keg or so and one rusted five-gallon oilcan which, to Lucas' horrified and sleep-dulled eyes, appeared capable of holding enough liquid to fill a ten-foot horse trough. He could even see it in the glass jars—a pale, colorless fluid in which still floated the shreds of corn-husks which George's tenth-hand still had not removed. "Whar was Nat last night?" he cried. He grasped his wife by the shoulder, shaking her. "Whar was Nat, old woman?"

"She left right behind you!" his wife cried. "She followed you again, like night before last! Didn't you know it?"

"I knows it now," Lucas said. "Get the axe!" he said. "Bust it! We aint got time to get it away." But there was not time for that either. Neither of them had yet moved when the sheriff of the county, followed by a deputy, came around the corner of the house—a tremendous man, fat, who obviously had been up all night and obviously still did not like it.

"Damn it, Lucas," he said. "I thought you had better sense than this."

"This aint none of mine," Lucas said. "You know it aint. Even if it was, would I have had it here? George Wilkins——"

"Never you mind about George Wilkins," the sheriff said. "I've got him too. He's out there in the car, with that girl of yours. Go get your pants on. We're going to town."

Two hours later he was in the commissioner's office in the federal courthouse in Jefferson. He was still inscrutable of face, blinking a little, listening to George Wilkins breathing hard beside him and to the voices of the white men.

"Confound it, Carothers," the commissioner said, "what the hell kind of Senegambian Montague and Capulet is this anyhow?"

"Ask them!" Edmonds said violently. "Ask them! Wilkins and that girl of Lucas' want to get married. Lucas wouldn't hear of it for some reason—I just seem to be finding out now why. So last night Lucas came to my house and told me George was running a still on my land because—" without even a pause to draw a fresh breath Edmonds began to roar again "—he knew damn well what I would do because I have been telling every nigger on my place for years just what I would do if I ever found one drop of that damn wildcat——"

"Yes, yes," the commissioner said; "all right, all right. So you telephoned the sheriff——"

"And we got the message—" it was one of the deputies, a plump man though nowhere as big as the sheriff, voluble, muddy about the lower legs and a little strained and weary in the face too "—and we went out there and Mr Roth told us where to look. But there aint no kettle in the gully where he said, so we set down and thought about just where would we hide a still if we was one of Mr Roth's niggers and we went and looked there and sho enough there it was, neat and careful as you please, all took to pieces and about half buried and covered with brush against a kind of mound in the creek bottom. Only it was getting toward daybreak then, so we decided to come on back to George's house and look under the kitchen floor like Mr Roth said, and then have a little talk with George. So we come on back to George's house, only there aint any George or nobody else in it and nothing under the kitchen floor neither and so we are coming on back toward Mr

Roth's house to ask him if maybe he aint got the wrong house in mind maybe; it's just about full daylight now and we are about a hundred yards from Lucas's house when what do we see but George and the gal legging it up the hill toward Lucas's cabin with a gallon jug in each hand, only George busted the jugs on a root before we could get to them. And about that time Lucas's wife starts to yelling in the house and we run around to the back and there is another still setting in Lucas's back yard and about forty gallons of whisky setting on his back gallery like he was fixing to hold a auction sale and Lucas standing there in his drawers and shirt-tail, hollering, 'Git the axe and bust it! Git the axe and bust it!' "

"Yes," the commissioner said. "But who do you charge? You went out there to catch George, but all your evidence is against Lucas."

"There was two stills," the deputy said. "And George and that gal both swear Lucas has been making and selling whisky right there in Edmonds' back yard for twenty years." For an instant Lucas looked up and met Edmonds' glare, not of reproach and no longer even of surprise, but of grim and furious outrage. Then he looked away, blinking, listening to George Wilkins breathing hard beside him like a man in the profoundest depths of sleep, and to the voices.

"But you cant make his own daughter testify against him," the commissioner said.

"George can, though," the deputy said. "George aint any kin to him. Not to mention being in a fix where George has got to think up something good to say and think of it quick."

"Let the court settle all that, Tom," the sheriff said. "I

was up all last night and I haven't even had my breakfast yet. I've brought you a prisoner and thirty or forty gallons of evidence and two witnesses. Let's get done with this."

"I think you've brought two prisoners," the commissioner said. He began to write on the paper before him. Lucas watched the moving hand, blinking. "I'm going to commit them both. George can testify against Lucas, and that girl can testify against George. She aint any kin to George either."

He could have posted his and George's appearance bonds without altering the first figure of his bank balance. When Edmonds had drawn his own check to cover them, they returned to Edmonds' car. This time George drove it, with Nat in front with him. It was seventeen miles back home. For those seventeen miles he sat beside the grim and seething white man in the back seat, with nothing to look at but those two heads—that of his daughter where she shrank as far as possible from George, into her corner, never once looking back; that of George, the ruined panama hat raked above his right ear, who still seemed to swagger even sitting down. *Leastways his face aint all full of teeth now like it used to be whenever it found anybody looking at it,* he thought viciously. But never mind that either, right now. So he sat in the car when it stopped at the carriage gate and watched Nat spring out and run like a frightened deer up the lane toward his house, still without looking back, never once looking at him. Then they drove on to the mule lot, the stable, and he and George got out and again he could hear George breathing behind him while Edmonds, behind the wheel now, leaned his elbow in the window and glared at them both.

"Get your mules!" Edmonds said. "What in hell are you waiting for?"

"I thought you were fixing to say something," Lucas said. "So a man's kinfolks cant tell on him in court."

"Never you mind about that!" Edmonds said. "George can tell plenty, and he aint any kin to you. And if he should begin to forget, Nat aint any kin to George and she can tell plenty. I know what you are thinking about. But you have waited too late. If George and Nat tried to buy a wedding license now, they would probably hang you and George both. Besides, damn that. I'm going to take you both to the penitentiary myself as soon as you are laid-by. Now you get on down to your south creek piece. By God, this is one time you will take advice from me. And here it is: dont come out until you have finished it. If dark catches you, dont let it worry you. I'll send somebody down there with a lantern."

He was done with the south creek piece before dark; he had intended to finish it today anyhow. He was back at the stable, his mules watered and rubbed down and stalled and fed while George was still unharnessing. Then he entered the lane and in the beginning of twilight walked toward his house above whose chimney the windless supper smoke stood. He didn't walk fast, neither did he look back when he spoke. "George Wilkins," he said.

"Sir," George said behind him. They walked on in single file and almost step for step, about five feet apart.

"Just what was your idea?"

"I dont rightly know, sir," George said. "It uz mostly Nat's. We never aimed to get you into no trouble. She say maybe ifn we took and fotch that kettle from whar you and Mister Roth told them shurfs it was and you would find it settin on yo back porch, maybe when we offered to help you git shet of it fo they got here, yo mind might change about loandin us the money to—I mean to leffen us get married."

"Hah," Lucas said. They walked on. Now he could smell the cooking meat. He reached the gate and turned. George stopped too, lean, wasp-waisted, foppish even in faded overalls below the swaggering rake of the hat. "There's more folks than just me in that trouble."

"Yes sir," George said. "Hit look like it is. I hope it gonter be a lesson to me."

"I hope so too," Lucas said. "When they get done sending you to Parchman you'll have plenty of time between working cotton and corn you aint going to get no third and fourth of even, to study it." They looked at one another.

"Yes sir," George said. "Especially wid you there to help me worry hit out."

"Hah," Lucas said. He didn't move; he hardly raised his voice even: "Nat." He didn't even look toward the house then as the girl came down the path, barefoot, in a clean, faded calico dress and a bright headrag. Her face was swollen from crying, but her voice was defiant, not hysterical.

"It wasn't me that told Mister Roth to telefoam them shurfs!" she cried. He looked at her for the first time. He looked at her until even the defiance began to fade, to be replaced by something alert and speculative. He saw her glance flick past his shoulder to where George stood and return.

"My mind done changed," he said. "I'm going to let you

and George get married." She stared at him. Again he watched her glance flick to George and return.

"It changed quick," she said. She stared at him. Her hand, the long, limber, narrow, light-palmed hand of her race, rose and touched for an instant the bright cotton which bound her head. Her inflection, the very tone and pitch of her voice had changed. "Me, marry George Wilkins and go to live in a house whar the whole back porch is done already fell off and whar I got to walk a half a mile and back from the spring to fetch water? He aint even got no stove!"

"My chimbley cooks good," George said. "And I can prop up the porch."

"And I can get used to walking a mile for two lard buckets full of water," she said. "I dont wants no propped-up porch. I wants a new porch on George's house and a cook-stove and a well. And how you gonter get um? What you gonter pay for no stove with, and a new porch, and somebody to help you dig a well?" Yet it was still Lucas she stared at, ceasing with no dying fall of her high, clear soprano voice, watching her father's face as if they were engaged with foils. His face was not grim and neither cold nor angry. It was absolutely expressionless, impenetrable. He might have been asleep standing, as a horse sleeps. When he spoke, he might have been speaking to himself.

"A cook-stove," he said. "The back porch fixed. A well."

"A new back porch," she said. He might not have even heard her. She might not have spoken even.

"The back porch fixed," he said. Then she was not looking at him. Again the hand rose, slender and delicate and markless of any labor, and touched the back of her head-kerchief. Lucas moved. "George Wilkins," he said.

"Sir," George said.

"Come into the house," Lucas said.

And so, in its own good time, the other day came at last. In their Sunday clothes he and Nat and George stood beside the carriage gate while the car came up and stopped. "Morning, Nat," Edmonds said. "When did you get home?"

"I got home yistiddy, Mister Roth."

"You stayed in Vicksburg a good while. I didn't know you were going until Aunt Molly told me you were already gone."

"Yassuh," she said. "I lef the next day after them shurfs was here.—I didn't know it neither," she said. "I never much wanted to go. It was pappy's idea for me to go and see my aunt——"

"Hush, and get in the car," Lucas said. "If I'm going to finish my crop in this county or finish somebody else's crop in Parchman county, I would like to know it soon as I can."

"Yes," Edmonds said. He spoke to Nat again. "You and George go on a minute. I want to talk to Lucas." Nat and George went on. Lucas stood beside the car while Edmonds looked at him. It was the first time Edmonds had spoken to him since that morning three weeks ago, as though it had required those three weeks for his rage to consume itself, or die down at least. Now the white man leaned in the window, looking at the impenetrable face with its definite strain of white blood, the same blood which ran in his own veins, which had not only come to the negro through male descent while it had come to him from a woman, but had reached the negro a generation sooner—a face composed, inscrutable, even a little haughty, shaped even in expression in the pattern of his great-grandfather McCaslin's face. "I reckon you know what's going to happen to you," he said. "When that federal lawyer gets through with Nat, and Nat gets through with George, and George gets through with you and Judge Gowan gets through with all of you. You have been on this place all your life, almost twice as long as I have. You knew all the McCaslins and Edmonds both that ever lived here, except old Carothers. Was that still and that whisky in your back yard yours?"

"You know it wasn't," Lucas said.

"All right," Edmonds said. "Was that still they found in the creek bottom yours?"

They looked at each other. "I aint being tried for that one," Lucas said.

"Was that still yours, Lucas?" Edmonds said. They looked at one another. Yet still the face which Edmonds saw was absolutely blank, impenetrable. Even the eyes appeared to have nothing behind them. He thought, and not for the first time: *I am not only looking at a face older than mine and which has seen and winnowed more, but at a man most of whose blood was pure ten thousand years when my own anonymous beginnings became mixed enough to produce me.*

"Do you want me to answer that?" Lucas said.

"No!" Edmonds said violently. "Get in the car!"

When they reached town, the streets leading into it and the Square itself were crowded with cars and wagons; the flag rippled and flew in the bright May weather above the federal courthouse. Following Edmonds, he and Nat and George crossed the thronged pavement, walking in a narrow lane of faces they knew—other people from their place, people from other places along the creek and in the neighborhood, come the seventeen miles also with no hope of getting into the courtroom itself but just to wait on the street and see them pass—and faces they only knew by hearsay: the rich white lawyers and judges and marshals talking to one another around their proud cigars, the haughty and powerful of the earth. They entered the marble foyer, crowded too and sonorous with voices, where George began to walk gingerly on the hard heels of his Sunday shoes. Then Lucas took from his coat the thick, soiled, folded document which had lain hidden under the loose brick in his fireplace for three weeks now and touched Edmonds' arm with it—the paper thick enough and soiled enough yet which of its own accord apparently fell open at a touch, stiffly but easily too along the old hand-smudged folds, exposing, presenting among the meaning less and unread lettering between salutation and seal the three phrases in the cramped script of whatever nameless clerk which alone of the whole mass of it Lucas at least had bothered to read: *George Wilkins* and *Nathalie Beauchamp* and a date in October of last year.

"Do you mean," Edmonds said, "that you have had this all the time? All these three weeks?" But still the face he glared at was impenetrable, almost sleepy looking.

"You hand it to Judge Gowan," Lucas said.

He and Nat and George sat quietly on a hard wooden bench in a small office, where an oldish white man—Lucas knew him though not particularly that he was a deputy marshal—chewed a toothpick and read a Memphis newspaper. Then a young, brisk, slightly harried white man in glasses opened the door and glinted his glasses an instant and vanished; then, following the old white man they crossed the foyer again, the marble cavern murmurously resonant with the constant slow feet and the voices, the faces watching them again as they mounted the stairs. They crossed the empty courtroom without pausing and entered another office but larger, finer, quieter. There was an angry-looking man whom Lucas did not know—the United States Attorney, who had moved to Jefferson only after the administration changed eight years ago, after Lucas had stopped coming to town very often anymore. But Edmonds was there, and behind the table sat a man whom Lucas did know, who had used to come out in old Cass' time forty and fifty years ago and stay for weeks during the quail season, shooting with Zack, with Lucas to hold the horses while they got down to shoot when the dogs pointed. It took hardly any time at all.

"Lucas Beauchamp?" the judge said. "With thirty gallons of whisky and a still sitting on his back porch in broad daylight? Nonsense."

"Then there you are," the angry man said, flinging out his hands. "I didn't know anything about this either until Edmonds—" But the judge was not even listening to him. He was looking at Nat.

"Come here, girl," he said. Nat moved forward and stopped. Lucas could see her trembling. She looked small, thin as a lath, young; she was their youngest and last—seventeen, born into his wife's old age and, it sometimes seemed to him, into his too. She was too young to be married and face all the troubles which married people had to get through in order to become old and find out for themselves the taste and savor of peace. Just a stove and a new back porch and a well were not enough. "You're Lucas's girl?" the judge said.

"Yassuh," Nat said in her high, sweet, chanting soprano. "I'm name Nat. Nat Wilkins, Gawge Wilkins' wife. There the paper fer hit in yo hand."

"I see it is," the judge said. "It's dated last October."

"Yes sir, Judge," George said. "We been had it since I sold my cotton last fall. We uz married then, only she wont come to live in my house unto Mister Lu—I mean I gots a stove and the porch fixed and a well dug."

"Have you got that now?"

"Yes sir, Judge," George said. "I got the money for hit now and I'm just fo gittin the rest of it, soon as I gits around to the hammerin and the diggin."

"I see," the judge said. "Henry," he said to the other old man, the one with the toothpick, "have you got that whisky where you can pour it out?"

"Yes, Judge," the other said.

"And both those stills where you can chop them to pieces, destroy them good?"

"Yes, Judge."

"Then clear my office. Get them out of here. Get that jimber-jawed clown out of here at least."

"He's talking about you, George Wilkins," Lucas murmured.

"Yes sir," George said. "Sound like he is."

4.

At first he thought that two or three days at the outside would suffice—or nights, that is, since George would have to be in his crop during the day, let alone getting himself and Nat settled for marriage in their house. But a week passed, and though Nat would come back home at least once during the day, usually to borrow something, he had not seen George at all. He comprehended the root of his impatience—the mound and its secret which someone, any-one else, might stumble upon by ·chance as he had, the rapid and daily shortening of the alloted span in which he had not only to find the treasure but to get any benefit and pleasure from it, all in abeyance until he could com-plete the petty business which had intervened, and nothing with which to pass the period of waiting—the good year, the good early season, and cotton and corn springing up almost in the planter's wheel-print, so that there was now nothing to do but lean on the fence and watch it grow;— on the one hand, that which he wanted to do and could not; on the other, that which he could have done and no need for. But at last, in the second week, when he knew that in one more day his patience would be completely gone, he stood just inside his kitchen door and watched George enter and cross the lot in the dusk and enter the stable and emerge with his mare and put her to the wagon and drive away. So the next morning he went no further than his first patch and leaned on the fence in the bright dew looking at his cotton until his wife began to shout at him from the house.

When he entered, Nat was sitting in his chair beside the hearth, bent forward, her long narrow hands dangling limp between her knees, her face swollen and puffed again with crying. "Yawl and your George Wilkins!" Molly said. "Go on and tell him."

"He aint started on the well or nothing," Nat said. "He aint even propped up the back porch. With all that money you give him, he aint even started. And I axed him and he just say he aint got around to it yet, and I waited and I

axed him again and he still just say he aint got around to
it yet. Unto I told him at last that ifn he didn't get started
like he promised, my mind gonter change about whatall I
seed that night them shurfs come out here and so last night
he say he gwine up the road a .piece and do I wants to
come back home and stay because he mought not get back
unto late and I say I can bar the door because I thought
he was going to fix to start on the well. And when I seed
him catch up pappy's mare and wagon, I knowed that was
it. And it aint unto almost daylight when he got back, and
he aint got nothing. Not nothing to dig with and no boards
to fix the porch, and he had done spent the money pappy
give him. And I told him what I was gonter do and I was
waiting at the house soon as Mister Roth got up and I told
Mister Roth my mind done changed about what I seed
that night and Mister Roth started in to cussing and say I
done waited too late because I'm Gawge's wife now and
the Law wont listen to me and for me to come and tell
you and Gawge both to be offen his place by sundown."

"There now!" Molly cried. "There's your George Wilkins!" Lucas was already moving toward the door. "Whar
you gwine?" she said. "Whar we gonter move to?"

"You wait to start worrying about where we will move to
when Roth Edmonds starts to worrying about why we aint
gone," Lucas said.

The sun was well up now. It was going to be hot today;
it was going to make cotton and corn both before the sun
went down. When he reached George's house, George
stood quietly out from behind the corner of it. Lucas
crossed the grassless and sunglared yard, the light dust
swept into the intricate and curving patterns which Molly
had taught Nat. "Where is it?" Lucas said.

"I hid hit in that gully where mine use to be," George said. "Since them shurfs never found nothing there the yuther time, they'll think hit aint no use to look there no more."

"You fool," Lucas said. "Dont you know a week aint going to pass from now to the next election without one of them looking in that gully just because Roth Edmonds told them there was a still in it once? And when they catch you this time, you aint going to have any witness you have already been married to since last fall."

"They aint going to catch me this time," George said. "I done had my lesson. I'm gonter run this one the way you tells me to."

"You better had," Lucas said. "As soon as dark falls you take that wagon and get that thing out of that gully. I'll show you where to put it. Hah," he said. "And I reckon this one looks enough like the one that was in that gully before not to even been moved at all."

"No sir," George said. "This is a good one. The worm in hit is almost brand-new. That's how come I couldn't git him down on the price he axed. That porch and well money liked two dollars of being enough, but I just made that up myself, without needing to bother you. But it aint worrying about gittin caught that troubles my mind. What I cant keep from studying about is what we gonter tell Nat about that back porch and that well."

"What *we* is?" Lucas said.

"What I is, then," George said. Lucas looked at him for a moment.

"George Wilkins," he said.

"Sir," George said.

"I dont give no man advice about his wife," Lucas said.

Chapter Two

Aʙᴏᴜᴛ a hundred yards before they reached the commissary, Lucas spoke over his shoulder without stopping. "You wait here," he said.

"No, no," the salesman said. "I'll talk to him myself. If I cant sell it to him, there aint a—" He stopped. He recoiled actually; another step and he would have walked full tilt into Lucas. He was young, not yet thirty, with the assurance, the slightly soiled snap and dash, of his calling, and a white man. Yet he even stopped talking and looked at the negro in battered overalls who stood looking down at him not only with dignity but with command.

"You wait here," Lucas said. So the salesman leaned against the fence in the bright August morning, while Lucas went on to the commissary. He mounted the steps, beside which a bright-coated young mare with a blaze and three stockings stood under a wide plantation saddle, and entered the long room with its ranked shelves of tinned food and tobacco and patent medicines, its hooks pendant with trace chains and collars and hames. Edmonds sat at a roll-top desk beside the front window, writing in a ledger. Lucas stood quietly looking at the back of Edmonds' neck until the other turned. "He's come," Lucas said.

Edmonds swivelled the chair around, back-tilted. He was already glaring before the chair stopped moving; he said with astonishing violence: "No!"

"Yes," Lucas said.

"No!"

"He brought it with him," Lucas said. "I saw with my own eyes——"

"Do you mean to tell me you wrote him to come down here after I told you I wouldn't advance you three hundred dollars nor three hundred cents nor even three cents——"

"I saw it, I tell you," Lucas said. "I saw it work with my own eyes. I buried a dollar in my back yard this morning and that machine went right straight to where it was and found it. We are going to find that money tonight and I will pay you back in the morning."

"Good!" Edmonds said. "Fine! You've got over three thousand dollars in the bank. Advance yourself the money. Then you wont even have to pay it back." Lucas looked at him. He didn't even blink. "Hah," Edmonds said. "And because why? Because you know damn well just like I know damn well that there aint any money buried around here. You've been here sixty-seven years. Did you ever hear of anybody in this country with enough money to bury? Can you imagine anybody in this country burying anything worth as much as two bits that some of his kinfolks or his friends or his neighbors aint dug up and spent before he could even get back home and put his shovel away?"

"You're wrong," Lucas said. "Folks find it. Didn't I tell you about them two strange white men that come in here after dark that night three or four years ago and dug up twenty-two thousand dollars in a old churn and got out again before anybody even laid eyes on them? I saw the hole where they filled it up again. And the churn."

"Yes," Edmonds said. "You told me. And you didn't believe it then either. But now you've changed your mind. Is that it?"

"They found it," Lucas said. "Got clean away before anybody even knowed it, knowed they was here even."

"Then how do you know it was twenty-two thousand dollars?" But Lucas merely looked at him. It was not stubbornness but an infinite, almost Jehovah-like patience, as if he were contemplating the antics of a lunatic child.

"Your father would have lent me three hundred dollars if he was here," he said.

"But I aint," Edmonds said. "And if I could keep you from spending any of your money on a damn machine to hunt buried gold with, I would do that too. But then, you aint going to use your money, are you? That's why you came to me. You've got better sense. You just hoped I didn't have. Didn't you?"

"It looks like I'm going to have to use mine," Lucas said. "I'm going to ask you one more time——"

"No!" Edmonds said. Lucas looked at him for a good minute this time. He did not sigh.

"All right," he said.

When he emerged from the commissary, he saw George too, the soiled gleam of the ruined panama hat where George and the salesman now squatted in the shade of a tree, squatting on their heels without any other support. *Hah*, he thought, *He mought talk like a city man and he mought even think he is one. But I know now where he was born at.* The salesman looked up as Lucas approached. He gave Lucas one rapid, hard look and rose, already moving toward the commissary. "Hell," he said, "I told you all the time to let me talk to him."

"No," Lucas said. "You stay out of there."

"Then what are you going to do?" the salesman said. "Here I've come all the way from Memphis—And how you ever persuaded them up there in Saint Louis to send this machine out without any downpayment in the first place, I still dont see. And I'll tell you right now, if I've got to take it back, turn in an expense account for this trip and not one damn thing to show for it, something is——"

"We aint doing any good standing here, at least," Lucas said. He went on, the others following him, back to the gate, the road where the salesman's car waited. The divining machine sat on the back seat and Lucas stood in the open door, looking at it—an oblong metal box with a handle for carrying at each end, compact and solid, efficient and business-like and complex with knobs and dials. He didn't touch it. He just leaned in the door and stood over it, blinking, bemused. He spoke to no one. "And I watched it work," he said. "I watched it with my own eyes."

"What did you expect?" the salesman said. "That's what it's supposed to do. That's why we want three hundred dollars for it. Well?" he said. "What are you going to do? I've got to know, so I can know what to do myself. Aint you got three hundred dollars? What about some of your kinfolks? Hasn't your wife got three hundred dollars hid under the mattress somewhere?" Lucas mused on the machine. He did not look up yet.

"We will find that money tonight," he said. "You put in the machine and I'll show you where to look, and we'll go halves in it."

"Ha, ha, ha," the salesman said harshly, with no muscle of his face moving save the ones which parted his lips. "Now I'll tell one." Lucas mused above the box.

"We bound to find hit, captain," George said suddenly. "Two white men slipped in here three years ago and dug up twenty-two thousand dollars in a old churn one night and got clean away fo daylight."

"You bet," the salesman said. "And you knew it was exactly twenty-two grand because you found where they had throwed away the odd cents they never wanted to bother with."

"Naw sir," George said. "Hit mought a been more than twenty-two thousand dollars. Hit wuz a big churn."

"George Wilkins," Lucas said. He was still half way inside the car. He didn't even turn his head.

"Sir," George said.

"Hush," Lucas said. He withdrew his head and upper body and turned and looked at the salesman. Again the young white man saw a face absolutely impenetrable, even a little cold. "I'll swap you a mule for it," Lucas said.

"A mule?"

"When we find that money tonight, I'll buy the mule back from you for the three hundred dollars." George drew in his breath with a faint hissing sound. The salesman glanced quickly at him, at the raked hat, the rapid batting of his eyes. Then the salesman looked back at Lucas. They looked at one another—the shrewd, suddenly sober, suddenly attentive face of the young white man, the absolutely expressionless one of the negro.

"Do you own the mule?"

"How could I swap it to you if I didn't?" Lucas said.

"Let's go see it," the salesman said.

"George Wilkins," Lucas said.

"Sir," George said.

"Go to my stable and get my halter."

2.

Edmonds found the mule was missing as soon as the lotmen, Dan and Oscar, brought the drove in from pasture that evening. She was a three-year-old, eleven-hundred-pound mare mule named Alice Ben Bolt, and he had refused three hundred dollars for her in the spring. He didn't even curse. He merely surrendered the mare to Dan and waited beside the lot fence while the rapid beat of the mare's feet died away in the dusk and then returned and Dan sprang down and handed him his flashlight and pistol. Then, himself on the mare and the two negroes on saddleless mules, they went back across the pasture, fording the creek, to the gap in the fence through which the mule had been led. From there they followed the tracks of the mule and the man in the soft earth along the edge of a cotton field, to the road. And here too they could follow them, Dan walking now and carrying the flashlight, where the man had led the unshod mule in the soft dirt which bordered the gravel. "That's Alice's foot," Dan said. "I'd know it anywhere."

Later Edmonds would realise that both the negroes had recognised the man's footprints too. But at the time his very fury and concern had short-circuited his normal sensitivity to negro behavior. They would not have told him who made the tracks even if he had demanded to know, but the realisation that they knew would have enabled him to make the correct divination and so save himself the four or five hours of mental turmoil and physical effort which he was about to enter.

They lost the tracks. He expected to find the marks where the mule had been loaded into a waiting truck; whereupon he would return home and telephone to the sheriff in Jefferson and to the Memphis police to watch the horse-and-mule markets tomorrow. There were no such marks. It took them almost an hour to find where the tracks had disappeared onto the gravel, crossing it, descending through the opposite roadside weeds, to re-appear in another field three hundred yards away. Supper-less, raging, the mare which had been under saddle all day unfed too, he followed the two shadowy mules, cursing Alice and the darkness and the single puny light on which they were forced to depend.

Two hours later they were in the creek bottom four miles from the house. He was walking too now, lest he dash his brains out against a limb, stumbling and thrashing among briers and undergrowth and rotting logs and tree-tops, leading the mare with one hand and fending his face with the other arm and trying to watch his feet, so that he walked into one of the mules, instinctively leaping in the right direction as it lashed viciously back at him with one hoof, before he discovered that the negroes had stopped. Then, cursing aloud now and leaping quickly again to avoid the invisible second mule which would be somewhere on that side, he realised that the flashlight was off now and he too saw the faint, smoky glare of a light-wood torch among the trees ahead. It was moving. "That's right," he said quickly. "Keep the light off." He called Oscar's name. "Give the mules to Dan and come back here and take the mare." He waited, watching the light, until the negro's hand fumbled at his. He relinquished the reins and moved around the mules, drawing the pistol and still watching the moving light. "Hand me the flashlight," he said. "You and Oscar wait here."

"I better come with you," Dan said.

"All right," Edmonds said, watching the light. "Let Oscar hold the mules." He went on without waiting, though he presently heard the negro close behind him, both of them moving as rapidly as they dared. The rage was not cold now. It was hot, and there was an eagerness upon him, a kind of vindictive exultation as he plunged on, heedless of underbrush or log, the flashlight in his left hand and the pistol in his right, gaining rapidly on the torch.

"It's the Old Injun's mound," Dan murmured behind him. "That's how come that light looked so high up. Him and George Wilkins ought to be pretty nigh through it by now."

"Him and George Wilkins?" Edmonds said. He stopped dead in his tracks. He whirled. He was not only about to perceive the whole situation in its complete and instantaneous entirety, as when the photographer's bulb explodes, but he knew now that he had seen it all the while and had refused to believe it purely and simply because he knew that when he did accept it, his brain would burst. "Lucas and George?"

"Digging down that mound," Dan said. "They been at it every night since Uncle Lucas found that thousand-dollar gold piece in it last spring."

"And you knew about it?"

"We all knowed about it. We been watching them. A thousand-dollar gold piece Uncle Lucas found that night when he was trying to hide his—" The voice died away.

Edmonds couldn't hear it any more, drowned by a rushing in his skull which, had he been a few years older, would have been apoplexy. He could neither breathe nor see for a moment. Then he whirled again. He said something in a hoarse strangled voice and sprang on, crashing at last from the undergrowth into the glade where the squat mound lifted the gaping yawn of its gutted flank like a photographer's backdrop before which the two arrested figures gaped at him—the one carrying before him what Edmonds might have taken for a receptacle containing feed except that he now knew neither of these had taken time to feed Alice or any other mule since darkness fell, the other holding the smoking pine-knot high above the ruined rake of the panama hat.

"You, Lucas!" he shouted. George flung the torch away, but Edmonds' flashlight already held them spitted. Then he saw the white man, the salesman, for the first time, snap-brim hat, necktie and all, just rising from beside a tree, his trousers rolled to his knees and his feet invisible in caked mud. "That's right," Edmonds said. "Go on, George. Run. I believe I can hit that hat without even touching you." He approached, the flashlight's beam contracting onto the metal box which Lucas held, gleaming and glinting among the knobs and dials. "So that's it," he said. "Three hundred dollars. I wish somebody would come into this country with a seed that had to be worked everyday from New Year's right on through Christmas. As soon as you niggers are laid-by, trouble starts. But never mind that. Because I aint going to worry about Alice tonight. And if you and George want to spend the rest of it walking around with that damn machine, that's your business. But that mule is going to be in her stall in my stable at sunup. Do you hear?" Now the salesman appeared suddenly at Lucas' elbow. Edmonds had forgotten about him.

"What mule is that?" he said. Edmonds turned the light on him for a moment.

"My mule, sir," he said.

"Is that so?" the other said. "I've got a bill of sale for that mule. Signed by Lucas here."

"Have you now?" Edmonds said. "You can make pipe lighters out of it when you get home."

"Is that so? Look here, Mister What's-your-name—" But Edmonds had already turned the light back to Lucas, who still held the divining machine before him as if it were some object symbolical and sanctified for a ceremony, a ritual.

"On second thought," Edmonds said, "I aint going to worry about that mule at all. I told you this morning what I thought about this business. But you are a grown man; if you want to fool with it, I cant stop you. By God, I dont even want to. But if that mule aint in her stall by sunup tomorrow, I'm going to telephone the sheriff. Do you hear me?"

"I hear you," Lucas said sullenly. Now the salesman spoke again.

"All right, big boy," he said. "If that mule is moved from where she's at until I'm ready to load her up and move out of here, I'm going to telephone the sheriff. Do you hear that too?" This time Edmonds jumped, flung, the light beam at the salesman's face.

"Were you talking to me, sir?" he said.

"No," the salesman said. "I'm talking to him. And he heard me." For a moment longer Edmonds held the beam on the other. Then he dropped it, so that only their legs

and feet showed, planted in the pool and its refraction as
if they stood in water. He put the pistol back into his
pocket.

"Well, you and Lucas have got till daylight to settle
that. Because that mule is going to be back in my stable
at sunup." He turned. Lucas watched him go back to
where Dan waited at the edge of the glade. Then the two
of them went on, the light swinging and flicking on among
the trees, the brush. Presently it vanished.

"George Wilkins," Lucas said.

"Sir," George said.

"Find the pine-knot and light it again." George did so;
once more the red glare streamed and stank away in thick
smoke, upward against the August stars of more than midnight. Lucas put the divining machine down and took the
torch. "Grab holt of that thing," he said. "I got to find
it now."

But when day broke they had not found it. The torch
paled in the wan, dew-heavy light. The salesman was
asleep on the wet ground now, drawn into a ball against the
dawn's wet chill, unshaven, the dashing city hat crumpled
beneath his cheek, his necktie wrenched sideways in the
collar of his soiled white shirt, his muddy trousers rolled
to his knees, the brightly-polished shoes of yesterday now
two shapeless lumps of caked mud. When they waked him
at last he sat up cursing. But he knew at once where he
was and why. "All right now," he said. "If that mule
moves one foot from that cottonhouse where we left her,
I'm going to get the sheriff."

"I just want one more night," Lucas said. "That money
is here."

"Take one more," the salesman said. "Take a hundred.

Spend the rest of your life here if you want to. Just tell me first what about that fellow that claims he owns that mule?"

"I'll tend to him," Lucas said. "I'll tend to him this morning. You dont need to worry about that. Besides, if you try to move the mule yourself today, that sheriff will take her away from you. You just leave her where she is and stop worrying yourself and me too. Let me have just one more night with this thing and I'll fix everything."

"All right," the salesman said. "But do you know what one more night is going to cost you? It's going to cost you exactly twenty-five dollars more. Now I'm going to town and go to bed."

They returned to the salesman's car. He put the divining machine back into the trunk of the car and locked it. He let Lucas and George out at Lucas' gate. The car went on down the road, already going fast. George batted his eyes rapidly after it. "Now whut we gonter do?" he said.

"Eat your breakfast quick as you can and get back here," Lucas said. "You are going to town and back by noon."

"I needs to go to bed too," George said. "I'm bad off to sleep too."

"You can sleep tomorrow," Lucas said. "Maybe most of tonight."

"I could have rid in and come back with him, if you had just said so sooner," George said.

"Hah," Lucas said. "But I didn't. You eat your breakfast quick as you can. Or if you think maybe you cant catch a ride to town, maybe you better start now without waiting for breakfast. Because it will be thirty-four miles to walk, and you are going to be back here by noon."

When George reached Lucas' gate ten minutes later, Lucas met him, the check already filled out in his laborious, cramped, though quite legible hand. It was for fifty dollars. "Get it in silver dollars," Lucas said. "And be back here by noon."

It was just dusk when the salesman's car stopped again at Lucas' gate, where Lucas and George waited. George carried a pick and a long-handled shovel. The salesman was freshly shaven and his face looked rested; the snap-brim hat had been brushed and his shirt was clean. But he wore now a pair of cotton khaki pants still bearing the manufacturer's stitched label and still showing the creases where they had lain folded on the store's shelf when it opened for business that morning. He gave Lucas a hard, jeering stare as Lucas and George approached. "I aint going to ask if my mule's all right," he said. "Because I dont need to. Do I?"

"It's all right," Lucas said. He and George got into the back seat. The divining machine now sat on the front seat beside the salesman. George stopped halfway in and blinked rapidly at it.

"I just happened to think how rich I'd be if I just knowed what it knows," he said. "All of us would be. We wouldn't need to be wasting no night after night hunting buried money then, would we?" He addressed the salesman now, affable, deferential, chatty: "Then you and Mister Lucas neither wouldn't care who owned no mule, nor even if there was ere mule to own, would you?"

"Hush, and get in the car," Lucas said. The salesman put the car into gear, but it did not move yet. He sat half-turned, looking back at Lucas.

"Well?" he said. "Where do you want to take your walk tonight? Same place?"

"Not there," Lucas said. "I'll show you where. We were looking in the wrong place. I misread the paper."

"You bet," the salesman said. "It's worth that extra twenty-five bucks to have found that out——" He had started the car. Now he stopped it so suddenly that Lucas and George, sitting gingerly on the edge of the seat, were flung forward against the back of the front one. "What did you say?" the salesman said. "You did what to the paper?"

"I misread it," Lucas said.

"Misread what?"

"The paper."

"You mean you've got a letter or something that tells where it was buried?"

"That's right," Lucas said. "I misread it yesterday."

"Where is it?"

"It's put away in my house."

"Go get it."

"Never mind," Lucas said. "We wont need it. I read it right this time." For a moment longer the salesman looked at Lucas over his shoulder. Then he turned his head and put his hand to the gear lever, but the car was already in gear.

"All right," he said. "Where's the place?"

"Drive on," Lucas said. "I'll show you."

It took them almost two hours to reach it, the road not even a road but a gullied overgrown path winding through hills, the place they sought not in the bottom but on a hill overlooking the creek—a clump of ragged cedars, the ruins of old cementless chimneys, a depression which was once a well or a cistern, the old wornout brier- and sedge-choked fields spreading away and a few snaggled trees of what had been an orchard, shadowy and dim beneath the moonless sky where the fierce stars of late summer swam. "It's in the orchard," Lucas said. "It's divided, buried in two separate places. One of them's in the orchard."

"Provided the fellow that wrote you the letter aint come back and joined them together again," the salesman said. "What are we waiting on? Here, Jack," he said to George, "grab that thing out of there." George lifted the divining machine from the car. The salesman had a flashlight now, quite new, thrust into his hip pocket, though he didn't put it on at once. He looked around at the dark horizon of other hills, visible even in the darkness for miles. "By God, you better find it first pop this time. There probably aint a man in ten miles that can walk that wont be up here inside of an hour, watching us."

"Dont tell me that," Lucas said. "Tell it to this three-hundred-and-twenty-five-dollar talking box I done bought that dont seem to know how to say nothing but No."

"You aint bought this box yet, big boy," the salesman said. "You say one of the places is in them trees there. All right. Where?"

Lucas, carrying the shovel, entered the orchard. The others followed. The salesman watched Lucas pause, squinting at the trees and sky to orient himself, moving on again. At last he stopped. "We can start here," he said. The salesman snapped on the flashlight, cupping the beam with his hand onto the box in George's hands.

"All right, Jack," he said. "Get going."

"I better tote it," Lucas said.

"No," the salesman said. "You're too old. I dont know yet that you can even keep up with us."

"I did last night," Lucas said.

"This aint last night," the salesman said. "Get on, Jack!" he said sharply. They moved on, George in the middle, carrying the machine, while all three of them watched the small cryptic dials in the flashlight's contracted beam as they worked back and forth across the orchard in parallel traverses, all three watching when the needles jerked into life and gyrated and spun for a moment, then stopped, quivering. Then Lucas held the box and watched George spading into the light's concentrated pool and saw the rusted can come up at last and the bright cascade of silver dollars glint and rush about the salesman's hands and heard the salesman's voice: "Well, by God. Well, by God." Lucas squatted also. He and the salesman squatted opposite one another across the pit.

"Well, I done found this much of it, anyhow," Lucas said. The salesman, one hand spread upon the scattered coins, made a slashing blow with the other as if Lucas had reached for the money. Squatting, he laughed harshly and steadily at Lucas.

"*You* found? This machine dont belong to you, old man."

"I bought it from you," Lucas said.

"With what?"

"A mule," Lucas said. The other laughed at him across the pit, harsh and steady. "I give you a billy sale for it," Lucas said.

"Which never was worth a damn," the salesman said. "It's in my car yonder. Go and get it whenever you want to. It was so worthless I never even bothered to tear it up."

He scrabbled the coins back into the can. The flashlight lay on the ground where he had dropped it, flung it, still burning. He rose quickly out of the light until only his lower legs showed, in the new creased cotton trousers, the low black shoes which had not been polished again but merely washed. "All right," he said. "This aint hardly any of it. You said it was divided, buried in two separate places. Where's the other one?"

"Ask your finding machine," Lucas said. "Aint it supposed to know? Aint that why you want three hundred dollars for it?" They faced one another in the darkness, two shadows, faceless. Lucas moved. "Then I reckon we can go home," he said. "George Wilkins."

"Sir," George said.

"Wait," the salesman said. Lucas paused. They faced one another again, invisible. "There wasn't over a hundred here," the salesman said. "Most of it is in the other place. I'll give you ten percent."

"It was my letter," Lucas said. "That aint enough."

"Twenty," the salesman said. "And that's all."

"I want half," Lucas said.

"Half?"

"And that mule paper back, and another paper saying that that machine is mine."

"Ha ha," the salesman said. "And ha ha ha. You say that letter said in the orchard. The orchard aint very big. And most of the night left, not to mention tomor——"

"I said it said some of it was in the orchard," Lucas said. They faced one another in the darkness.

"Tomorrow," the salesman said.

"Now," Lucas said.

"Tomorrow."

"Now," Lucas said. The invisible face stared at his own invisible face. Both he and George seemed to feel the windless summer air moving to the white man's trembling

"Jack," the salesman said, "how much did you say them other fellows found?" But Lucas answered before George could speak.

"Twenty-two thousand dollars."

"Hit mought er been more than twenty-two thousand," George said. "Hit was a big——"

"All right," the salesman said. "I'll give you a bill of sale for it as soon as we finish."

"I want it now," Lucas said. They returned to the car. Lucas held the flashlight. They watched the salesman rip open his patent brief case and jerk out of it and fling toward Lucas the bill of sale for the mule. Then they watched his jerking hand fill in the long printed form with its carbon duplicates and sign it and rip out one of the duplicates.

"You get possession tomorrow morning," he said. "It belongs to me until then." He sprang out of the car. "Come on."

"And half it finds is mine," Lucas said.

"How in hell is it going to be any half or any nothing, with you standing there running your mouth?" the salesman said. "Come on." But Lucas didn't move.

"What about them fifty dollars we done already found then?" he said. "Dont I get half of them?" This time the salesman merely stood laughing at him, harsh and steady and without mirth. Then he was gone. He hadn't even closed the brief case. He snatched the machine from George and the flashlight from Lucas and ran back toward the orchard, the light jerking and leaping as he ran. "George Wilkins," Lucas said.

"Sir," George said.

"Take that mule back where you got it. Then go tell Roth Edmonds he can quit worrying folks about it."

3.

He mounted the gnawed steps beside which the bright mare stood under the wide saddle, and entered the long room with its ranked shelves of tinned food, the hooks from which hung collars and traces and hames and plow-lines, its smell of molasses and cheese and leather and kerosene. Edmonds swivelled the chair around from the desk. "Where've you been?" he said. "I sent word to you two days ago I wanted to see you. Why didn't you come?"

"I was in bed, I reckon," Lucas said. "I been up all night long for the last three nights. I cant stand it any more like when I was a young man. You wont neither when you are my age."

"And I've got better sense at half your age than to try it. And maybe when you get twice mine, you'll have too. But that's not what I wanted. I want to know about that damn Saint Louis drummer. Dan says he's still here. What's he doing?"

"Hunting buried money," Lucas said.

For a moment Edmonds didn't speak. Then he said, "What? Hunting what? What did you say?"

"Hunting buried money," Lucas said. He let himself go easily back against the edge of the counter. He took from his vest pocket a small tin of snuff and uncapped it and filled the cap carefully and exactly with snuff and drew his lower lip outward between thumb and finger and tilted the snuff into it and capped the tin and put it back in his vest pocket. "Using my finding box. He rents it from me by the night. That's why I've been having to stay up all night, to see I got the box back. But last night he never turned up, so I got a good night's sleep for a change. So I reckon he's done gone back wherever it was he come from."

Edmonds sat in the swivel chair and stared at Lucas. "Rents it from you? The same machine you stole my—that you—the same machine——"

"For twenty-five dollars a night," Lucas said. "That's what he charged me to use it one night. So I reckon that's the regular rent on them. He sells them; he ought to know. Leastways, that's what I charges." Edmonds put his hands on the chair arms, but he didn't move yet. He sat perfectly still, leaning forward a little, staring at the negro leaning against the counter, in whom only the slight shrinkage of the jaws revealed the old man, in threadbare mohair trousers such as Grover Cleveland or President Taft might have worn in the summertime, a white stiff-bosomed collarless shirt beneath a pique vest yellow with age and looped across by a heavy gold watchchain, and the sixty-dollar handmade beaver hat which Edmonds' grandfather had given him fifty years ago above the face which was not sober and not grave but wore no expression at all. "Because he was looking in the wrong place," he said. "He was hunting up there on that hill. That money is buried down yonder by the creek somewhere. Them two white men that slipped in here that night four years ago and got clean away with twenty-two thousand dollars——" Now Edmonds got himself out of the chair and onto his feet.

He drew a long deep breath and began to walk steadily toward Lucas. "And now we·done got shut of him, me and George Wilkins—" Walking steadily toward him, Edmonds expelled his breath. He had believed it would be a shout but it was not much more than a whisper.

"Get out of here," he said. "Go home. And dont come back. Dont ever come back. When you need supplies, send Aunt Molly after them."

Chapter Three

When Edmonds glanced up from the ledger and saw the old woman coming up the road, he did not recognise her. He returned to the ledger and it was not until he heard her toiling up the steps and saw her enter the commissary itself, that he knew who it was. Because for something like four or five years now he had never seen her outside her own gate. He would pass the house on his mare while riding his crops and see her sitting on the gallery, her shrunken face collapsed about the reed stem of a clay pipe, or moving about the washing-pot and clothes-line in the back yard, moving slowly and painfully, as the very old move, appearing to be much older even to Edmonds, when he thought about it at all, than Edmonds certainly knew her to be. And regularly once a month he would get down and tie the mare to the fence and enter the house with a tin of tobacco and a small sack of the soft cheap candy which she loved, and visit with her for a half hour. He called it a libation to his luck, as the centurion spilled first a little of the wine he drank, though actually it was to his ancestors and to the conscience which he would have probably affirmed he did not possess, in the form, the person, of the negro woman who had been the only mother he ever knew, who had not only delivered him on that night of rain and flood when her husband had very nearly lost his life fetching the doctor who arrived too late, but moved into the very house, bringing her own child, the white child and the black one sleeping in the same room with her so she could suckle them both until he was weaned, and never out of the house very long at a time until he went off to school at twelve—a small woman, almost tiny, who in the succeeding forty years seemed to have grown even smaller, in the same clean white headcloth and aprons which he first remembered, whom he knew to be actually younger than Lucas but who looked much older, incredibly old, who during the last few years had begun to call him by his father's name, or even by the title which the older negroes referred to his grandfather.

"Good Lord," he said. "What are you doing away over here? Why didn't you send Lucas? He ought to know better than to let you ———"

"He's in bed asleep now," she said. She was panting a little from the walk. "That's how I had a chance to come. I dont want nothing. I come to talk to you." She turned a little toward the window. Then he saw the myriad-wrinkled face.

"Why, what is it?" he said. He rose from the swivel chair and drew the other one, a straight chair with wire-braced legs, out from behind the desk. "Here," he said. But she only looked from him to the chair with the same blind look until he took her by the arm which, beneath the two or three layers of clothing beneath the faded, perfectly clean dress, felt no larger than the reed stem of the pipe she smoked. He led her to the chair and lowered her into it, the voluminous layer on layer of her skirts and underskirts spreading. Immediately she bowed her head and turned it aside and raised one gnarled hand, like a tiny clump of dried and blackened roots, before her eyes.

"The light hurts them," she said. He helped her up and turned the chair until its back was toward the window. This time she found it herself and sat down. Edmonds returned to the swivel chair.

"All right," he said. "What is it?"

"I want to leave Lucas," she said. "I want one of them . . . one of them . . ." Edmonds sat perfectly motionless, staring at the face which now he could not distinctly see.

"You what?" he said. "A divorce? After forty-five years, at your age? What will you do? How will you get along without somebody——"

"I can work. I will ——"

"Damn that," Edmonds said. "You know I didn't mean that. Even if father hadn't fixed it in his will to take care of you for the rest of your life. I mean what will you do? Leave the house that belongs to you and Lucas and go live with Nat and George?"

"That will be just as bad," she said. "I got to go clean away. Because he's crazy. Ever since he got that machine, he's done went crazy. Him and—and . . ." Even though he had just spoken it, he realised that she couldn't even think of George's name. She spoke again, immobile, looking at nothing as far as he could tell, her hands like two cramped ink-splashes on the lap of the immaculate apron: "—stays out all night long every night with it, hunting that buried money. He dont even take care of his own stock right no more. I feeds the mare and the hogs and milks, tries to. But that's all right. I can do that. I'm glad to do that when he is sick in the body. But he's sick in the mind now.

Bad sick. He dont even get up to go to church on Sunday no more. He'd bad sick, marster. He's doing a thing the Lord aint meant for folks to do. And I'm afraid."

"Afraid of what?" Edmonds said. "Lucas is strong as a horse. He's a better man than I am, right now. He's all laid-by now, with nothing to do until his crop makes. It wont hurt him to stay up all night walking up and down that creek with George for a while. He'll have to quit next month to pick his cotton."

"It aint that I'm afraid of."

"Then what?" he said. "What is it?"

"I'm afraid he's going to find it."

Again Edmonds sat in his chair, looking at her. "Afraid he's going to find it?" Still she looked at nothing that he could see, motionless, tiny, like a doll, an ornament.

"Because God say, 'What's rendered to My earth, it belong to Me unto I resurrect it. And let him or her touch it, and beware.' And I'm afraid. I got to go. I got to be free of him."

"There aint any buried money in this country," Edmonds said. "Hasn't he been poking around in the bottom ever since last spring, hunting for it? And that machine aint going to find it either. I tried my best to keep him from buying it. I did everything I knew except have that damn agent arrested for trespass. I wish now I had done that. If I had just foreseen— But that wouldn't have done any good. Lucas would just have met him down the road somewhere and bought it. But he aint going to find any more buried money with it than he found walking up and down the creek, making George Wilkins dig where he thought it ought to be. Even he'll believe that soon. He'll quit. Then he'll be all right."

"No," she said. "Lucas is an old man. He dont look it, but he's sixty-seven years old. And when a man that old takes up money-hunting, it's like when he takes up gambling or whisky or women. He aint going to have time to quit. And then he's gonter be lost, lost. . . ." She ceased. She did not move on the hard chair, not even the depthless splotches of her knotted hands against the apron's blanched spread. *Damn, damn, damn,* Edmonds thought.

"I could tell you how to cure him in two days," he said. "If you were twenty years younger. But you couldn't do it now."

"Tell me. I can do it."

"No," he said. "You are too old now."

"Tell me. I can do it."

"Wait till he comes in with that thing tomorrow morning, then take it yourself and go down to the creek and hunt buried money. Do it the next morning, and the one after that. Let him find out that's what you are doing— using his machine while he is asleep, all the time he is asleep and cant watch it, cant hunt himself. Let him come in and find there's no breakfast ready for him, wake up and find there's no supper ready because you're still down in the creek bottom, hunting buried money with his machine. That'll cure him. But you're too old. You couldn't stand it. You go back home and when Lucas wakes up, you and he— No, that's too far for you to walk twice in one day. Tell him I said to wait there for me. I'll come after supper and talk to him."

"Talking wont change him. I couldn't. And you cant. All I can do is to go clean away from him."

"Maybe it cant," Edmonds said. "But I can damn sure

try it: And he will damn sure listen. I'll be there after supper. You tell him to wait."

She rose then. He watched her toil back down the road toward home, tiny, almost like a doll. It was not just concern, and, if he had told himself the truth, not concern for her at all. He was raging—an abrupt boiling-over of an accumulation of floutings and outrages covering not only his span but his father's lifetime too, back into the time of his grandfather McCaslin Edmonds. Lucas was not only the oldest person living on the place, older even than Edmonds' father would have been, there was that quarter strain not only of white blood and not even Edmonds blood, but of old Carothers McCaslin himself, from whom Lucas was descended not only by a male line but in only two generations, while Edmonds was descended by a female line and five generations back; even as a child the boy remarked how Lucas always referred to his father as Mr Edmonds, never as Mister Zack, as the other negroes did, and how with a cold and deliberate calculation he evaded having to address the white man by any name whatever when speaking to him.

Yet it was not that Lucas made capital of his white or even his McCaslin blood, but the contrary. It was as if he were not only impervious to that blood, he was indifferent to it. He didn't even need to strive with it. He didn't even have to bother to defy it. He resisted it simply by being the composite of the two races which made him, simply by possessing it. Instead of being at once the battle-ground and victim of the two strains, he was a vessel, durable, ancestryless, nonconductive, in which the toxin and its anti stalemated one another, seetheless, unrumored in the outside air. There had been three of them once: James, then a sister named Fonsiba, then Lucas, children of Aunt Tomey's Turl, old Carothers McCaslin's son, and Tennie Beauchamp, whom Edmonds' great-uncle Amodeus McCaslin won from a neighbor in a poker game in 1859. Fonsiba married and went to Arkansas to live and never returned, though Lucas continued to hear from her until her death. But James, the eldest, ran away before he became of age and didn't stop until he had crossed the Ohio River and they never heard from or of him again at all— that is, that his white kindred ever knew. It was as though he had not only (as his sister was later to do) put running water between himself and the land of his grandmother's betrayal and his father's nameless birth, but he had interposed latitude and geography too, shaking from his feet forever the very dust of the land where his white ancestor could acknowledge or repudiate him from one day to another, according to his whim, but where he dared not even repudiate the white ancestor save when it met the white man's humor of the moment.

But Lucas remained. He didn't have to stay. Of the three children, he not only had no material shackles (nor, as Carothers Edmonds began to comprehend later, moral ones either) holding him to the place, he alone was equipped beforehand with financial independence to have departed forever at any time after his twenty-first birthday. It was known father to son to son among the Edmonds until it came to Carothers in his turn, how when in the early fifties old Carothers McCaslin's twin sons, Amodeus and Theophilus, first put into operation their scheme for the manumission of their father's slaves, there was made an especial provision (hence a formal acknowledgment, even though only by inference and only from his white

half-brothers) for their father's negro son. It was a sum
of money, with the accumulated interest, to become the
negro son's on his verbal demand but which Tomey's Turl,
who elected to remain even after his constitutional liber-
ation, never availed himself of. And he died, and old Carothers McCaslin was dead more than fifty years then, and
Amodeus and Theophilus were dead too, at seventy and
better, in the same year as they had been born in the same
year, and McCaslin Edmonds now had the land, the plantation, in fee and title both, relinquished to him by Isaac
McCaslin, Theophilus' son, for what reason, what con-
sideration other than the pension which McCaslin and his
son Zachary and his son Carothers still paid to Isaac in his
little jerry-built bungalow in Jefferson, no man certainly
knew. But relinquished it certainly was, somehow and
somewhere back in that dark time in Mississippi when a
man had to be hard and ruthless to get a patrimony to leave
behind himself and strong and hard to keep it until he
could bequeath it;—relinquished, repudiated even, by its
true heir (Isaac, 'Uncle Ike', childless, a widower now, living in his dead wife's house the title to which he likewise
declined to assume, born into his father's old age and himself born old and became steadily younger and younger
until, past seventy himself and at least that many years
nearer eighty than he ever admitted any more, he had
acquired something of a young boy's high and selfless inno-
cence) who had retained of the patrimony, and by his own
request, only the trusteeship of the legacy which his negro
uncle still could not quite seem to comprehend was his
for the asking.

He never asked for it. He died. Then his first son,
James, fled, quitted the cabin he had been born in, the

plantation, Mississippi itself, by night and with nothing save the clothes he walked in. When Isaac McCaslin heard about it in town he drew a third of the money, the legacy, with its accumulated interest, in cash and departed also and was gone a week and returned and put the money back into the bank. Then the daughter, Fonsiba, married and moved to Arkansas. This time Isaac went with them and transferred a third of the legacy to a local Arkansas bank and arranged for Fonsiba to draw three dollars of it each week, no more and no less, and returned home. Then one morning Isaac was at home, looking at a newspaper, not reading it, looking at it, when he realised what it was and why. It was the date. *It's somebody's birthday*, he thought. He said aloud, "It's Lucas's. He's twenty-one today," as his wife entered. She was a young woman then; they had been married only a few years but he had already come to know the expression which her face wore, looking at it always as he did now: peacefully and with pity for her and regret too, for her, for both of them, knowing the tense bitter indomitable voice as well as he did the expression:

"Lucas Beauchamp is in the kitchen. He wants to see you. Maybe your cousin has sent you word he has decided to stop even that fifty dollars a month he swapped you for your father's farm." But it was all right. It didn't matter. He could ask her forgiveness as loudly thus as if he had shouted, express his pity and grief; husband and wife did not need to speak words to one another, not just from the old habit of living together but because in that one long-ago instant at least out of the long and shabby stretch of their human lives, even though they knew at the time it wouldn't and couldn't last, they had touched and become as God when they voluntarily and in advance forgave one another for all that each knew the other could never be. Then Lucas was in the room, standing just inside the door, his hat in one hand against his leg—the face the color of a used saddle, the features Syriac, not in a racial sense but as the heir to ten centuries of desert horsemen. It was not at all the face of their grandfather, Carothers McCaslin. It was the face of the generation which had just preceded them: the composite tintype face of ten thousand undefeated Confederate soldiers almost indistinguishably caricatured, composed, cold, colder than his, more ruthless than his, with more bottom than he had.

"Many happy returns!" Isaac said. "I godfrey, I was just about——"

"Yes," Lucas said. "The rest of that money. I wants it."

"Money?" Isaac said. "Money?"

"That Old Marster left for pappy. If it's still ourn. If you're going to give it to us."

"It's not mine to give or withhold either. It was your father's. All any of you had to do was to ask for it. I tried to find Jim after he——"

"I'm asking now," Lucas said.

"All of it? Half of it is Jim's."

"I can keep it for him same as you been doing."

"Yes," Isaac said. "You're going too," he said. "You're leaving too."

"I aint decided yet," Lucas said. "I might. I'm a man now. I can do what I want. I want to know I can go when I decide to."

"You could have done that at any time. Even if grandpa hadn't left money for Tomey's Turl. All you, any of you, would have had to do would be to come to me. . . ." His voice died. He thought, *Fifty dollars a month. He knows*

*that's all. That I reneged, cried calf-rope, sold my birth-
right, betrayed my blood, for what he too calls not peace
but obliteration, and a little food.* "It's in the bank," he
said. "We'll go and get it."

Only Zachary Edmonds and, in his time, his son Carothers knew that part of it. But what followed most of the
town of Jefferson knew, so that the anecdote not only took
its place in the Edmonds family annals, but in the minor
annals of the town too:—how the white and the negro
cousins went side by side to the bank that morning and
Lucas said, "Wait. It's a heap of money."

"It's too much," the white man said. "Too much to keep
hidden under a break in a hearth. Let me keep it for you.
Let me keep it."

"Wait," Lucas said. "Will the bank keep it for a black
man same as for a white?"

"Yes," the white man said. "I will ask them to."

"How can I get it back?" Lucas said. The white man
explained about the check. "All right," Lucas said. They
stood side by side at the window while the white man had
the account transferred and the new pass-book filled out;
again Lucas said "Wait" and then they stood side by side
at the ink-splashed wooden shelf while Lucas wrote out
the check, writing it steadily under the white man's direction in the cramped though quite legible hand which the
white man's mother had taught him and his brother and
sister too. Then they stood again at the grille while the
teller cashed the check and Lucas, still blocking the single
window, counted the money tediously and deliberately
through twice and pushed it back to the teller beyond the
grille. "Now you can put it back," he said. "And gimme my
paper."

But he didn't leave. Within the year he married, not a country woman, a farm woman, but a town woman, and McCaslin Edmonds built a house for them and allotted Lucas a specific acreage to be farmed as he saw fit as long as he lived or remained on the place. Then McCaslin Edmonds died and his son married and on that spring night of flood and isolation the boy Carothers was born. Still in infancy, he had already accepted the black man as an adjunct to the woman who was the only mother he would remember, as simply as he accepted his black foster-brother, as simply as he accepted his father as an adjunct to his existence. Even before he was out of infancy, the two houses had become interchangeable: himself and his foster-brother sleeping on the same pallet in the white man's house or in the same bed in the negro's and eating of the same food at the same table in either, actually preferring the negro house, the hearth on which even in summer a little fire always burned, centering the life in it, to his own. It did not even need to come to him as a part of his family's chronicle that his white father and his foster-brother's black one had done the same; it never even occurred to him that they in their turn and simultaneously had not had the first of remembering projected upon a single woman whose skin was likewise dark. One day he knew, without wondering or remembering when or how he had learned that either, that the black woman was not his mother, and did not regret it; he knew that his own mother was dead and did not grieve. There was still the black woman, constant, steadfast, and the black man of whom he saw as much and even more than of his own father, and the negro's house, the strong warm negro smell, the night-time hearth and the fire even in summer on it, which he still preferred to his own. And besides, he was no longer an infant. He and his foster-brother rode the plantation horses and mules, they had a pack of small hounds to hunt with and promise of a gun in another year or so; they were sufficient, complete, wanting, as all children do, not to be understood, leaping in mutual embattlement before any threat to privacy, but only to love, to question and examine unchallenged, and to be let alone.

Then one day the old curse of his fathers, the old haughty ancestral pride based not on any value but on an accident of geography, stemmed not from courage and honor but from wrong and shame, descended to him. He did not recognise it then. He and his foster-brother, Henry, were seven years old. They had finished supper at Henry's house and Molly was just sending them to bed in the room across the hall where they slept when there, when suddenly he said, "I'm going home."

"Les stay here," Henry said. "I thought we was going to get up when pappy did and go hunting."

"You can," he said. He was already moving toward the door. "I'm going home."

"All right," Henry said, following him. And he remembered how they walked that half mile to his house in the first summer dark, himself walking just fast enough that the negro boy never quite came up beside him, entering the house in single file and up the stairs and into the room with the bed and the pallet on the floor which they slept on when they passed the night here, and how he undressed just slow enough for Henry to beat him to the pallet and lie down. Then he went to the bed and lay down on it, rigid, staring up at the dark ceiling even after he heard Henry raise onto one elbow, looking toward the bed with slow and equable astonishment. "Are you going to sleep up there?" Henry said. "Well, all right. This here pallet sleeps all right to me, but I reckon I just as lief to if you wants to," and rose and approached the bed and stood over the white boy, waiting for him to move over and make room until the boy said, harsh and violent though not loud:

"No!"

Henry didn't move. "You mean you dont want me to sleep in the bed?" Nor did the boy move. He didn't answer, rigid on his back, staring upward. "All right," Henry said quietly and went back to the pallet and lay down again. The boy heard him, listened to him; he couldn't help it, lying clenched and rigid and open-eyed, hearing the slow equable voice: "I reckon on a hot night like tonight we will sleep cooler if we——"

"Shut up!" the boy said. "How'm I or you neither going to sleep if you keep on talking?" Henry hushed then. But the boy didn't sleep, long after Henry's quiet and untroubled breathing had begun, lying in a rigid fury of the grief he could not explain, the shame he would not admit. Then he slept and it seemed to him he was still awake, waked and did not know he had slept until he saw in the gray of dawn the empty pallet on the floor. They did not hunt that morning. They never slept in the same room again and never again ate at the same table because he admitted to himself it was shame now and he did not go to Henry's house and for a month he only saw Henry at a distance, with Lucas in the field, walking beside his father and holding the reins of the team while Lucas plowed. Then one day he knew it was grief and was ready to admit it was shame also, wanted to admit it only it was too late then, forever and forever too late. He went to

Molly's house. It was already late afternoon; Henry and Lucas would be coming up from the field at any time now. Molly was there, looking at him from the kitchen door as he crossed the yard. There was nothing in her face; he said it the best he could for that moment, because later he would be able to say it all right, say it once and forever so that it would be gone forever, facing her before he entered her house yet, stopping, his feet slightly apart, trembling a little, lordly, peremptory: "I'm going to eat supper with you all tonight."

It was all right. There was nothing in her face. He could say it almost any time now, when the time came. "Course you is," she said. "I'll cook you a chicken."

Then it was as if it had never happened at all. Henry came almost at once; he must have seen him from the field, and he and Henry killed and dressed the chicken. Then Lucas came and he went to the barn with Henry and Lucas while Henry milked. Then they were busy in the yard in the dusk, smelling the cooking chicken, until Molly called Henry and then a little later himself, the voice as it had always been, peaceful and steadfast: "Come and eat your supper."

But it was too late. The table was set in the kitchen where it always was and Molly stood at the stove drawing the biscuit out as she always stood, but Lucas was not there and there was just one chair, one plate, his glass of milk beside it, the platter heaped with untouched chicken, and even as he sprang back, gasping, for an instant blind as the room rushed and swam, Henry was turning toward the door to go out of it.

"Are you ashamed to eat when I eat?" he cried.

Henry paused, turning his head a little to speak in the

voice slow and without heat: "I aint shamed of nobody," he said peacefully. "Not even me."

So he entered his heritage. He ate its bitter fruit. He listened as Lucas referred to his father as Mr Edmonds, never as Mister Zack; he watched him avoid having to address the white man directly by any name at all with a calculation so coldly and constantly alert, a finesse so deliberate and unflagging, that for a time he could not tell if even his father knew that the negro was refusing to call him mister. At last he spoke to his father about it. The other listened gravely, with something in his face which the boy could not read and which at the moment he paid little attention to since he was still young then, still a child; he had not yet divined that there was something between his father and Lucas, something more than difference in race could account for since it did not exist between Lucas and any other white man, something more than the white blood, even the McCaslin blood, could account for since it was not there between his uncle Isaac McCaslin and Lucas. "You think that because Lucas is older than I am, old enough even to remember Uncle Buck and Uncle Buddy a little, and is a descendant of the people who lived on this place where we Edmonds are usurpers, yesterday's mushrooms, is not reason enough for him not to want to say mister to me?" his father said. "We grew up together, we ate and slept together and hunted and fished together, like you and Henry. We did it until we were grown men. Except that I always beat him shooting except one time. And as it turned out, I even beat him then. You think that's not reason enough?"

"We're not usurpers," the boy said, cried almost. "Our grandmother McCaslin was as much kin to old Carothers

as Uncle Buck and Buddy. Uncle Isaac himself gave—
Uncle Isaac himself says . . ." He ceased. His father
watched him. "No, sir," he said harshly. "That's not
enough."

"Ah," his father said. Then the boy could read what
was in his face. He had seen it before, as all children had
—that moment when, enveloped and surrounded still by
the warmth and confidence, he discovers that the reserve
which he had thought to have passed had merely retreated and set up a new barrier, still impregnable;—that
instant when the child realises with both grief and outrage
that the parent antedates it, has experienced things, shames
and triumphs both, in which it can have no part. "I'll make
a trade with you. You let me and Lucas settle how he is to
treat me, and I'll let you and him settle how he is to treat
you."

Then, in adolescence, he knew what he had seen in his
father's face that morning, what shadow, what stain, what
mark—something which had happened between Lucas and
his father, which nobody but they knew and would ever
know if the telling depended on them—something which
had happened because they were themselves, men, not
stemming from any difference of race nor because one blood
strain ran in them both. Then, in his late teens, almost a
man, he even knew what it had been. *It was a woman,* he
thought. *My father and a nigger, over a woman. My father
and a nigger man over a nigger woman,* because he simply
declined even to realise that he had even refused to think
a white woman. He didn't even think Molly's name. That
didn't matter. *And by God Lucas beat him,* he thought.
Edmonds, he thought, harshly and viciously. *Edmonds.
Even a nigger McCaslin is a better man, better than all of*

*us. Old Carothers got his nigger bastards right in his back
yard and I would like to have seen the husband or anybody
else that said him nay.—Yes, Lucas beat him, else Lucas
wouldn't be here. If father had beat Lucas, he couldn't have
let Lucas stay here even to forgive him. It will only be
Lucas who could have stayed because Lucas is impervious
to anybody, even to forgiving them, even to having to harm
them.*

Impervious to time too. Zachary Edmonds died, and in
his turn he inherited the plantation the true heir to which,
by male descent and certainly morally and, if the truth
were known, probably legally too, was still alive, living on
the doled pittance which his great-nephew now in his turn
sent him each month. For twenty years now he had run
it, tried to even with the changed times, as his father and
grandfather and great-grandfather had done before him.
Yet when he looked back over those twenty years, they
seemed to him one long and unbroken course of outrageous
trouble and conflict, not with the land or weather (or even
lately, with the federal government) but with the old negro
who in his case did not even bother to remember not to
call him mister, who called him Mr Edmonds and Mister
Carothers or Carothers or Roth or son or spoke to him in
a group of younger negroes, lumping them all together,
as "you boys." There were the years during which Lucas
had continued to farm his acreage in the same clumsy old
fashion which Carothers McCaslin himself had probably
followed, declining advice, refusing to use improved im-
plements, refusing to let a tractor so much as cross the land
which his McCaslin forbears had given him without recourse for life, refusing even to allow the pilot who dusted
the rest of the cotton with weevil poison, even fly his laden

aeroplane through the air above it, yet drawing supplies from the commissary as if he farmed, and at an outrageous and incredible profit, a thousand acres, having on the commissary books an account dating thirty years back which Edmonds knew he would never pay for the good and simple reason that Lucas would not only outlive the present Edmonds as he had outlived the two preceding him, but would probably outlast the very ledgers which held the account. Then the still which Lucas had run almost in his, Edmonds', back yard for at least twenty years, according to his daughter, until his own avarice exposed him, and the three-hundred-dollar mule which he had stolen from not only his business partner and guarantor but actually from his own blood relation and swapped for a machine for divining the hiding-place of buried money; and now this: breaking up after forty-five years the home of the woman who had been the only mother he, Edmonds, ever knew, who had raised him, fed him from her own breast as she was actually doing her own child, who had surrounded him always with care for his physical body and for his spirit too, teaching him his manners, behavior—to be gentle with his inferiors, honorable with his equals, generous to the weak and considerate of the aged, courteous, truthful and brave to all—who had given him, the motherless, without stint or expectation of reward that constant and abiding devotion and love which existed nowhere else in this world for him;—breaking up her home who had no other kin save an old brother in Jefferson whom she had not even seen in ten years, and the eighteen-year-old married daughter with whom she would doubtless refuse to live since the daughter's husband likewise had lain himself liable to the curse which she believed her own husband had incurred.

Impervious to time too. It seemed to Edmonds, sitting at his solitary supper which he couldn't eat, that he could actually see Lucas standing there in the room before him—the face which at sixty-seven looked actually younger than his own at forty-three, showed less of the ravages of passions and thought and satieties and frustrations than his own—the face which was not at all a replica even in caricature of his grandfather McCaslin's but which had heired and now reproduced with absolute and shocking fidelity the old ancestor's entire generation and thought—the face which, as old Isaac McCaslin had seen it that morning forty-five years ago, was a composite of a whole generation of fierce and undefeated young Confederate soldiers, embalmed and slightly mummified—and he thought with amazement and something very like horror: *He's more like old Carothers than all the rest of us put together, including old Carothers. He is both heir and prototype simultaneously of all the geography and climate and biology which sired old Carothers and all the rest of us and our kind, myriad, countless, faceless, even nameless now except himself who fathered himself, intact and complete, contemptuous, as old Carothers must have been, of all blood black white yellow or red, including his own.*

2.

It was full dark when he tied the mare to Lucas' fence and walked up the rock path neatly bordered with broken brick and upended bottles and such set into the earth, and mounted the steps and entered. Lucas was waiting, standing in the door with his hat on, in silhouette against the firelight on the hearth. The old woman did not rise. She sat as in the commissary that afternoon, motionless, only bent a little forward, her tiny gnarled hands immobile again on the white apron, the shrunken and tragic mask touched here and there into highlight by the fire, and for the first time in his memory he was seeing her in or about the house without the clay pipe in her mouth. Lucas drew up a chair for him. But Lucas did not sit down. He went and stood at the other side of the hearth, the firelight touching him too—the broad sweep of the hand-made beaver hat which Edmonds' grandfather had given him fifty years ago, the faintly Syriac features, the heavy gold watch-chain looped across the unbuttoned vest. "Now what's all this?" Edmonds said.

"She wants a voce," Lucas said. "All right."

"All right?" Edmonds said. "All right?"

"Yes. What's it going to cost me?"

"I see," Edmonds said. "If you got to pay out money for it, she cant have one. Well, this is one thing you aint going to swangdangle anybody out of. You aint buying or selling a gold-finding machine either now, old man. She dont want any mule."

"She can have it," Lucas said. "I just want to know how much it will cost me. Why cant you declare us voced like you done Oscar and that yellow slut he fotched out here from Memphis last summer? You not only declared them voced, you took her back to town yourself and bought her a railroad ticket back to Memphis."

"Because they were not married very hard," Edmonds said. "And sooner or later she was going to take a lick at him with that razor she carried. And if she had ever missed or fumbled, Oscar would have torn her head off. He was just waiting for a chance to. That's why I did it. But you aint Oscar. This is different. Listen to me, Lucas. You are an older man than me; I admit that. You may have more money than I've got, which I think you have, and you may have more sense than I've got, as you think you have. But you cant do this."

"Dont tell me," Lucas said. "Tell her. This aint my doing. I'm satisfied like this."

"Yes. Sure. As long as you can do like you want to—spend all the time you aint sleeping and eating making George Wilkins walk up and down that creek bottom, toting that damn—that damn—" Then he stopped and started over, holding his voice not down only but back too, for a while yet at least: "I've told you and told you there aint any money buried around here. That you are just wasting your time. But that's all right. You and George Wilkins both could walk around down there until you drop, for all of me. But Aunt Molly——"

"I'm a man," Lucas said. "I'm the man here. I'm the one to say in my house, like you and your paw and his paw were the ones to say in his. You aint got any complaints about the way I farm my land and make my crop, have you?"

"No complaints?" Edmonds said. "No complaints?" The other didn't even pause.

"Long as I do that, I'm the one to say about my private business, and your father would be the first to tell you so if he was here. Besides, I will have to quit hunting every night soon now, to get my cotton picked. Then I'll just hunt Saturday and Sunday night." Up to now he had been speaking to the ceiling apparently. Now he looked at Edmonds. "But them two nights is mine. On them two nights I dont farm nobody's land, I dont care who he is that claims to own it."

"Well," Edmonds said. "Two nights a week. You'll have to start that next week, because some of your cotton is ready." He turned to the old woman. "There, Aunt Molly," he said. "Two nights a week, and he's bound, even Lucas, to come to his senses soon ———"

"I dont axes him to stop hunting but two nights a week," she said. She hadn't moved, speaking in a monotonous sing-song, looking at neither of them. "I dont axes him to stop hunting for it at all. Because it's too late now. He cant help himself now. And I gots to be free."

Edmonds looked up again at the impassive, the impenetrable face under the broad, old-fashioned hat. "Do you want her to go?" he said. "Is that it?"

"I'm going to be the man in this house," Lucas said. It was not stubborn. It was quiet: final. His stare was as steady as Edmonds' was, and immeasurably colder.

"Listen," Edmonds said. "You're getting along. You aint got a lot more time here. You said something about father a minute ago. All right. But when his time came and he laid down to die, he laid down in peace. Because he never *had anything* Jesus, he had almost said it aloud. *Damn damn damn* he thought *had anything about his wife in her old age to have to say God forgive me for doing that.* Almost aloud; he just caught it. "And you time's coming to want to lay down in peace, and you dont know when."

"Nor does you."

"That's correct. But I'm forty-three. You are sixty-seven." They stared at one another. Still the face beneath the hat

was impassive, impenetrable. Then Lucas moved. He
turned and spat neatly into the fire.

"All right," he said quietly. "I want to lay down in peace
too. I'll get shut of the machine. I'll give it to George Wilkins—" That was when the old woman moved. When
Edmonds looked around she was trying to rise from the
chair, trying to thrust herself up with one hand, the other
arm outstretched, not to ward Lucas off but toward him,
Edmonds.

"No!" she cried. "Mister Zack! Cant you see? Not that
he would keep on using it just the same as if he had kept
it, but he would fotch onto Nat, my last one and least one,
the curse of God that's gonter destroy him or her that
touches what's done been rendered back to Him? I wants
him to keep it! That's why I got to go, so he can keep it
and not have to even think about giving it to George! Dont
you see?"

Edmonds had risen too, his chair crashing over backward. He was trembling, glaring at Lucas. "So you'll try
your tricks on me too. On me," he said in a shaking voice.
"All right. You're not going to get any divorce. And you're
going to get rid of that machine. You bring that thing up
to my house the first thing in the morning. You hear me?"

He returned home, or to the stable. There was a moon
now, blanched upon the open cotton almost ready for
picking. The curse of God. He knew what she meant, what
she had been fumbling toward. Granted the almost unbelievable circumstance that there should be as much as a
thousand dollars buried and forgotten somewhere within
Lucas' radius, and granted the even more impossible circumstance that Lucas should find it: what it might do to
him, even to a man sixty-seven years old, who had, as Ed-

monds knew, three times that sum in a Jefferson bank; even a thousand dollars on which there was no sweat, at least none of his own. And to George, the daughter's husband, who had not a dollar anywhere, who was not yet twenty-five and with an eighteen-year-old wife expecting a child next spring.

There was no one to take the mare; he had told Dan not to wait. He unsaddled himself and rubbed her down and opened the gate to the pasture lane and slipped the bridle and slapped her moon-bright rump as she rushed suddenly away, cantering, curvetting, her three stockings and the blaze glinting moonward for an instant as she turned. "God damn it," he said, "I wish to hell either me or Lucas Beauchamp was a horse. Or a mule."

Lucas did not appear the next morning with the divining machine. When Edmonds himself departed at nine oclock (it was Sunday) he still had not appeared. Edmonds was driving his car now; for a moment he thought of going to Lucas' house, stopping there on his way. But it was Sunday; it seemed to him that he had been worrying and stewing over Lucas' affairs for six days a week since last May and very likely he would resume stewing and fretting over them at sunup tomorrow, and since Lucas himself had stated that beginning next week he would devote only Saturdays and Sundays to the machine, possibly until that time he would consider himself under his own dispensation to refrain from it on those two days. So he went on. He was gone all that day—to church five miles away, then to Sunday dinner with some friends three miles further on, where he spent the afternoon looking at other men's cotton and adding his voice to the curses at governmental interference with the raising and marketing of it. So it was after dark when he

reached his own gate again and remembered Lucas and
Molly and the divining machine once more. Lucas would
not have left it at the empty house in his absence, so he
turned and drove on to Lucas' cabin. It was dark; when he
shouted there was no answer. So he drove on the quarter-
mile to George's and Nat's, but it was dark too, no answer
there to his voice. *Maybe it's all right now,* he thought.
*Maybe they've all gone to church. Anyway, it'll be tomor-
row in another twelve hours I'll have to start in worrying
about Lucas and something and so it might as well be this,
something at least I am familiar with, accustomed to.*

Then the next morning, Monday, he had been in the
stable for almost an hour and neither Dan nor Oscar had
appeared. He had opened the stalls himself and turned the
mule drove into the lane to the pasture and was just coming out of the mare's stall with the feed basket as Oscar
came into the hallway, not running but trotting wearily and
steadily. Then Edmonds saw that he still wore his Sunday
clothes—a bright shirt and a tie, serge trousers with a long
tear in one leg and splashed to the knees with mud. "It's
Aunt Molly Beauchamp," Oscar said. "She been missing
since yestiddy sometime. We been hunting her all night.
We found where she went down to the creek and we been
tracking her. Only she so little and light she dont hardly
make a foot on the ground. Uncle Luke and George and
Nat and Dan and some others are still hunting."

"I'll saddle the mare," Edmonds said. "I've turned the
mules out; you'll have to go to the pasture and catch one.
Hurry."

The mules, free in the big pasture, were hard to catch;
it was almost an hour before Oscar returned bareback on
one of them. And it was two hours more before they over-

took Lucas and George and Nat and Dan and another man where they followed and lost and hunted and found and followed again the faint, light prints of the old woman's feet as they seemed to wander without purpose among the jungle of brier and rotted logs along the creek. It was almost noon when they found her, lying on her face in the mud, the once immaculate apron and the clean faded skirts stained and torn, one hand still grasping the handle of the divining-machine as she had fallen with it. She was not dead. When Oscar picked her up she opened her eyes, looking at no one, at nothing, and closed them again. "Run," Edmonds told Dan. "Take the mare. Go back for the car and go get Doctor Rideout. Hurry.—Can you carry her?"

"I can tote her," Oscar said. "She dont weigh hardly nothing. Not nigh as much as that finding-box."

"I'll tote her," George said. "Bein as she's Nat's—" Edmonds turned on him, on Lucas too.

"You tote that box," he said. "Both of you tote it. Hope it finds something between here and the house. Because if those needles ever move on my place afterward, neither of you all will be looking at them.—I'm going to see about that divorce," he said to Lucas. "Before she kills herself. Before you and that machine kill her between you. By God, I'm glad I aint walking in your shoes right now. I'm glad I aint going to lie in your bed tonight, thinking about what you're going to think about."

The day came. The cotton was all in and ginned and baled and frost had fallen, completing the firing of the corn which was being gathered and measured into the cribs. With Lucas and Molly in the back seat, he drove in to Jefferson and stopped before the county courthouse where the Chancellor was sitting. "You dont need to come in," he told Lucas. "They probably wouldn't let you in. But you be around close. I'm not going to wait for you. And remember. Aunt Molly gets the house, and half your crop this year and half of it every year as long as you stay on my place."

"You mean every year I keep on farming my land."

"I mean every damned year you stay on my place. Just what I said."

"Cass Edmonds give me that land to be mine long as I——"

"You heard me," Edmonds said. Lucas looked at him. He blinked.

"Do you want me to move off of it?" he said.

"Why?" Edmonds said. "What for? When you are going to be on it all night long every night, hunting buried money? You might as well sleep on it all day too. Besides, you'll have to stay on it to make Aunt Molly's half-crop. And I dont mean just this year. I mean every——"

"She can have all of it," Lucas said. "I'll raise it all right. And she can have all of it. I got them three thousand dollars old Carothers left me, right there in that bank yonder. They'll last me out my time—unless you done decided to give half of them to somebody. And when me and George Wilkins find that money——"

"Get out of the car," Edmonds said. "Go on. Get out of it."

The Chancellor was sitting in his office—a small detached building beside the courthouse proper. As they walked toward it Edmonds suddenly had to take the old woman's arm, catching her just in time, feeling again the thin, almost fleshless arm beneath the layers of sleeve, dry and light and brittle and frail as a rotted stick. He stopped, holding her up. "Aunt Molly," he said, "do you still want to do this? You dont have to. I'll take that thing away from him. By God, I——"

She tried to go on, tugging at his hand. "I got to," she said. "He'll get another one. Then he'll give that one to George the first thing to keep you from taking it. And they'll find it some day and maybe I'll be gone then and cant help. And Nat was my least and my last one. I wont never see the others before I die."

"Come on," Edmonds said. "Come on then."

There were a few people going in and out of the office; a few inside, not many. They waited quietly at the back of the room until their turn came. Then he found that he actually was holding her up. He led her forward, still supporting her, believing that if he released her for an instant even she would collapse into a bundle of dried and lifeless sticks, covered by the old, faded, perfectly clean garments, at his feet. "Ah, Mr Edmonds," the Chancellor said. "This is the plaintiff?"

"Yes, sir," Edmonds said. The Chancellor (he was quite old) slanted his head to look at Molly above his spectacles. Then he shifted them up his nose and looked at her through them. He made a clucking sound. "After forty-five years. You cant do anything about it?"

"No, sir," Edmonds said. "I tried. I . . ." The Chancellor made the clucking sound again. He looked down at the bill which the clerk laid before him.

"She will be provided for, of course."

"Yes, sir. I'll see to that."

The Chancellor mused upon the bill. "There's no contest, I suppose."

"No, sir," Edmonds said. And then—and he did not

even know Lucas had followed them until he saw the
Chancellor slant his head again and look past them this
time across the spectacles, and saw the clerk glance up and
heard him say, "You, nigger! Take off your hat!"—then
Lucas thrust Molly aside and came to the table, removing
his hat as he did so.

"We aint gonter have no contest or no voce neither," he
said.

"You what?" the Chancellor said. "What's this?" Lucas
had not once looked at Edmonds. As far as Edmonds could
tell, he was not looking at the Chancellor either. Edmonds
thought idiotically how it must have been years since he
had seen Lucas uncovered; in fact, he could not remember
at all being aware previously that Lucas' hair was gray.

"We dont want no voce," Lucas said. "I done changed
my mind."

"Are you the husband?" the Chancellor said.

"That's right," Lucas said.

"Say sir to the court!" the clerk said. Lucas glanced at
the clerk.

"What?" he said. "I dont want no court. I done changed
my——"

"Why, you uppity——" the clerk began.

"Wait," the Chancellor said. He looked at Lucas. "You
have waited too late. This bill has been presented in due
form and order. I am about to pronounce on it."

"Not now," Lucas said. "We dont want no voce. Roth
Edmonds knows what I mean."

"What? Who does?"

"Why, the uppity——" the clerk said. "Your Honor——"
Again the Chancellor raised his hand slightly toward the
clerk. He still looked at Lucas.

"Mister Roth Edmonds," Lucas said. Edmonds moved forward quickly, still holding the old woman's arm. The Chancellor looked at him.

"Yes, Mr Edmonds?"

"Yes, sir," Edmonds said. "That's right. We dont want it now."

"You wish to withdraw the bill?"

"Yes, sir. If you please, sir."

"Ah," the Chancellor said. He folded the bill and handed it to the clerk. "Strike this off the docket, Mr Hulett," he said.

When they were out of the office, he was almost carrying her, though she was trying to walk. "Here," he said, almost roughly, "it's all right now. Didn't you hear the judge? Didn't you hear Lucas tell the judge that Roth Edmonds knows what he means?"

He lifted her into the car almost bodily, Lucas just behind them. But instead of getting in, Lucas said, "Wait a minute."

"Wait a minute?" Edmonds said. "Hah!" he said. "You've bankrupted your waiting. You've already spent—" But Lucas had gone on. And Edmonds waited. He stood beside the car and watched Lucas cross the Square, toward the stores, erect beneath the old, fine, well-cared-for hat, walking with that unswerving and dignified deliberation which every now and then, and with something sharp at the heart, Edmonds recognised as having come from his own ancestry too as the hat had come. He was not gone long. He returned, unhurried, and got into the car. He was carrying a small sack—obviously candy, a nickel's worth. He put it into Molly's hand.

"Here," he said. "You aint got no teeth left but you can still gum it."

3.

It was cool that night. He had a little fire, and for supper the first ham from the smokehouse, and he was sitting at his solitary meal, eating with more appetite than it seemed to him he had had in months, when he heard the knocking from the front of the house—the rapping of knuckles on the edge of the veranda, not loud, not hurried, merely peremptory. He spoke to the cook through the kitchen door: "Tell him to come in here," he said. He went on eating. He was eating when Lucas entered and passed him and set the divining machine on the other end of the table. It was clean of mud now; it looked as though it had been polished, at once compact and complex and efficient-looking with its bright cryptic dials and gleaming knobs. Lucas stood looking down at it for a moment. Then he turned away. Until he left the room he did not once look toward it again. "There it is," he said. "Get rid of it."

"All right. I'll put it away in the attic. Maybe by next spring Aunt Molly will forget about it and you can——"

"No. Get rid of it."

"For good?"

"Yes. Clean off this place, where I wont never see it again. Just dont tell me where. Sell it if you can and keep the money. But sell it a far piece away, where I wont never see it nor hear tell of it again."

"Well," Edmonds said. "Well." He thrust his chair back from the table and sat looking up at the other, at the old man who had emerged out of the tragic complexity of his motherless childhood as the husband of the woman who had been the only mother he ever knew, who had never once said "sir" to his white skin and whom he knew even called him Roth behind his back, let alone to his face. "Look here," he said. "You dont have to do that. Aunt Molly's old, and she's got some curious notions. But what she dont know— Because you aint going to find any money, buried or not, around here or anywhere else. And if you want to take that damn thing out now and then, say once or twice a month, and spend the night walking up and down that damn creek——"

"No," Lucas said. "Get rid of it. I dont want to never see it again. Man has got three score and ten years on this earth, the Book says. He can want a heap in that time and a heap of what he can want is due to come to him, if he just starts in soon enough. I done waited too late to start. That money's there. Them two white men that slipped in here that night three years ago and dug up twenty-two thousand dollars and got clean away with it before anybody saw them. I know. I saw the hole where they filled it up again, and the churn it was buried in. But I am near to the end of my three score and ten, and I reckon to find that money aint for me."

Pantaloon in Black

I.

HE STOOD in the worn, faded clean overalls which Mannie herself had washed only a week ago, and heard the first clod stride the pine box. Soon he had one of the shovels himself, which in his hands (he was better than six feet and weighed better than two hundred pounds) resembled the toy shovel a child plays with at the shore, its half cubic foot of flung dirt no more than the light gout of sand the child's shovel would have flung. Another member of his sawmill gang touched his arm and said, "Lemme have hit, Rider." He didn't even falter. He released one hand in midstroke and flung it backward, striking the other across the chest, jolting him back a step, and restored the hand to the moving shovel, flinging the dirt with that effortless fury so that the mound seemed to be rising of its own volition, not built up from above but thrusting visibly upward out of the earth itself, until at last the grave, save for its rawness, resembled any other marked off without order about the barren plot by shards of pottery and broken bottles and old brick and other objects insignificant to sight but actually of a profound meaning and fatal to touch, which no white man could have read. Then he straightened up and with one hand flung the shovel quivering upright in the mound like a javelin and turned and began to walk away, walking on even when an old woman came out of the meagre clump of his kin and friends and a few old people who had known him and his dead wife both since they were born, and grasped his forearm. She was his aunt. She had raised him. He could not remember his parents at all.

"Whar you gwine?" she said.

"Ah'm goan home," he said.

"You dont wants ter go back dar by yoself," she said. "You needs to eat. You come on home and eat."

"Ah'm goan home," he repeated, walking out from under her hand, his forearm like iron, as if the weight on it were no more than that of a fly, the other members of the mill gang whose head he was giving way quietly to let him pass. But before he reached the fence one of them overtook him; he did not need to be told it was his aunt's messenger.

"Wait, Rider," the other said. "We gots a jug in de bushes——" Then the other said what he had not intended to say, what he had never conceived of himself saying in circumstances like these, even though everybody knew it—the dead who either will not or cannot quit the earth yet although the flesh they once lived in has been returned to it, let the preachers tell and reiterate and affirm how they left it not only without regret but with joy, mounting toward glory: "You dont wants ter go back dar. She be wawkin yit."

He didn't pause, glancing down at the other, his eyes red at the inner corners in his high, slightly backtilted head. "Lemme lone, Acey," he said. "Doan mess wid me now," and went on, stepping over the three-strand wire fence without even breaking his stride, and crossed the road and

entered the woods. It was middle dusk when he emerged
from them and crossed the last field, stepping over that
fence too in one stride, into the lane. It was empty at this
hour of Sunday evening—no family in wagon, no rider, no
walkers churchward to speak to him and carefully refrain
from looking after him when he had passed—the pale,
powder-light, powder-dry dust of August from which the
long week's marks of hoof and wheel had been blotted by
the strolling and unhurried Sunday shoes, with somewhere
beneath them, vanished but not gone, fixed and held in the
annealing dust, the narrow, splay-toed prints of his wife's
bare feet where on Saturday afternoons she would walk
to the commissary to buy their next week's supplies while
he took his bath; himself, his own prints, setting the period
now as he strode on, moving almost as fast as a smaller
man could have trotted, his body breasting the air her body
had vacated, his eyes touching the objects—post and tree
and field and house and hill—her eyes had lost.

The house was the last one in the lane, not his but
rented from Carothers Edmonds, the local white land-
owner. But the rent was paid promptly in advance, and
even in just six months he had refloored the porch and re-
built and roofed the kitchen, doing the work himself on
Saturday afternoon and Sunday with his wife helping him,
and bought the stove. Because he made good money: saw-
milling ever since he began to get his growth at fifteen and
sixteen and now, at twenty-four, head of the timber gang
itself because the gang he headed moved a third again as
much timber between sunup and sundown as any other
moved, handling himself at times out of the vanity of his
own strength logs which ordinarily two men would have
handled with canthooks; never without work even in the

old days when he had not actually needed the money, when a lot of what he wanted, needed perhaps, didn't cost money —the women bright and dark and for all purposes nameless he didn't need to buy and it didn't matter to him what he wore and there was always food for him at any hour of day or night in the house of his aunt who didn't even want to take the two dollars he gave her each Saturday—so there had been only the Saturday and Sunday dice and whiskey that had to be paid for until that day six months ago when he saw Mannie, whom he had known all his life, for the first time and said to himself: "Ah'm thu wid all dat," and they married and he rented the cabin from Carothers Edmonds and built a fire on the hearth on their wedding night as the tale told how Uncle Lucas Beauchamp, Edmonds' oldest tenant, had done on his forty-five years ago and which had burned ever since; and he would rise and dress and eat his breakfast by lamplight to walk the four miles to the mill by sunup, and exactly one hour after sundown he would enter the house again, five days a week, until Saturday. Then the first hour would not have passed noon when he would mount the steps and knock, not on post or doorframe but on the underside of the gallery roof itself, and enter and ring the bright cascade of silver dollars onto the scrubbed table in the kitchen where his dinner simmered on the stove and the galvanised tub of hot water and the baking powder can of soft soap and the towel made of scalded flour sacks sewn together and his clean overalls and shirt waited, and Mannie would gather up the money and walk the half-mile to the commissary and buy their next week's supplies and bank the rest of the money in Edmonds' safe and return and they would eat once again without haste or hurry after five days

—the sidemeat, the greens, the cornbread, the buttermilk from the well-house, the cake which she baked every Saturday now that she had a stove to bake in.

But when he put his hand on the gate it seemed to him suddenly that there was nothing beyond it. The house had never been his anyway, but now even the new planks and sills and shingles, the hearth and stove and bed, were all a part of the memory of somebody else, so that he stopped in the half-open gate and said aloud, as though he had gone to sleep in one place and then waked suddenly to find himself in another: "Whut's Ah doin hyar?" before he went on. Then he saw the dog. He had forgotten it. He remembered neither seeing nor hearing it since it began to howl just before dawn yesterday—a big dog, a hound with a strain of mastiff from somewhere (he had told Mannie a month after they married: "Ah needs a big dawg. You's de onliest least thing whut ever kep up wid me one day, leff alone fo weeks.") coming out from beneath the gallery and approaching, not running but seeming rather to drift across the dusk until it stood lightly against his leg, its head raised until the tips of his fingers just touched it, facing the house and making no sound; whereupon, as if the animal controlled it, had lain guardian before it during his absence and only this instant relinquished, the shell of planks and shingles facing him solidified, filled, and for the moment he believed that he could not possibly enter it. "But Ah needs to eat," he said. "Us bofe needs to eat," he said, moving on though the dog did not follow until he turned and cursed it. "Come on hyar!" he said. "Whut you skeered of? She lacked you too, same as me," and they mounted the steps and crossed the porch and entered the house—the dusk-filled single room where all those six months were now crammed and crowded into one instant of time until there was no space left for air to breathe, crammed and crowded about the hearth where the fire which was to have lasted to the end of them, before which in the days before he was able to buy the stove he would enter after his four-mile walk from the mill and find her, the shape of her narrow back and haunches squatting, one narrow spread hand shielding her face from the blaze over which the other hand held the skillet, had already fallen to a dry, light soilure of dead ashes when the sun rose yesterday—and himself standing there while the last of light died about the strong and indomitable beating of his heart and the deep steady arch and collapse of his chest which walking fast over the rough going of woods and fields had not increased and standing still in the quiet and fading room had not slowed down.

Then the dog left him. The light pressure went off his flank; he heard the click and hiss of its claws on the wooden floor as it surged away and he thought at first that it was fleeing. But it stopped just outside the front door, where he could see it now, and the upfling of its head as the howl began, and then he saw her too. She was standing in the kitchen door, looking at him. He didn't move. He didn't breathe nor speak until he knew his voice would be all right, his face fixed too not to alarm her. "Mannie," he said. "Hit's awright. Ah aint afraid." Then he took a step toward her, slow, not even raising his hand yet, and stopped. Then he took another step. But this time as soon as he moved she began to fade. He stopped at once, not breathing again, motionless, willing his eyes to see that she had stopped too. But she had not stopped. She was fading, going. "Wait," he said, talking as sweet as he had ever heard his voice speak to a woman: "Den lemme go wid you, honey." But she was going. She was going fast now, he could actually feel between them the insuperable barrier of that very strength which could handle alone a log which would have taken any two other men to handle, of the blood and bones and flesh too strong, invincible for life, having learned at least once with his own eyes how tough, even in sudden and violent death, not a young man's bones and flesh perhaps but the will of that bone and flesh to remain alive, actually was.

Then she was gone. He walked through the door where she had been standing, and went to the stove. He did not light the lamp. He needed no light. He had set the stove up himself and built the shelves for the dishes, from among which he took two plates by feel and from the pot sitting cold on the cold stove he ladled onto the plates the food which his aunt had brought yesterday and of which he had eaten yesterday though now he did not remember when he had eaten it nor what it was, and carried the plates to the scrubbed bare table beneath the single small fading window and drew two chairs up and sat down, waiting again until he knew his voice would be what he wanted it to be. "Come on hyar, now," he said roughly. "Come on hyar and eat yo supper. Ah aint gonter have no—" and ceased, looking down at his plate, breathing the strong, deep pants, his chest arching and collapsing until he stopped it presently and held himself motionless for perhaps a half minute, and raised a spoonful of the cold and glutinous peas to his mouth. The congealed and lifeless mass seemed to bounce on contact with his lips. Not even warmed from mouth-heat, peas and spoon spattered and rang upon the plate; his chair crashed backward and he was standing, feeling the muscles of his jaw beginning to drag his mouth open, tugging upward the top half of his head. But he stopped that too before it became sound, holding himself again while he rapidly scraped the food from his plate onto the other and took it up and left the kitchen, crossed the other room and the gallery and set the plate on the bottom step and went on toward the gate.

The dog was not there, but it overtook him within the first half mile. There was a moon then, their two shadows flitting broken and intermittent among the trees or slanted long and intact across the slope of pasture or old abandoned fields upon the hills, the man moving almost as fast as a horse could have moved over that ground, altering his course each time a lighted window came in sight, the dog trotting at heel while their shadows shortened to the moon's curve until at last they trod them and the last far lamp had vanished and the shadows began to lengthen on the other hand, keeping to heel even when a rabbit burst from almost beneath the man's foot, then lying in the gray of dawn beside the man's prone body, beside the labored heave and collapse of the chest, the loud harsh snoring which sounded not like groans of pain but like someone engaged without arms in prolonged single combat.

When he reached the mill there was nobody there but the fireman—an older man just turning from the wood-pile, watching quietly as he crossed the clearing, striding as if he were going to walk not only through the boiler shed but through (or over) the boiler too, the overalls which had been clean yesterday now draggled and soiled and drenched to the knees with dew, the cloth cap flung onto the side of his head, hanging peak downward over his ear as he always wore it, the whites of his eyes rimmed with red and with something urgent and strained about them. "Whar yo bucket?" he said. But before the fireman could answer he had stepped past him and lifted the polished lard pail down from a nail in a post. "Ah just wants a biscuit," he said.

"Eat hit all," the fireman said. "Ah'll eat outen de yuthers' buckets at dinner. Den you gawn home and go to bed. You dont looks good."

"Ah aint come hyar to look," he said, sitting on the ground, his back against the post, the open pail between his knees, cramming the food into his mouth with his hands, wolfing it—peas again, also gelid and cold, a fragment of yesterday's Sunday fried chicken, a few rough chunks of this morning's fried sidemeat, a biscuit the size of a child's cap—indiscriminate, tasteless. The rest of the crew was gathering now, with voices and sounds of movement outside the boiler shed; presently the white foreman rode into the clearing on a horse. He did not look up, setting the empty pail aside, rising, looking at no one, and went to the branch and lay on his stomach and lowered his face to the water, drawing the water into himself with the same deep, strong, troubled inhalations that he had snored with, or as when he had stood in the empty house at dusk yesterday, trying to get air.

Then the trucks were rolling. The air pulsed with the rapid beating of the exhaust and the whine and clang of the saw, the trucks rolling one by one up to the skidway, he mounting the trucks in turn, to stand balanced on the load he freed, knocking the chocks out and casting loose the shackle chains and with his cant-hook squaring the sticks of cypress and gum and oak one by one to the incline and holding them until the next two men of his gang were ready to receive and guide them, until the discharge of each truck became one long rumbling roar punctuated by grunting shouts and, as the morning grew and the sweat came, chanted phrases of song tossed back and forth. He did not sing with them. He rarely ever did, and this morning might have been no different from any other—himself man-height again above the heads which carefully refrained from looking at him, stripped to the waist now, the shirt removed and the overalls knotted about his hips by the suspender straps, his upper body bare except for the handkerchief about his neck and the cap clapped and clinging somehow over his right ear, the mounting sun sweat-glinted steel-blue on the midnight-colored bunch and slip of muscles until the whistle blew for noon and he said to the two men at the head of the skidway: "Look out. Git out de way," and rode the log down the incline, balanced erect upon it in short rapid backward-running steps above the headlong thunder.

His aunt's husband was waiting for him—an old man, as tall as he was, but lean, almost frail, carrying a tin pail in one hand and a covered plate in the other; they too sat in the shade beside the branch a short distance from where the others were opening their dinner pails. The bucket contained a fruit jar of buttermilk packed in a clean damp towsack. The covered dish was a peach pie, still warm. "She baked hit fer you dis mawin," the uncle said. "She say fer you to come home." He didn't answer, bent forward a little, his elbows on his knees, holding the pie in both hands, wolfing at it, the syrupy filling smearing and trickling down his chin, blinking rapidly as he chewed, the whites of his eyes covered a little more by the creeping red. "Ah went to yo house last night, but you want dar. She sont me. She wants you to come on home. She kept de lamp burnin all last night fer you."

"Ah'm awright," he said.

"You aint awright. De Lawd guv, and He tuck away. Put yo faith and trust in Him. And she kin help you."

"Whut faith and trust?" he said. "Whut Mannie ever done ter Him? Whut He wanter come messin wid me and ——"

"Hush!" the old man said. "Hush!"

Then the trucks were rolling again. Then he could stop needing to invent to himself reasons for his breathing, until after a while he began to believe he had forgot about breathing since now he could not hear it himself above the steady thunder of the rolling logs; whereupon as soon as he found himself believing he had forgotten it, he knew that he had not, so that instead of tipping the final log onto the skidway he stood up and cast his cant-hook away as if it were a burnt match and in the dying reverberation of the last log's rumbling descent he vaulted down between the two slanted tracks of the skid, facing the log which still lay on the truck. He had done it before—taken a log from the truck onto his hands, balanced, and turned with it and tossed it onto the skidway, but never with a stick of this size, so that in a complete cessation of all sound save the pulse of the exhaust and the light free-running whine of the disengaged saw since every eye there, even that of the white foreman, was upon him, he nudged the log to the edge of the truckframe and squatted and set his palms against the underside of it. For a time there was no movement at all. It was as if the unrational and inanimate wood had invested, mesmerised the man with some of its own primal inertia. Then a voice said quietly: "He got hit.

Hit's off de truck," and they saw the crack and gap of air, watching the infinitesimal straightening of the braced legs until the knees locked, the movement mounting infinitesimally through the belly's insuck, the arch of the chest, the neck cords, lifting the lip from the white clench of teeth in passing, drawing the whole head backward and only the bloodshot fixity of the eyes impervious to it, moving on up the arms and the straightening elbows until the balanced log was higher than his head. "Only he aint gonter turn wid dat un," the same voice said. "And when he try to put hit back on de truck, hit gonter kill him." But none of them moved. Then—there was no gathering of supreme effort—the log seemed to leap suddenly backward over his head of its own volition, spinning, crashing and thundering down the incline; he turned and stepped over the slanting track in one stride and walked through them as they gave way and went on across the clearing toward the woods even though the foreman called after him: "Rider!" and again: "You, Rider!"

At sundown he and the dog were in the river swamp four miles away—another clearing, itself not much larger than a room, a hut, a hovel partly of planks and partly of canvas, an unshaven white man standing in the door beside which a shotgun leaned, watching him as he approached, his hand extended with four silver dollars on the palm. "Ah wants a jug," he said.

"A jug?" the white man said. "You mean a pint. This is Monday. Aint you all running this week?"

"Ah laid off," he said. "Whar's my jug?" waiting, looking at nothing apparently, blinking his bloodshot eyes rapidly in his high, slightly back-tilted head, then turning, the jug hanging from his crooked middle finger against his leg,

at which moment the white man looked suddenly and
sharply at his eyes as though seeing them for the first time
—the eyes which had been strained and urgent this morning and which now seemed to be without vision too and
in which no white showed at all—and said,

"Here. Gimme that jug. You dont need no gallon. I'm
going to give you that pint, give it to you. Then you get out
of here and stay out. Dont come back until—" Then the
white man reached and grasped the jug, whereupon the
other swung it behind him, sweeping his other arm up and
out so that it struck the white man across the chest.

"Look out, white folks," he said. "Hit's mine. Ah done
paid you."

The white man cursed him. "No you aint. Here's your
money. Put that jug down, nigger."

"Hit's mine," he said, his voice quiet, gentle even, his
face quiet save for the rapid blinking of the red eyes. "Ah
done paid for hit," turning on, turning his back on the
man and the gun both, and recrossed the clearing to where
the dog waited beside the path to come to heel again. They
moved rapidly on between the close walls of impenetrable
cane-stalks which gave a sort of blondness to the twilight
and possessed something of that oppression, that lack of
room to breathe in, which the walls of his house had had.
But this time, instead of fleeing it, he stopped and raised
the jug and drew the cob stopper from the fierce duskreek
of uncured alcohol and drank, gulping the liquid solid and
cold as ice water, without either taste or heat until he lowered the jug and the air got in. "Hah," he said. "Dat's right.
Try me. Try me, big boy. Ah gots something hyar now dat
kin whup you."

And, once free of the bottom's unbreathing blackness,

there was the moon again, his long shadow and that of the lifted jug slanting away as he drank and then held the jug poised, gulping the silver air into his throat until he could breathe again, speaking to the jug: "Come on now. You always claim you's a better man den me. Come on now. Prove it." He drank again, swallowing the chill liquid tamed of taste or heat either while the swallowing lasted, feeling it flow solid and cold with fire, past then enveloping the strong steady panting of his lungs until they too ran suddenly free as his moving body ran in the silver solid wall of air he breasted. And he was all right, his striding shadow and the trotting one of the dog travelling swift as those of two clouds along the hill; the long cast of his motionless shadow and that of the lifted jug slanting across the slope as he watched the frail figure of his aunt's husband toiling up the hill.

"Dey tole me at de mill you was gone," the old man said. "Ah knowed whar to look. Come home, son. Dat ar cant help you."

"Hit done awready hope me," he said. "Ah'm awready home. Ah'm snakebit now and pizen cant hawm me."

"Den stop and see her. Leff her look at you. Dat's all she axes: just leff her look at you—" But he was already moving. "Wait!" the old man cried. "Wait!"

"You cant keep up," he said, speaking into the silver air, breasting aside the silver solid air which began to flow past him almost as fast as it would have flowed past a moving horse. The faint frail voice was already lost in the night's infinitude, his shadow and that of the dog scudding the free miles, the deep strong panting of his chest running free as air now because he was all right.

Then, drinking, he discovered suddenly that no more of the liquid was entering his mouth. Swallowing, it was no longer passing down his throat, his throat and mouth filled now with a solid and unmoving column which without reflex or revulsion sprang, columnar and intact and still retaining the mold of his gullet, outward glinting in the moonlight, splintering, vanishing into the myriad murmur of the dewed grass. He drank again. Again his throat merely filled solidly until two icy rills ran from his mouth-corners; again the intact column sprang silvering, glinting, shivering, while he panted the chill of air into his throat, the jug poised before his mouth while he spoke to it: "Awright. Ah'm ghy try you again. Soon as you makes up yo mind to stay whar I puts you, Ah'll leff you alone." He drank, filling his gullet for the third time and lowered the jug one instant ahead of the bright intact repetition, panting, indrawing the cool of air until he could breathe. He stoppered the cob carefully back into the jug and stood, panting, blinking, the long cast of his solitary shadow slanting away across the hill and beyond, across the mazy infinitude of all the night-bound earth. "Awright," he said. "Ah just misread de sign wrong. Hit's done done me all de help Ah needs. Ah'm awright now. Ah doan needs no mo of hit."

He could see the lamp in the window as he crossed the pasture, passing the black-and-silver yawn of the sandy ditch where he had played as a boy with empty snuff-tins and rusted harness-buckles and fragments of trace-chains and now and then an actual wheel, passing the garden patch where he had hoed in the spring days while his aunt stood sentry over him from the kitchen window, crossing

the grassless yard in whose dust he had sprawled and crept
before he learned to walk. He entered the house, the room,
the light itself, and stopped in the door, his head back-
tilted a little as if he could not see, the jug hanging from
his crooked finger, against his leg. "Unc Alec say you
wanter see me," he said.

"Not just to see you," his aunt said. "To come home,
whar we kin help you."

"Ah'm awright," he said. "Ah doan needs no help."

"No," she said. She rose from the chair and came and
grasped his arm as she had grasped it yesterday at the
grave. Again, as on yesterday, the forearm was like iron
under her hand. "No! When Alec come back and tole me
how you had wawked off de mill and de sun not half down,
Ah knowed why and whar. And dat cant help you."

"Hit done awready hope me. Ah'm awright now."

"Dont lie to me," she said. "You aint never lied to me.
Dont lie to me now."

Then he said it. It was his own voice, without either
grief or amazement, speaking quietly out of the tremendous panting of his chest which in a moment now would
begin to strain at the walls of this room too. But he would
be gone in a moment.

"Nome," he said, "Hit aint done me no good."

"And hit cant! Cant nothing help you but Him! Ax
Him! Tole Him about hit! He wants to hyar you and help
you!"

"Efn He God, Ah dont needs to tole Him. Efn He God,
He awready know hit. Awright. Hyar Ah is. Leff Him
come down hyar and do me some good."

"On yo knees!" she cried. "On yo knees and ax Him!"

But it was not his knees on the floor, it was his feet. And for a space he could hear her feet too on the planks of the hall behind him and her voice crying after him from the door: "Spoot! Spoot!"—crying after him across the moon-dappled yard the name he had gone by in his childhood and adolescence, before the men he worked with and the bright dark nameless women he had taken in course and forgotten until he saw Mannie that day and said, "Ah'm thu wid all dat," began to call him Rider.

It was just after midnight when he reached the mill. The dog was gone now. This time he could not remember when nor where. At first he seemed to remember hurling the empty jug at it. But later the jug was still in his hand and it was not empty, although each time he drank now the two icy runnels streamed from his mouth-corners, sopping his shirt and overalls until he walked constantly in the fierce chill of the liquid tamed now of flavor and heat and odor too even when the swallowing ceased. "Sides that," he said, "Ah wouldn't thow nothin at him. Ah mout kick him cfn he needed hit and was close enough. But Ah wouldn't ruint no dog chunkin hit."

The jug was still in his hand when he entered the clearing and paused among the mute soaring of the moon-blond lumber-stacks. He stood in the middle now of the unimpeded shadow which he was treading again as he had trod it last night, swaying a little, blinking about at the stacked lumber, the skidway, the piled logs waiting for tomorrow, the boiler-shed all quiet and blanched in the moon. And then it was all right. He was moving again. But he was not moving, he was drinking, the liquid cold and swift and tasteless and requiring no swallowing, so that he could not tell if it were going down inside or outside. But it was all right. And now he was moving, the jug gone now and he didn't know the when or where of that either. He crossed the clearing and entered the boiler shed and went on through it, crossing the junctureless backloop of time's trepan, to the door of the tool-room, the faint glow of the lantern beyond the plank-joints, the surge and fall of living shadow, the mutter of voices, the mute click and scutter of the dice, his hand loud on the barred door, his voice loud too: "Open hit. Hit's me. Ah'm snakebit and bound to die."

Then he was through the door and inside the tool-room. They were the same faces—three members of his timber gang, three or four others of the mill crew, the white night-watchman with the heavy pistol in his hip pocket and the small heap of coins and worn bills on the floor before him, one who was called Rider and was Rider standing above the squatting circle, swaying a little, blinking, the dead muscles of his face shaped into smiling while the white man stared up at him. "Make room, gamblers," he said. "Make room. Ah'm snakebit and de pizen cant hawm me."

"You're drunk," the white man said. "Get out of here. One of you niggers open the door and get him out of here."

"Dass awright, boss-man," he said, his voice equable, his face still fixed in the faint rigid smiling beneath the blink-ing of the red eyes; "Ah aint drunk. Ah just cant wawk straight fer dis yar money weighin me down."

Now he was kneeling too, the other six dollars of his last week's pay on the floor before him, blinking, still smiling at the face of the white man opposite, then, still smiling, he watched the dice pass from hand to hand around the circle as the white man covered the bets, watching the

soiled and palm-worn money in front of the white man
gradually and steadily increase, watching the white man
cast and win two doubled bets in succession then lose on
for twenty-five cents, the dice coming to him at last, the
cupped snug clicking of them in his fist. He spun a coin
into the center.

"Shoots a dollar," he said, and cast, and watched the
white man pick up the dice and flip them back to him.
"Ah lets hit lay," he said. "Ah'm snakebit. Ah kin pass
wid anything," and cast, and this time one of the negroes
flipped the dice back. "Ah lets hit lay," he said, and cast,
and moved as the white man moved, catching the white
man's wrist before his hand reached the dice, the two of
them squatting, facing each other above the dice and the
money, his left hand grasping the white man's wrist, his
face still fixed in the rigid and deadened smiling, his voice
equable, almost deferential: "Ah kin pass even wid miss-
outs. But dese hyar yuther boys—" until the white man's
hand sprang open and the second pair of dice clattered
onto the floor beside the first two and the white man
wrenched free and sprang up and back and reached the
hand backward toward the pocket where the pistol was.

The razor hung between his shoulder-blades from a loop
of cotton string round his neck inside his shirt. The same
motion of the hand which brought the razor forward over
his shoulder flipped the blade open and freed it from the
cord, the blade opening on until the back edge of it lay
across the knuckles of his fist, his thumb pressing the
handle into his closing fingers, so that in the second before
the half-drawn pistol exploded he actually struck at the
white man's throat not with the blade but with a sweeping

blow of his fist, following through in the same motion so that not even the first jet of blood touched his hand or arm.

2.

After it was over—it didn't take long; they found the prisoner on the following day, hanging from the bell-rope in a negro schoolhouse about two miles from the sawmill, and the coroner had pronounced his verdict of death at the hands of a person or persons unknown and surrendered the body to its next of kin all within five minutes—the sheriff's deputy who had been officially in charge of the business was telling his wife about it. They were in the kitchen. His wife was cooking supper. The deputy had been out of bed and in motion ever since the jail delivery shortly before midnight of yesterday and had covered considerable ground since, and he was spent now from lack of sleep and hurried food at hurried and curious hours and, sitting in a chair beside the stove, a little hysterical too.

"Them damn niggers," he said. "I swear to godfrey, it's a wonder we have as little trouble with them as we do. Because why? Because they aint human. They look like a man and they walk on their hind legs like a man, and they can talk and you can understand them and you think they are understanding you, at least now and then. But when it comes to the normal human feelings and sentiments of human beings, they might just as well be a damn herd of wild buffaloes. Now you take this one today——"

"I wish you would," his wife said harshly. She was a stout woman, handsome once, graying now and with a neck definitely too short, who looked not harried at all but composed in fact, only choleric. Also, she had attended a club rook-party that afternoon and had won the first, the fifty-cent, prize until another member had insisted on a recount of the scores and the ultimate throwing out of one entire game. "Take him out of my kitchen, anyway. You sheriffs! Sitting around that courthouse all day long, talking. It's no wonder two or three men can walk in and take prisoners out from under your very noses. They would take your chairs and desks and window sills too if you ever got your feet and backsides off of them that long."

"It's more of them Birdsongs than just two or three," the deputy said. "There's forty-two active votes in that connection. Me and Maydew taken the poll-list and counted them one day. But listen——" The wife turned from the stove, carrying a dish. The deputy snatched his feet rapidly out of the way as she passed him, passed almost over him, and went into the dining room. The deputy raised his voice a little to carry the increased distance: "His wife dies on him. All right. But does he grieve? He's the biggest and busiest man at the funeral. Grabs a shovel before they even got the box into the grave they tell me, and starts throwing dirt onto her faster than a slip scraper could have done it. But that's all right——" His wife came back. He moved his feet again and altered his voice again to the altered range: "——maybe that's how he felt about her. There aint any law against a man rushing his wife into the ground, provided he never had nothing to do with rushing her to the cemetery too. But here the next day he's the first man back at work except the fireman, getting back to the mill before the fireman had his fire going, let alone steam up; five minutes earlier and he could even have helped the fireman wake Birdsong up so Birdsong could go home and go back to bed again, or he could even have cut Birdsong's throat then and saved everybody trouble.

"So he comes to work, the first man on the job, when McAndrews and everybody else expected him to take the day off since even a nigger couldn't want no better excuse for a holiday than he had just buried his wife, when a white man would have took the day off out of pure respect no matter how he felt about his wife, when even a little child would have had sense enough to take a day off when he would still get paid for it too. But not him. The first man there, jumping from one log truck to another before the starting whistle quit blowing even, snatching up ten-foot cypress logs by himself and throwing them around like matches. And then, when everybody had finally decided that that's the way to take him, the way he wants to be took, he walks off the job in the middle of the afternoon without by-your-leave or much obliged or goodbye to Mc-Andrews or nobody else, gets himself a whole gallon of bust-skull white-mule whisky, comes straight back to the mill and to the same crap game where Birdsong has been running crooked dice on them mill niggers for fifteen years, goes straight to the same game where he has been peacefully losing a probably steady average ninety-nine percent of his pay ever since he got big enough to read the spots on them miss-out dice, and cuts Birdsong's throat clean to the neckbone five minutes later." The wife passed him again and went to the dining room. Again he drew his feet back and raised his voice:

"So me and Maydew go out there. Not that we expected to do any good, as he had probably passed Jackson, Tennessee, about daylight; and besides, the simplest way to find him would be just to stay close behind them Birdsong boys.

Of course there wouldn't be nothing hardly worth bringing back to town after they did find him, but it would close
the case. So it's just by the merest chance that we go by
his house; I dont even remember why we went now, but
we did; and there he is. Sitting behind the barred front
door with a open razor on one knee and a loaded shotgun
on the other? No. He was asleep. A big pot of field peas et
clean empty on the stove, and him laying in the back yard
asleep in the broad sun with just his head under the edge
of the porch in the shade and a dog that looked like a cross
between a bear and a Polled Angus steer yelling fire and
murder from the back door. And we wake him and he
sets up and says, 'Awright, white folks. Ah done it. Jest
dont lock me up,' and Maydew says, 'Mr Birdsong's kinfolks aint going to lock you up neither. You'll have plenty
of fresh air when they get hold of you,' and he says, 'Ah
done it. Jest dont lock me up'—advising, instructing the
sheriff not to lock him up; he done it all right and it's too
bad but it aint convenient for him to be cut off from the
fresh air at the moment. So we loaded him into the car,
when here come the old woman—his ma or aunt or something—panting up the road at a dog-trot, wanting to come
with us too, and Maydew trying to explain to her what
would maybe happen to her too if them Birdsong kin
catches us before we can get him locked up, only she is
coming anyway, and like Maydew says, her being in the
car too might be a good thing if the Birdsongs did happen
to run into us, because after all interference with the law
cant be condoned even if the Birdsong connection did
carry that beat for Maydew last summer.

"So we brought her along too and got him to town and
into the jail all right and turned him over to Ketcham and

Ketcham taken him on up stairs and the old woman coming too, right on up to the cell, telling Ketcham, 'Ah tried to raise him right. He was a good boy. He aint never been in no trouble till now. He will suffer for what he done. But dont let the white folks get him,' until Ketcham says, 'You and him ought to thought of that before he started barbering white men without using no later first.' So he locked them both up in the cell because he felt like Maydew did, that her being in there with him might be a good influence on the Birdsong boys if anything started if he should happen to be running for sheriff or something when Maydew's term was up. So Ketcham come on back down stairs and pretty soon the chain gang come in and went on up to the bull pen and he thought things had settled down for a while when all of a sudden he begun to hear the yelling, not howling: yelling, though there wasn't no words in it, and he grabbed his pistol and run back up stairs to the bull pen where the chain gang was and Ketcham could see into the cell where the old woman was kind of squinched down in one corner and where that nigger had done tore that iron cot clean out of the floor it was bolted to and was standing in the middle of the cell, holding the cot over his head like it was a baby's cradle, yelling, and says to the old woman, 'Ah aint goan hurt you,' and throws the cot against the wall and comes and grabs holt of that steel barred door and rips it out of the wall, bricks hinges and all, and walks out of the cell toting the door over his head like it was a gauze window-screen, hollering, "It's awright. It's awright. Ah aint trying to git away.'

"Of course Ketcham could have shot him right there, but like he said, if it wasn't going to be the law, then them Birdsong boys ought to have the first lick at him. So

Ketcham dont shoot. Instead, he jumps in behind where them chain gang niggers was kind of backed off from that steel door, hollering, 'Grab him! Throw him down!' except the niggers hung back at first too until Ketcham gets in where he can kick the ones he can reach, batting at the others with the flat of the pistol until they rush him. And Ketcham says that for a full minute that nigger would grab them as they come in and fling them clean across the room like they was rag dolls, saying, 'Ah aint tryin to git out. Ah aint tryin to git out,' until at last they pulled him down —a big mass of nigger heads and arms and legs boiling around on the floor and even then Ketcham says every now and then a nigger would come flying out and go sailing through the air across the room, spraddled out like a flying squirrel and with his eyes sticking out like car head-lights, until at last they had him down and Ketcham went in and begun peeling away niggers until he could see him laying there under the pile of them, laughing, with tears big as glass marbles running across his face and down past his ears and making a kind of popping sound on the floor like somebody dropping bird eggs, laughing and laughing and saying, 'Hit look lack Ah just cant quit thinking. Look lack Ah just cant quit.' And what do you think of that?"

"I think if you eat any supper in this house you'll do it in the next five minutes," his wife said from the dining room. "I'm going to clear this table then and I'm going to the picture show."

The Old People

I.

At first there was nothing. There was the faint, cold, steady rain, the gray and constant light of the late November dawn, with the voices of the hounds converging somewhere in it and toward them. Then Sam Fathers, standing just behind the boy as he had been standing when the boy shot his first running rabbit with his first gun and almost with the first load it ever carried, touched his shoulder and he began to shake, not with any cold. Then the buck was there. He did not come into sight; he was just there, looking not like a ghost but as if all of light were condensed in him and he were the source of it, not only moving in it but disseminating it, already running, seen first as you always see the deer, in that split second after he has already seen you, already slanting away in that first soaring bound, the antlers even in that dim light looking like a small rocking-chair balanced on his head.

"Now," Sam Fathers said, "shoot quick, and slow."

The boy did not remember that shot at all. He would live to be eighty, as his father and his father's twin brother and their father in his turn had lived to be, but he would never hear that shot nor remember even the shock of the gun-butt. He didn't even remember what he did with the gun afterward. He was running. Then he was standing over the buck where it lay on the wet earth still in the attitude of speed and not looking at all dead, standing over it shaking and jerking, with Sam Fathers beside him again, extending the knife. "Dont walk up to him in front," Sam said. "If he aint dead, he will cut you all to pieces with his feet. Walk up to him from behind and take him by the horn first, so you can hold his head down until you can jump away. Then slip your other hand down and hook your fingers in his nostrils."

The boy did that—drew the head back and the throat taut and drew Sam Fathers' knife across the throat and Sam stooped and dipped his hands in the hot smoking blood and wiped them back and forth across the boy's face. Then Sam's horn rang in the wet gray woods and again and again; there was a boiling wave of dogs about them, with Tennie's Jim and Boon Hogganbeck whipping them back after each had had a taste of the blood, then the men, the true hunters—Walter Ewell whose rifle never missed, and Major de Spain and old General Compson and the boy's cousin, McCaslin Edmonds, grandson of his father's sister, sixteen years his senior and, since both he and Mc-Caslin were only children and the boy's father had been nearing seventy when he was born, more his brother than his cousin and more his father than either—sitting their horses and looking down at them: at the old man of seventy who had been a negro for two generations now but whose face and bearing were still those of the Chickasaw chief who had been his father; and the white boy of twelve with the prints of the bloody hands on his face, who had nothing to do now but stand straight and not let the trembling show.

"Did he do all right, Sam?" his cousin McCaslin said.

"He done all right," Sam Fathers said.

They were the white boy, marked forever, and the old dark man sired on both sides by savage kings, who had marked him, whose bloody hands had merely formally consecrated him to that which, under the man's tutelage, he had already accepted, humbly and joyfully, with abnegation and with pride too; the hands, the touch, the first worthy blood which he had been found at last worthy to draw, joining him and the man forever, so that the man would continue to live past the boy's seventy years and then eighty years, long after the man himself had entered the earth as chiefs and kings entered it;—the child, not yet a man, whose grandfather had lived in the same country and in almost the same manner as the boy himself would grow up to live, leaving his descendants in the land in his turn as his grandfather had done, and the old man past seventy whose grandfathers had owned the land long before the white men ever saw it and who had vanished from it now with all their kind, what of blood they left behind them running now in another race and for a while even in bondage and now drawing toward the end of its alien and irrevocable course, barren, since Sam Fathers had no children.

His father was Ikkemotubbe himself, who had named himself Doom. Sam told the boy about that—how Ikkemotubbe, old Issetibbeha's sister's son, had run away to New Orleans in his youth and returned seven years later with a French companion calling himself the Chevalier Soeur-Blonde de Vitry, who must have been the Ikkemotubbe of his family too and who was already addressing Ikkemotubbe as *Du Homme*;—returned, came home again, with

his foreign Aramis and the quadroon slave woman who
was to be Sam's mother, and a gold-laced hat and coat and
a wicker wine-hamper containing a litter of month-old puppies and a gold snuff-box filled with a white powder resembling fine sugar. And how he was met at the River
landing by three or four companions of his bachelor youth,
and while the light of a smoking torch gleamed on the glit-
tering braid of the hat and coat Doom squatted in the mud
of the land and took one of the puppies from the hamper
and put a pinch of the white powder on its tongue and
the puppy died before the one who was holding it could
cast it away. And how they returned to the Plantation
where Issetibbeha, dead now, had been succeeded by his
son, Doom's fat cousin Moketubbe, and the next day Moketubbe's eight-year-old son died suddenly and that afternoon,
in the presence of Moketubbe and most of the others (the
People, Sam Fathers called them) Doom produced another
puppy from the wine-hamper and put a pinch of the white
powder on its tongue and Moketubbe abdicated and
Doom became in fact The Man which his French friend
already called him. And how on the day after that, during
the ceremony of accession, Doom pronounced a marriage
between the pregnant quadroon and one of the slave men
which he had just inherited (that was how Sam Fathers got
his name, which in Chickasaw had been Had-Two-Fathers)
and two years later sold the man and woman and the child
who was his own son to his white neighbor, Carothers
McCaslin.

That was seventy years ago. The Sam Fathers whom
the boy knew was already sixty—a man not tall, squat
rather, almost sedentary, flabby-looking though he actually
was not, with hair like a horse's mane which even at sev-

enty showed no trace of white and a face which showed
no age until he smiled, whose only visible trace of negro
blood was a slight dullness of the hair and the fingernails,
and something else which you did notice about the eyes,
which you noticed because it was not always there, only in
repose and not always then—something not in their shape
nor pigment but in their expression, and the boy's cousin
McCaslin told him what that was: not the heritage of
Ham, not the mark of servitude but of bondage; the
knowledge that for a while that part of his blood had been
the blood of slaves. "Like an old lion or a bear in a cage,"
McCaslin said. "He was born in the cage and has been in
it all his life; he knows nothing else. Then he smells
something. It might be anything, any breeze blowing past
anything and then into his nostrils. But there for a second
was the hot sand or the cane-brake that he never even saw
himself, might not even know if he did see it and probably does know he couldn't hold his own with it if he
got back to it. But that's not what he smells then. It was
the cage he smelled. He hadn't smelled the cage until that
minute. Then the hot sand or the brake blew into his nostrils and blew away, and all he could smell was the cage.
That's what makes his eyes look like that."

"Then let him go!" the boy cried. "Let him go!"

His cousin laughed shortly. Then he stopped laughing,
making the sound that is. It had never been laughing. "His
cage aint McCaslins," he said. "He was a wild man. When
he was born, all his blood on both sides, except the little
white part, knew things that had been tamed out of our
blood so long ago that we have not only forgotten them,
we have to live together in herds to protect ourselves from
our own sources. He was the direct son not only of a war-

rior but of a chief. Then he grew up and began to learn things, and all of a sudden one day he found out that he had been betrayed, the blood of the warriors and chiefs had been betrayed. Not by his father," he added quickly. "He probably never held it against old Doom for selling him and his mother into slavery, because he probably believed the damage was already done before then and it was the same warriors' and chiefs' blood in him and Doom both that was betrayed through the black blood which his mother gave him. Not betrayed by the black blood and not wilfully betrayed by his mother, but betrayed by her all the same, who had bequeathed him not only the blood of slaves but even a little of the very blood which had enslaved it; himself his own battleground, the scene of his own vanquishment and the mausoleum of his defeat. His cage aint us," McCaslin said. "Did you ever know anybody yet, even your father and Uncle Buddy, that ever told him to do or not do anything that he ever paid any attention to?"

That was true. The boy first remembered him as sitting in the door of the plantation blacksmith-shop, where he sharpened plow-points and mended tools and even did rough carpenter-work when he was not in the woods. And sometimes, even when the woods had not drawn him, even with the shop cluttered with work which the farm waited on, Sam would sit there, doing nothing at all for half a day or a whole one, and no man, neither the boy's father and twin uncle in their day nor his cousin McCaslin after he became practical though not yet titular master, ever to say to him, "I want this finished by sundown" or "why wasn't this done yesterday?" And once each year, in the late fall, in November, the boy would watch the wagon, the hooped canvas top erected now, being loaded—the food, hams and sausage from the smokehouse, coffee and flour and molasses from the commissary, a whole beef killed just last night for the dogs until there would be meat in camp, the crate containing the dogs themselves, then the bedding, the guns, the horns and lanterns and axes, and his cousin McCaslin and Sam Fathers in their hunting clothes would mount to the seat and with Tennie's Jim sitting on the dog-crate they would drive away to Jefferson, to join Major de Spain and General Compson and Boon Hogganbeck and Walter Ewell and go on into the big bottom of the Tallahatchie where the deer and bear were, to be gone two weeks. But before the wagon was even loaded the boy would find that he could watch no longer. He would go away, running almost, to stand behind the corner where he could not see the wagon and nobody could see him, not crying, holding himself rigid except for the trembling, whispering to himself: "Soon now. Soon now. Just three more years" (or two more or one more) "and I will be ten. Then Cass said I can go."

White man's work, when Sam did work. Because he did nothing else: farmed no alloted acres of his own, as the other ex-slaves of old Carothers McCaslin did, performed no field-work for daily wages as the younger and newer negroes did—and the boy never knew just how that had been settled between Sam and old Carothers, or perhaps with old Carothers' twin sons after him. For, although Sam lived among the negroes, in a cabin among the other cabins in the quarters, and consorted with negroes (what of consorting with anyone Sam did after the boy got big enough to walk alone from the house to the blacksmith-shop and then to carry a gun) and dressed like them and talked like

them and even went with them to the negro church now
and then, he was still the son of that Chickasaw chief and
the negroes knew it. And, it seemed to the boy, not only
negroes. Boon Hogganbeck's grandmother had been a
Chickasaw woman too, and although the blood had run
white since and Boon was a white man, it was not chief's
blood. To the boy at least, the difference was apparent immediately you saw Boon and Sam together, and even Boon
seemed to know it was there—even Boon, to whom in his
tradition it had never occurred that anyone might be better
born than himself. A man might be smarter, he admitted
that, or richer (luckier, he called it) but not better born.
Boon was a mastiff, absolutely faithful, dividing his fidelity equally between Major de Spain and the boy's cousin
McCaslin, absolutely dependent for his very bread and dividing that impartially too between Major de Spain and
McCaslin, hardy, generous, courageous enough, a slave to
all the appetites and almost unratiocinative. In the boy's
eyes at least it was Sam Fathers, the negro, who bore himself not only toward his cousin McCaslin and Major de
Spain but toward all white men, with gravity and dignity
and without servility or recourse to that impenetrable wall
of ready and easy mirth which negroes sustain between
themselves and white men, bearing himself toward his
cousin McCaslin not only as one man to another but as
an older man to a younger.

He taught the boy the woods, to hunt, when to shoot
and when not to shoot, when to kill and when not to kill,
and better, what to do with it afterward. Then he would
talk to the boy, the two of them sitting beneath the close
fierce stars on a summer hilltop while they waited for the
hounds to bring the fox back within hearing, or beside

a fire in the November or December woods while the dogs
worked out a coon's trail along the creek, or fireless in the
pitch dark and heavy dew of April mornings while they
squatted beneath a turkey-roost. The boy would never
question him; Sam did not react to questions. The boy
would just wait and then listen and Sam would begin,
talking about the old days and the People whom he had
not had time ever to know and so could not remember (he
did not remember ever having seen his father's face), and
in place of whom the other race into which his blood had
run supplied him with no substitute.

And as he talked about those old times and those dead
and vanished men of another race from either that the
boy knew, gradually to the boy those old times would
cease to be old times and would become a part of the boy's
present, not only as if they had happened yesterday but
as if they were still happening, the men who walked
through them actually walking in breath and air and
casting an actual shadow on the earth they had not quitted.
And more: as if some of them had not happened yet but
would occur tomorrow, until at last it would seem to the
boy that he himself had not come into existence yet, that
none of his race nor the other subject race which his people
had brought with them into the land had come here yet;
that although it had been his grandfather's and then his
father's and uncle's and was now his cousin's and someday would be his own land which he and Sam hunted
over, their hold upon it actually was as trivial and without
reality as the now faded and archaic script in the chancery
book in Jefferson which allocated it to them and that it was
he, the boy, who was the guest here and Sam Father's
voice the mouthpiece of the host.

Until three years ago there had been two of them, the other a full-blood Chickasaw, in a sense even more incredibly lost than Sam Fathers. He called himself Jobaker, as if it were one word. Nobody knew his history at all. He was a hermit, living in a foul little shack at the forks of the creek five miles from the plantation and about that far from any other habitation. He was a market hunter and fisherman and he consorted with nobody, black or white; no negro would even cross his path and no man dared approach his hut except Sam. And perhaps once a month the boy would find them in Sam's shop—two old men squatting on their heels on the dirt floor, talking in a mixture of negroid English and flat hill dialect and now and then a phrase of that old tongue which as time went on and the boy squatted there too listening, he began to learn. Then Jobaker died. That is, nobody had seen him in some time. Then one morning Sam was missing, nobody, not even the boy, knew when nor where, until that night when some negroes hunting in the creek bottom saw the sudden burst of flame and approached. It was Jobaker's hut, but before they got anywhere near it, someone shot at them from the shadows beyond it. It was Sam who fired, but nobody ever found Jobaker's grave.

The next morning, sitting at breakfast with his cousin, the boy saw Sam pass the dining-room window and he remembered then that never in his life before had he seen Sam nearer the house than the blacksmith-shop. He stopped eating even; he sat there and he and his cousin both heard the voices from beyond the pantry door, then the door opened and Sam entered, carrying his hat in his hand but without knocking as anyone else on the place except a house servant would have done, entered just far enough for the door to close behind him and stood looking at neither of them—the Indian face above the nigger clothes, looking at something over their heads or at something not even in the room.

"I want to go," he said. "I want to go to the Big Bottom to live."

"To live?" the boy's cousin said.

"At Major de Spain's and your camp, where you go to hunt," Sam said. "I could take care of it for you all while you aint there. I will build me a little house in the woods, if you rather I didn't stay in the big one."

"What about Isaac here?" his cousin said. "How will you get away from him? Are you going to take him with you?" But still Sam looked at neither of them, standing just inside the room with that face which showed nothing, which showed that he was an old man only when it smiled.

"I want to go," he said. "Let me go."

"Yes," the cousin said quietly. "Of course. I'll fix it with Major de Spain. You want to go soon?"

"I'm going now," Sam said. He went out. And that was all. The boy was nine then; it seemed perfectly natural that nobody, not even his cousin McCaslin, should argue with Sam. Also, since he was nine now, he could understand that Sam could leave him and their days and nights in the woods together without any wrench. He believed that he and Sam both knew that this was not only temporary but that the exigencies of his maturing, of that for which Sam had been training him all his life some day to dedicate himself, required it. They had settled that one night last summer while they listened to the hounds bringing a fox back up the creek valley; now the boy dis-

cerned in that very talk under the high, fierce August
stars a presage, a warning, of this moment today. "I done
taught you all there is of this settled country," Sam said.
"You can hunt it good as I can now. You are ready for
the Big Bottom now, for bear and deer. Hunter's meat,"
he said. "Next year you will be ten. You will write your
age in two numbers and you will be ready to become a
man. Your pa" (Sam always referred to the boy's cousin as
his father, establishing even before the boy's orphanhood
did that relation between them not of the ward to his
guardian and kinsman and chief and head of his blood, but
of the child to the man who sired his flesh and his thinking
too.) "promised you can go with us then." So the boy
could understand Sam's going. But he couldn't understand
why now, in March, six months before the moon for
hunting.

"If Jobaker's dead like they say," he said, "and Sam
hasn't got anybody but us at all kin to him, why does he
want to go to the Big Bottom now, when it will be six
months before we get there?"   •

"Maybe that's what he wants," McCaslin said. "Maybe
he wants to get away from you a little while."

But that was all right. McCaslin and other grown people
often said things like that and he paid no attention to them,
just as he paid no attention to Sam saying he wanted to
go to the Big Bottom to live. After all, he would have to
live there for six months, because there would be no use
in going at all if he was going to turn right around and
come back. And, as Sam himself had told him, he already
knew all about hunting in this settled country that Sam
or anybody else could teach him. So it would be all right.
Summer, then the bright days after the first frost, then the

cold and himself on the wagon with McCaslin this time
and the moment would come and he would draw the blood,
the big blood which would make him a man, a hunter, and
Sam would come back home with them and he too would
have outgrown the child's pursuit of rabbits and 'possums.
Then he too would make one before the winter fire, talking
of the old hunts and the hunts to come as hunters talked.

So Sam departed. He owned so little that he could
carry it. He walked. He would neither let McCaslin send
him in the wagon, nor take a mule to ride. No one saw his
go even. He was just gone one morning, the cabin which
had never had very much in it, vacant and empty, the shop
in which there never had been very much done, standing
idle. Then November came at last, and now the boy made
one—himself and his cousin McCaslin and Tennie's Jim,
and Major de Spain and General Compson and Walter
Ewell and Boon and old Uncle Ash to do the cooking,
waiting for them in Jefferson with the other wagon, and
the surrey in which he and McCaslin and General Compson and Major de Spain would ride.

Sam was waiting at the camp to meet them. If he was
glad to see them, he did not show it. And if, when they
broke camp two weeks later to return home, he was sorry
to see them go, he did not show that either. Because he did
not come back with them. It was only the boy who returned, returning solitary and alone to the settled familiar
land, to follow for eleven months the childish business of
rabbits and such while he waited to go back, having brought
with him, even from his brief first sojourn, an unforgettable
sense of the big woods—not a quality dangerous or particularly inimical, but profound, sentient, gigantic and brooding, amid which he had been permitted to go to and fro

at will, unscathed, why he knew not, but dwarfed and, until he had drawn honorably blood worthy of being drawn, alien.

Then November, and they would come back. Each morning Sam would take the boy out to the stand allotted him. It would be one of the poorer stands of course, since he was only ten and eleven and twelve and he had never even seen a deer running yet. But they would stand there, Sam a little behind him and without a gun himself, as he had been standing when the boy shot the running rabbit when he was eight years old. They would stand there in the November dawns, and after a while they would hear the dogs. Sometimes the chase would sweep up and past quite close, belling and invisible; once they heard the two heavy reports of Boon Hogganbeck's old gun with which he had never killed anything larger than a squirrel and that sitting, and twice they heard the flat unreverberant clap of Walter Ewell's rifle, following which you did not even wait to hear his horn.

"I'll never get a shot," the boy said. "I'll never kill one."

"Yes you will," Sam said. "You wait. You'll be a hunter. You'll be a man."

But Sam wouldn't come out. They would leave him there. He would come as far as the road where the surrey waited, to take the riding horses back, and that was all. The men would ride the horses and Uncle Ash and Tennie's Jim and the boy would follow in the wagon with Sam, with the camp equipment and the trophies, the meat, the heads, the antlers, the good ones, the wagon winding on among the tremendous gums and cypresses and oaks where no axe save that of the hunter had ever sounded, between the impenetrable walls of cane and brier—the two changing yet constant walls just beyond which the

wilderness whose mark he had brought away forever on
his spirit even from that first two weeks seemed to lean,
stooping a little, watching them and listening, not quite
inimical because they were too small, even those such as
Walter and Major de Spain and old General Compson who
had killed many deer and bear, their sojourn too brief and
too harmless to excite to that, but just brooding, secret,
tremendous, almost inattentive.

Then they would emerge, they would be out of it, the
line as sharp as the demarcation of a doored wall. Suddenly skeleton cotton- and corn-fields would flow away
on either hand, gaunt and motionless beneath the gray
rain; there would be a house, barns, fences, where the
hand of man had clawed for an instant, holding, the wall
of the wilderness behind them now, tremendous and still
and seemingly impenetrable in the gray and fading light,
the very tiny orifice through which they had emerged apparently swallowed up. The surrey would be waiting, his
cousin McCaslin and Major de Spain and General Compson and Walter and Boon dismounted beside it. Then
Sam would get down from the wagon and mount one of the
horses and, with the others on a rope behind him, he
would turn back. The boy would watch him for a while
against that tall and secret wall, growing smaller and
smaller against it, never looking back. Then he would
enter it, returning to what the boy believed, and thought
that his cousin McCaslin believed, was his loneliness and
solitude.

2.

So the instant came. He pulled trigger and Sam Fathers
marked his face with the hot blood which he had spilled

and he ceased to be a child and became a hunter and a
man. It was the last day. They broke camp that afternoon
and went out, his cousin and Major de Spain and General
Compson and Boon on the horses, Walter Ewell and the
negroes in the wagon with him and Sam and his hide and
antlers. There could have been (and were) other trophies
in the wagon. But for him they did not exist, just as for
all practical purposes he and Sam Fathers were still alone
together as they had been that morning. The wagon wound
and jolted between the slow and shifting yet constant walls
from beyond and above which the wilderness watched them
pass, less than inimical now and never to be inimical again
since the buck still and forever leaped, the shaking gun-
barrels coming constantly and forever steady at last, crashing, and still out of his instant of immortality the buck
sprang, forever immortal;—the wagon jolting and bouncing
on, the moment of the buck, the shot, Sam Fathers and
himself and the blood with which Sam had marked him
forever one with the wilderness which had accepted him
since Sam said that he had done all right, when suddenly
Sam reined back and stopped the wagon and they all
heard the unmistakable and unforgettable sound of a deer
breaking cover.

Then Boon shouted from beyond the bend of the trail
and while they sat motionless in the halted wagon, Walter
and the boy already reaching for their guns, Boon came
galloping back, flogging his mule with his hat, his face
wild and amazed as he shouted down at them. Then the
other riders came around the bend, also spurring.

"Get the dogs!" Boon cried. "Get the dogs! If he had a
nub on his head, he had fourteen points! Laying right
there by the road in that pawpaw thicket! If I'd a knowed

he was there, I could have cut his throat with my pocket knife!"

"Maybe that's why he run," Walter said. "He saw you never had your gun." He was already out of the wagon with his rifle. Then the boy was out too with his gun, and the other riders came up and Boon got off his mule somehow and was scrabbling and clawing among the duffel in the wagon, still shouting, "Get the dogs! Get the dogs!" And it seemed to the boy too that it would take them forever to decide what to do—the old men in whom the blood ran cold and slow, in whom during the intervening years between them and himself the blood had become a different and colder substance from that which ran in him and even in Boon and Walter.

"What about it, Sam?" Major de Spain said. "Could the dogs bring him back?"

"We wont need the dogs," Sam said. "If he dont hear the dogs behind him, he will circle back in here about sundown to bed."

"All right," Major de Spain said. "You boys take the horses. We'll go on out to the road in the wagon and wait there." He and General Compson and McCaslin got into the wagon and Boon and Walter and Sam and the boy mounted the horses and turned back and out of the trail. Sam led them for an hour through the gray and unmarked afternoon whose light was little different from what it had been at dawn and which would become darkness without any graduation between. Then Sam stopped them.

"This is far enough," he said. "He'll be coming upwind, and he dont want to smell the mules." They tied the mounts in a thicket. Sam led them on foot now, unpathed through the markless afternoon, the boy pressing close behind him, the two others, or so it seemed to the boy, on his heels. But they were not. Twice Sam turned his head slightly and spoke back to him across his shoulder, still walking: "You got time. We'll get there fore he does."

So he tried to go slower. He tried deliberately to decelerate the dizzy rushing of time in which the buck which he had not even seen was moving, which it seemed to him must be carrying the buck farther and farther and more and more irretrievably away from them even though there were no dogs behind him now to make him run, even though, according to Sam, he must have completed his circle now and was heading back toward them. They went on; it could have been another hour or twice that or less than half, the boy could not have said. Then they were on a ridge. He had never been in here before and he could not see that it was a ridge. He just knew that the earth had risen slightly because the underbrush had thinned a little, the ground sloping invisibly away toward a dense wall of cane. Sam stopped. "This is it," he said. He spoke to Walter and Boon: "Follow this ridge and you will come to two crossings. You will see the tracks. If he crosses, it will be at one of these three."

Walter looked about for a moment. "I know it," he said. "I've even seen your deer. I was in here last Monday. He aint nothing but a yearling."

"A yearling?" Boon said. He was panting from the walking. His face still looked a little wild. "If the one I saw was any yearling, I'm still in kindergarden."

"Then I must have seen a rabbit," Walter said. "I always heard you quit school altogether two years before the first grade."

Boon glared at Walter. "If you dont want to shoot him,
get out of the way," he said. "Set down somewhere. By
God, I——"

"Aint nobody going to shoot him standing here," Sam
said quietly.

"Sam's right," Walter said. He moved, slanting the
worn, silver-colored barrel of his rifle downward to walk
with it again. "A little more moving and a little more quiet
too. Five miles is still Hogganbeck range, even if we wasn't
downwind." They went on. The boy could still hear Boon
talking, though presently that ceased too. Then once more
he and Sam stood motionless together against a tremendous pin oak in a little thicket, and again there was nothing.
There was only the soaring and sombre solitude in the dim
light, there was the thin murmur of the faint cold rain
which had not ceased all day. Then, as if it had waited for
them to find their positions and become still, the wilderness breathed again. It seemed to lean inward above them,
above himself and Sam and Walter and Boon in their
separate lurking-places, tremendous, attentive, impartial and
omniscient, the buck moving in it somewhere, not running
yet since he had not been pursued, not frightened yet and
never fearsome but just alert also as they were alert, perhaps already circling back, perhaps quite near, perhaps
conscious also of the eye of the ancient immortal Umpire.
Because he was just twelve then, and that morning something had happened to him: in less than a second he had
ceased forever to be the child he was yesterday. Or perhaps that made no difference, perhaps even a city-bred
man, let alone a child, could not have understood it;
perhaps only a country-bred one could comprehend loving
the life he spills. He began to shake again.

"I'm glad it's started now," he whispered. He did not move to speak; only his lips shaped the expiring words: "Then it will be gone when I raise the gun——"

Nor did Sam. "Hush," he said.

"Is he that near?" the boy whispered. "Do you think——"

"Hush," Sam said. So he hushed. But he could not stop the shaking. He did not try, because he knew it would go away when he needed the steadiness—had not Sam Fathers already consecrated and absolved him from weakness and regret too?—not from love and pity for all which lived and ran and then ceased to live in a second in the very midst of splendor and speed, but from weakness and regret. So they stood motionless, breathing deep and quiet and steady. If there had been any sun, it would be near to setting now; there was a condensing, a densifying, of what he had thought was the gray and unchanging light until he realised suddenly that it was his own breathing, his heart, his blood—something, all things, and that Sam Fathers had marked him indeed, not as a mere hunter, but with something Sam had had in his turn of his vanished and forgotten people. He stopped breathing then; there was only his heart, his blood, and in the following silence the wilderness ceased to breathe also, leaning, stooping overhead with its breath held, tremendous and impartial and waiting. Then the shaking stopped too, as he had known it would, and he drew back the two heavy hammers of the gun.

Then it had passed. It was over. The solitude did not breathe again yet; it had merely stopped watching him and was looking somewhere else, even turning its back on him, looking on away up the ridge at another point, and the boy knew as well as if he had seen him that the buck had come to the edge of the cane and had either seen or scented them and faded back into it. But the solitude did not breathe again. It should have suspired again then but it did not. It was still facing, watching, what it had been watching and it was not here, not where he and Sam stood; rigid, not breathing himself, he thought, cried *No! No!*, knowing already that it was too late, thinking with the old despair of two and three years ago: *I'll never get a shot.* Then he heard it—the flat single clap of Walter Ewell's rifle which never missed. Then the mellow sound of the horn came down the ridge and something went out of him and he knew then he had never expected to get the shot at all.

"I reckon that's it," he said. "Walter got him." He had raised the gun slightly without knowing it. He lowered it again and had lowered one of the hammers and was already moving out of the thicket when Sam spoke.

"Wait."

"Wait?" the boy cried. And he would remember that —how he turned upon Sam in the truculence of a boy's grief over the missed opportunity, the missed luck. "What for? Dont you hear that horn?"

And he would remember how Sam was standing. Sam had not moved. He was not tall, squat rather and broad, and the boy had been growing fast for the past year or so and there was not much difference between them in height, yet Sam was looking over the boy's head and up the ridge toward the sound of the horn and the boy knew that Sam did not even see him; that Sam knew he was still there beside him but he did not see the boy. Then the boy saw

the buck. It was coming down the ridge, as if it were
walking out of the very sound of the horn which related
its death. It was not running, it was walking, tremendous,
unhurried, slanting and tilting its head to pass the antlers
through the undergrowth, and the boy standing with Sam
beside him now instead of behind him as Sam always stood,
and the gun still partly aimed and one of the hammers
still cocked.

Then it saw them. And still it did not begin to run.
It just stopped for an instant, taller than any man, looking at them; then its muscles suppled, gathered. It did not
even alter its course, not fleeing, not even running, just
moving with that winged and effortless ease with which
deer move, passing within twenty feet of them, its head high
and the eye not proud and not haughty but just full and
wild and unafraid, and Sam standing beside the boy now,
his right arm raised at full length, palm-outward, speaking
in that tongue which the boy had learned from listening to
him and Joe Baker in the blacksmith shop, while up the
ridge Walter Ewell's horn was still blowing them in to a
dead buck.

"Oleh, Chief," Sam said. "Grandfather."

When they reached Walter, he was standing with his
back toward them, quite still, bemused almost, looking
down at his feet. He didn't look up at all.

"Come here, Sam," he said quietly. When they reached
him he still did not look up, standing above a little spike
buck which had still been a fawn last spring. "He was so
little I pretty near let him go," Walter said. "But just look
at the track he was making. It's pretty near big as a cow's.
If there were any more tracks here besides the ones he is

laying in, I would swear there was another buck here that I never even saw."

3.

It was dark when they reached the road where the surrey waited. It was turning cold, the rain had stopped, and the sky was beginning to blow clear. His cousin and Major de Spain and General Compson had a fire going. "Did you get him?" Major de Spain said.

"Got a good-sized swamp-rabbit with spike horns," Walter said. He slid the little buck down from his mule. The boy's cousin McCaslin looked at it.

"Nobody saw the big one?" he said.

"I dont even believe Boon saw it," Walter said. "He probably jumped somebody's straw cow in that thicket." Boon started cursing, swearing at Walter and at Sam for not getting the dogs in the first place and at the buck and all.

"Never mind," Major de Spain said. "He'll be here for us next fall. Let's get started home."

It was after midnight when they let Walter out at his gate two miles from Jefferson and later still when they took General Compson to his house and then returned to Major de Spain's, where he and McCaslin would spend the rest of the night, since it was still seventeen miles home. It was cold, the sky was clear now; there would be a heavy frost by sunup and the ground was already frozen beneath the horses' feet and the wheels and beneath their own feet as they crossed Major de Spain's yard and entered the house, the warm dark house, feeling their way up the dark stairs until Major de Spain found a candle and lit it, and

into the strange room and the big deep bed, the still cold
sheets until they began to warm to their bodies and at last
the shaking stopped and suddenly he was telling McCaslin about it while McCaslin listened, quietly until he had
finished. "You dont believe it," the boy said. "I know
you dont——"

"Why not?" McCaslin said. "Think of all that has happened here, on this earth. All the blood hot and strong
for living, pleasuring, that has soaked back into it. For
grieving and suffering too, of course, but still getting something out of it for all that, getting a lot out of it, because
after all you dont have to continue to bear what you believe is suffering; you can always choose to stop that, put
an end to that. And even suffering and grieving is better
than nothing; there is only one thing worse than not being
alive, and that's shame. But you cant be alive forever, and
you always wear out life long before you have exhausted the
possibilities of living. And all that must be somewhere; all
that could not have been invented and created just to be
thrown away. And the earth is shallow; there is not a great
deal of it before you come to the rock. And the earth
dont want to just keep things, hoard them; it wants to
use them again. Look at the seed, the acorns, at what
happens even to carrion when you try to bury it: it re-
fuses too, seethes and struggles too until it reaches light
and air again, hunting the sun still. And they——" the boy
saw his hand in silhouette for a moment against the window
beyond which, accustomed to the darkness now, he could
see sky where the scoured and icy stars glittered "——they
dont want it, need it. Besides, what would it want, itself,
knocking around out there, when it never had enough
time about the earth as it was, when there is plenty of room

about the earth, plenty of places still unchanged from what they were when the blood used and pleasured in them while it was still blood?"

"But we want them," the boy said. "We want them too. There is plenty of room for us and them too."

"That's right," McCaslin said. "Suppose they dont have substance, cant cast a shadow——"

"But I saw it!" the boy cried. "I saw him!"

"Steady," McCaslin said. For an instant his hand touched the boy's flank beneath the covers. "Steady. I know you did. So did I. Sam took me in there once after I killed my first deer."

The Bear

I.

THERE was a man and a dog too this time. Two beasts, counting Old Ben, the bear, and two men, counting Boon Hogganbeck, in whom some of the same blood ran which ran in Sam Fathers, even though Boon's was·a plebeian strain of it and only Sam and Old Ben and the mongrel Lion were taintless and incorruptible.

He was sixteen. For six years now he had been a man's hunter. For six years now he had heard the best of all talking. It was of the wilderness, the big woods, bigger and older than any recorded document:—of white man fatuous enough to believe he had bought any fragment of it, of Indian ruthless enough to pretend that any fragment of it had been his to convey; bigger than Major de Spain and the scrap he pretended to, knowing better; older than old Thomas Sutpen of whom Major de Spain had had it and who knew better; older even than old Ikkemotubbe, the Chickasaw chief, of whom old Sutpen had had it and who knew better in his turn. It was of the men, not white nor black nor red but men, hunters, with the will and ·hardihood to endure and the humility and skill to survive, and the dogs and the bear and deer juxtaposed and reliefed against it, ordered and compelled by and within the wilder-

ness in the ancient and unremitting contest according to
the ancient and immitigable rules which voided all regrets
and brooked no quarter;—the best game of all, the best of
all breathing and forever the best of all listening, the voices
quiet and weighty and deliberate for retrospection and
recollection and exactitude among the concrete trophies—
the racked guns and the heads and skins—in the libraries
of town houses or the offices of plantation houses or (and
best of all) in the camps themselves where the intact and
still-warm meat yet hung, the men who had slain it sitting
before the burning logs on hearths when there were houses
and hearths or about the smoky blazing of piled wood in
front of stretched tarpaulins when there were not. There
was always a bottle present, so that it would seem to him
that those fine fierce instants of heart and brain and courage and wiliness and speed were concentrated and distilled
into that brown liquor which not women, not boys and
children, but only hunters drank, drinking not of the blood
they spilled but some condensation of the wild immortal
spirit, drinking it moderately, humbly even, not with the
pagan's base and baseless hope of acquiring thereby the
virtues of cunning and strength and speed but in salute
to them. Thus it seemed to him on this December morning not only natural but actually fitting that this should
have begun with whisky.

He realised later that it had begun long before that. It
had already begun on that day when he first wrote his age
in two ciphers and his cousin McCaslin brought him for
the first time to the camp, the big woods, to earn for himself from the wilderness the name and state of hunter
provided he in his turn were humble and enduring enough.
He had already inherited then, without ever having seen

it, the big old bear with one trap-ruined foot that in an
area almost a hundred miles·square had earned for himself a name, a definite designation like a living man:—
the long legend of corn-cribs broken down and rifled, of
shoats and grown pigs and even calves carried bodily into
the woods and devoured and traps and deadfalls over-
thrown and dogs mangled and slain and shotgun and even
rifle shots delivered at point-blank range yet with no more
effect than so many peas blown through a tube by a
child—a corridor of wreckage and destruction beginning
back before the boy was born, through which sped, not
fast but rather with the ruthless and irresistible deliberation of a locomotive, the shaggy tremendous shape. It ran
in his knowledge before he ever saw it. It loomed and
towered in his dreams before he even saw the unaxed
woods where it left its crooked print, shaggy, tremendous,
red-eyed, not malevolent but just big, too big for the
dogs which tried to bay it, for the horses which tried to
ride it down, for the men and the bullets they fired into
it; too big for the very country which was its constricting
scope. It was as if the boy had already divined what his
senses and intellect had not encompassed yet: that doomed
wilderness whose edges were being constantly and punily
gnawed at by men with plows and axes who feared it because it was wilderness, men myriad and nameless even to
one another in the land where the old bear had earned·
a name, and through which ran not even a mortal beast but
an anachronism indomitable and invincible out of an old
dead time, a phantom, epitome and apotheosis of the old
wild life which the little puny humans swarmed and
hacked at in a fury of abhorrence and fear like pygmies
about the ankles of a drowsing elephant;—the old bear,

solitary, indomitable, and alone; widowered childless and absolved of mortality—old. Priam reft of his old wife and outlived all his sons.

Still a child, with three years then two years then one year yet before he too could make one of them, each November he would watch the wagon containing the dogs and the bedding and food and guns and his cousin Mc-Caslin and Tennie's Jim and Sam Fathers too until Sam moved to the camp to live, depart for the Big Bottom, the big woods. To him, they were going not to hunt bear and deer but to keep yearly rendezvous with the bear which they did not even intend to kill. Two weeks later they would return, with no trophy, no skin. He had not expected it. He had not even feared that it might be in the wagon this time with the other skins and heads. He did not even tell himself that in three years or two years or one year more he would be present and that it might even be his gun. He believed that only after he had served his apprenticeship in the woods which would prove him worthy to be a hunter, would he even be permitted to distinguish the crooked print, and that even then for two November weeks he would merely make another minor one, along with his cousin and Major de Spain and General Compson and Walter Ewell and Boon and the dogs which feared to bay it and the shotguns and rifles which failed even to bleed it, in the yearly pageant-rite of the old bear's furious immortality.

His day came at last. In the surrey with his cousin and Major de Spain and General Compson he saw the wilderness through a slow drizzle of November rain just above the ice point as it seemed to him later he always saw it or at least always remembered it—the tall and endless wall

of dense November woods under the dissolving afternoon
and the year's death, sombre, impenetrable (he could not
even discern yet how, at what point they could possibly
hope to enter it even though he knew that Sam Fathers
was waiting there with the wagon), the surrey moving
through the skeleton stalks of cotton and corn in the last
of open country, the last trace of man's puny gnawing at the
immemorial flank, until, dwarfed by that perspective into
an almost ridiculous diminishment, the surrey itself seemed
to have ceased to move (this too to be completed later,
years later, after he had grown to a man and had seen the
sea) as a solitary small boat hangs in lonely immobility,
merely tossing up and down, in the infinite waste of the
ocean while the water and then the apparently impenetrable land which it nears without appreciable progress,
swings slowly and opens the widening inlet which is the
anchorage. He entered it. Sam was waiting, wrapped in a
quilt on the wagon seat behind the patient and steaming
mules. He entered his novitiate to the true wilderness with
Sam beside him as he had begun his apprenticeship in miniature to manhood after the rabbits and such with Sam
beside him, the two of them wrapped in the damp, warm,
negro-rank quilt while the wilderness closed behind his
entrance as it had opened momentarily to accept him, opening before his advancement as it closed behind his progress,
no fixed path the wagon followed but a channel non-
existent ten yards ahead of it and ceasing to exist ten
yards after it had passed, the wagon progressing not by
its own volition but by attrition of their intact yet fluid
circumambience, drowsing, earless, almost lightless.

It seemed to him that at the age of ten he was witnessing
his own birth. It was not even strange to him. He had ex-

perienced it all before, and not merely in dreams. He saw the camp—a paintless six-room bungalow set on piles above the spring high-water—and he knew already how it was going to look. He helped in the rapid orderly disorder of their establishment in it and even his motions were familiar to him, foreknown. Then for two weeks he ate the coarse rapid food—the shapeless sour bread, the wild strange meat, venison and bear and turkey and coon which he had never tasted before—which men ate, cooked by men who were hunters first and cooks afterward; he slept in harsh sheetless blankets as hunters slept. Each morning the gray of dawn found him and Sam Fathers on the stand, the crossing, which had been allotted him. It was the poorest one, the most barren. He had expected that; he had not dared yet to hope even to himself that he would even hear the running dogs this first time. But he did hear them. It was on the third morning—a murmur, sourceless, almost indistinguishable, yet he knew what it was although he had never before heard that many dogs running at once, the murmur swelling into separate and distinct voices until he could call the five dogs which his cousin owned from among the others. "Now," Sam said, "slant your gun up a little and draw back the hammers and then stand still."

But it was not for him, not yet. The humility was there; he had learned that. And he could learn the patience. He was only ten, only one week. The instant had passed. It seemed to him that he could actually see the deer, the buck, smoke-colored, elongated with speed, vanished, the woods, the gray solitude still ringing even when the voices of the dogs had died away; from far away across the sombre woods and the gray half-liquid morning there came two shots. "Now let your hammers down," Sam said.

He did so. "You knew it too," he said.

"Yes," Sam said. "I want you to learn how to do when you didn't shoot. It's after the chance for the bear or the deer has done already come and gone that men and dogs get killed."

"Anyway, it wasn't him," the boy said. "It wasn't even a bear. It was just a deer."

"Yes," Sam said, "it was just a deer."

Then one morning, it was in the second week, he heard the dogs again. This time before Sam even spoke he readied the too-long, too-heavy, man-size gun as Sam had taught him, even though this time he knew the dogs and the deer were coming less close than ever, hardly within hearing even. They didn't sound like any running dogs he had ever heard before even. Then he found that Sam, who had taught him first of all to cock the gun and take position where he could see best in all directions and then never to move again, had himself moved up beside him. "There," he said. "Listen." The boy listened, to no ringing chorus strong and fast on a free scent but a moiling yapping an octave too high and with something more than indecision and even abjectness in it which he could not yet recognise, reluctant, not even moving very fast, taking a long time to pass out of hearing, leaving even then in the air that echo of thin and almost human hysteria, abject, almost humanly grieving, with this time nothing ahead of it, no sense of a fleeing unseen smoke-colored shape. He could hear Sam breathing at his shoulder. He saw the arched curve of the old man's inhaling nostrils.

"It's Old Ben!" he cried, whispering.

Sam didn't move save for the slow gradual turning of his head as the voices faded on and the faint steady rapid arch and collapse of his nostrils. "Hah," he said. "Not even running. Walking."

"But up here!" the boy cried. "Way up here!"

"He do it every year," Sam said. "Once. Ash and Boon say he comes up here to run the other little bears away. Tell them to get to hell out of here and stay out until the hunters are gone. Maybe." The boy no longer heard anything at all, yet still Sam's head continued to turn gradually and steadily until the back of it was toward him. Then it turned back and looked down at him—the same face, grave, familiar, expressionless until it smiled, the same old man's eyes from which as he watched there faded slowly a quality darkly and fiercely lambent, passionate and proud. "He dont care no more for bears than he does for dogs or men neither. He come to see who's here, who's new in camp this year, whether he can shoot or not, can stay or not. Whether we got the dog yet that can bay and hold him until a man gets there with a gun. Because he's the head bear. He's the man." It faded, was gone; again they were the eyes as he had known them all his life. "He'll let them follow him to the river. Then he'll send them home. We might as well go too; see how they look when they get back to camp."

The dogs were there first, ten of them huddled back under the kitchen, himself and Sam squatting to peer back into the obscurity where they crouched, quiet, the eyes rolling and luminous, vanishing, and no sound, only that effluvium which the boy could not quite place yet, of something more than dog, stronger than dog and not just animal, just beast even. Because there had been nothing in front of the abject and painful yapping except the solitude, the wilderness, so that when the eleventh hound got back about mid-afternoon and he and Tennie's Jim held the passive and still trembling bitch while Sam daubed her tattered ear and raked shoulder with turpentine and axle-grease, it was still no living creature but only the wilderness which, leaning for a moment, had patted lightly once her temerity. "Just like a man," Sam said. "Just like folks. Put off as long as she could having to be brave, knowing all the time that sooner or later she would have to be brave once so she could keep on calling herself a dog, and knowing beforehand what was going to happen when she done it."

He did not know just when Sam left. He only knew that he was gone. For the next three mornings he rose and ate breakfast and Sam was not waiting for him. He went to his stand alone; he found it without help now and stood on it as Sam had taught him. On the third morning he heard the dogs again, running strong and free on a true scent again, and he readied the gun as he had learned to do and heard the hunt sweep past on since he was not ready yet, had not deserved other yet in just one short period of two weeks as compared to all the long life which he had already dedicated to the wilderness with patience and humility; he heard the shot again, one shot, the single clapping report of Walter Ewell's rifle. By now he could not only find his stand and then return to camp without guidance, by using the compass his cousin had given him he reached Walter waiting beside the buck and the moiling of dogs over the cast entrails before any of the others except Major de Spain and Tennie's Jim on the horses, even before Uncle Ash arrived with the one-eyed wagon-mule which did not mind the smell of blood or even, so they said, of bear.

It was not Uncle Ash on the mule. It was Sam, returned. And Sam was waiting when he finished his dinner and, himself on the one-eyed mule and Sam on the other one of the wagon team, they rode for more than three hours through the rapid shortening sunless afternoon, following no path, no trail even that he could discern, into a section of country he had never seen before. Then he understood why Sam had made him ride the one-eyed mule which would not spook at the smell of blood, of wild animals. The other one, the sound one, stopped short and tried to whirl and bolt even as Sam got down, jerking and wrenching at the rein while Sam held it, coaxing it forward with his voice since he did not dare risk hitching it, drawing it forward while the boy dismounted from the marred one which would stand. Then, standing beside Sam in the thick great gloom of ancient woods and the winter's dying afternoon, he looked quietly down at the rotted log scored and gutted with claw-marks and, in the wet earth beside it, the print of the enormous warped two-toed foot. Now he knew what he had heard in the hounds' voices in the woods that morning and what he had smelled when he peered under the kitchen where they huddled. It was in him too, a little different because they were brute beasts and he was not, but only a little different—an eagerness, passive; an abjectness, a sense of his own fragility and impotence against the timeless woods, yet without doubt or dread; a flavor like brass in the sudden run of saliva in his mouth, a hard sharp constriction either in his brain or his stomach, he could not tell which and it did not matter; he knew only that for the first time he realised that the bear which had run in his listening and loomed in his dreams since before he could remember and which therefore must have existed in the listening and the dreams of his cousin and Major de Spain and even old General Compson before they began to remember in their turn, was a mortal animal and that they had departed for the camp each November with no actual intention of slaying it, not because it could not be slain but because so far they had no actual hope of being able to. "It will be tomorrow," he said.

"You mean we will try tomorrow," Sam said. "We aint got the dog yet."

"We've got eleven," he said. "They ran him Monday."

"And you heard them," Sam said. "Saw them too. We aint got the dog yet. It wont take but one. But he aint there. Maybe he aint nowhere. The only other way will be for him to run by accident over somebody that had a gun and knowed how to shoot it."

"That wouldn't be me," the boy said. "It would be Walter or Major or——"

"It might," Sam said. "You watch close tomorrow. Because he's smart. That's how come he has lived this long. If he gets hemmed up and has got to pick out somebody to run over, he will pick out you."

"How?" he said. "How will he know. . . ." He ceased. "You mean he already knows me, that I aint never been to the big bottom before, aint had time to find out yet whether I . . ." He ceased again, staring at Sam; he said humbly, not even amazed: "It was me he was watching. I dont reckon he did need to come but once."

"You watch tomorrow," Sam said. "I reckon we better start back. It'll be long after dark now before we get to camp."

The next morning they started three hours earlier than they had ever done. Even Uncle Ash went, the cook, who

called himself by profession a camp cook and who did little
else save cook for Major de Spain's hunting and camping
parties, yet who had been marked by the wilderness from
simple juxtaposition to it until he responded as they all
did, even the boy who until two weeks ago had never
even seen the wilderness, to a hound's ripped ear and
shoulder and the print of a crooked foot in a patch of wet
earth. They rode. It was too far to walk: the boy and Sam
and Uncle Ash in the wagon with the dogs, his cousin and
Major de Spain and General Compson and Boon and Walter and Tennie's Jim riding double on the horses; again
the first gray light found him, as on that first morning two
weeks ago, on the stand where Sam had placed and left
him. With the gun which was too big for him, the breech-
loader which did not even belong to him but to Major de
Spain and which he had fired only once, at a stump on
the first day to learn the recoil and how to reload it with
the paper shells, he stood against a big gum tree beside a
little bayou whose black still water crept without motion out
of a cane-brake, across a small clearing and into the cane
again, where, invisible, a bird, the big woodpecker called
Lord-to-God by negroes, clattered at a dead trunk. It was a
stand like any other stand, dissimilar only in incidentals
to the one where he had stood each morning for two weeks;
a territory new to him yet no less familiar than that other
one which after two weeks he had come to believe he
knew a little—the same solitude, the same loneliness
through which frail and timorous man had merely passed
without altering it, leaving no mark nor scar, which looked
exactly as it must have looked when the first ancestor of
Sam Fathers' Chickasaw predecessors crept into it and looked
about him, club or stone axe or bone arrow drawn and

ready, different only because, squatting at the edge of the kitchen, he had smelled the dogs huddled and cringing beneath it and saw the raked ear and side of the bitch that, as Sam had said, had to be brave once in order to keep on calling herself a dog, and saw yesterday in the earth beside the gutted log, the print of the living foot. He heard no dogs at all. He never did certainly hear them. He only heard the drumming of the woodpecker stop short off, and knew that the bear was looking at him. He never saw it. He did not know whether it was facing him from the cane or behind him. He did not move, holding the useless gun which he knew now he would never fire at it, now or ever, tasting in his saliva that taint of brass which he had smelled in the huddled dogs when he peered under the kitchen.

Then it was gone. As abruptly as it had stopped, the woodpecker's dry hammering set up again, and after a while he believed he even heard the dogs—a murmur, scarce a sound even, which he had probably been hearing for a time, perhaps a minute or two, before he remarked it, drifting into hearing and then out again, dying away. They came nowhere near him. If it was dogs he heard, he could not have sworn to it; if it was a bear they ran, it was another bear. It was Sam himself who emerged from the cane and crossed the bayou, the injured bitch following at heel as a bird dog is taught to walk. She came and crouched against his leg, trembling. "I didn't see him," he said. "I didn't, Sam."

"I know it," Sam said. "He done the looking. You didn't hear him neither, did you?"

"No," the boy said. "I——"

"He's smart," Sam said. "Too smart." Again the boy

saw in his eyes that quality of dark and brooding lambence
as Sam looked down at the bitch trembling faintly and
steadily against the boy's leg. From her raked shoulder a
few drops of fresh blood clung like bright berries. "Too
big. We aint got the dog yet. But maybe some day."

Because there would be a next time, after and after.
He was only ten. It seemed to him that he could see them,
the two of them, shadowy in the limbo from which time
emerged and became time: the old bear absolved of mortality and himself who shared a little of it. Because he
recognised now what he had smelled in the huddled dogs
and tasted in his own saliva, recognised fear as a boy, a
youth, recognises the existence of love and passion and
experience which is his heritage but not yet his patrimony,
from entering by chance the presence or perhaps even
merely the bedroom of a woman who has loved and been
loved by many men. *So I will have to see him,* he thought,
without dread or even hope. *I will have to look at him.* So
it was in June of the next summer. They were at the camp
again, celebrating Major de Spain's and General Compson's birthdays. Although the one had been born in September and the other in the depth of winter and almost
thirty years earlier, each June the two of them and Mc-
Caslin and Boon and Walter Ewell (and the boy too from
now on) spent two weeks at the camp, fishing and shooting
squirrels and turkey and running coons and wildcats with
the dogs at night. That is, Boon and the negroes (and the
boy too now) fished and shot squirrels and ran the coons
and cats, because the proven hunters, not only Major de
Spain and old General Compson (who spent those two
weeks sitting in a rocking chair before a tremendous iron
pot of Brunswick stew, stirring and tasting, with Uncle

Ash to quarrel with about how he was making it and Tennie's Jim to pour whisky into the tin dipper from which he drank it) but even McCaslin and Walter Ewell who were still young enough, scorned such other than shooting the wild gobblers with pistols for wagers or to test their marksmanship.

That is, his cousin McCaslin and the others thought he was hunting squirrels. Until the third evening he believed that Sam Fathers thought so too. Each morning he would leave the camp right after breakfast. He had his own gun now, a new breech-loader, a Christmas gift; he would own and shoot it for almost seventy years, through two new pairs of barrels and locks and one new stock, until all that remained of the original gun was the silver-inlaid triggerguard with his and McCaslin's engraved names and the date in 1878. He found the tree beside the little bayou where he had stood that morning. Using the compass he ranged from that point; he was teaching himself to be better than a fair woodsman without even knowing he was doing it. On the third day he even found the gutted log where he had first seen the print. It was almost completely crumbled now, healing with unbelievable speed, a passionate and almost visible relinquishment, back into the earth from which the tree had grown. He ranged the summer woods now, green with gloom, if anything actually dimmer than they had been in November's gray dissolution, where even at noon the sun fell only in windless dappling upon the earth which never completely dried and which crawled with snakes—moccasins and watersnakes and rattlers, themselves the color of the dappled gloom so that he would not always see them until they moved; returning to camp later and later and later, first day, second

day, passing in the twilight of the third evening the little
log pen enclosing the log barn where Sam was putting
up the stock for the night. "You aint looked right yet,"
Sam said.

He stopped. For a moment he didn't answer. Then he
said peacefully, in a peaceful rushing burst, as when a
boy's miniature dam in a little brook gives way: "All right.
Yes. But how? I went to the bayou. I even found that log
again. I ———"

"I reckon that was all right. Likely he's been watching
you. You never saw his foot?"

"I . . ." the boy said. "I didn't . . . I never thought
. . ."

"It's the gun," Sam said. He stood beside the fence,
motionless, the old man, son of a negro slave and a Chickasaw chief, in the battered and faded overalls and the
frayed five-cent straw hat which had been the badge of
the negro's slavery and was now the regalia of his freedom. The camp—the clearing, the house, the barn and its
tiny lot with which Major de Spain in his turn had scratched
punily and evanescently at the wilderness—faded in the
dusk, back into the immemorial darkness of the woods. *The
gun*, the boy thought. *The gun.* "You will have to choose,"
Sam said.

He left the next morning before light, without breakfast, long before Uncle Ash would wake in his quilts on
the kitchen floor and start the fire. He had only the compass and a stick for the snakes. He could go almost a mile
before he would need to see the compass. He sat on a log,
the invisible compass in his hand, while the secret night-
sounds which had ceased at his movements, scurried again
and then fell still for good and the owls ceased and gave

over to the waking day birds and there was light in the
gray wet woods and he could see the compass. He went
fast yet still quietly, becoming steadily better and better
as a woodsman without yet having time to realise it; he
jumped a doe and a fawn, walked them out of the bed,
close enough to see them—the crash of undergrowth, the
white scut, the fawn scudding along behind her, faster
than he had known it could have run. He was hunting
right, upwind, as Sam had taught him, but that didn't
matter now. He had left the gun; by his own will and relinquishment he had accepted not a gambit, not a choice,
but a condition in which not only the bear's heretofore inviolable anonymity but all the ancient rules and balances
of hunter and hunted had been abrogated. He would not
even be afraid, not even in the moment when the fear
would take him completely: blood, skin, bowels, bones,
memory from the long time before it even became his
memory—all save that thin clear quenchless lucidity which
alone differed him from this bear and from all the other
bears and bucks he would follow during almost seventy
years, to which Sam had said: "Be scared. You cant help
that. But dont be afraid. Aint nothing in the woods going
to hurt you if you dont corner it or it dont smell that you
are afraid. A bear or a deer has got to be scared of a coward
the same as a brave man has got to be."

By noon he was far beyond the crossing on the little
bayou, farther into the new and alien country than he had
ever been, travelling now not only by the compass but by
the old, heavy, biscuit-thick silver watch which had been
his father's. He had left the camp nine hours ago; nine
hours from now, dark would already have been an hour
old. He stopped, for the first time since he had risen from

the log when he could see the compass face at last, and
looked about, mopping his sweating face on his sleeve. He
had already relinquished, of his will, because of his need,
in humility and peace and without regret, yet apparently
that had not been enough, the leaving of the gun was not
enough. He stood for a moment—a child, alien and lost
in the green and soaring gloom of the markless wilderness.
Then he relinquished completely to it. It was the watch
and the compass. He was still tainted. He removed the
linked chain of the one and the looped thong of the other
from his overalls and hung them on a bush and leaned the
stick beside them and entered it.

When he realised he was lost, he did as Sam had coached
and drilled him: made a cast to cross his backtrack. He
had not been going very fast for the last two or three hours,
and he had gone even less fast since he left the compass
and watch on the bush. So he went slower still now, since
the tree could not be very far; in fact, he found it before he
really expected to and turned and went to it. But there
was no bush beneath it, no compass nor watch, so he did
next as Sam had coached and drilled him: made this next
circle in the opposite direction and much larger, so that the
pattern of the two of them would bisect his track somewhere, but crossing no trace nor mark anywhere of his
feet or any feet, and now he was going faster though still
not panicked, his heart beating a little more rapidly but
strong and steady enough, and this time it was not even
the tree because there was a down log beside it which he
had never seen before and beyond the log a little swamp,
a seepage of moisture somewhere between earth and water,
and he did what Sam had coached and drilled him as the
next and the last, seeing as he sat down on the log the

crooked print, the warped indentation in the wet ground which while he looked at it continued to fill with water until it was level full and the water began to overflow and the sides of the print began to dissolve away. Even as he looked up he saw the next one, and, moving, the one beyond it; moving, not hurrying, running, but merely keeping pace with them as they appeared before him as though they were being shaped out of thin air just one constant pace short of where he would lose them forever and be lost forever himself, tireless, eager, without doubt or dread, panting a little above the strong rapid little hammer of his heart, emerging suddenly into a little glade and the wilderness coalesced. It rushed, soundless, and solidified—the tree, the bush, the compass and the watch glinting where a ray of sunlight touched them. Then he saw the bear. It did not emerge, appear: it was just there, immobile, fixed in the green and windless noon's hot dappling, not as big as he had dreamed it but as big as he had expected, bigger, dimensionless against the dappled obscurity, looking at him. Then it moved. It crossed the glade without haste, walking for an instant into the sun's full glare and out of it, and stopped again and looked back at him across one shoulder. Then it was gone. It didn't walk into the woods. It faded, sank back into the wilderness without motion as he had watched a fish, a huge old bass, sink back into the dark depths of its pool and vanish without even any movement of its fins.

2.

So he should have hated and feared Lion. He was thirteen then. He had killed his buck and Sam Fathers had marked his face with the hot blood, and in the next November he killed a bear. But before that accolade he had become as competent in the woods as many grown men with the same experience. By now he was a better woodsman than most grown men with more. There was no territory within twenty-five miles of the camp that he did not know—bayou, ridge, landmark trees and path; he could have led anyone direct to any spot in it and brought him back. He knew game trails that even Sam Fathers had never seen; in the third fall he found a buck's beddingplace by himself and unbeknown to his cousin he borrowed Walter Ewell's rifle and lay in wait for the buck at dawn and killed it when it walked back to the bed as Sam had told him how the old Chickasaw fathers did.

By now he knew the old bear's footprint better than he did his own, and not only the crooked one. He could see any one of the three sound prints and distinguish it at once from any other, and not only because of its size. There were other bears within that fifty miles which left tracks almost as large, or at least so near that the one would have appeared larger only by juxtaposition. It was more than that. If Sam Fathers had been his mentor and the backyard rabbits and squirrels his kindergarten, then the wilderness the old bear ran was his college and the old male bear itself, so long unwifed and childless as to have become its own ungendered progenitor, was his alma mater.

He could find the crooked print now whenever he wished, ten miles or five miles or sometimes closer than that, to the camp. Twice while on stand during the next three years he heard the dogs strike its trail and once even jump it by chance, the voices high, abject, almost human in their hysteria. Once, still-hunting with Walter Ewell's rifle, he saw it cross a long corridor of down timber where a tornado had passed. It rushed through rather than across the tangle of trunks and branches as a locomotive would, faster than he had ever believed it could have moved, almost as fast as a deer even because the deer would have spent most of that distance in the air; he realised then why it would take a dog not only of abnormal courage but size and speed too ever to bring it to bay. He had a little dog at home, a mongrel, of the sort called fyce by negroes, a ratter, itself not much bigger than a rat and possessing that sort of courage which had long since stopped being bravery and had become foolhardiness. He brought it with him one June and, timing them as if they were meeting an appointment with another human being, himself carrying the fyce with a sack over its head and Sam Fathers with a brace of the hounds on a rope leash, they lay downwind of the trail and actually ambushed the bear. They were so close that it turned at bay although he realised later this might have been from surprise and amazement at the shrill and frantic uproar of the fyce. It turned at bay against the trunk of a big cypress, on its hind feet; it seemed to the boy that it would never stop rising, taller and taller, and even the two hounds seemed to have taken a kind of desperate and despairing courage from the fyce. Then he realised that the fyce was actually not going to stop. He flung the gun down and ran. When he overtook and grasped the shrill, frantically pinwheeling little dog, it seemed to him that he was directly under the bear. He could smell it, strong and hot and rank. Sprawling, he looked up where it loomed and towered over him like a thunderclap. It was quite familiar, until he remembered: this was the way he had used to dream about it.

Then it was gone. He didn't see it go. He knelt, holding
the frantic fyce with both hands, hearing the abased wailing of the two hounds drawing further and further away,
until Sam came up, carrying the gun. He laid it quietly
down beside the boy and stood looking down at him.
"You've done seed him twice now, with a gun in your
hands," he said. "This time you couldn't have missed him."

The boy rose. He still held the fyce. Even in his arms
it continued to yap frantically, surging and straining toward
the fading sound of the hounds like a collection of live-
wire springs. The boy was panting a little. "Neither could
you," he said. "You had the gun. Why didn't you shoot
him?"

Sam didn't seem to have heard. He put out his hand
and touched the little dog in the boy's arms which still
yapped and strained even though the two hounds were out
of hearing now. "He's done gone," Sam said. "You can
slack off and rest now, until next time." He stroked the
little dog until it began to grow quiet under his hand.
"You's almost the one we wants," he said. "You just aint
big enough. We aint got that one yet. He will need to be
just a little bigger than smart, and a little braver than
either." He withdrew his hand from the fyce's head and
stood looking into the woods where the bear and the hounds
had vanished. "Somebody is going to, some day."

"I know it," the boy said. "That's why it must be one
of us. So it wont be until the last day. When even he dont
want it to last any longer."

So he should have hated and feared Lion. It was in
the fourth summer, the fourth time he had made one in
the celebration of Major de Spain's and General Compson's birthday. In the early spring Major de Spain's mare

l foaled a horse colt. One evening when Sam brought
: horses and mules up to stable them for the night, the
t was missing and it was all he could do to get the frantic
re into the lot. He had thought at first to let the mare
d him back to where she had become separated from the
l. But she would not do it. She would not even feint to-
rd any particular part of the woods or even in any par-
ular direction. She merely ran, as if she couldn't see, still
ntic with terror. She whirled and ran at Sam once, as if
attack him in some ultimate desperation, as if she could
t for the moment realise that he was a man and a long-
niliar one. He got her into the lot at last. It was too dark
that time to back-track her, to unravel the erratic course
e had doubtless pursued.

He came to the house and told Major de Spain. It was
animal, of course, a big one, and the colt was dead now,
erever it was. They all knew that. "It's a panther," Gen-
l Compson said at once. "The same one. That doe and
vn last March." Sam had sent Major de Spain word of
when Boon Hogganbeck came to the camp on a routine
it to see how the stock had wintered—the doe's throat
n out, and the beast had run down the helpless fawn
d killed it too.

"Sam never did say that was a panther," Major de Spain
d. Sam said nothing now, standing behind Major de
ain where they sat at supper, inscrutable, as if he were
st waiting for them to stop talking so he could go home.
e didn't even seem to be looking at anything. "A panther
ght jump a doe, and he wouldn't have much trouble
:ching the fawn afterward. But no panther would have
mped that colt with the dam right there with it. It was
d Ben," Major de Spain said. "I'm disappointed in him.

He has broken the rules. I didn't think he would have do
that. He has killed mine and McCaslin's dogs, but that w
all right. We gambled the dogs against him; we gave ea
other warning. But now he has come into my house a
destroyed my property, out of season too. He broke t
rules. It was Old Ben, Sam." Still Sam said nothing, star
ing there until Major de Spain should stop talking. "We
back-track her tomorrow and see," Major de Spain said.

Sam departed. He would not live in the camp; he h
built himself a little hut something like Joe Baker's, or
stouter, tighter, on the bayou a quarter-mile away, an
stout log crib where he stored a little corn for the shoat
raised each year. The next morning he was waiting wh
they waked. He had already found the colt. They did n
even wait for breakfast. It was not far, not five hundr
yards from the stable—the three-months' colt lying on
side, its throat torn out and the entrails and one ham par
eaten. It lay not as if it had been dropped but as if it h
been struck and hurled, and no cat-mark, no claw-ma
where a panther would have gripped it while finding
throat. They read the tracks where the frantic mare h
circled and at last rushed in with that same ultimate de
peration with which she had whirled on Sam Fathers ye
terday evening, and the long tracks of dead and terrifi
running and those of the beast which had not even rushe
at her when she advanced but had merely walked thr
or four paces toward her until she broke, and Gener
Compson said, "Good God, what a wolf!"

Still Sam said nothing. The boy watched him while t
men knelt, measuring the tracks. There was something
Sam's face now. It was neither exultation nor joy nor hop
Later, a man, the boy realised what it had been, and th

Sam had known all the time what had made the tracks and what had torn the throat out of the doe in the spring and killed the fawn. It had been foreknowledge in Sam's face that morning. *And he was glad,* he told himself. *He was old. He had no children, no people, none of his blood anywhere above earth that he would ever meet again. And even if he were to, he could not have touched it, spoken to it, because for seventy years now he had had to be a negro. It was almost over now and he was glad.*

They returned to camp and had breakfast and came back with guns and the hounds. Afterward the boy realised that they also should have known then what killed the colt as well as Sam Fathers did. But that was neither the first nor the last time he had seen men rationalise from and even act upon their misconceptions. After Boon, standing astride the colt, had whipped the dogs away from it with his belt, they snuffed at the tracks. One of them, a young dog hound without judgment yet, bayed once, and they ran for a few feet on what seemed to be a trail. Then they stopped, looking back at the men, eager enough, not baffled, merely questioning, as if they were asking "Now what?" Then they rushed back to the colt, where Boon, still astride it, slashed at them with the belt.

"I never knew a trail to get cold that quick," General Compson said.

"Maybe a single wolf big enough to kill a colt with the dam right there beside it dont leave scent," Major de Spain said.

"Maybe it was a hant," Walter Ewell said. He looked at Tennie's Jim. "Hah, Jim?"

Because the hounds would not run it, Major de Spain had Sam hunt out and find the tracks a hundred yards

farther on and they put the dogs on it again and again
the young one bayed and not one of them realised then
that the hound was not baying like a dog striking game but
was merely bellowing like a country dog whose yard has
been invaded. General Compson spoke to the boy and Boon
and Tennie's Jim: to the squirrel hunters. "You boys keep
the dogs with you this morning. He's probably hanging
around somewhere, waiting to get his breakfast off the colt.
You might strike him."

But they did not. The boy remembered how Sam stood
watching them as they went into the woods with the
leashed hounds—the Indian face in which he had never
seen anything until it smiled, except that faint arching of
the nostrils on that first morning when the hounds had
found Old Ben. They took the hounds with them on the
next day, though when they reached the place where they
hoped to strike a fresh trail, the carcass of the colt was gone.
Then on the third morning Sam was waiting again, this
time until they had finished breakfast. He said, "Come." He
led them to his house, his little hut, to the corn-crib beyond it. He had removed the corn and had made a dead-
fall of the door, baiting it with the colt's carcass; peering
between the logs, they saw an animal almost the color of
a gun or pistol barrel, what little time they had to examine
its color or shape. It was not crouched nor even standing.
It was in motion, in the air, coming toward them—a heavy
body crashing with tremendous force against the door so
that the thick door jumped and clattered in its frame, the
animal, whatever it was, hurling itself against the door
again seemingly before it could have touched the floor and
got a new purchase to spring from. "Come away," Sam said,
"fore he break his neck." Even when they retreated the

heavy and measured crashes continued, the stout door jumping and clattering each time, and still no sound from the
beast itself—no snarl, no cry.

"What in hell's name is it?" Major de Spain said.

"It's a dog," Sam said, his nostrils arching and collapsing
faintly and steadily and that faint, fierce milkiness in his
eyes again as on that first morning when the hounds had
struck the old bear. "It's the dog."

"*The* dog?" Major de Spain said.

"That's gonter hold Old Ben."

"Dog the devil," Major de Spain said. "I'd rather have
Old Ben himself in my pack than that brute. Shoot him."

"No," Sam said.

"You'll never tame him. How do you ever expect to make
an animal likc that afraid of you?"

"I dont want him tame," Sam said; again the boy watched
his nostrils and the fierce milky light in his eyes. "But I
almost rather he be tame than scared, of me or any man
or any thing. But he wont be ncither, of nothing."

"Then what are you going to do with it?"

"You can watch," Sam said.

Each morning through the second week they would go
to Sam's crib. He had removed a few shingles from the roof
and had put a rope on the colt's carcass and had drawn it
out when the trap fell. Each morning they would watch
him lower a pail of water into the crib while the dog
hurled itself tirelessly against the door and dropped back
and leaped again. It never made any sound and there was
nothing frenzied in the act but only a cold and grim indomitable determination. Toward the end of the week it
stopped jumping at the door. Yet it had not weakened ap-
preciably and it was not as if it had rationalised· the fact

that the door was not going to give. It was as if for that
time it simply disdained to jump any longer. It was not
down. None of them had ever seen it down. It stood, and
they could see it now—part mastiff, something of Airedale
and something of a dozen other strains probably, better
than thirty inches at the shoulders and weighing as they
guessed almost ninety pounds, with cold yellow eyes and
a tremendous chest and over all that strange color like a
blued gun-barrel.

Then the two weeks were up. They prepared to break
camp. The boy begged to remain and his cousin let him.
He moved into the little hut with Sam Fathers. Each morning he watched Sam lower the pail of water into the crib.
By the end of that week the dog was down. It would rise
and half stagger, half crawl to the water and drink and
collapse again. One morning it could not even reach the
water, could not raise its forequarters even from the floor.
Sam took a short stick and prepared to enter the crib.
"Wait," the boy said. "Let me get the gun——"

"No," Sam said. "He cant move now." Nor could it. It
lay on its side while Sam touched it, its head and the
gaunted body, the dog lying motionless, the yellow eyes
open. They were not fierce and there was nothing of petty
malevolence in them, but a cold and almost impersonal
malignance like some natural force. It was not even looking
at Sam nor at the boy peering at it between the logs.

Sam began to feed it again. The first time he had to
raise its head so it could lap the broth. That night he left
a bowl of broth containing lumps of meat where the dog
could reach it. The next morning the bowl was empty and
the dog was lying on its belly, its head up, the cold yellow
eyes watching the door as Sam entered, no change what-

ever in the cold yellow eyes and still no sound from it even when it sprang, its aim and co-ordination still bad from weakness so that Sam had time to strike it down with the stick and leap from the crib and slam the door as the dog, still without having had time to get its feet under it to jump again seemingly, hurled itself against the door as if the two weeks of starving had never been.

At noon that day someone came whooping through the woods from the direction of the camp. It was Boon. He came and looked for a while between the logs, at the tremendous dog lying again on its belly, its head up, the yellow eyes blinking sleepily at nothing: the indomitable and unbroken spirit. "What we better do," Boon said, "is to let that son of a bitch go and catch Old Ben and run him on the dog." He turned to the boy his weather-reddened and beetling face. "Get your traps together. Cass says for you to come on home. You been in here fooling with that horse-eating varmint long enough."

Boon had a borrowed mule at the camp; the buggy was waiting at the edge of the bottom. He was at home that night. He told McCaslin about it. "Sam's going to starve him again until he can go in and touch him. Then he will feed him again. Then he will starve him again, if he has to."

"But why?" McCaslin said. "What for? Even Sam will never tame that brute."

"We dont want him tame. We want him like he is. We just want him to find out at last that the only way he can get out of that crib and stay out of it is to do what Sam or somebody tells him to do. He's the dog that's going to stop Old Ben and hold him. We've already named him. His name is Lion."

Then November came at last. They returned to the camp. With General Compson and Major de Spain and his cousin and Walter and Boon he stood in the yard among the guns and bedding and boxes of food and watched Sam Fathers and Lion come up the lane from the lot—the Indian, the old man in battered overalls and rubber boots and a worn sheepskin coat and a hat which had belonged to the boy's father; the tremendous dog pacing gravely beside him. The hounds rushed out to meet them and stopped, except the young one which still had but little of judgment. It ran up to Lion, fawning. Lion didn't snap at it. He didn't even pause. He struck it rolling and yelping for five or six feet with a blow of one paw as a bear would have done and came on into the yard and stood, blinking sleepily at nothing, looking at no one, while Boon said, "Jesus. Jesus.—Will he let me touch him?"

"You can touch him," Sam said. "He dont care. He dont care about nothing or nobody."

The boy watched that too. He watched it for the next two years from that moment when Boon touched Lion's head and then knelt beside him, feeling the bones and muscles, the power. It was as if Lion were a woman—or perhaps Boon was the woman. That was more like it—the big, grave, sleepy-seeming dog which, as Sam Fathers said, cared about no man and no thing; and the violent, insensitive, hard-faced man with his touch of remote Indian blood and the mind almost of a child. He watched Boon take over Lion's feeding from Sam and Uncle Ash both. He would see Boon squatting in the cold rain beside the kitchen while Lion ate. Because Lion neither slept nor ate with the other dogs though none of them knew where he did sleep until in the second November, thinking until then that Lion slept in his kennel beside Sam Fathers' hut, when the boy's cousin McCaslin said something about it to Sam by sheer chance and Sam told him. And that night the boy and Major de Spain and McCaslin with a lamp entered the back room where Boon slept—the little, tight, airless room rank with the smell of Boon's unwashed body and his wet hunting-clothes—where Boon, snoring on his back, choked and waked and Lion raised his head beside him and looked back at them from his cold, slumbrous yellow eyes.

"Damn it, Boon," McCaslin said. "Get that dog out of here. He's got to run Old Ben tomorrow morning. How in hell do you expect him to smell anything fainter than a skunk after breathing you all night?"

"The way I smell aint hurt my nose none that I ever noticed," Boon said.

"It wouldn't matter if it had," Major de Spain said. "We're not depending on you to trail a bear. Put him outside. Put him under the house with the other dogs."

Boon began to get up. "He'll kill the first one that happens to yawn or sneeze in his face or touches him."

"I reckon not," Major de Spain said. "None of them are going to risk yawning in his face or touching him either, even asleep. Put him outside. I want his nose right tomorrow. Old Ben fooled him last year. I dont think he will do it again."

Boon put on his shoes without lacing them; in his long soiled underwear, his hair still tousled from sleep, he and Lion went out. The others returned to the front room and the poker game where McCaslin's and Major de Spain's hands waited for them on the table. After a while McCaslin said, "Do you want me to go back and look again?"

"No," Major de Spain said. "I call," he said to Walter Ewell. He spoke to McCaslin again. "If you do, dont tell me. I am beginning to see the first sign of my increasing age: I dont like to know that my orders have been disobeyed, even when I knew when I gave them that they would be.—A small pair," he said to Walter Ewell.

"How small?" Walter said.

"Very small," Major de Spain said.

And the boy, lying beneath his piled quilts and blankets waiting for sleep, knew likewise that Lion was already back in Boon's bed, for the rest of that night and the next one and during all the nights of the next November and the next one. He thought then: *I wonder what Sam thinks. He could have Lion with him, even if Boon is a white man. He could ask Major or McCaslin either. And more than that. It was Sam's hand that touched Lion first and Lion knows it.* Then he became a man and he knew that too. It had been all right. That was the way it should have been. Sam was the chief, the prince; Boon, the plebeian, was his huntsman. Boon should have nursed the dogs.

On the first morning that Lion led the pack after Old Ben, seven strangers appeared in the camp. They were swampers: gaunt, malaria-ridden men appearing from nowhere, who ran trap-lines for coons or perhaps farmed little patches of cotton and corn along the edge of the bottom, in clothes but little better than Sam Fathers' and nowhere near as good as Tennie's Jim's, with worn shotguns and rifles, already squatting patiently in the cold drizzle in the side yard when day broke. They had a spokesman; afterward Sam Fathers told Major de Spain how all during the past summer and fall they had drifted into the camp singly or in pairs and threes, to look quietly at Lion for a while and then go away: "Mawnin, Major. We heerd you was aimin to put that ere blue dawg on that old two-toed bear this mawnin. We figgered we'd come up and watch, if you dont mind. We wont do no shooting, lessen he runs over us."

"You are welcome," Major de Spain said. "You are welcome to shoot. He's more your bear than ours."

"I reckon that aint no lie. I done fed him enough cawn to have a sheer in him. Not to mention a shoat three years ago."

"I reckon I got a sheer too," another said. "Only it aint in the bear." Major de Spain looked at him. He was chewing tobacco. He spat. "Hit was a heifer calf. Nice un too. Last year. When I finally found her, I reckon she looked about like that colt of yourn looked last June."

"Oh," Major de Spain said. "Be welcome. If you see game in front of my dogs, shoot it."

Nobody shot Old Ben that day. No man saw him. The dogs jumped him within a hundred yards of the glade where the boy had seen him that day in the summer of his eleventh year. The boy was less than a quarter-mile away. He heard the jump but he could distinguish no voice among the dogs that he did not know and therefore would be Lion's, and he thought, believed, that Lion was not among them. Even the fact that they were going much faster than he had ever heard them run behind Old Ben before and that the high thin note of hysteria was missing now from their voices was not enough to disabuse him. He didn't comprehend until that night, when Sam told him that Lion would never cry on a trail. "He gonter growl when he catches Old Ben's throat," Sam said. "But he aint gonter never holler, no more than he ever done when he was jumping at that two-inch door. It's that blue dog in him. What you call it?"

"Airedale," the boy said.

Lion was there; the jump was just too close to the river. When Boon returned with Lion about eleven that night, he swore that Lion had stopped Old Ben once but that the hounds would not go in and Old Ben broke away and took to the river and swam for miles down it and he and Lion went down one bank for about ten miles and crossed and came up the other but it had begun to get dark before they struck any trail where Old Ben had come up out of the water, unless he was still in the water when he passed the ford where they crossed. Then he fell to cursing the hounds and ate the supper Uncle Ash had saved for him and went off to bed and after a while the boy opened the door of the little stale room thunderous with snoring and the great grave dog raised its head from Boon's pillow and blinked at him for a moment and lowered its head again.

When the next November came and the last day, the day on which it was now becoming traditional to save for Old Ben, there were more than a dozen strangers waiting. They were not all swampers this time. Some of them were townsmen, from other county seats like Jefferson, who had heard about Lion and Old Ben and had come to watch the great blue dog keep his yearly rendezvous with the old two-toed bear. Some of them didn't even have guns and the hunting-clothes and boots they wore had been on a store shelf yesterday.

This time Lion jumped Old Ben more than five miles from the river and bayed and held him and this time the hounds went in, in a sort of desperate emulation. The boy heard them; he was that near. He heard Boon whooping;

he heard the two shots when General Compson delivered both barrels, one containing five buckshot, the other a single ball, into the bear from as close as he could force his almost unmanageable horse. He heard the dogs when the bear broke free again. He was running now; panting, stumbling, his lungs bursting, he reached the place where General Compson had fired and where Old Ben had killed two of the hounds. He saw the blood from General Compson's shots, but he could go no further. He stopped, leaning against a tree for his breathing to ease and his heart to slow, hearing the sound of the dogs as it faded on and died away.

In camp that night—they had as guests five of the still terrified strangers in new hunting coats and boots who had been lost all day until Sam Fathers went out and got them —he heard the rest of it: how Lion had stopped and held the bear again but only the one-eyed mule which did not mind the smell of wild blood would approach and Boon was riding the mule and Boon had never been known to hit anything. He shot at the bear five times with his pump gun, touching nothing, and Old Ben killed another hound and broke free once more and reached the river and was gone. Again Boon and Lion hunted as far down one bank as they dared. Too far; they crossed in the first of dusk and dark overtook them within a mile. And this time Lion found the broken trail, the blood perhaps, in the darkness where Old Ben had come up out of the water, but Boon had him on a rope, luckily, and he got down from the mule and fought Lion hand-to-hand until he got him back to camp. This time Boon didn't even curse. He stood in the door, muddy, spent, his huge gargoyle's face tragic and still amazed. "I missed him," he said. "I was in twenty-five feet of him and I missed him five times."

"But we have drawn blood," Major de Spain said. "General Compson drew blood. We have never done that before."

"But I missed him," Boon said. "I missed him five times. With Lion looking right at me."

"Never mind," Major de Spain said. "It was a damned fine race. And we drew blood. Next year we'll let General Compson or Walter ride Katie, and we'll get him."

Then McCaslin said, "Where is Lion, Boon?"

"I left him at Sam's," Boon said. He was already turning away. "I aint fit to sleep with him."

So he should have hated and feared Lion. Yet he did not. It seemed to him that there was a fatality in it. It seemed to him that something, he didn't know what, was beginning; had already begun. It was like the last act on a set stage. It was the beginning of the end of something, he didn't know what except that he would not grieve. He would be humble and proud that he had been found worthy to be a part of it too or even just to see it too.

3.

It was December. It was the coldest December he had ever remembered. They had been in camp four days over two weeks, waiting for the weather to soften so that Lion and Old Ben could run their yearly race. Then they would break camp and go home. Because of these unforeseen additional days which they had had to pass waiting on the weather, with nothing to do but play poker, the whisky had given out and he and Boon were being sent to Memphis with a suitcase and a note from Major de Spain to Mr Semmes, the distiller, to get more. That is, Major de Spain and McCaslin were sending Boon to get the whisky and sending him to see that Boon got back with it or most of it or at least some of it.

Tennie's Jim waked him at three. He dressed rapidly, shivering, not so much from the cold because a fresh fire already boomed and roared on the hearth, but in that dead winter hour when the blood and the heart are slow and sleep is incomplete. He crossed the gap between house and kitchen, the gap of iron earth beneath the brilliant and rigid night where dawn would not begin for three hours yet, tasting, tongue palate and to the very bottom of his lungs the searing dark, and entered the kitchen, the lamp-lit warmth where the stove glowed, fogging the windows, and where Boon already sat at the table at breakfast, hunched over his plate, almost in his plate, his working jaws blue with stubble and his face innocent of water and his coarse, horse-mane hair innocent of comb—the quarter Indian, grandson of a Chickasaw squaw, who on occasion resented with his hard and furious fists the intimation of one single drop of alien blood and on others, usually after whisky, affirmed with the same fists and the same fury that his father had been the full-blood Chickasaw and even a chief and that even his mother had been only half white. He was four inches over six feet; he had the mind of a child, the heart of a horse, and little hard shoe-button eyes without depth or meanness or generosity or viciousness or gentleness or anything else, in the ugliest face the boy had ever seen. It looked like somebody had found a walnut a little larger than a football and with a machinist's hammer had shaped features into it and then painted it, mostly red;

not Indian red but a fine bright ruddy color which whisky might have had something to do with but which was mostly just happy and violent out-of-doors, the wrinkles in it not the residue of the forty years it had survived but from squinting into the sun or into the gloom of cane-brakes where game had run, baked into it by the camp fires before which he had lain trying to sleep on the cold November or December ground while waiting for daylight so he could rise and hunt again, as though time were merely something he walked through as he did through air, aging him no more than air did. He was brave, faithful, improvident and unreliable; he had neither profession job nor trade and owned one vice and one virtue: whisky, and that absolute and unquestioning fidelity to Major de Spain and the boy's cousin McCaslin. "Sometimes I'd call them both virtues," Major de Spain said once. "Or both vices," McCaslin said.

He ate his breakfast, hearing the dogs under the kitchen, wakened by the smell of frying meat or perhaps by the feet overhead. He heard Lion once, short and peremptory, as the best hunter in any camp has only to speak once to all save the fools, and none other of Major de Spain's and McCaslin's dogs were Lion's equal in size and strength and perhaps even in courage, but they were not fools; Old Ben had killed the last fool among them last year.

Tennie's Jim came in as they finished. The wagon was outside. Ash decided he would drive them over to the log-line where they would flag the outbound log-train and let Tennie's Jim wash the dishes. The boy knew why. It would not be the first time he had listened to old Ash badgering Boon.

It was cold. The wagon wheels banged and clattered on the frozen ground; the sky was fixed and brilliant. He was not shivering, he was shaking, slow and steady and hard, the food he had just eaten still warm and solid inside him while his outside shook slow and steady around it as though his stomach floated loose. "They wont run this morning," he said. "No dog will have any nose today."

"Cep Lion," Ash said. "Lion dont need no nose. All he need is a bear." He had wrapped his feet in towsacks and he had a quilt from his pallet bed on the kitchen floor drawn over his head and wrapped around him until in the thin brilliant starlight he looked like nothing at all that the boy had ever seen before. "He run a bear through a thousand-acre ice-house. Catch him too. Them other dogs dont matter because they aint going to keep up with Lion nohow, long as he got a bear in front of him."

"What's wrong with the other dogs?" Boon said. "What the hell do you know about it anyway? This is the first time you've had your tail out of that kitchen since we got here except to chop a little wood."

"Aint nothing wrong with them," Ash said. "And long as it's left up to them, aint nothing going to be. I just wish I had knowed all my life how to take care of my health good as them hounds knows."

"Well, they aint going to run this morning," Boon said. His voice was harsh and positive. "Major promised they wouldn't until me and Ike get back."

"Weather gonter break today. Gonter soft up. Rain by night." Then Ash laughed, chuckled, somewhere inside the quilt which concealed even his face. "Hum up here, mules!" he said, jerking the reins so that the mules leaped forward and snatched the lurching and banging wagon for several feet before they slowed again into their quick, short-paced, rapid plodding. "Sides, I like to know why Major

need to wait on you. It's Lion he aiming to use. I aint never
heard tell of you bringing no bear nor no other kind of
meat into this camp."

Now Boon's going to curse Ash or maybe even hit him,
the boy thought. But Boon never did, never had; the boy
knew he never would even though four years ago Boon had
shot five times with a borrowed pistol at a negro on the
street in Jefferson, with the same result as when he had
shot five times at Old Ben last fall. "By God," Boon said,
"he aint going to put Lion or no other dog on nothing until
I get back tonight. Because he promised me. Whip up
them mules and keep them whipped up. Do you want me
to freeze to death?"

They reached the log-line and built a fire. After a while
the log train came up out of the woods under the paling
east and Boon flagged it. Then in the warm caboose the
boy slept again while Boon and the conductor and brakeman talked about Lion and Old Ben as people later would
talk about Sullivan and Kilrain and, later still, about Demp-
sey and Tunney. Dozing, swaying as the springless caboose lurched and clattered, he would hear them still talking, about the shoats and calves Old Ben had killed and
the cribs he had rifled and the traps and deadfalls he had
wrecked and the lead he probably carried under his hide—
Old Ben, the two-toed bear in a land where bears with
trap-ruined feet had been called Two-Toe or Three-Toe or
Cripple-Foot for fifty years, only Old Ben was an extra
bear (the head bear, General Compson called him) and so
had earned a name such as a human man could have worn
and not been sorry.

They reached Hoke's at sunup. They emerged from the
warm caboose in their hunting clothes, the muddy boots

and stained khaki and Boon's blue unshaven jowls. But that was all right. Hoke's was a sawmill and commissary and two stores and a loading-chute on a sidetrack from the main line, and all the men in it wore boots and khaki too. Presently the Memphis train came. Boon bought three packages of popcorn-and-molasses and a bottle of beer from the news butch and the boy went to sleep again to the sound of his chewing.

But in Memphis it was not all right. It was as if the high buildings and the hard pavements, the fine carriages and the horse cars and the men in starched collars and neckties made their boots and khaki look a little rougher and a little muddier and made Boon's beard look worse and more unshaven and his face look more and more like he should never have brought it out of the woods at all or at least out of reach of Major de Spain or McCaslin or someone who knew it and could have said, "Dont be afraid. He wont hurt you." He walked through the station, on the slick floor, his face moving as he worked the popcorn out of his teeth with his tongue, his legs spraddled and stiff in the hips as if he were walking on buttered glass, and that blue stubble on his face like the filings from a new gun-barrel. They passed the first saloon. Even through the closed doors the boy could seem to smell the sawdust and the reek of old drink. Boon began to cough. He coughed for something less than a minute. "Damn this cold," he said. "I'd sure like to know where I got it."

"Back there in the station," the boy said.

Boon had started to cough again. He stopped. He looked at the boy. "What?" he said.

"You never had it when we left camp nor on the train

either." Boon looked at him, blinking. Then he stopped blinking. He didn't cough again. He said quietly:

"Lend me a dollar. Come on. You've got it. If you ever had one, you've still got it. I dont mean you are tight with your money because you aint. You just dont never seem to ever think of nothing you want. When I was sixteen a dollar bill melted off of me before I even had time to read the name of the bank that issued it." He said quietly: "Let me have a dollar, Ike."

"You promised Major. You promised McCaslin. Not till we get back to camp."

"All right," Boon said in that quiet and patient voice. "What can I do on just one dollar? You aint going to lend me another."

"You're damn right I aint," the boy said, his voice quiet too, cold with rage which was not at Boon, remembering: Boon snoring in a hard chair in the kitchen so he could watch the clock and wake him and McCaslin and drive them the seventeen miles in to Jefferson to catch the train to Memphis; the wild, never-bridled Texas paint pony which he had persuaded McCaslin to let him buy and which he and Boon had bought at auction for four dollars and seventy-five cents and fetched home wired between two gentle old mares with pieces of barbed wire and which had never even seen shelled corn before and didn't even know what it was unless the grains were bugs maybe and at last (he was ten and Boon had been ten all his life) Boon said the pony was gentled and with a towsack over its head and four negroes to hold it they backed it into an old two-wheeled cart and hooked up the gear and he and Boon got up and Boon said, "All right, boys. Let him go" and one of the negroes—it was Tennie's Jim—snatched the towsack off and leaped for his life and they lost the first wheel against a post of the open gate only at that moment Boon caught him by the scruff of the neck and flung him into the roadside ditch so he only saw the rest of it in fragments: the other wheel as it slammed through the side gate and crossed the back yard and leaped up onto the gallery and scraps of the cart here and there along the road and Boon vanishing rapidly on his stomach in the leaping and spurting dust and still holding the reins until they broke too and two days later they finally caught the pony seven miles away still wearing the hames and the headstall of the bridle around its neck like a duchess with two necklaces at one time. He gave Boon the dollar.

"All right," Boon said. "Come on in out of the cold."

"I aint cold," he said.

"You can have some lemonade."

"I dont want any lemonade."

The door closed behind him. The sun was well up now. It was a brilliant day, though Ash had said it would rain before night. Already it was warmer; they could run tomorrow. He felt the old lift of the heart, as pristine as ever, as on the first day; he would never lose it, no matter how old in hunting and pursuit: the best, the best of all breathing, the humility and the pride. He must stop thinking about it. Already it seemed to him that he was running, back to the station, to the tracks themselves: the first train going south; he must stop thinking about it. The street was busy. He watched the big Norman draft horses, the Percherons; the trim carriages from which the men in the fine overcoats and the ladies rosy in furs descended and entered the station. (They were still next door to it but one.) Twenty years ago his father had ridden into Memphis as a member of Colonel Sartoris' horse in Forrest's command, up Main street and (the tale told) into the lobby of the Gayoso Hotel where the Yankee officers sat in the leather chairs spitting into the tall bright cuspidors and then out again, scot-free——

The door opened behind him. Boon was wiping his mouth on the back of his hand. "All right," he said. "Let's go tend to it and get the hell out of here."

They went and had the suitcase packed. He never knew where or when Boon got the other bottle. Doubtless Mr Semmes gave it to him. When they reached Hoke's again at sundown, it was empty. They could get a return train to Hoke's in two hours; they went straight back to the station as Major de Spain and then McCaslin had told Boon to do and then ordered him to do and had sent the boy along to see that he did. Boon took the first drink from his bottle in the wash room. A man in a uniform cap came to tell him he couldn't drink there and looked at Boon's face once and said nothing. The next time he was pouring into his water glass beneath the edge of a table in the restaurant when the manager (she was a woman) did tell him he couldn't drink there and he went back to the wash-room. He had been telling the negro waiter and all the other people in the restaurant who couldn't help but hear him and who had never heard of Lion and didn't want to, about Lion and Old Ben. Then he happened to think of the zoo. He had found out that there was another train to Hoke's at three oclock and so they would spend the time at the zoo and take the three oclock train until he came back from the washroom for the third time. Then they would take the first train back to camp, get Lion and come back to the zoo where, he said, the bears were fed on ice cream and lady fingers and he would match Lion against them all.

So they missed the first train, the one they were supposed to take, but he got Boon onto the three oclock train and they were all right again, with Boon not even going to the wash-room now but drinking in the aisle and talking about Lion and the men he buttonholed no more daring to tell Boon he couldn't drink there than the man in the station had dared.

When they reached Hoke's at sundown, Boon was asleep. The boy waked him at last and got him and the suitcase off the train and he even persuaded him to eat some supper at the sawmill commissary. So he was all right when they got in the caboose of the log-train to go back into the woods, with the sun going down red and the sky already overcast. and the ground would not freeze tonight. It was the boy who slept now, sitting behind the ruby stove while the springless caboose jumped and clattered and Boon and the brakeman and the conductor talked about Lion and Old Ben because they knew what Boon was talking about because this was home. "Overcast and already thawing," Boon said. "Lion will get him tomorrow."

It would have to be Lion, or somebody. It would not be Boon. He had never hit anything bigger than a squirrel that anybody ever knew, except the negro woman that day when he was shooting at the negro man. He was a big negro and not ten feet away but Boon shot five times with the pistol he had borrowed from Major de Spain's negro coachman and the negro he was shooting at outed with a dollar-and-a-half mail-order pistol and would have burned Boon down with it only it never went off, it just went snicksnicksnicksnicksnick five times and Boon still blasting away and he broke a plate-glass window that cost McCaslin forty-five dollars and hit a negro woman who happened to be passing in the leg only Major de Spain paid for that; he and McCaslin cut cards, the plate-glass window against the negro woman's leg. And the first day on stand this year, the first morning in camp, the buck ran right over Boon; he heard Boon's old pump gun go whow. whow. whow. whow. whow. and then his voice: "God damn, here he comes! Head him! Head him!" and when he got there the buck's tracks and the five exploded shells were not twenty paces apart.

There were five guests in camp that night, from Jefferson: Mr Bayard Sartoris and his son and General Compson's son and two others. And the next morning he looked out the window, into the gray thin drizzle of daybreak which Ash had predicted, and there they were, standing and squatting beneath the thin rain, almost two dozen of them who had fed Old Ben corn and shoats and even calves for ten years, in their worn hats and hunting coats and overalls which any town negro would have thrown away or burned and only the rubber boots strong and sound, and the worn and blueless guns and some even without guns. While they ate breakfast a dozen more arrived, mounted and on foot: loggers from the camp thirteen miles below and sawmill men from Hoke's and the only gun among them that one which the log-train conductor carried: so that when they went into the woods this morning Major de Spain led a party almost as strong, excepting that some of them were not armed, as some he had led in the last darkening days of '64 and '65. The little yard would not hold them. They overflowed it, into the lane where Major de Spain sat his mare while Ash in his dirty apron thrust the greasy cartridges into his carbine and passed it up to him and the great grave blue dog stood at his stirrup not as a dog stands but as a horse stands, blinking his sleepy topaz eyes at nothing, deaf even to the yelling of the hounds which Boon and Tennie's Jim held on leash.

"We'll put General Compson on Katie this morning," Major de Spain said. "He drew blood last year; if he'd had a mule then that would have stood, he would have——"

"No," General Compson said. "I'm too old to go helling through the woods on a mule or a horse or anything else any more. Besides, I had my chance last year and missed it. I'm going on a stand this morning. I'm going to let that boy ride Katie."

"No, wait," McCaslin said. "Ike's got the rest of his life to hunt bears in. Let somebody else——"

"No," General Compson said. "I want Ike to ride Katie. He's already a better woodsman than you or me either and in another ten years he'll be as good as Walter."

At first he couldn't believe it, not until Major de Spain spoke to him. Then he was up, on the one-eyed mule which would not spook at wild blood, looking down at the dog motionless at Major de Spain's stirrup, looking in the gray streaming light bigger than a calf, bigger than he knew it actually was—the big head, the chest almost as big as his own, the blue hide beneath which the muscles flinched or quivered to no touch since the heart which drove blood to them loved no man and no thing, standing as a horse stands yet different from a horse which infers only weight and speed while Lion inferred not only courage and all else that went to make up the will and desire to pursue and kill, but endurance, the will and desire to endure beyond all imaginable limits of flesh in order to overtake and slay. Then the dog looked at him. It moved its head and looked at him across the trivial uproar of the hounds, out of the yellow eyes as depthless as Boon's, as free as Boon's of meanness or generosity or gentleness or viciousness. They were just cold and sleepy. Then it blinked, and he knew it was not looking at him and never had been, without even bothering to turn its head away.

That morning he heard the first cry. Lion had already vanished while Sam and Tennie's Jim were putting saddles on the mule and horse which had drawn the wagon and he watched the hounds as they crossed and cast, snuffing and whimpering, until they too disappeared. Then he and Major de Spain and Sam and Tennie's Jim rode after them and heard the first cry out of the wet and thawing woods not two hundred yards ahead, high, with that abject, almost human quality he had come to know, and the other hounds joining in until the gloomed woods rang and clamored. They rode then. It seemed to him that he could actually see the big blue dog boring on, silent, and the bear too: the thick, locomotive-like shape which he had seen that day four years ago crossing the blow-down, crashing on ahead of the dogs faster than he had believed it could have moved, drawing away even from the running mules. He heard a shotgun, once. The woods had opened, they were going fast, the clamor faint and fading on ahead; they passed the man who had fired—a swamper, a pointing arm, a gaunt face, the small black orifice of his yelling studded with rotten teeth.

He heard the changed note in the hounds' uproar and two hundred yards ahead he saw them. The bear had turned. He saw Lion drive in without pausing and saw the bear strike him aside and lunge into the yelling hounds and kill one of them almost in its tracks and whirl and run again. Then they were in a streaming tide of dogs. He heard Major de Spain and Tennie's Jim shouting and the pistol sound of Tennie's Jim's leather thong as he tried to turn them. Then he and Sam Fathers were riding alone. One of the hounds had kept on with Lion though. He recognised its voice. It was the young hound which even a year ago had had no judgment and which, by the lights of the other hounds anyway, still had none. *Maybe that's what courage is,* he thought. "Right," Sam said behind him. "Right. We got to turn him from the river if we can."

Now they were in cane: a brake. He knew the path through it as well as Sam did. They came out of the undergrowth and struck the entrance almost exactly. It would traverse the brake and come out onto a high open ridge above the river. He heard the flat clap of Walter Ewell's rifle, then two more. "No," Sam said. "I can hear the hound. Go on."

They emerged from the narrow roofless tunnel of snapping and hissing cane, still galloping, onto the open ridge below which the thick yellow river, reflectionless in the gray and streaming light, seemed not to move. Now he could hear the hound too. It was not running. The cry was a high frantic yapping and Boon was running along the edge of the bluff, his old gun leaping and jouncing against his back on its sling made of a piece of cotton plowline. He whirled and ran up to them, wild-faced, and flung himself onto the mule behind the boy. "That damn boat!" he cried. "It's on the other side! He went straight across! Lion was too close to him! That little hound too! Lion was so close I couldn't shoot! Go on!" he cried, beating his heels into the mule's flanks. "Go on!"

They plunged down the bank, slipping and sliding in the thawed earth, crashing through the willows and into the water. He felt no shock, no cold, he on one side of the swimming mule, grasping the pommel with one hand and holding his gun above the water with the other, Boon opposite him. Sam was behind them somewhere, and then the river, the water about them, was full of dogs. They swam faster than the mules; they were scrabbling up the bank before the mules touched bottom. Major de Spain was whooping from the bank they had just left and, looking back, he saw Tennie's Jim and the horse as they went into the water.

Now the woods ahead of them and the rain-heavy air were one uproar. It rang and clamored; it echoed and broke against the bank behind them and reformed and clamored and rang until it seemed to the boy that all the hounds which had ever bayed game in this land were yelling down at him. He got his leg over the mule as it came up out of the water. Boon didn't try to mount again. He grasped one stirrup as they went up the bank and crashed through the undergrowth which fringed the bluff and saw the bear, on its hind feet, its back against a tree while the bellowing hounds swirled around it and once more Lion drove in, leaping clear of the ground.

This time the bear didn't strike him down. It caught the dog in both arms, almost loverlike, and they both went down. He was off the mule now. He drew back both hammers of the gun but he could see nothing but moiling spotted houndbodies until the bear surged up again. Boon was yelling something, he could not tell what; he could see Lion still clinging to the bear's throat and he saw the bear, half erect, strike one of the hounds with one paw and hurl it five or six feet and then, rising and rising as though it would never stop, stand erect again and begin to rake at Lion's belly with its forepaws. Then Boon was running. The boy saw the gleam of the blade in his hand and watched him leap among the hounds, hurdling them, kicking them aside as he ran, and fling himself astride the bear as he had hurled himself onto the mule, his legs locked around the bear's belly, his left arm under the bear's throat where Lion clung, and the glint of the knife as it rose and fell.

It fell just once. For an instant they almost resembled a piece of statuary: the clinging dog, the bear, the man stride its back, working and probing the buried blade. Then they went down, pulled over backward by Boon's weight, Boon underneath. It was the bear's back which reappeared first but at once Boon was astride it again. He had never released the knife and again the boy saw the almost infinitesimal movement of his arm and shoulder as he probed and sought; then the bear surged erect, raising with it the man and the dog too, and turned and still carrying the man and the dog it took two or three steps toward the woods on its hind feet as a man would have walked and crashed down. It didn't collapse, crumple. It fell all of a piece, as a tree falls, so that all three of them, man dog and bear, seemed to bounce once.

He and Tennie's Jim ran forward. Boon was kneeling at the bear's head. His left ear was shredded, his left coat sleeve was completely gone, his right boot had been ripped from knee to instep; the bright blood thinned in the thin rain down his leg and hand and arm and down the side of his face which was no longer wild but was quite calm. Together they prized Lion's jaws from the bear's throat.

"Easy, goddamn it," Boon said. "Cant you see his guts are all out of him?" He began to remove his coat. He spoke to Tennie's Jim in that calm voice: "Bring the boat up. It's about a hundred yards down the bank there. I saw it." Tennie's Jim rose and went away. Then, and he could not remember if it had been a call or an exclamation from Tennie's Jim or if he had glanced up by chance, he saw Tennie's Jim stooping and saw Sam Fathers lying motionless on his face in the trampled mud.

The mule had not thrown him. He remembered that Sam was down too even before Boon began to run. There was no mark on him whatever and when he and Boon turned him over, his eyes were open and he said something in that tongue which he and Joe Baker had used to speak together. But he couldn't move. Tennie's Jim brought the skiff up; they could hear him shouting to Major de Spain across the river. Boon wrapped Lion in his hunting coat and carried him down to the skiff and they carried Sam down and returned and hitched the bear to the one-eyed mule's saddle-bow with Tennie's Jim's leash-thong and dragged him down to the skiff and got him into it and left Tennie's Jim to swim the horse and the two mules back across. Major de Spain caught the bow of the skiff as Boon jumped out and past him before it touched the bank. He looked at Old Ben and said quietly: "Well." Then he walked into the water and leaned down and touched Sam and Sam looked up at him and said something in that old tongue he and Joe Baker spoke. "You dont know what happened?" Major de Spain said.

"No, sir," the boy said. "It wasn't the mule. It wasn't anything. He was off the mule when Boon ran in on the bear. Then we looked up and he was lying on the ground."

Boon was shouting at Tennie's Jim, still in the middle of the river.

"Come on, goddamn it!" he said. "Bring me that mule!"

"What do you want with a mule?" Major de Spain said.

Boon didn't even look at him. "I'm going to Hoke's to get the doctor," he said in that calm voice, his face quite calm beneath the steady thinning of the bright blood.

"You need a doctor yourself," Major de Spain said. "Tennie's Jim——"

"Damn that," Boon said. He turned on Major de Spain. His face was still calm, only his voice was a pitch higher. "Cant you see his goddamn guts are all out of him?"

"Boon!" Major de Spain said. They looked at one another. Boon was a good head taller than Major de Spain; even the boy was taller now than Major de Spain.

"I've got to get the doctor," Boon said. "His goddamn guts——"

"All right," Major de Spain said. Tennie's Jim came up out of the water. The horse and the sound mule had already scented Old Ben; they surged and plunged all the way up to the top of the bluff, dragging Tennie's Jim with them, before he could stop them and tie them and come back. Major de Spain unlooped the leather thong of his compass from his buttonhole and gave it to Tennie's Jim. "Go straight to Hoke's," he said. "Bring Doctor Crawford back with you. Tell him there are two men to be looked at. Take my mare. Can you find the road from here?"

"Yes, sir," Tennie's Jim said.

"All right," Major de Spain said. "Go on." He turned to the boy. "Take the mules and the horse and go back and get the wagon. We'll go on down the river in the boat to Coon bridge. Meet us there. Can you find it again?"

"Yes, sir," the boy said.

"All right. Get started."

He went back to the wagon. He realised then how far they had run. It was already afternoon when he put the mules into the traces and tied the horse's lead-rope to the tail-gate. He reached Coon bridge at dusk. The skiff was already there. Before he could see it and almost before he could see the water he had to leap from the tilting wagon, still holding the reins, and work around to where he could grasp the bit and then the ear of the plunging sound mule and dig his heels and hold it until Boon came up the bank. The rope of the led horse had already snapped and it had already disappeared up the road toward camp. They turned the wagon around and took the mules out and he led the sound mule a hundred yards up the road and tied it. Boon had already brought Lion up to the wagon and Sam was sitting up in the skiff now and when they raised him he tried to walk, up the bank and to the wagon and he tried to climb into the wagon but Boon did not wait; he picked Sam up bodily and set him on the seat. Then they hitched Old Ben to the one-eyed mule's saddle again and dragged him up the bank and set two skid-poles into the open tail-gate and got him into the wagon and he went and got the sound mule and Boon fought it into the traces, striking it across its hard hollow-sounding face until it came into position and stood trembling. Then the rain came down, as though it had held off all day waiting on them.

They returned to camp through it, through the streaming and sightless dark, hearing long before they saw any light the horn and the spaced shots to guide them. When they came to Sam's dark little hut he tried to stand up. He spoke again in the tongue of the old fathers; then he said clearly: "Let me out. Let me out."

"He hasn't got any fire," Major said. "Go on!" he said sharply.

But Sam was struggling now, trying to stand up. "Let me out, master," he said. "Let me go home."

So he stopped the wagon and Boon got down and lifted Sam out. He did not wait to let Sam try to walk this time. He carried him into the hut and Major de Spain got light on a paper spill from the buried embers on the hearth and lit the lamp and Boon put Sam on his bunk and drew off his boots and Major de Spain covered him and the boy was not there, he was holding the mules, the sound one which was trying again to bolt since when the wagon stopped Old Ben's scent drifted forward again along the streaming blackness of air, but Sam's eyes were probably open again on that profound look which saw further than them or the hut, further than the death of a bear and the dying of a dog. Then they went on, toward the long wailing of the horn and the shots which seemed each to linger intact somewhere in the thick streaming air until the next spaced report joined and blended with it, to the lighted house, the bright streaming windows, the quiet faces as Boon entered, bloody and quite calm, carrying the bundled coat. He laid Lion, blood coat and all, on his stale sheetless pallet bed which not even Ash, as deft in the house as a woman, could ever make smooth.

The sawmill doctor from Hoke's was already there. Boon would not let the doctor touch him until he had seen to Lion. He wouldn't risk giving Lion chloroform. He put the entrails back and sewed him up without it while Major de

Spain held his head and Boon his feet. But he never tried
to move. He lay there, the yellow eyes open upon nothing
while the quiet men in the new hunting clothes and in the
old ones crowded· into the little airless room rank with the
smell of Boon's body and garments, and watched. Then
the doctor cleaned and disinfected Boon's face and arm and
leg and bandaged them and, the boy in front with a lantern
and the doctor and McCaslin and Major de Spain and
General Compson following, they went to Sam Fathers'
hut. Tennie's Jim had built up the fire; he squatted before
it, dozing. Sam had not moved since Boon had put him
in the bunk and Major de Spain had covered him with the
blankets, yet he opened his eyes and looked from one to
another of the faces and when McCaslin touched his shoulder and said, "Sam. The doctor wants to look at you," he
even drew his hands out of the blanket and began to
fumble at his shirt buttons until McCaslin said, "Wait.
We'll do it." They undressed him. He lay there—the
copper-brown, almost hairless body, the old man's body,
the old man, the wild man not even one generation from
the woods, childless, kinless, peopleless—motionless, his
eyes open but no longer looking at any of them, while the
doctor examined him and drew the blankets up and put
the stethoscope back into his bag and snapped the bag and
only the boy knew that Sam too was going to die.

"Exhaustion," the doctor said. "Shock maybe. A man his
age swimming rivers in December. He'll be all right. Just
make him stay in bed for a day or two. Will there be somebody here with him?"

"There will be somebody here," Major de Spain said.

They went back to the house, to the rank little room
where Boon still sat on the pallet bed with Lion's head

under his hand while the men, the ones who had hunted behind Lion and the ones who had never seen him before today, came quietly in to look at him and went away. Then it was dawn and they all went out into the yard to look at Old Ben, with his eyes open too and his lips snarled back from his worn teeth and his mutilated foot and the little hard lumps under his skin which were the old bullets (there were fifty-two of them, buckshot rifle and ball) and the single almost invisible slit under his left shoulder where Boon's blade had finally found his life. Then Ash began to beat on the bottom of the dishpan with a heavy spoon to call them to breakfast and it was the first time he could remember hearing no sound from the dogs under the kitchen while they were eating. It was as if the old bear, even dead there in the yard, was a more potent terror still than they could face without Lion between them.

The rain had stopped during the night. By midmorning the thin sun appeared, rapidly burning away mist and cloud, warming the air and the earth; it would be one of those windless Mississippi December days which are a sort of Indian summer's Indian summer. They moved Lion out to the front gallery, into the sun. It was Boon's idea. "God-damn it," he said, "he never did want to stay in the house until I made him. You know that." He took a crowbar and loosened the floor boards under his pallet bed so it could be raised, mattress and all, without disturbing Lion's position, and they carried him out to the gallery and put him down facing the woods.

Then he and the doctor and McCaslin and Major de Spain went to Sam's hut. This time Sam didn't open his eyes and his breathing was so quiet, so peaceful that they could hardly see that he breathed. The doctor didn't even take out his stethoscope nor even touch him. "He's all right," the doctor said. "He didn't even catch cold. He just quit."

"Quit?" McCaslin said.

"Yes. Old people do that sometimes. Then they get a good night's sleep or maybe it's just a drink of whisky, and they change their minds."

They returned to the house. And then they began to arrive—the swamp-dwellers, the gaunt men who ran trap-lines and lived on quinine and coons and river water, the farmers of little corn- and cotton-patches along the bottom's edge whose fields and cribs and pig-pens the old bear had rifled, the loggers from the camp and the sawmill men from Hoke's and the town men from further away than that, whose hounds the old bear had slain and traps and deadfalls he had wrecked and whose lead he carried. They came up mounted and on foot and in wagons, to enter the yard and look at him and then go on to the front where Lion lay, filling the little yard and overflowing it until there were almost a hundred of them squatting and stand-ing in the warm and drowsing sunlight, talking quietly of hunting, of the game and the dogs which ran it, of hounds and bear and deer and men of yesterday vanished from the earth, while from time to time the great blue dog would open his eyes, not as if he were listening to them but as though to look at the woods for a moment before closing his eyes again, to remember the woods or to see that they were still there. He died at sundown.

Major de Spain broke camp that night. They carried Lion into the woods, or Boon carried him that is, wrapped in a quilt from his bed, just as he had refused to let anyone else touch Lion yesterday until the doctor got there; Boon carrying Lion, and the boy and General Compson and Walter and still almost fifty of them following with lanterns and lighted pine-knots—men from Hoke's and even further, who would have to ride out of the bottom in the dark, and swampers and trappers who would have to walk even, scattering toward the little hidden huts where they lived. And Boon would let nobody else dig the grave either and lay Lion in it and cover him and then General Compson stood at the head of it while the blaze and smoke of the pine-knots streamed away among the winter branches and spoke as he would have spoken over a man. Then they returned to camp. Major de Spain and McCaslin and Ash had rolled and tied all the bedding. The mules were hitched to the wagon and pointed out of the bottom and the wagon was already loaded and the stove in the kitchen was cold and the table was set with scraps of cold food and bread and only the coffee was hot when the boy ran into the kitchen where Major de Spain and McCaslin had already eaten. "What?" he cried. "What? I'm not going."

"Yes," McCaslin said, "we're going out tonight. Major wants to get on back home."

"No!" he said. "I'm going to stay."

"You've got to be back in school Monday. You've already missed a week more than I intended. It will take you from now until Monday to catch up. Sam's all right. You heard Doctor Crawford. I'm going to leave Boon and Tennie's Jim both to stay with him until he feels like getting up."

He was panting. The others had come in. He looked rapidly and almost frantically around at the other faces. Boon had a fresh bottle. He upended it and started the cork by striking the bottom of the bottle with the heel of his hand and drew the cork with his teeth and spat it out and drank. "You're damn right you're going back to school," Boon said. "Or I'll burn the tail off of you myself if Cass dont, whether you are sixteen or sixty. Where in hell do you expect to get without education? Where would Cass be? Where in hell would I be if I hadn't never went to school?"

He looked at McCaslin again. He could feel his breath coming shorter and shorter and shallower and shallower, as if there were not enough air in the kitchen for that many to breathe. "This is just Thursday. I'll come home Sunday night on one of the horses. I'll come home Sunday, then. I'll make up the time I lost studying Sunday night. McCaslin," he said, without even despair.

"No, I tell you," McCaslin said. "Sit down here and eat your supper. We're going out to——"

"Hold up, Cass," General Compson said. The boy did not know General Compson had moved until he put his hand on his shoulder. "What is it, bud?" he said.

"I've got to stay," he said. "I've got to."

"All right," General Compson said. "You can stay. If missing an extra week of school is going to throw you so far behind you'll have to sweat to find out what some hired pedagogue put between the covers of a book, you better quit altogether.—And you shut up, Cass," he said, though McCaslin had not spoken. "You've got one foot straddled into a farm and the other foot straddled into a bank; you aint even got a good hand-hold where this boy was already an old man long before you damned Sartorises and Edmondses invented farms and banks to keep yourselves from having to find out what this boy was born knowing and fearing too maybe but without being afraid, that could go ten miles on a compass because he wanted to look at a bear none of us had ever got near enough to put a bullet in and looked at the bear and came the ten miles back on the compass in the dark; maybe by God that's the why and the wherefore of farms and banks.—I reckon you still aint going to tell what it is?"

But still he could not. "I've got to stay," he said.

"All right," General Compson said. "There's plenty of grub left. And you'll come home Sunday, like you promised McCaslin? Not Sunday night: Sunday."

"Yes, sir," he said.

"All right," General Compson said. "Sit down and eat, boys," he said. "Let's get started. It's going to be cold before we get home."

They ate. The wagon was already loaded and ready to depart; all they had to do was to get into it. Boon would drive them out to the road, to the farmer's stable where the surrey had been left. He stood beside the wagon, in silhouette on the sky, turbaned like a Paythan and taller than any there, the bottle tilted. Then he flung the bottle from his lips without even lowering it, spinning and glinting in the faint starlight, empty. "Them that's going," he said, "get in the goddamn wagon. Them that aint, get out of the goddamn way." The others got in. Boon mounted to the seat beside General Compson and the wagon moved, on into the obscurity until the boy could no longer see it, even the moving density of it amid the greater night. But he could still hear it, for a long while: the slow, deliberate banging of the wooden frame as it lurched from rut to rut. And he could hear Boon even when he could no longer hear the wagon. He was singing, harsh, tuneless, loud.

That was Thursday. On Saturday morning Tennie's

Jim left on McCaslin's woods-horse which had not been
out of the bottom one time now in six years, and late that
afternoon rode through the gate on the spent horse and on
to the commissary where McCaslin was rationing the ten-
ants and the wage-hands for the coming week, and this time
McCaslin forestalled any necessity or risk of having to wait
while Major de Spain's surrey was being horsed and har-
nessed. He took their own, and with Tennie's Jim already
asleep in the back seat he drove in to Jefferson and waited
while Major de Spain changed to boots and put on his
overcoat, and they drove the thirty miles in the dark of
that night and at daybreak on Sunday morning they
swapped to the waiting mare and mule and as the sun rose
they rode out of the jungle and onto the low ridge where
they had buried Lion: the low mound of unannealed
earth where Boon's spade-marks still showed and beyond
the grave the platform of freshly cut saplings bound between four posts and the blanket-wrapped bundle upon the
platform and Boon and the boy squatting between the
platform and the grave until Boon, the bandage removed,
ripped, from his head so that the long scoriations of Old
Ben's claws resembled crusted tar in the sunlight, sprang
up and threw down upon them with the old gun with
which he had never been known to hit anything although
McCaslin was already off the mule, kicked both feet free
of the irons and vaulted down before the mule had stopped,
walking toward Boon.

"Stand back," Boon said. "By God, you wont touch him.
Stand back, McCaslin." Still McCaslin came on, fast yet
without haste.

"Cass!" Major de Spain said. Then he said "Boon! You,
Boon!" and he was down too and the boy rose too, quickly,

and still McCaslin came on not fast but steady and walked
up to the grave and reached his hand steadily out, quickly
yet still not fast, and took hold the gun by the middle so
that he and Boon faced one another across Lion's grave,
both holding the gun, Boon's spent indomitable amazed
and frantic face almost a head higher than McCaslin's
beneath the black scoriations of beast's claws and then
Boon's chest began to heave as though there were not
enough air in all the woods, in all the wilderness, for all
of them, for him and anyone else, even for him alone.

"Turn it loose, Boon," McCaslin said.

"You damn little spindling—" Boon said. "Dont you
know I can take it away from you? Dont you know I can
tie it around your neck like a damn cravat?"

"Yes," McCaslin said. "Turn it loose, Boon."

"This is the way he wanted it. He told us. He told us
exactly how to do it. And by God you aint going to move
him. So we did it like he said, and I been sitting here ever
since to keep the damn wildcats and varmints away from
him and by God—" Then McCaslin had the gun, down-
slanted while he pumped the slide, the five shells snicking
out of it so fast that the last one was almost out before the
first one touched the ground and McCaslin dropped the
gun behind him without once having taken his eyes from
Boon's.

"Did you kill him, Boon?" he said. Then Boon moved.
He turned, he moved like he was still drunk and then
for a moment blind too, one hand out as he blundered toward the big tree and seemed to stop walking before he
reached the tree so that he plunged, fell toward it, flinging up both hands and catching himself against the tree and
turning until his back was against it, backing with the tree's

trunk his wild spent scoriated face and the tremendous heave and collapse of his chest, McCaslin following, facing him again, never once having moved his eyes from Boon's eyes. "Did you kill him, Boon?"

"No!" Boon said. "No!"

"Tell the truth," McCaslin said. "I would have done it if he had asked me to." Then the boy moved. He was between them, facing McCaslin; the water felt as if it had burst and sprung not from his eyes alone but from his whole face, like sweat.

"Leave him alone!" he cried. "Goddamn it! Leave him alone!"

4.

then he was twenty-one. He could say it, himself and his cousin juxtaposed not against the wilderness but against the tamed land which was to have been his heritage, the land which old Carothers McCaslin his grandfather had bought with white man's money from the wild men whose grandfathers without guns hunted it, and tamed and ordered or believed he had tamed and ordered it for the reason that the human beings he held in bondage and in the power of life and death had removed the forest from it and in their sweat scratched the surface of it to a depth of perhaps fourteen inches in order to grow something out of it which had not been there before and which could be translated back into the money he who believed he had bought it had had to pay to get it and hold it and a reasonable profit too: and for which reason old Carothers McCaslin, knowing better, could raise his children, his descendants and heirs, to believe the land was his to hold and bequeath since the strong and ruthless man has a cynical foreknowledge of his own vanity and pride and strength and a contempt for all his get: just as, knowing better, Major de Spain and his fragment of that wilderness which was bigger and older than any recorded deed: just as, knowing better, old Thomas Sutpen, from whom Major de Spain had had his fragment for money: just as Ikkemotubbe, the Chickasaw chief, from whom Thomas Sutpen had had the fragment for money or rum or whatever it was, knew in his turn that not even a fragment of it had been his to relinquish or sell

not against the wilderness but against the land, not in pursuit and lust but in relinquishment, and in the commissary as it should have been, not the heart perhaps but certainly the solar-plexus of the repudiated and relinquished: the square, galleried, wooden building squatting like a portent above the fields whose laborers it still held in thrall '65 or no and placarded over with advertisements for snuff and cures for chills and salves and potions manufactured and sold by white men to bleach the pigment and straighten the hair of negroes that they might resemble the very race which for two hundred years had held them in bondage and from which for another hundred years not even a bloody civil war would have set them completely free

himself and his cousin amid the old smells of cheese and salt meat and kerosene and harness, the ranked shelves of tobacco and overalls and bottled medicine and thread and plow-bolts, the barrels and kegs of flour and meal and molasses and nails, the wall pegs dependant with plowlines and plow-collars and hames and trace-chains, and the desk and the shelf above it on which rested the ledgers in which McCaslin recorded the slow outward trickle of food and supplies and equipment which returned each fall as cotton made and ginned and sold (two threads frail as truth and impalpable as equators yet cable-strong to bind for life them who made the cotton to the land their sweat fell on), and the older ledgers clumsy and archaic in size and shape, on the yellowed pages of which were recorded in the faded hand of his father Theophilus and his uncle Amodeus during the two decades before the Civil War, the manumission in title at least of Carothers McCaslin's slaves:

'Relinquish,' McCaslin said. 'Relinquish. You, the direct male descendant of him who saw the opportunity and took it, bought the land, took the land, got the land no matter how, held it to bequeath, no matter how, out of the old grant, the first patent, when it was a wilderness of wild beasts and wilder men, and cleared it, translated it into something to bequeath to his children, worthy of bequeathment for his descendants' ease and security and pride and to perpetuate his name and accomplishments. Not only the male descendant but the only and last descendant in the male line and in the third generation, while I am not only four generations from old Carothers, I derived through a woman and the very McCaslin in my name is mine only by sufferance and courtesy and my grandmother's pride in what that man accomplished whose legacy and monument you think you can repudiate.' and he

'I cant repudiate it. It was never mine to repudiate. It was never Father's and Uncle Buddy's to bequeath me to repudiate because it was never Grandfather's to bequeath them to bequeath me to repudiate because it was never old Ikkemotubbe's to sell to Grandfather for bequeathment and repudiation. Because it was never Ikkemotubbe's fathers' fathers' to bequeath Ikkemotubbe to sell to Grandfather or any man because on the instant when Ikkemotubbe discovered, realised, that he could sell it for money, on that instant it ceased ever to have been his forever, father to father to father, and the man who bought it bought nothing.'

'Bought nothing?' and he

'Bought nothing. Because He told in the Book how He created the earth, made it and looked at it and said it was all right, and then He made man. He made the earth first and peopled it with dumb creatures, and then He created man to be His overseer on the earth and to hold suzerainty over the earth and the animals on it in His name, not to hold for himself and his descendants inviolable title forever, generation after generation, to the oblongs and squares of the earth, but to hold the earth mutual and intact in the communal anonymity of brotherhood, and all the fee He asked was pity and humility and sufferance and endurance and the sweat of his face for bread. And I know what you are going to say,' he said: 'That nevertheless Grandfather—' and McCaslin

'—did own it. And not the first. Not alone and not the first since, as your Authority states, man was dispossessed of Eden. Nor yet the second and still not alone, on down through the tedious and shabby chronicle of His chosen sprung from Abraham, and of the sons of them who dispossessed Abraham, and of the five hundred years during which half the known world and all it contained was chattel to one city as this plantation and all the life it contained was chattel and revokeless thrall to this commissary store and those ledgers yonder during your grandfather's life, and the next thousand years while men fought over the fragments of that collapse until at last even the fragments

were exhausted and men snarled over the gnawed bones of
the old world's worthless evening until an accidental egg
discovered to them a new hemisphere. So let me say it:
That nevertheless and notwithstanding old Carothers did
own it. Bought it, got it, no matter; kept it, held it, no matter; bequeathed it: else why do you stand here relinquishing and repudiating? Held it, kept it for fifty years until
you could repudiate it, while He—this Arbiter, this Archi-
tect, this Umpire—condoned—or did He? looked down
and saw—or did He? Or at least did nothing: saw, and
could not, or did not see; saw, and would not, or perhaps
He would not see—perverse, impotent, or blind: which?'
and he

'Dispossessed.' and McCaslin

'What?' and he

'Dispossessed. Not impotent: He didn't condone; not
blind, because He watched it. And let me say it. Dispossessed of Eden. Dispossessed of Canaan, and those who dispossessed him dispossessed him dispossessed, and the five
hundred years of absentee landlords in the Roman bagnios,
and the thousand years of wild men from the northern woods
who dispossessed them and devoured their ravished substance ravished in turn again and then snarled in what you
call the old world's worthless twilight over the old world's
gnawed bones, blasphemous in His name until He used a
simple egg to discover to them a new world where a nation
of people could be founded in humility and pity and sufferance and pride of one to another. And Grandfather did own
the land nevertheless and notwithstanding because He
permitted it, not impotent and not condoning and not
blind because He ordered and watched it. He saw the
land already accursed even as Ikkemotubbe and Ikkemo-

tubbe's father old Issetibbeha and old Issetibbeha's fathers too held it, already tainted even before any white man owned it by what Grandfather and his kind, his fathers, had brought into the new land which He had vouchsafed them out of pity and sufferance, on condition of pity and humility and sufferance and endurance, from that old world's corrupt and worthless twilight as though in the sailfuls of the old world's tainted wind which drove the ships—' and McCaslin

'Ah.'

'—and no hope for the land anywhere so long as Ikkemotubbe and Ikkemotubbe's descendants held it in unbroken succession. Maybe He saw that only by voiding the land for a time of Ikkemotubbe's blood and substituting for it another blood, could He accomplish His purpose. Maybe He knew already what that other blood would be, maybe it was more than justice that only the white man's blood was available and capable to raise the white man's curse, more than vengeance when—' and McCaslin

'Ah.'

'—when He used the blood which had brought in the evil to destroy the evil as doctors use fever to burn up fever, poison to slay poison. Maybe He chose Grandfather out of all of them He might have picked. Maybe He knew that Grandfather himself would not serve His purpose because Grandfather was born too soon too, but that Grandfather would have descendants, the right descendants; maybe He had foreseen already the descendants Grandfather would have, maybe He saw already in Grandfather the seed progenitive of the three generations He saw it would take to set at least some of His lowly people free—' and McCaslin

'The sons of Ham. You who quote the Book: the sons of Ham.' and he

'There are some things He said in the Book, and some things reported of Him that He did not say. And I know what you will say now: That if truth is one thing to me and another thing to you, how will we choose which is truth? You dont need to choose. The heart already knows. He didn't have His Book written to be read by what must elect and choose, but by the heart, not by the wise of the earth because maybe they dont need it or maybe the wise no longer have any heart, but by the doomed and lowly of the earth who have nothing else to read with but the heart. Because the men who wrote his Book for Him were writing about truth and there is only one truth and it covers all things that touch the heart.' and McCaslin

'So these men who transcribed His Book for Him were sometime liars.' and he

'Yes. Because they were human men. They were trying to write down the heart's truth out of the heart's driving complexity, for all the complex and troubled hearts which would beat after them. What they were trying to tell, what He wanted said, was too simple. Those for whom they transcribed His words could not have believed them. It had to be expounded in the everyday terms which they were familiar with and could comprehend, not only those who listened but those who told it too, because if they who were that near to Him as to have been elected from among all who breathed and spoke language to transcribe and relay His words, could comprehend truth only through the complexity of passion and lust and hate and fear which drives the heart, what distance back to truth must they traverse whom truth could only reach by word-of-mouth?' and McCaslin

'I might answer that, since you have taken to proving your points and disproving mine by the same text, I dont know. But I dont say that, because you have answered yourself: No time at all if, as you say, the heart knows truth, the infallible and unerring heart. And perhaps you are right, since although you admitted three generations from old Carothers to you, there were not three. There were not even completely two. Uncle Buck and Uncle Buddy. And they not the first and not alone. A thousand other Bucks and Buddies in less than two generations and sometimes less than one in this land which so you claim God created and man himself cursed and tainted. Not to mention 1865.' and he

'Yes. More men that Father and Uncle Buddy,' not even glancing toward the shelf above the desk, nor did McCaslin. They did not need to. To him it was as though the ledgers in their scarred cracked leather bindings were being lifted down one by one in their fading sequence and spread open on the desk or perhaps upon some apocryphal Bench or even Altar or perhaps before the Throne Itself for a last perusal and contemplation and refreshment of the Allknowledgeable before the yellowed pages and the brown thin ink in which was recorded the injustice and a little at least of its amelioration and restitution faded back forever into the anonymous communal original dust

the yellowed pages scrawled in fading ink by the hand first of his grandfather and then of his father and uncle, bachelors up to and past fifty and then sixty, the one who ran the plantation and the farming of it and the other who did the housework and the cooking and continued

to do it even after his twin married and the boy himself
was born

the two brothers who as soon as their father was buried
moved out of the tremendously-conceived, the almost barn-
like edifice which he had not even completed, into a one-
room log cabin which the two of them built themselves
and added other rooms to while they lived in it, refusing
to allow any slave to touch any timber of it other than the
actual raising into place the logs which two men alone
could not handle, and domiciled all the slaves in the big
house some of the windows of which were still merely
boarded up with odds and ends of plank or with the skins
of bear and deer nailed over the empty frames: each sundown the brother who superintended the farming would
parade the negroes as a first sergeant dismisses a company,
and herd them willynilly, man woman and child, without
question protest or recourse, into the tremendous abortive
edifice scarcely yet out of embryo, as if even old Carothers
McCaslin had paused aghast at the concrete indication of
his own vanity's boundless conceiving: he would call his
mental roll and herd them in and with a hand-wrought
nail as long as a flenching-knife and suspended from a short
deer-hide thong attached to the door-jamb for that purpose, he would nail to the door of that house which lacked
half its windows and had no hinged back door at all, so
that presently and for fifty years afterward, when the boy
himself was big to hear and remember it, there was in the
land a sort of folk-tale: of the countryside all night long
full of skulking McCaslin slaves dodging the moonlit roads
and the Patrol-riders to visit other plantations, and of the
unspoken gentlemen's agreement between the two white
men and the two dozen black ones that, after the white

man had counted them and driven the home-made nail into
the front door at sundown, neither of the white men would
go around behind the house and look at the back door,
provided that all the negroes were behind the front one
when the brother who drove it drew out the nail again at
daybreak

the twins who were identical even in their handwriting,
unless you had specimens side by side to compare, and even
when both hands appeared on the same page (as often happened, as if, long since past any oral intercourse, they had
used the diurnally advancing pages to conduct the un-
avoidable business of the compulsion which had traversed
all the waste wilderness of North Mississippi in 1830 and
'40 and singled them out to drive) they both looked as
though they had been written by the same perfectly normal ten-year-old boy, even to the spelling, except that the
spelling did not improve as one by one the slaves which
Carothers McCaslin had inherited and purchased— Ros-
cius and Phoebe and Thucydides and Eunice and their
descendants, and Sam Fathers and his mother for both of
whom he had swapped an underbred trotting gelding to
old Ikkemotubbe, the Chickasaw chief from whom he had
likewise bought the land, and Tennie Beauchamp whom
the twin Amodeus had won from a neighbor in a poker-
game, and the anomaly calling itself Percival Brownlee
which the twin Theophilus had purchased, neither he nor
his brother ever knew why apparently, from Bedford Forrest while he was still only a slave-dealer and not yet a
general (It was a single page, not long and covering less
than a year, not seven months in fact, begun in the hand
which the boy had learned to distinguish as that of his
father:

*Percavil Brownly 26yr Old. cleark @ Bookepper.
bought from N.B.Forest at Cold Water 3 Mar 1856
$265. dolars*

and beneath that, in the same hand:

*5 mar 1856 No bookepper any way Cant read. Can
write his Name but I already put that down My self
Says he can Plough but dont look like it to Me. sent
to Feild to day Mar 5 1856*

and the same hand:

*6 Mar 1856 Cant plough either Says he aims to be a
Precher so may be he can lead live stock to Crick to
Drink*

and this time it was the other, the hand which he now
recognised as his uncle's when he could see them both on
the same page:

*Mar 23th 1856 Cant do that either Except one at a
Time Get shut of him*

then the first again:

24 Mar 1856 Who in hell would buy him

then the second:

*19th of Apr 1856 Nobody You put yourself out of
Market at Cold Water two months ago I never said
sell him Free him*

the first:

22 Apr 1856 Ill get it out of him

the second:

> Jun 13th 1856 How $1 per yr 265$ 265 yrs Wholl
> sign his Free paper

then the first again:

> 1 Oct 1856 Mule josephine Broke Leg @ shot Wrong
> stall wrong niger wrong everything $100. dolars

and the same:

> 2 Oct 1856 Freed Debit McCaslin @ McCaslin $265.
> dolars

then the second again:

> Oct 3th Debit Theophilus McCaslin Niger 265$
> Mule 100$ 365$ He hasnt gone yet Father should be
> here

then the first:

> 3 Oct 1856 Son of a bitch wont leave What would
> father done

the second:

> 29th of Oct 1856 Renamed him

the first:

> 31 Oct 1856 Renamed him what

the second:

> Chrstms 1856 Spintrius

) took substance and even a sort of shadowy life with their
passions and complexities too as page followed page and

year year; all there, not only the general and condoned
injustice and its slow amortization but the specific tragedy
which had not been condoned and could never be amortized,
the new page and the new ledger, the hand which he
could now recognise at first glance as his father's:

> Father dide Lucius Quintus Carothers McCaslin, Cal-
> lina 1772 Missippy 1837. Dide and burid 27 June
> 1837
> Roskus. rased by Granfather in Callina Dont know
> how old. Freed 27 June 1837 Dont want to leave. Dide
> and Burid 12 Jan 1841
> Fibby Roskus Wife. bought by granfather in Callina
> says Fifty Freed 27 June 1837 Dont want to leave.
> Dide and burd 1 Aug 1849
> Thucydus Roskus @ Fibby Son born in Callina 1779.
> Refused 10acre peace fathers Will 28 Jun 1837 Re-
> fused Cash offer $200. dolars from A.@ T. McCaslin
> 28 Jun 1837 Wants to stay and work it out

and beneath this and covering the next five pages and
almost that many years, the slow, day-by-day accrument
of the wages allowed him and the food and clothing—the
molasses and meat and meal, the cheap durable shirts and
jeans and shoes and now and then a coat against rain and
cold—charged against the slowly yet steadily mounting
sum of balance (and it would seem to the boy that he could
actually see the black man, the slave whom his white owner
had forever manumitted by the very act from which the
black man could never be free so long as memory lasted,
entering the commissary, asking permission perhaps of the
white man's son to see the ledger-page which he could not
even read, not even asking for the white man's word, which

he would have had to accept for the reason that there was absolutely no way under the sun for him to test it, as to how the account stood, how much longer before he could go and never return, even if only as far as Jefferson seventeen miles away) on to the double pen-stroke closing the final entry:

> *3 Nov 1841 By Cash to Thucydus McCaslin $200.*
> *dolars Set Up blaksmith in J. Dec 1841 Dide and*
> *burid in J. 17 feb 1854*
> *Eunice Bought by Father in New Orleans 1807 $650.*
> *dolars. Marrid to Thucydus 1809 Drownd in Crick*
> *Cristmas Day 1832*

and then the other hand appeared, the first time he had seen it in the ledger to distinguish it as his uncle's, the cook and housekeeper whom even McCaslin, who had known him and the boy's father for sixteen years before the boy was born, remembered as sitting all day long in the rocking chair from which he cooked the food, before the kitchen fire on which he cooked it:

> *June 21th 1833 Drownd herself*

and the first:

> *23 Jun 1833 Who in hell ever heard of a niger drownd-*
> *ing him self*

and the second, unhurried, with a complete finality; the two identical entries might have been made with a rubber stamp save for the date:

> *Aug 13th 1833 Drownd herself*

and he thought *But why? But why?* He was sixteen then.

It was neither the first time he had been alone in the commissary nor the first time he had taken down the old ledgers familiar on their shelf above the desk ever since he could remember. As a child and even after nine and ten and eleven, when he had learned to read, he would look up at the scarred and cracked backs and ends but with no particular desire to open them, and though he intended to examine them someday because he realised that they probably contained a chronological and much more comprehensive though doubtless tedious record than he would ever get from any other source, not alone of his own flesh and blood but of all his people, not only the whites but the black one too, who were as much a part of his ancestry as his white progenitors, and of the land which they had all held and used in common and fed from and on and would continue to use in common without regard to color or titular ownership, it would only be on some idle day when he was old and perhaps even bored a little since what the old books contained would be after all these years fixed immutably, finished, unalterable, harmless. Then he was sixteen. He knew what he was going to find before he found it. He got the commissary key from McCaslin's room after midnight while McCaslin was asleep and with the commissary door shut and locked behind him and the forgotten lantern stinking anew the rank dead icy air, he leaned above the yellowed page and thought not Why drowned herself, but thinking what he believed his father had thought when he found his brother's first comment: Why did Uncle Buddy think she had drowned herself? finding, beginning to find on the next succeeding page what he knew he would find, only this was still not it because he already knew this:

*Tomasina called Tomy Daughter of Thucydus @
Eunice Born 1810 dide in Child bed June 1833 and
Burd. Yr stars fell*

nor the next:

*Turl Son of Thucydus @ Eunice Tomy born Jun 1833
yr stars fell Fathers will*

and nothing more, no tedious recording filling this page
of wages day by day and food and clothing charged against
them, no entry of his death and burial because he had outlived his white half-brothers and the books which McCaslin
kept did not include obituaries: just *Fathers will* and he
had seen that too: old Carothers' bold cramped hand far
less legible than his sons' even and not much better in
spelling, who while capitalising almost every noun and
verb, made no effort to punctuate or construct whatever,
just as he made no effort either to explain or obfuscate the
thousand-dollar legacy to the son of an unmarried slave-
girl, to be paid only at the child's coming-of-age, bearing
the consequence of the act of which there was still no
definite incontrovertible proof that he acknowledged, not
out of his own substance but penalising his sons with it,
charging them a cash forfeit on the accident of their own
paternity; not even a bribe for silence toward his own fame
since his fame would suffer only after he was no longer
present to defend it, flinging almost contemptuously, as he
might a cast-off hat or pair of shoes, the thousand dollars
which could have had no more reality to him under those
conditions than it would have to the negro, the slave who
would not even see it until he came of age, twenty-one
years too late to begin to learn what money was. *So I
reckon that was cheaper than saying My son to a nigger*

he thought. *Even if My son wasn't but just two words.
But there must have been* love he thought. *Some sort
of love. Even what he would have called love: not just an
afternoon's or a night's spittoon.* There was the old man,
old, within five years of his life's end, long a widower and,
since his sons were not only bachelors but were approaching middleage, lonely in the house and doubtless even
bored since his plantation was established now and func-
tioning and there was enough money now, too much of
it probably for a man whose vices even apparently remained below his means; there was the girl, husbandless
and young, only twenty-three when the child was born:
perhaps he had sent for her at first out of loneliness, to
have a young voice and movement in the house, sum-
moned her, bade her mother send her each morning to
sweep the floors and make the beds and the mother
acquiescing since that was probably already understood,
already planned: the only child of a couple who were not
field hands and who held themselves something above
the other slaves not alone for that reason but because
the husband and his father and mother too had been
inherited by the white man from his father, and the white
man himself had travelled three hundred miles and better
to New Orleans in a day when men travelled by horseback
or steamboat, and bought the girl's mother as a wife for

and that was all. The old frail pages seemed to turn of
their own accord even while he thought *His own daughter
His own daughter. No No Not even him* back to that one
where the white man (not even a widower then) who never
went anywhere any more than his sons in their time ever
did and who did not need another slave, had gone all the
way to New Orleans and bought one. And Tomey's Terrel

was still alive when the boy was ten years old and he knew
from his own observation and memory that there had already been some white in Tomey's Terrel's blood before
his father gave him the rest of it; and looking down at the
yellowed page spread beneath the yellow glow of the lantern smoking and stinking in that rank chill midnight room
fifty years later, he seemed to see her actually walking into
the icy creek on that Christmas day six months before her
daughter's and her lover's (*Her first lover's* he thought.
Her first) child was born, solitary, inflexible, griefless,
ceremonial, in formal and succinct repudiation of grief
and despair who had already had to repudiate belief and
hope

that was all. He would never need look at the ledgers
again nor did he; the yellowed pages in their fading and
implacable succession were as much a part of his conscious-
ness and would remain so forever, as the fact of his own
nativity:

> *Tennie Beauchamp 21yrs Won by Amodeus McCaslin
> from Hubert Beauchamp Esqre Possible Strait against
> three Treys in sigt Not called 1859 Marrid to Tomys
> Turl 1859*

and no date of freedom because her freedom, as well as
that of her first surviving child, derived not from Buck and
Buddy McCaslin in the commissary but from a stranger in
Washington and no date of death and burial, not only because McCaslin kept no obituaries in his books, but because in this year 1883 she was still alive and would
remain so to see a grandson by her last surviving child:

> *Amodeus McCaslin Beauchamp Son of tomys Turl
> @ Tennie Beauchamp 1859 dide 1859*

then his uncle's hand entire, because his father was now
a member of the cavalry command of that man whose
name as a slave-dealer he could not even spell: and not
even a page and not even a full line:

> *Dauter Tomes Turl and tenny 1862*

and not even a line and not even a sex and no cause given
though the boy could guess it because McCaslin was thirteen then and he remembered how there was not always
enough to eat in more places than Vicksburg:

> *Child of tomes Turl and Tenny 1863*

and the same hand again and this one lived, as though
Tennie's perseverance and the fading and diluted ghost
of old Carothers' ruthlessness had at last conquered even
starvation: and clearer, fuller, more carefully written and
spelled than the boy had yet seen it, as if the old man,
who should have been a woman to begin with, trying to
run what was left of the plantation in his brother's absence
in the intervals of cooking and caring for himself and
the fourteen-year-old orphan, had taken as an omen for
renewed hope the fact that this nameless inheritor of slaves
was at least remaining alive long enough to receive a name:

> *James Thucydus Beauchamp Son of Tomes Turl and
> Tenny Beauchamp Born 29th december 1864 and both
> Well Wanted to call him Theophilus but Tride Amo-
> deus McCaslin and Callina McCaslin and both dide
> so Disswaded Them Born at Two clock A,m, both
> Well*

but no more, nothing; it would be another two years yet
before the boy, almost a man now, would return from the

abortive trip into Tennessee with the still-intact third of
old Carothers' legacy to his Negro son and his descendants,
which as the three surviving children established at last
one by one their apparent intention of surviving, their white
half-uncles had increased to a thousand dollars each, conditions permitting, as they came of age, and completed the
page himself as far as it would even be completed when
that day was long passed beyond which a man born in
1864 (or 1867 either, when he himself saw light) could
have expected or himself hoped or even wanted to be
still alive; his own hand now, queerly enough resembling
neither his father's nor his uncle's nor even McCaslin's,
but like that of his grandfather's save for the spelling:

> *Vanished sometime on night of his twenty-first birth-*
> *day Dec 29 1885. Traced by Isaac McCaslin to Jack-*
> *son Tenn. and there lost. His third of legacy $1000.00*
> *returned to McCaslin Edmonds Trustee this day Jan*
> *12 1886*

but not yet: that would be two years yet, and now his
father's again, whose old commander was now quit of
soldiering and slave-trading both; once more in the ledger
and then not again and more illegible than ever, almost
indecipherable at all from the rheumatism which now crip-
pled him and almost completely innocent now even of any
sort of spelling as well as punctuation, as if the four
years during which he had followed the sword of the
only man ever breathing who ever sold him a negro, let
alone beat him in a trade, had convinced him not only of
the vanity of faith and hope but of orthography too:

> *Miss sophonsiba b dtr t t @ t 1869*

but not of belief and will because it was there, written, as
McCaslin had told him, with the left hand, but there in the
ledger one time more and then not again, for the boy
himself was a year old, and when Lucas was born six
years later, his father and uncle had been dead inside the
same twelve-months almost five years; his own hand again,
who was there and saw it, 1886, she was just seventeen,
two years younger than himself, and he was in the commissary when McCaslin entered out of the first of dusk
and said, 'He wants to marry Fonsiba,' like that: and he
looked past McCaslin and saw the man, the stranger, taller
than McCaslin and wearing better clothes than McCaslin
and most of the other white men the boy knew habitually
wore, who entered the room like a white man and stood
in it like a white man, as though he had let McCaslin
precede him into it not because McCaslin's skin was white
but simply because McCaslin lived there and knew the
way, and who talked like a white man too, looking at him
past McCaslin's shoulder rapidly and keenly once and
then no more, without further interest, as a mature and
contained white man not impatient but just pressed for
time might have looked. 'Marry Fonsiba?' he cried. 'Marry
Fonsiba?' and then no more either, just watching and
listening while McCaslin and the Negro talked:

'To live in Arkansas, I believe you said.'

'Yes. I have property there. A farm.'

'Property? A farm? You own it?'

'Yes.'

'You dont say Sir, do you?'

'To my elders, yes.'

'I see. You are from the North.'

'Yes. Since a child.'

'Then your father was a slave.'

'Yes. Once.'

'Then how do you own a farm in Arkansas?'

'I have a grant. It was my father's. From the United States. For military service.'

'I see,' McCaslin said. 'The Yankee army.'

'The United States army,' the stranger said; and then himself again, crying it at McCaslin's back:

'Call aunt Tennie! I'll go get her! I'll—' But McCaslin was not even including him; the stranger did not even glance back toward his voice, the two of them speaking to one another again as if he were not even there:

'Since you seem to have it all settled,' McCaslin said, 'why have you bothered to consult my authority at all?'

'I dont,' the stranger said. 'I acknowledge your authority only so far as you admit your responsibility toward her as a female member of the family of which you are the head. I dont ask your permission. I ——'

'That will do!' McCaslin said. But the stranger did not falter. It was neither as if he were ignoring McCaslin nor as if he had failed to hear him. It was as though he were making, not at all an excuse and not exactly a justification, but simply a statement which the situation absolutely required and demanded should be made in McCaslin's hearing whether McCaslin listened to it or not. It was as if he were talking to himself, for himself to hear the words spoken aloud. They faced one another, not close yet at slightly less than foils' distance, erect, their voices not raised, not impactive, just succinct:

'—I inform you, notify you in advance as chief of her family. No man of honor could do less. Besides, you have, in your way, according to your lights and upbringing——'

'That's enough, I said,' McCaslin said. 'Be off this place by full dark. Go.' But for another moment the other did not move, contemplating McCaslin with that detached and heatless look, as if he were watching reflected in McCaslin's pupils the tiny image of the figure he was sustaining.

'Yes,' he said. 'After all, this is your house. And in your fashion you have. . . . But no matter. You are right. This is enough.' He turned back toward the door; he paused again but only for a second, already moving while he spoke: 'Be easy. I will be good to her.' Then he was gone.

'But how did she ever know him?' the boy cried. 'I never even heard of him before! And Fonsiba, that's never been off this place except to go to church since she was born——'

'Ha,' McCaslin said. 'Even their parents dont know until too late how seventeen-year-old girls ever met the men who marry them too, if they are lucky.' And the next morning they were both gone, Fonsiba too. McCaslin never saw her again, nor did he, because the woman he found at last five months later was no one he had ever known. He carried a third of the three-thousand-dollar fund in gold in a money-belt, as when he had vainly traced Tennie's Jim into Tennessee a year ago. They—the man—had left an address of some sort with Tennie, and three months later a letter came, written by the man although McCaslin's wife Alice had taught Fonsiba to read and write too a little. But it bore a different postmark from the address the man had left with Tennie, and he travelled by rail as far as he could and then by contracted stage and then by a hired livery rig and then by rail again for a distance: an

experienced traveller by now and an experienced blood-
hound too and a successful one this time because he would
have to be; as the slow interminable empty muddy December miles crawled and crawled and night followed night in
hotels, in roadside taverns of rough logs and containing little
else but a bar, and in the cabins of strangers and the hay
of lonely barns, in none of which he dared undress because
of his secret golden girdle like that of a disguised one of
the Magi travelling incognito and not even hope to draw
him but only determination and desperation, he would tell
himself: *I will have to find her. I will have to. We have
already lost one of them. I will have to find her this time.*
He did. Hunched in the slow and icy rain, on a spent hired
horse splashed to the chest and higher, he saw it—a single
log edifice with a clay chimney which seemed in process
of being flattened by the rain to a nameless and valueless
rubble of dissolution in that roadless and even pathless
waste of unfenced fallow and wilderness jungle—no barn,
no stable, not so much as a hen-coop: just a log cabin built
by hand and no clever hand either, a meagre pile of clum-
sily-cut firewood sufficient for about one day and not even
a gaunt hound to come bellowing out from under the house
when he rode up—a farm only in embryo, perhaps a good
farm, maybe even a plantation someday, but not now, not
for years yet and only then with labor, hard and enduring
and unflagging work and sacrifice; he shoved open the
crazy kitchen door in its awry frame and entered an icy
gloom where not even a fire for cooking burned and after
another moment saw, crouched into the wall's angle behind
a crude table, the coffee-colored face which he had known
all his life but knew no more, the body which had been
born within a hundred yards of the room that he was born

in and in which some of his own blood ran but which was
now completely inheritor of generation after generation
to whom an unannounced white man on a horse was a
white man's hired Patroller wearing a pistol sometimes
and a blacksnake whip always; he entered the next room,
the only other room the cabin owned, and found, sitting
in a rocking chair before the hearth, the man himself, reading—sitting there in the only chair in the house, before
that miserable fire for which there was not wood sufficient
to last twenty-four hours, in the same ministerial clothing
in which he had entered the commissary five months ago
and a pair of gold-framed spectacles which, when he looked
up and then rose to his feet, the boy saw did not even
contain lenses, reading a book in the midst of that desola-
tion, that muddy waste fenceless and even pathless and
without even a walled shed for stock to stand beneath:
and over all, permeant, clinging to the man's very clothing
and exuding from his skin itself, that rank stink of baseless and imbecile delusion, that boundless rapacity and
folly, of the carpet-bagger followers of victorious armies.

'Dont you see?' he cried. 'Dont you see? This whole land,
the whole South, is cursed, and all of us who derive from
it, whom it ever suckled, white and black both, lie under
the curse? Granted that my people brought the curse onto
the land: maybe for that reason their descendants alone
can—not resist it, not combat it—maybe just endure and
outlast it until the curse is lifted. Then your peoples' turn
will come because we have forfeited ours. But not now.
Not yet. Dont you see?'

The other stood now, the unfrayed garments still ministerial even if not quite so fine, the book closed upon one
finger to keep the place, the lenseless spectacles held like

a music master's wand in the other workless hand while the owner of it spoke his measured and sonorous imbecility of the boundless folly and the baseless hope: 'You're wrong. The curse you whites brought into this land has been lifted. It has been voided and discharged. We are seeing a new era, an era dedicated, as our founders intended it, to freedom, liberty and equality for all, to which this country will be the new Canaan——'

'Freedom from what? From work? Canaan?' He jerked his arm, comprehensive, almost violent: whereupon it all seemed to stand there about them, intact and complete and visible in the drafty, damp, heatless, negro-stale negro-rank sorry room—the empty fields without plow or seed to work them, fenceless against the stock which did not exist within or without the walled stable which likewise was not there. 'What corner of Canaan is this?'

'You are seeing it at a bad time. This is winter. No man farms this time of year.'

'I see. And of course her need for food and clothing will stand still while the land lies fallow.'

'I have a pension,' the other said. He said it as a man might say *I have grace* or *I own a gold mine.* 'I have my father's pension too. It will arrive on the first of the month. What day is this?'

'The eleventh,' he said. 'Twenty days more. And until then?'

'I have a few groceries in the house from my credit account with the merchant in Midnight who banks my pension check for me. I have executed to him a power of attorney to handle it for me as a matter of mutual——'

'I see. And if the groceries dont last the twenty days?'

'I still have one more hog.'

'Where?'

'Outside,' the other said. 'It is customary in this country to allow stock to range free during the winter for food. It comes up from time to time. But no matter if it doesn't; I can probably trace its footprints when the need——'

'Yes!' he cried. 'Because no matter: you still have the pension check. And the man in Midnight will cash it and pay himself out of it for what you have already eaten and if there is any left over, it is yours. And the hog will be eaten by then or you still cant catch it, and then what will you do?'

'It will be almost spring then,' the other said. 'I am planning in the spring——'

'It will be January,' he said. 'And then February. And then more than half of March—' and when he stopped again in the kitchen she had not moved, she did not even seem to breathe or to be alive except her eyes watching him; when he took a step toward her it was still not movement because she could have retreated no further: only the tremendous fathomless ink-colored eyes in the narrow, thin, too thin coffee-colored face watching him without alarm, without recognition, without hope. 'Fonsiba,' he said. 'Fonsiba. Are you all right?'

'I'm free,' she said. Midnight was a tavern, a livery stable, a big store (that would be where the pension check banked itself as a matter of mutual elimination of bother and fret, he thought) and a little one, a saloon and a blacksmith shop. But there was a bank there too. The president (the owner, for all practical purposes) of it was a translated Mississippian who had been one of Forrest's men too: and his body lightened of the golden belt for the first time since he left home eight days ago, with pencil and

paper he multiplied three dollars by twelve months and
divided it into one thousand dollars; it would stretch that
way over almost twenty-eight years and for twenty-eight
years at least she would not starve, the banker promising
to send the three dollars himself by a trusty messenger on
the fifteenth of each month and put it into her actual hand,
and he returned home and that was all because in 1874
his father and his uncle were both dead and the old ledgers
never again came down from the shelf above the desk to
which his father had returned them for the last time that
day in 1869. But he could have completed it:

> *Lucas Quintus Carothers McCaslin Beauchamp. Last
> surviving son and child of Tomey's Terrel and Ten-
> nie Beauchamp. March 17, 1874*

except that there was no need: not *Lucius Quintus @c @c
@c,* but *Lucas Quintus,* not refusing to be called Lucius,
because he simply eliminated that word from the name;
not denying, declining the name itself, because he used
three quarters of it; but simply taking the name and changing, altering it, making it no longer the white man's but
his own, by himself composed, himself selfprogenitive and
nominate, by himself ancestored, as, for all the old ledgers
recorded to the contrary, old Carothers himself was

and that was all: 1874 the boy; 1888 the man, repudiated denied and free; 1895 and husband but no father,
unwidowered but without a wife, and found long since
that no man is ever free and probably could not bear it if
he were; married then and living in Jefferson in the little
new jerrybuilt bungalow which his wife's father had given
them: and one morning Lucas stood suddenly in the door-
way of the room where he was reading the Memphis paper

and he looked at the paper's dateline and thought *It's his birthday. He's twenty-one today* and Lucas said: 'Whar's the rest of that money old Carothers left? I wants it. All of it.'

that was all: and McCaslin

'More men than that one Buck and Buddy to fumble-heed that truth so mazed for them that spoke it and so confused for them that heard yet still there was 1865:' and he

'But not enough. Not enough of even Father and Uncle Buddy to fumble-heed in even three generations not even three generations fathered by Grandfather not even if there had been nowhere beneath His sight any but Grand-father and so He would not even have needed to elect and choose. But He tried and I know what you will say. That having Himself created them He could have known no more of hope than He could have pride and grief but He didn't hope He just waited because He had made them: not just because He had set them alive and in motion but because He had already worried with them so long: wor-ried with them so long because He had seen how in indi-vidual cases they were capable of anything any height or depth remembered in mazed incomprehension out of heaven where hell was created too and so He must admit them or else admit His equal somewhere and so be no longer God and therefore must accept responsibility for what He Himself had done in order to live with Himself in His lonely and paramount heaven. And He probably knew it was vain but He had created them and knew them capable of all things because He had shaped them out of the primal Absolute which contained all and had watched them since in their individual exaltation and baseness and they them-

selves not knowing why nor how nor even when: until at
last He saw that they were all Grandfather all of them and
that even from them the elected and chosen the best the
very best He could expect (not hope mind; not hope)
would be Bucks and Buddies and not even enough of them
and in the third generation not even Bucks and Buddies
but—' and McCaslin

'Ah:' and he

'Yes. If He could see Father and Uncle Buddy in Grandfather He must have seen me too. —an Isaac born into a
later life than Abraham's and repudiating immolation:
fatherless and therefore safe declining the altar because
maybe this time the exasperated Hand might not supply
the kid—' and McCaslin

'Escape:' and he

'All right. Escape.—Until one day He said what you
told Fonsiba's husband that afternoon here in this room:
This will do. This is enough: not in exasperation or rage or
even just sick to death as you were sick that day: just *This
is enough* and looked about for one last time, for one time
more since He had created them, upon this land this
South for which He had done so much with woods for
game and streams for fish and deep rich soil for seed and
lush springs to sprout it and long summers to mature it and
serene falls to harvest it and short mild winters for men
and animals and saw no hope anywhere and looked beyond
it where hope should have been, where to East North and
West lay illimitable that whole hopeful continent dedicated
as a refuge and sanctuary of liberty and freedom from what
you called the old world's worthless evening and saw the
rich descendants of slavers, females of both sexes, to whom
the black they shrieked of was another specimen another

example like the Brazilian macaw brought home in a cage
by a traveller, passing resolutions about horror and outrage in warm and air-proof halls: and the thundering can-
nonade of politicians earning votes and the medicine-shows
of pulpiteers earning Chatauqua fees, to whom the outrage
and the injustice were as much abstractions as Tariff or
Silver or Immortality and who employed the very shackles
of its servitude and the sorry rags of its regalia as they did
the other beer and banners and mottoes redfire and brim-
stone and sleight-of-hand and musical handsaws: and the
whirling wheels which manufactured for a profit the pristine
replacements of the shackles and shoddy garments as they
wore out and spun the cotton and made the gins which
ginned it and the cars and ships which hauled it, and
the men who ran the wheels for that profit and established
and collected the taxes it was taxed with and the rates for
hauling it and the commissions for selling it: and He could
have repudiated them since they were his creation now
and forever more throughout all their generations until not
only that old world from which He had rescued them
but this new one too which He had revealed and led them
to as a sanctuary and refuge were become the same worthless tideless rock cooling in the last crimson evening except
that out of all that empty sound and bootless fury one
silence, among that loud and moiling all of them just one
simple enough to believe that horror and outrage were
first and last simply horror and outrage and was crude
enough to act upon that, illiterate and had no words for
talking or perhaps was just busy and had no time to, one
out of them all who did not bother Him with cajolery and
adjuration then pleading then threat and had not even
bothered to inform Him in advance what he was about so

that a lesser than He might have even missed the simple act
of lifting the long ancestral musket down from the deer-
horns above the door, whereupon He said *My name is
Brown too* and the other *So is mine* and He *Then mine
or yours cant be because I am against it* and the other *So
am I* and He triumphantly *Then where are you going
with that gun?* and the other told him in one sentence one
word and He: amazed: Who knew neither hope nor pride
nor grief *But your Association, your Committee, your
Officers. Where are your Minutes, your Motions, your
Parliamentary Procedures?* and the other *I aint against
them. They are all right I reckon for them that have the
time. I am just against the weak because they are niggers
being held in bondage by the strong just because they are
white.* So He turned once more to this land which He still
intended to save because He had done so much for it—'
and McCaslin

'What?' and he

'—to these people He was still committed to because
they were his creations—' and McCaslin

'Turned back to us? His face to us?' and he

'—whose wives and daughters at least made soups and
jellies for them when they were sick and carried the trays
through the mud and the winter too into the stinking cabins
and sat in the stinking cabins and kept fires going until
crises came and passed but that was not enough: and when
they were very sick had them carried into the big house
itself into the company room itself maybe and nursed them
there which the white man would have done too for any
other of his cattle that was sick but at least the man who
hired one from a livery wouldn't have and still that was
not enough: so that He said and not in grief either Who

had made them and so could know no more of grief than
He could of pride or hope: *Apparently they can learn
nothing save through suffering, remember nothing save
when underlined in blood*—' and McCaslin

'Ashby on an afternoon's ride, to call on some remote
maiden cousins of his mother or maybe just acquaintances
of hers, comes by chance upon a minor engagement of out-
posts and dismounts and with his crimson-lined cloak for
target leads a handful of troops he never saw before against
an entrenched position of backwoods-trained riflemen. Lee's
battle-order, wrapped maybe about a handful of cigars and
doubtless thrown away when the last cigar was smoked,
found by a Yankee Intelligence officer on the floor of a
saloon behind the Yankee lines after Lee had already
divided his forces before Sharpsburg. Jackson on the Plank
Road, already rolled up the flank which Hooker believed
could not be turned and, waiting only for night to pass to
continue the brutal and incessant slogging which would
fling that whole wing back into Hooker's lap where he sat
on a front gallery in Chancellorsville drinking rum toddies
and telegraphing Lincoln that he had defeated Lee, is shot
from among a whole covey of minor officers and in the blind
night by one of his own patrols, leaving as next by seniority
Stuart that gallant man born apparently already horsed and
sabred and already knowing all there was to know about
war except the slogging and brutal stupidity of it: and that
same Stuart off raiding Pennsylvania hen-roosts when Lee
should have known of all of Meade just where Hancock
was on Cemetery Ridge: and Longstreet too at Gettysburg
and that same Longstreet shot out of saddle by his own men
in the dark by mistake just as Jackson was. His face to
us? His face to us?' and he

'How else have made them fight? Who else but Jack-
sons and Stuarts and Ashbys and Morgans and Forrests?—
the farmers of the central and middle-west, holding land
by the acre instead of the tens or maybe even the hun-
dreds, farming it themselves and to no single crop of cotton or tobacco or cane, owning no slaves and needing and
wanting none and already looking toward the Pacific coast,
not always as long as two generations there and having
stopped where they did stop only through the fortuitous
mischance that an ox died or a wagon-axle broke. And the
New England mechanics who didn't even own land and
measured all things by the weight of water and the cost
of turning wheels and the narrow fringe of traders and
ship-owners still looking backward across the Atlantic and
attached to the continent only by their counting-houses.
And those who should have had the alertness to see: the
wildcat manipulators of mythical wilderness townsites; and
the astuteness to rationalise: the bankers who held the
mortgages on the land which the first were only waiting
to abandon and on the railroads and steamboats to carry
them still further west, and on the factories and the wheels
and the rented tenements those who ran them lived in; and
the leisure and scope to comprehend and fear in time and
even anticipate: the Boston-bred (even when not born in
Boston) spinster descendants of long lines of similarly-bred
and likewise spinster aunts and uncles whose hands knew
no callus except that of the indicting pen, to whom the
wilderness itself began at the top of tide and who looked,
if at anything other than Beacon Hill, only toward heaven
—not to mention all the loud rabble of the camp-followers
of pioneers: the bellowing of politicians, the mellifluous
choiring of self-styled men of God, the—' and McCaslin

'Here, here. Wait a minute:' and he

'Let me talk now. I'm trying to explain to the head of my family something which I have got to do which I dont quite understand myself, not in justification of it but to explain it if I can. I could say I dont know why I must do it but that I do know I have got to because I have got myself to have to live with for the rest of my life and all I want is peace to do it in. But you are the head of my family. More. I knew a long time ago that I would never have to miss my father, even if you are just finding out that you have missed your son.—the drawers of bills and the shavers of notes and the schoolmasters and the self-ordained to teach and lead and all that horde of the semi-literate with a white shirt but no change for it, with one eye on themselves and watching each other with the other one. Who else could have made them fight: could have struck them so aghast with fear and dread as to turn shoulder to shoulder and face one way and even stop talking for a while and even after two years of it keep them still so wrung with terror that some among them would seriously propose moving their very capital into a foreign country lest it be ravaged and pillaged by a people whose entire white male population would have little more than filled any one of their larger cities: except Jackson in the Valley and three separate armies trying to catch him and none of them ever knowing whether they were just retreating from a battle or just running into one and Stuart riding his whole command entirely around the biggest single armed force this continent ever saw in order to see what it looked like from behind and Morgan leading a cavalry charge against a stranded man-of-war. Who else could have declared a war against a power with ten times the area and

a hundred times the men and a thousand times the re-
sources, except men who could believe that all necessary to
conduct a successful war was not acumen nor shrewdness
nor politics nor diplomacy nor money nor even integrity
and simple arithmetic but just love of land and courage——'

'And an unblemished and gallant ancestry and the
ability to ride a horse,' McCaslin said. 'Dont leave that out.'
It was evening now, the tranquil sunset of October mazy
with windless woodsmoke. The cotton was long since picked
and ginned, and all day now the wagons loaded with gathered corn moved between field and crib, processional across
the enduring land. 'Well, maybe that's what He wanted. At
least, that's what He got.' This time there was no yellowed procession of fading and harmless ledger-pages. This
was chronicled in a harsher book and McCaslin, fourteen
and fifteen and sixteen, had seen it and the boy himself
had inherited it as Noah's grandchildren had inherited the
Flood although they had not been there to see the deluge:
that dark corrupt and bloody time while three separate
peoples had tried to adjust not only to one another but
to the new land which they had created and inherited too
and must live in for the reason that those who had lost it
were no less free to quit it than those who had gained
it were:——those upon whom freedom and equality had
been dumped overnight and without warning or prepara-
tion or any training in how to employ it or even just endure it and who misused it not as children would nor
yet because they had been so long in bondage and then so
suddenly freed, but misused it as human beings always
misuse freedom, so that he thought *Apparently there is a
wisdom beyond even that learned through suffering neces-*

sary for a man to distinguish between liberty and license;
those who had fought for four years and lost to preserve a
condition under which that franchisement was anomaly
and paradox, not because they were opposed to freedom as
freedom but for the old reasons for which man (not the
generals and politicians but man) has always fought and
died in wars: to preserve a status quo or to establish a better future one to endure for his children; and lastly, as if
that were not enough for bitterness and hatred and fear,
that third race even more alien to the people whom they
resembled in pigment and in whom even the same blood
ran, than to the people whom they did not,—that race
threefold in one and alien even among themselves save for
a single fierce will for rapine and pillage, composed of the
sons of middleaged Quartermaster lieutenants and Army
sutlers and contractors in military blankets and shoes and
transport mules, who followed the battles they themselves
had not fought and inherited the conquest they themselves
had not helped to gain, sanctioned and protected even if
not blessed, and left their bones and in another generation
would be engaged in a fierce economic competition of small
sloven farms with the black men they were supposed to
have freed and the white descendants of fathers who had
owned no slaves anyway whom they were supposed to have
disinherited and in the third generation would be back
once more in the little lost county seats as barbers and ga-
rage mechanics and deputy sheriffs and mill- and gin-hands
and power-plant firemen, leading, first in mufti then later
in an actual formalised regalia of hooded sheets and pass-
words and fiery christian symbols, lynching mobs against
the race their ancestors had come to save: and of all that
other nameless horde of speculators in human misery, ma-

nipulators of money and politics and land, who follow
catastrophe and are their own protection as grasshoppers
are and need no blessing and sweat no plow or axe-helve
and batten and vanish and leave no bones, just as they
derived apparently from no ancestry, no mortal flesh, no
act even of passion or even of lust: and the Jew who came
without protection too since after two thousand years he
had got out of the habit of being or needing it, and solitary, without even the solidarity of the locusts and in this
a sort of courage since he had come thinking not in terms
of simple pillage but in terms of his great-grandchildren,
seeking yet some place to establish them to endure even
though forever alien: and unblessed: a pariah about the
face of the Western earth which twenty centuries later
was still taking revenge on him for the fairy tale with
which he had conquered it. McCaslin had actually seen it,
and the boy even at almost eighty would never be able
to distinguish certainly between what he had seen and
what had been told him: a lightless and gutted and empty
land where women crouched with the huddled children
behind locked doors and men armed in sheets and masks
rode the silent roads and the bodies of white and black
both, victims not so much of hate as of desperation and
despair, swung from lonely limbs: and men shot dead in
polling-booths with the still wet pen in one hand and the
unblotted ballot in the other: and a United States marshal
in Jefferson who signed his official papers with a crude
cross, an ex-slave called Sickymo, not at all because his
ex-owner was a doctor and apothecary but because, still
a slave, he would steal his master's grain alcohol and di-
lute it with water and peddle it in pint bottles from a
cache beneath the roots of a big sycamore tree behind the

drug store, who had attained his high office because his half-white sister was the concubine of the Federal A.P.M.: and this time McCaslin did not even say Look but merely lifted one hand, not even pointing, not even specifically toward the shelf of ledgers but toward the desk, toward the corner where it sat beside the scuffed patch on the floor where two decades of heavy shoes had stood while the white man at the desk added and multiplied and subtracted. And again he did not need to look because he had seen this himself and, twenty-three years after the Surrender and twenty-four after the Proclamation, was still watching it: the ledgers, new ones now and filled rapidly, succeeding one another rapidly · and containing more names than old Carothers or even his father and Uncle Buddy had ever dreamed of; new names and new faces to go with them, among which the old names and faces that even his father and uncle would have recognised, were lost, vanished—Tomey's Terrel dead, and even the tragic and miscast Percival Brownlee, who couldn't keep books and couldn't farm either, found his true niche at last, reappeared in 1862 during the boy's father's absence and had apparently been living on the plantation for at least a month before his uncle found out about it, conducting impromptu revival meetings among negroes, preaching and leading the singing also in his high sweet true soprano voice and disappeared again on foot and at top speed, not behind but ahead of a body of raiding Federal horse and reappeared for the third and last time in the entourage of a travelling Army paymaster, the two of them passing through Jefferson in a surrey at the exact moment when the boy's father (it was 1866) also happened to be crossing the Square, the surrey and its occu-

pants traversing rapidly that quiet and bucolic scene and
even in that fleeting moment and to others beside the
boy's father giving an illusion of flight and illicit holiday
like a man on an excursion during his wife's absence with
his wife's personal maid, until Brownlee glanced up and
saw his late co-master and gave him one defiant female
glance and then broke again, leaped from the surrey and
disappeared this time for good and it was only by chance
that McCaslin, twenty years later, heard of him again,
an old man now and quite fat, as the well-to-do proprietor
of a select New Orleans brothel; and Tennie's Jim gone,
nobody knew where, and Fonsiba in Arkansas with her
three dollars each month and the scholar-husband with
his lenseless spectacles and frock coat and his plans for
the spring; and only Lucas was left, the baby, the last
save himself of old Carothers' doomed and fatal blood
which in the male derivation seemed to destroy all it
touched, and even he was repudiating and at least hoping
to escape it;—Lucas, the boy of fourteen whose name
would not even appear for six years yet among those rapid
pages in the bindings new and dustless too since McCaslin
lifted them down daily now to write into them the continu-
ation of that record which two hundred years had not been
enough to complete and another hundred would not be
enough to discharge; that chronicle which was a whole
land in miniature, which multiplied and compounded was
the entire South, twenty-three years after surrender and
twenty-four from emancipation—that slow trickle of molasses and meal and meat, of shoes and straw hats and overalls, of plowlines and collars and heel-bolts and buckheads
and clevises, which returned each fall as cotton—the two
threads frail as truth and impalpable as equators yet cable-

strong to bind for life them who made the cotton to the land their sweat fell on: and he

'Yes. Binding them for a while yet, a little while yet. Through and beyond that life and maybe through and beyond the life of that life's sons and maybe even through and beyond that of the sons of those sons. But not always, because they will endure. They will outlast us because they are—' it was not a pause, barely a falter even, possibly appreciable only to himself, as if he couldn't speak even to McCaslin, even to explain his repudiation, that which to him too, even in the act of escaping (and maybe this was the reality and the truth of his need to escape) was heresy: so that even in escaping he was taking with him more of that evil and unregenerate old man who could summon, because she was his property, a human being because she was old enough and female, to his widower's house and get a child on her and then dismiss her because she was of an inferior race, and then bequeath a thousand dollars to the infant because he would be dead then and wouldn't have to pay it, than even he had feared. 'Yes. He didn't want to. He had to. Because they will endure. They are better than we are. Stronger than we are. Their vices are vices aped from white men or that white men and bondage have taught them: improvidence and intemperance and evasion—not laziness: evasion: of what white men had set them to, not for their aggrandisement or even comfort but his own—' and McCaslin

'All right. Go on: Promiscuity. Violence. Instability and lack of control. Inability to distinguish between mine and thine—' and he

'How distinguish, when for two hundred years mine did not even exist for them?' and McCaslin

'All right. Go on. And their virtues—' and he

'Yes. Their own. Endurance—' and McCaslin

'So have mules:' and he

'—and pity and tolerance and forbearance and fidelity
and love of children—' and McCaslin

'So have dogs:' and he

'—whether their own or not or black or not. And more:
what they got not only not from white people but not
even despite white people because they had it already
from the old free fathers a longer time free than us because we have never been free—' and it was in McCaslin's
eyes too, he had only to look at McCaslin's eyes and it
was there, that summer twilight seven years ago, almost a
week after they had returned from the camp before he
discovered that Sam Fathers had told McCaslin: an old
bear, fierce and ruthless not just to stay alive but ruthless
with the fierce pride of liberty and freedom, jealous and
proud enough of liberty and freedom to see it threatened
not with fear nor even alarm but almost with joy, seeming
deliberately to put it into jeopardy in order to savor it and
keep his old strong bones and flesh supple and quick to
defend and preserve it; an old man, son of a Negro slave
and an Indian king, inheritor on the one hand of the long
chronicle of a people who had learned humility through
suffering and learned pride through the endurance which
survived the suffering, and on the other side the chronicle
of a people even longer in the land than the first, yet who
now existed there only in the solitary brotherhood of an
old and childless Negro's alien blood and the wild and
invincible spirit of an old bear; a boy who wished to learn
humility and pride in order to become skillful and worthy
in the woods but found himself becoming so skillful so

fast that he feared he would never become worthy because
he had not learned humility and pride though he had tried,
until one day an old man who could not have defined either
led him as though by the hand to where an old bear and
a little mongrel dog showed him that, by possessing one
thing other, he would possess them both; and a little dog,
nameless and mongrel and many-fathered, grown yet
weighing less than six pounds, who couldn't be dangerous because there was nothing anywhere much smaller,
not fierce because that would have been called just noise,
not humble because it was already too near the ground to
genuflect, and not proud because it would not have been
close enough for anyone to discern what was casting that
shadow and which didn't even know it was not going to
heaven since they had already decided it had no immortal
soul, so that all it could be was brave even though they
would probably call that too just noise. 'And you didn't
shoot,' McCaslin said. 'How close were you?'

'I dont know,' he said. 'There was a big wood tick just
inside his off hind leg. I saw that. But I didn't have the
gun then.'

'But you didn't shoot when you had the gun,' McCaslin
said. 'Why?' But McCaslin didn't wait, rising and crossing
the room, across the pelt of the bear he had killed two
years ago and the bigger one McCaslin had killed before
he was born, to the bookcase beneath the mounted head
of his first buck, and returned with the book and sat down
again and opened it. 'Listen,' he said. He read the five
stanzas aloud and closed the book on his finger and looked
up. 'All right,' he said. 'Listen,' and read again, but only
one stanza this time and closed the book and laid it on the

table. 'She cannot fade, though thou hast not thy bliss,'
McCaslin said: 'Forever wilt thou love, and she be fair.'

'He's talking about a girl,' he said.

'He had to talk about something,' McCaslin said. Then
he said, 'He was talking about truth. Truth is one. It
doesn't change. It covers all things which touch the heart
—honor and pride and pity and justice and courage and
love. Do you see now?' He didn't know. Somehow it had
seemed simpler than that, simpler than somebody talking
in a book about a young man and a girl he would never
need to grieve over because he could never approach any
nearer and would never have to get any further away. He
had heard about an old bear and finally got big enough to
hunt it and he hunted it four years and at last met it with
a gun in his hands and he didn't shoot. Because a little dog
—But he could have shot long before the fyce covered the
twenty yards to where the bear waited, and Sam Fathers
could have shot at any time during the interminable minute
while Old Ben stood on his hind legs over them. . . . He
ceased. McCaslin watched him, still speaking, the voice,
the words as quiet as the twilight itself was: 'Courage and
honor and pride, and pity and love of justice and of liberty.
They all touch the heart, and what the heart holds to be-
comes truth, as far as we know truth. Do you see now?'
and he could still hear them, intact in this twilight as in
that one seven years ago, no louder still because they did
not need to be because they would endure: and he had
only to look at McCaslin's eyes beyond the thin and bitter
smiling, the faint lip-lift which would have had to be
called smiling;—his kinsman, his father almost, who had
been born too late into the old time and too soon for the
new, the two of them juxtaposed and alien now to each

other against their ravaged patrimony, the dark and ravaged
fatherland still prone and panting from its etherless operation:

'Habet then.—So this land is, indubitably, of and by
itself cursed:' and he

'Cursed:' and again McCaslin merely lifted one hand,
not even speaking and not even toward the ledgers: so that,
as the stereopticon condenses into one instantaneous field
the myriad minutia of its scope, so did that slight and
rapid gesture establish in the small cramped and cluttered
twilit room not only the ledgers but the whole plantation
in its mazed and intricate entirety—the land, the fields
and what they represented in terms of cotton ginned and
sold, the men and women whom they fed and clothed and
even paid a little cash money at Christmas-time in return
for the labor which planted and raised and picked and
ginned the cotton, the machinery and mules and gear with
which they raised it and their cost and upkeep and re-
placement—that whole edifice intricate and complex and
founded upon injustice and erected by ruthless rapacity
and carried on even yet with at times downright savagery
not only to the human beings but the valuable animals too,
yet solvent and efficient and, more than that: not only still
intact but enlarged, increased; brought still intact by Mc-
Caslin, himself little more than a child then, through and
out of the debacle and chaos of twenty years ago where
hardly one in ten survived, and enlarged and increased
and would continue so, solvent and efficient and intact and
still increasing so long as McCaslin and his McCaslin successors lasted, even though their surnames might not even
be Edmonds then: and he: 'Habet too. Because that's it:
not the land, but us. Not only the blood, but the name

too; not only its color but its designation: Edmonds, white, but, a female line, could have no other but the name his father bore; Beauchamp, the elder line and the male one, but, black, could have had any name he liked and no man would have cared, except the name his father bore who had no name—' and McCaslin

'And since I know too what you know I will say now, once more let me say it: And one other, and in the third generation too, and the male, the eldest, the direct and sole and white and still McCaslin even, father to son to son—' and he

'I am free:' and this time McCaslin did not even gesture, no inference of fading pages, no postulation of the stereoptic whole, but the frail and iron thread strong as truth and impervious as evil and longer than life itself and reaching beyond record and patrimony both to join him with the lusts and passions, the hopes and dreams and griefs, of bones whose names while still fleshed and capable even old Carothers' grandfather had never heard: and he: 'And of that too:' and McCaslin

'Chosen, I suppose (I will concede it) out of all your time by Him as you say Buck and Buddy were from theirs. And it took Him a bear and an old man and four years just for you. And it took you fourteen years to reach that point and about that many, maybe more, for Old Ben, and more than seventy for Sam Fathers. And you are just one. How long then? How long?' and he

'It will be long. I have never said otherwise. But it will be all right because they will endure—' and McCaslin

'And anyway, you will be free.—No, not now nor ever, we from them nor they from us. So I repudiate too. I would deny even if I knew it were true. I would have to. Even

you can see that I could do no else. I am what I am; I will
be always what I was born and have always been. And
more than me. More than me, just as there were more
than Buck and Buddy in what you called His first plan
which failed:' and he

'And more than me:' and McCaslin

'No. Not even you. Because mark. You said how on that
instant when Ikkemotubbe realised that he could sell the
land to Grandfather, it ceased forever to have been his.
All right; go on: Then it belonged to Sam Fathers, old
Ikkemotubbe's son. And who inherited from Sam Fathers,
if not you? co-heir perhaps with Boon, if not of his life
maybe, at least of his quitting it?' and he

'Yes. Sam Fathers set me free.' And Isaac McCaslin, not
yet Uncle Ike, a long time yet before he would be uncle
to half a county and still father to none, living in one
small cramped fireless rented room in a Jefferson boarding-
house where petit juries were domiciled during court terms
and itinerant horse- and mule-traders stayed, with his kit
of brand-new carpenter's tools and the shotgun McCaslin
had given him with his name engraved in silver and old
General Compson's compass (and, when the General died,
his silver-mounted horn too) and the iron cot and mattress
and the blankets which he would take each fall into the
woods for more than sixty years and the bright tin coffee-
pot

there had been a legacy, from his Uncle Hubert Beauchamp, his godfather, that bluff burly roaring childlike
man from whom Uncle Buddy had won Tomey's Terrel's
wife Tennie in the poker-game in 1859—'posible strait
against three Treys in sigt Not called'—; no pale sentence
or paragraph scrawled in cringing fear of death by a weak

and trembling hand as a last desperate sop flung backward
at retribution, but a Legacy, a Thing, possessing weight to
the hand and bulk to the eye and even audible: a silver
cup filled with gold pieces and wrapped in burlap and
sealed with his godfather's ring in the hot wax, which
(intact still) even before his Uncle Hubert's death and
long before his own majority, when it would be his, had
become not only a legend but one of the family lares.
After his father's and his Uncle Hubert's sister's marriage
they moved back into the big house, the tremendous cavern which old Carothers had started and never finished,
cleared the remaining negroes out of it and with his
mother's dowry completed it, at least the rest of the windows and doors and moved into it, all of them save Uncle
Buddy who declined to leave the cabin he and his twin
had built, the move being the bride's notion and more than
just a notion and none ever to know if she really wanted to
live in the big house or if she knew before hand that Uncle
Buddy would refuse to move: and two weeks after his
birth in 1867, the first time he and his mother came down
stairs, one night and the silver cup sitting on the cleared
dining-room table beneath the bright lamp and while his
mother and his father and McCaslin and Tennie (his
nurse: carrying him)—all of them again but Uncle Buddy
—watched, his Uncle Hubert rang one by one into the
cup the bright and glinting mintage and wrapped it into
the burlap envelope and heated the wax and sealed it and
carried it back home with him where he lived alone now
without even his sister either to hold him down as Mc-
Caslin said or to try to raise him up as Uncle Buddy said,
and (dark times then in Mississippi) Uncle Buddy said
most of the niggers gone and the ones that didn't go even

Hub Beauchamp could not have wanted: but the dogs remained and Uncle Buddy said Beauchamp fiddled while
Nero fox-hunted

they would go and see it there; at last his mother would
prevail and they would depart in the surrey, once more all
save Uncle Buddy and McCaslin to keep Uncle Buddy
company until one winter Uncle Buddy began to fail and
from then on it was himself, beginning to remember now,
and his mother and Tennie and Tomey's Terrel to drive:
the twenty-two miles into the next county, the twin gate-
posts on one of which McCaslin could remember the half-
grown boy blowing a fox-horn at breakfast dinner and sup-
per-time and jumping down to open to any passer who
happened to hear it but where there were no gates at all
now, the shabby and overgrown entrance to what his
mother still insisted that people call Warwick because her
brother was if truth but triumphed and justice but pre-
vailed the rightful earl of it, the paintless house which outwardly did not change but which on the inside seemed
each time larger because he was too little to realise then
that there was less and less in it of the fine furnishings, the
rosewood and mahogany and walnut which for him had
never existed anywhere anyway save in his mother's tear-
ful lamentations and the occasional piece small enough to
be roped somehow onto the rear or the top of the carriage
on their return (And he remembered this, he had seen it:
an instant, a flash, his mother's soprano 'Even my dress!
Even my dress!' loud and outraged in the barren unswept
hall; a face young and female and even lighter in color
than Tomey's Terrel's for an instant in a closing door; a
swirl, a glimpse of the silk gown and the flick and glint of
an ear-ring: an apparition rapid and tawdry and illicit yet

somehow even to the child, the infant still almost, breathless and exciting and evocative: as though, like two limpid
and pellucid streams meeting, the child which he still was
had made serene and absolute and perfect rapport and
contact through that glimpsed nameless illicit hybrid female
flesh with the boy which had existed at that stage of inviolable and immortal adolescence in his uncle for almost
sixty years; the dress, the face, the ear-rings gone in that
same aghast flash and his uncle's voice: 'She's my cook!
She's my new cook! I had to have a cook, didn't I?' then
the uncle himself, the face alarmed and aghast too yet still
innocently and somehow even indomitably of a boy, they
retreating in their turn now, back to the front gallery, and
his uncle again, pained and still amazed, in a sort of desperate resurgence if not of courage at least of self-assertion:
'They're free now! They're folks too just like we are!' and
his mother: 'That's why! That's why! My mother's house!
Defiled! Defiled!' and his uncle: 'Damn it, Sibbey, at least
give her time to pack her grip:' then over, finished, the
loud uproar and all, himself and Tennie and he remembered Tennie's inscrutable face at the broken shutterless
window of the bare room which had once been the parlor
while they watched, hurrying down the lane at a stumbling
trot, the routed compounder of his uncle's uxory: the back,
the nameless face which he had seen only for a moment,
the once-hooped dress ballooning and flapping below a man's
overcoat, the worn heavy carpet-bag jouncing and banging
against her knee, routed and in retreat true enough and
in the empty lane solitary young-looking and forlorn yet
withal still exciting and evocative and wearing still the
silken banner captured inside the very citadel of respect-
ability, and unforgettable.)

the cup, the sealed inscrutable burlap, sitting on the shelf in the locked closet, Uncle Hubert unlocking the door and lifting it down and passing it from hand to hand: his mother, his father, McCaslin and even Tennie, insisting that each take it in turn and heft it for weight and shake it again to prove the sound, Uncle Hubert himself standing spraddled before the cold unswept hearth in which the very bricks themselves were crumbling into a litter of soot and dust and mortar and the droppings of chimneysweeps, still roaring and still innocent and still indomitable: and for a long time he believed nobody but himself had noticed that his uncle now put the cup only into his hands, unlocked the door and lifted it down and put it into his hands and stood over him until he had shaken it obediently until it sounded then took it from him and locked it back into the closet before anyone else could have offered to touch it, and even later, when competent not only to remember but to rationalise, he could not say what it was or even if it had been anything because the parcel was still heavy and still rattled, not even when, Uncle Buddy dead and his father, at last and after almost seventy-five years in bed after the sun rose, said: 'Go get that damn cup. Bring that damn Hub Beauchamp too if you have to:' because it still rattled though his uncle no longer put it even into his hands now but carried it himself from one to the other, his mother, McCaslin, Tennie, shaking it before each in turn, saying: 'Hear it? Hear it?' his face still innocent, not quite baffled but only amazed and not very amazed and still indomitable: and, his father and Uncle Buddy both gone now, one day without reason or any warning the almost completely empty house in which his uncle and Tennie's ancient and quarrelsome great-

grandfather (who claimed to have seen Lafayette and
McCaslin said in another ten years would be remembering
God) lived, cooked and slept in one single room, burst
into peaceful conflagration, a tranquil instantaneous sourceless unanimity of combustion, walls floors and roof: at
sunup it stood where his uncle's father had built it sixty
years ago, at sundown the four blackened and smokeless
chimneys rose from a light white powder of ashes and a
few charred ends of planks which did not even appear to
have been very hot: and out of the last of evening, the last
one of the twenty-two miles, on the old white mare which
was the last of that stable which McCaslin remembered,
the two old men riding double up to the sister's door, the
one wearing his fox-horn on its braided deerhide thong
and the other carrying the burlap parcel wrapped in a
shirt, the tawny wax-daubed shapeless lump sitting again
and on an almost identical shelf and his uncle holding the
half-opened door now, his hand not only on the knob but
one foot against it and the key waiting in the other hand,
the face urgent and still not baffled but still and even indomitably not very amazed and himself standing in the
half-opened door looking quietly up at the burlap shape
become almost three times its original height and a good
half less than its original thickness and turning away and
he would remember not his mother's look this time nor yet
Tennie's inscrutable expression but McCaslin's dark and
aquiline face grave insufferable and bemused: then one
night they waked him and fetched him still half-asleep into
the lamp light, the smell of medicine which was familiar
by now in that room and the smell of something else which
he had not smelled before and knew at once and would
never forget, the pillow, the worn and ravaged face from

which looked out still the boy innocent and immortal and
amazed and urgent, looking at him and trying to tell him
until McCaslin moved and leaned over the bed and drew
from the top of the night shirt the big iron key on the greasy
cord which suspended it, the eyes saying Yes Yes Yes now,
and cut the cord and unlocked the closet and brought the
parcel to the bed, the eyes still trying to tell him even when
he took the parcel so that was still not it, the hands still clinging to the parcel even while relinquishing it, the eyes more
urgent than ever trying to tell him but they never did;
and he was ten and his mother was dead too and McCaslin said, 'You are almost halfway now. You might as well
open it:' and he: 'No. He said twenty-one:' and he was
twenty-one and McCaslin shifted the bright lamp to the
center of the cleared dining-room table and set the parcel
beside it and laid his open knife beside the parcel and stood
back with that expression of old grave intolerant and repudiating and he lifted it, the burlap lump which fifteen
years ago had changed its shape completely overnight,
which shaken gave forth a thin weightless not-quite-musical
curiously muffled clatter, the bright knife-blade hunting
amid the mazed intricacy of string, the knobby gouts of
wax bearing his uncle's Beauchamp seal rattling onto the
table's polished top and, standing amid the collapse of burlap folds, the unstained tin coffee-pot still brand new, the
handful of copper coins and now he knew what had given
them the muffled sound: a collection of minutely-folded
scraps of paper sufficient almost for a rat's nest, of good
linen bond, of the crude ruled paper such as negroes use,
of raggedly-torn ledger-pages and the margins of news-
papers and once the paper label from a new pair of overalls, all dated and all signed, beginning with the first one

not six months after they had watched him seal the silver cup into the burlap on this same table in this same room by the light even of this same lamp almost twenty-one years ago:

> *I owe my Nephew Isaac Beauchamp McCaslin five (5) pieces Gold which I.O.U constitues My note of hand with Interest at 5 percent.*
>
> > *Hubert Fitz-Hubert Beauchamp*
>
> *at Warwick 27 Nov 1867*

and he: 'Anyway he called it Warwick:' once at least, even if no more. But there was more:

> *Isaac 24 Dec 1867 I.O.U. 2 pieces Gold H.Fh.B.*
> *I.O.U. Isaac 1 piece Gold 1 Jan 1868 H.Fh.B.*

then five again then three then one then one then a long time and what dream, what dreamed splendid recoup, not of any injury or betrayal of trust because it had been merely a loan: nay, a partnership:

> *I.O.U. Beauchamp McCaslin or his heirs twenty-five (25) pieces Gold This & All preceeding constituting My notes of hand at twenty (20) percentum compounded annually. This date of 19th January 1873*
>
> > *Beauchamp*

no location save that in time and signed by the single not name but word as the old proud earl himself might have scrawled Nevile: and that made forty-three and he could not remember himself of course but the legend had it at fifty, which balanced: one: then one: then one: then one and then the last three and then the last chit, dated after he came to live in the house with them and written in the shaky hand not of a beaten old man because he had never been beaten to know it but of a tired old man maybe and even at that tired only on the outside and still indomitable, the simplicity of the last one the simplicity not of resignation but merely of amazement, like a simple comment or remark, and not very much of that:

> *One silver cup. Hubert Beauchamp*

and McCaslin: 'So you have plenty of coppers anyway. But they are still not old enough yet to be either rarities or heirlooms. So you will have to take the money:' except that he didn't hear McCaslin, standing quietly beside the table and looking peacefully at the coffee-pot and the pot sitting one night later on the mantel above what was not even a fireplace in the little cramped icelike room in Jefferson as McCaslin tossed the folded banknotes onto the bed and, still standing (there was nowhere to sit save on the bed) did not even remove his hat and overcoat: and he

'As a loan. From you. This one:' and McCaslin

'You cant. I have no money that I can lend to you. And you will have to go to the bank and get it next month because I wont bring it to you:' and he could not hear Mc-Caslin now either, looking peacefully at McCaslin, his kinsman, his father almost yet no kin now as, at the last, even fathers and sons are no kin: and he

'It's seventeen miles, horseback and in the cold. We could both sleep here:' and McCaslin

'Why should I sleep here in my house when you wont sleep yonder in yours?' and gone, and he looking at the bright rustless unstained tin and thinking and not for the first time how much it takes to compound a man (Isaac McCaslin for instance) and of the devious intricate choosing yet unerring path that man's (Isaac McCaslin's for instance) spirit takes among all that mass to make him at last what he is to be, not only to the astonishment of them (the ones who sired the McCaslin who sired his father and Uncle Buddy and their sister, and the ones who sired the Beauchamp who sired his Uncle Hubert and his Uncle Hubert's sister) who believed they had shaped him, but to Isaac McCaslin too

as a loan and used it though he would not have had to: Major de Spain offered him a room in his house as long as he wanted it and asked nor would ever ask any question, and old General Compson more than that, to take him into his own room, to sleep in half of his own bed and more than Major de Spain because he told him baldly why: 'You sleep with me and before this winter is out, I'll know the reason. You'll tell me. Because I dont believe you just quit. It looks like you just quit but I have watched you in the woods too much and I dont believe you just quit even if it does look damn like it:' using it as a loan, paid his board and rent for a month and bought the tools, not simply because he was good with his hands because he had intended to use his hands and it could have been with horses, and not in mere static and hopeful emulation of the Nazarene as the young gambler buys a spotted shirt because the old gambler won in one yesterday, but (without the arrogance of false humility and without the false humbleness of pride, who intended to earn his bread, didn't especially want to earn it but had to earn it and for more than just bread) because if the Nazarene had found carpentering good for the life and ends He had assumed and elected to serve, it would be all right too for Isaac McCaslin even though Isaac McCaslin's ends, although simple enough in their apparent motivation, were and would be always incomprehensible to him, and his life, invincible enough in its needs, if he could have helped himself, not being the Nazarene, he would not have chosen it: and paid it back. He had forgotten the thirty dollars which McCaslin would put into the bank in his name each month, fetched it in to him and flung it onto the bed that first one time but no more; he had a partner now or rather he was the partner: a blasphemous profane clever old dipsomaniac who had built blockade-runners in Charleston in '62 and '3 and had been a ship's carpenter since and appeared in Jefferson two years ago nobody knew from where nor why and spent a good part of his time since recovering from delirium tremens in the jail; they had put a new roof on the stable of the bank's president and (the old man in jail again still celebrating that job) he went to the bank to collect for it and the president said, 'I should borrow from you instead of paying you:' and it had been seven months now and he remembered for the first time, two-hundred-and-ten dollars, and this was the first job of any size and when he left the bank the account stood at two-twenty, two-forty to balance, only twenty dollars more to go, then it did balance though by then the total had increased to three hundred and thirty and he said, 'I will transfer it now:' and the president said, 'I cant do that. McCaslin told me not to. Haven't you got another initial you could use and open another account?' but that was all right, the coins the silver and the bills as they accumulated knotted into a handkerchief and the coffee-pot wrapped in an old shirt as when Tennie's great-grandfather had fetched it from Warwick eighteen years ago, in the bottom of the iron-bound trunk which old Carothers had brought from Carolina and his landlady said,

'Not even a lock! And you dont even lock your door, not even when you leave!' and himself looking at her as peacefully as he had looked at McCaslin that first night in this same room, no kin to him at all yet more than kin as those who serve you even for pay are your kin and those who injure you are more than brother or wife

and had the wife now, got the old man out of jail and fetched him to the rented room and sobered him by superior strength, did not even remove his own shoes for twentyfour hours, got him up and got food into him and they built the barn this time from the ground up and he married her: an only child, a small girl yet curiously bigger than she seemed at first, solider perhaps, with dark eyes and a passionate heart-shaped face, who had time even on that farm to watch most of the day while he sawed timbers to the old man's measurements: and she: 'Papa told me about you. That farm is really yours, isn't it?' and he

'And McCaslin's:' and she

'Was there a will leaving half of it to him?' and he

'There didn't need to be a will. His grandmother was my father's sister. We were the same as brothers:' and she

'You are the same as second cousins and that's all you ever will be. But I dont suppose it matters:' and they were married, they were married and it was the new country, his heritage too as it was the heritage of all, out of the earth, beyond the earth yet of the earth because his too was of the earth's long chronicle, his too because each must share with another in order to come into it and in the sharing they become one: for that while, one: for that little while at least, one: indivisible, that while at least irrevocable and unrecoverable, living in a rented room still but for just a little while and that room wall-less and top-

less and floorless in glory for him to leave each morning and
return to at night; her father already owned the lot in
town and furnished the material and he and his partner
would build it, her dowry from one:. her wedding-present
from three, she not to know it until the bungalow was
finished and ready to be moved into and he never know
who told her, not her father and not his partner and not
even in drink though for a while he believed that, himself
coming home from work and just time to wash and rest a
moment before going down to supper, entering no rented
cubicle since it would still partake of glory even after they
would have grown old and lost it: and he saw her face
then, just before she spoke: 'Sit down:' the two of them
sitting on the bed's edge, not even touching yet, her face
strained and terrible, her voice a passionate and expiring
whisper of immeasurable promise: 'I love you. You know
I love you. When are we going to move?' and he

'I didn't—I didn't know—Who told you—' the hot fierce
palm clapped over his mouth, crushing his lips into his
teeth, the fierce curve of fingers digging into his cheek and
only the palm slacked off enough for him to answer:

'The farm. Our farm. Your farm:' and he

'I—' then the hand again, finger and palm, the whole
enveloping weight of her although she still was not touching him save the hand, the voice: 'No! No!' and the fingers
themselves seeming to follow through the cheek the im-
pulse to speech as it died in his mouth, then the whisper,
the breath again, of love and of incredible promise, the
palm slackening again to let him answer:

'When?' and he

'I—' then she was gone, the hand too, standing, her back
to him and her head bent, the voice so calm now that for

an instant it seemed no voice of hers that he ever remembered: 'Stand up and turn your back and shut your eyes:'
and repeated before he understood and stood himself with
his eyes shut and heard the bell ring for supper below stairs
and the calm voice again: 'Lock the door:' and he did so
and leaned his forehead against the cold wood, his eyes
closed, hearing his heart and the sound he had begun to
hear before he moved until it ceased and the bell rang again
below stairs and he knew it was for them this time and he
heard the bed and turned and he had never seen her naked
before, he had asked her to once, and why: that he wanted
to see her naked because he loved her and he wanted to
see her looking at him naked because he loved her but
after that he never mentioned it again, even turning his
face when she put the nightgown on over her dress to
undress at night and putting the dress on over the gown
to remove it in the morning and she would not let him get
into bed beside her until the lamp was out and even in
the heat of summer she would draw the sheet up over them
both before she would let him turn to her: and the landlady came up the stairs up the hall and rapped on the door
and then called their names but she didn't move, lying still
on the bed outside the covers, her face turned away on the
pillow, listening to nothing, thinking of nothing, not of him
anyway he thought then the landlady went away and she
said, 'Take off your clothes:' her head still turned away,
looking at nothing, thinking of nothing, waiting for nothing, not even him, her hand moving as though with volition and vision of its own, catching his wrist at the exact
moment when he paused beside the bed so that he never
paused but merely changed the direction of moving, downward now, the hand drawing him and she moved at last,

shifted, a movement one single complete inherent not practiced and one time older than man, looking at him now, drawing him still downward with the one hand down and down and he neither saw nor felt it shift, palm flat against his chest now and holding him away with the same apparent lack of any effort or any need for strength, and not looking at him now, she didn't need to, the chaste woman, the wife, already looked upon all the men who ever rutted and now her whole body had changed, altered, he had never seen it but once and now it was not even the one he had seen but composite of all woman-flesh since man that ever of its own will reclined on its back and opened, and out of it somewhere, without any movement of lips even, the dying and invincible whisper: 'Promise:' and he

'Promise?'

'The farm.' He moved. He had moved, the hand shifting from his chest once more to his wrist, grasping it, the arm still lax and only the light increasing pressure of the fingers as though arm and hand were a piece of wire cable with one looped end, only the hand tightening as he pulled against it. 'No,' he said. 'No:' and she was not looking at him still but not like the other but still the hand: 'No, I tell you. I wont. I cant. Never:' and still the hand and he said, for the last time, he tried to speak clearly and he knew it was still gently and he thought, *She already knows more than I with all the man-listening in camps where there was nothing to read ever even heard of. They are born already bored with what a boy approaches only at fourteen and fifteen with blundering and aghast trembling:* 'I cant. Not ever. Remember:' and still the steady and invincible hand and he said Yes and he thought, *She is lost. She was born lost. We were all born lost* then he stopped

thinking and even saying Yes, it was like nothing he had
ever dreamed, let alone heard in mere man-talking until
after a no-time he returned and lay spent on the insatiate
immemorial beach and again with a movement one time
more older than man she turned and freed herself and on
their wedding night she had cried and he thought she was
crying now at first, into the tossed and wadded pillow, the
voice coming from somewhere between the pillow and the
cachinnation: 'And that's all. That's all from me. If this
dont get you that son you talk about, it wont be mine:'
lying on her side, her back to the empty rented room,
laughing and laughing

5.

He went back to the camp one more time before the
lumber company moved in and began to cut the timber.
Major de Spain himself never saw it again. But he made
them welcome to use the house and hunt the land whenever they liked, and in the winter following the last hunt
when Sam Fathers and Lion died, General Compson and
Walter Ewell invented a plan to corporate themselves, the
old group, into a club and lease the camp and the hunting
privileges of the woods—an invention doubtless of the
somewhat childish old General but actually worthy of
Boon Hogganbeck himself. Even the boy, listening, recognised it for the subterfuge it was: to change the leopard's
spots when they could not alter the leopard, a baseless and
illusory hope to which even McCaslin seemed to subscribe
for a while, that once they had persuaded Major de Spain
to return to the camp he might revoke himself, which even
the boy knew he would not do. And he did not. The boy

never knew what occurred when Major de Spain declined. He was not present when the subject was broached and McCaslin never told him. But when June came and the time for the double birthday celebration there was no mention of it and when November came no one spoke of using Major de Spain's house and he never knew whether or not Major de Spain knew they were going on the hunt though without doubt old Ash probably told him: he and McCaslin and General Compson (and that one was the General's last hunt too) and Walter and Boon and Tennie's Jim and old Ash loaded two wagons and drove two days and almost forty miles beyond any country the boy had ever seen before and lived in tents for the two weeks. And the next spring they heard (not from Major de Spain) that he had sold the timber-rights to a Memphis lumber company and in June the boy came to town with McCaslin one Saturday and went to Major de Spain's office—the big, airy, book-lined second-storey room with windows at one end opening upon the shabby hinder purlieus of stores and at the other a door giving onto the railed balcony above the Square, with its curtained alcove where sat a cedar water-bucket and a sugar-bowl and spoon and tumbler and a wicker-covered demijohn of whiskey, and the bamboo-and-paper punkah swinging back and forth above the desk while old Ash in a tilted chair beside the entrance pulled the cord.

"Of course," Major de Spain said. "Ash will probably like to get off in the woods himself for a while, where he wont have to eat Daisy's cooking. Complain about it, anyway. Are you going to take anybody with you?"

"No sir," he said. "I thought that maybe Boon—" For six months now Boon had been town-marshall at Hoke's;

Major de Spain had compounded with the lumber company—or perhaps compromised was closer, since it was the lumber company who had decided that Boon might be better as a town-marshall than head of a logging gang.

"Yes," Major de Spain said. "I'll wire him today. He can meet you at Hoke's. I'll send Ash on by the train and they can take some food in and all you will have to do will be to mount your horse and ride over."

"Yes sir," he said. "Thank you." And he heard his voice again. He didn't know he was going to say it yet he did know, he had known it all the time: "Maybe if you . . ." His voice died. It was stopped, he never knew how because Major de Spain did not speak and it was not until his voice ceased that Major de Spain moved, turned back to the desk and the papers spread on it and even that without moving because he was sitting at the desk with a paper in his hand when the boy entered, the boy standing there looking down at the short plumpish grey-haired man in sober fine broadcloth and an immaculate glazed shirt whom he was used to seeing in boots and muddy corduroy, unshaven, sitting the shaggy powerful long-hocked mare with the worn Winchester carbine across the saddlebow and the great blue dog standing motionless as bronze at the stirrup, the two of them in that last year and to the boy anyway coming to resemble one another somehow as two people competent for love or for business who have been in love or in business together for a long time sometimes do. Major de Spain did not look up again.

"No. I will be too busy. But good luck to you. If you have it, you might bring me a young squirrel."

"Yes sir," he said. "I will."

He rode his mare, the three-year-old filly he had bred

and raised and broken himself. He left home a little after
midnight and six hours later, without even having sweated
her, he rode into Hoke's, the tiny log-line junction which
he had always thought of as Major de Spain's property too
although Major de Spain had merely sold the company
(and that many years ago) the land on which the sidetracks
and loading-platforms and the commissary store stood, and
looked about in shocked and grieved amazement even
though he had had forewarning and had believed himself
prepared: a new planing-mill already half completed which
would cover two or three acres and what looked like miles
and miles of stacked steel rails red with the light bright
rust of newness and of piled crossties sharp with creosote,
and wire corrals and feeding-troughs for two hundred
mules at least and the tents for the men who drove them;
so that he arranged for the care and stabling of his mare as
rapidly as he could and did not look any more, mounted
into the log-train caboose with his gun and climbed into
the cupola and looked no more save toward the wall of
wilderness ahead within which he would be able to hide
himself from it once more anyway.

Then the little locomotive shrieked and began to move:
a rapid churning of exhaust, a lethargic deliberate clashing of slack couplings traveling backward along the train,
the exhaust changing to the deep slow clapping bites of
power as the caboose too began to move and from the
cupola he watched the train's head complete the first and
only curve in the entire line's length and vanish into the
wilderness, dragging its length of train behind it so that
it resembled a small dingy harmless snake vanishing into
weeds, drawing him with it too until soon it ran once more
at its maximum clattering speed between the twin walls of

unaxed wilderness as of old. It had been harmless once.
Not five years ago Walter Ewell had shot a six-point buck
from this same moving caboose, and there was the story
of the half-grown bear: the train's first trip in to the cutting
thirty miles away, the bear between the rails, its rear end
elevated like that of a playing puppy while it dug to see
what sort of ants or bugs they might contain or perhaps
just to examine the curious symmetrical squared barkless
logs which had appeared apparently from nowhere in one
endless mathematical line overnight, still digging until the
driver on the braked engine not fifty feet away blew the
whistle at it, whereupon it broke frantically and took the
first tree it came to: an ash sapling not much bigger than
a man's thigh and climbed as high as it could and clung
there, its head ducked between its arms as a man (a woman
perhaps) might have done while the brakeman threw
chunks of ballast at it, and when the engine returned three
hours later with the first load of outbound logs the bear was
halfway down the tree and once more scrambled back up
as high as it could and clung again while the train passed
and was still there when the engine went in again in the
afternoon and still there when it came back out at dusk;
and Boon had been in Hoke's with the wagon after a barrel
of flour that noon when the train-crew told about it and
Boon and Ash, both twenty years younger then, sat under
the tree all that night to keep anybody from shooting it and
the next morning Major de Spain had the log-train held
at Hoke's and just before sundown on the second day, with
not only Boon and Ash but Major de Spain and General
Compson and Walter and McCaslin, twelve then, watching, it came down the tree after almost thirty-six hours
without even water and McCaslin told him how for a min-

ute they thought it was going to stop right there at the
barrow-pit where they were standing and drink, how it
looked at the water and paused and looked at them and at
the water again, but did not, gone, running, as bears run,
the two sets of feet, front and back, tracking two separate
though parallel courses.

It had been harmless then. They would hear the passing
log-train sometimes from the camp; sometimes, because nobody bothered to listen for it or not. They would hear it
going in, running light and fast, the light clatter of the
trucks, the exhaust of the diminutive locomotive and its
shrill peanut-parcher whistle flung for one petty moment
and absorbed by the brooding and inattentive wilderness
without even an echo. They would hear it going out,
loaded, not quite so fast now yet giving its frantic and
toylike illusion of crawling speed, not whistling now to
conserve steam, flinging its bitten laboring miniature puff-
ing into the immemorial woodsface with frantic and bootless vainglory, empty and noisy and puerile, carrying to no
destination or purpose sticks which left nowhere any scar
or stump as the child's toy loads and transports and unloads
its dead sand and rushes back for more, tireless and unceas-
ing and rapid yet never quite so fast as the Hand which
plays with it moves the toy burden back to load the toy
again. But it was different now. It was the same train,
engine cars and caboose, even the same enginemen brakeman and conductor to whom Boon, drunk then sober then
drunk again then fairly sober once more all in the space
of fourteen hours, had bragged that day two years ago
about what they were going to do to Old Ben tomorrow,
running with its same illusion of frantic rapidity between
the same twin walls of impenetrable and impervious woods,

passing the old landmarks, the old game crossings over which he had trailed bucks wounded and not wounded and more than once seen them, anything but wounded, bot out of the woods and up and across the embankment which bore the rails and ties then down and into the woods again as the earth-bound supposedly move but crossing as arrows travel, groundless, elongated, three times its actual length and even paler, different in color, as if there were a point between immobility and absolute motion where even mass chemically altered, changing without pain or agony not only in bulk and shape but in color too, approaching the color of wind, yet this time it was as though the train (and not only the train but himself, not only his vision which had seen it and his memory which remembered it but his clothes too, as garments carry back into the clean edgeless blowing of air the lingering effluvium of a sick-room or of death) had brought with it into the doomed wilderness even before the actual axe the shadow and portent of the new mill not even finished yet and the rails and ties which were not even laid; and he knew now what he had known as soon as he saw Hoke's this morning but had not yet thought into words: why Major de Spain had not come back, and that after this time he himself, who had had to see it one time other, would return no more.

Now they were near. He knew it before the engine-driver whistled to warn him. Then he saw Ash and the wagon, the reins without doubt wrapped once more about the brake-lever as within the boy's own memory Major de Spain had been forbidding him for eight years to do, the train slowing, the slackened couplings jolting and clashing again from car to car, the caboose slowing past the wagon as he swung down with his gun, the conductor leaning out above him to signal the engine, the caboose still slowing, creeping, although the engine's exhaust was already slatting in mounting tempo against the unechoing wilderness, the crashing of draw-bars once more travelling backward along the train, the caboose picking up speed at last. Then it was gone. It had not been. He could no longer hear it. The wilderness soared, musing, inattentive, myriad, eternal, green; older than any mill-shed, longer than any spur-line. "Mr Boon here yet?" he said.

"He beat me in," Ash said. "Had the wagon loaded and ready for me at Hoke's yistiddy when I got there and setting on the front steps at camp last night when I got in. He already been in the woods since fo daylight this morning. Said he gwine up to the Gum Tree and for you to hunt up that way and meet him." He knew where that was: a single big sweet-gum just outside the woods, in an old clearing; if you crept up to it very quietly this time of year and then ran suddenly into the clearing, sometimes you caught as many as a dozen squirrels in it, trapped, since there was no other tree near they could jump to. So he didn't get into the wagon at all.

"I will," he said.

"I figured you would," Ash said, "I fotch you a box of shells." He passed the shells down and began to unwrap the lines from the brake-pole.

"How many times up to now do you reckon Major has told you not to do that?" the boy said.

"Do which?" Ash said. Then he said: "And tell Boon Hogganbeck dinner gonter be on the table in a hour and if yawl want any to come on and eat it."

"In an hour?" he said. "It aint nine oclock yet." He

drew out his watch and extended it face-toward Ash.
"Look." Ash didn't even look at the watch.

"That's town time. You aint in town now. You in the woods."

"Look at the sun then."

"Nemmine the sun too," Ash said. "If you and Boon Hogganbeck want any dinner, you better come on in and get it when I tole you. I aim to get done in that kitchen because I got my wood to chop. And watch your feet. They're crawling."

"I will," he said.

Then he was in the woods, not alone but solitary; the solitude closed about him, green with summer. They did not change, and, timeless, would not, anymore than would the green of summer and the fire and rain of fall and the iron cold and sometimes even snow

the day, the morning when he killed the buck and Sam marked his face with its hot blood, they returned to camp and he remembered old Ash's blinking and disgruntled and even outraged disbelief until at last McCaslin had had to affirm the fact that he had really killed it: and that night Ash sat snarling and unapproachable behind the stove so that Tennie's Jim had to serve the supper and waked them with breakfast already on the table the next morning and it was only half-past one oclock and at last out of Major de Spain's angry cursing and Ash's snarling and sullen rejoinders the fact emerged that Ash not only wanted to go into the woods and shoot a deer also but he intended to and Major de Spain said, 'By God, if we dont let him we will probably have to do the cooking from now on:' and Walter Ewell said, 'Or get up at midnight to eat what Ash cooks:' and since he had already killed his buck for this

*hunt and was not to shoot again unless they needed meat,
he offered his gun to Ash until Major de Spain took command and allotted that gun to Boon for the day and gave
Boon's unpredictable pump gun to Ash, with two buckshot
shells but Ash said, 'I got shells:' and showed them, four:
one buck, one of number three shot for rabbits, two of bird-
shot and told one by one their history and their origin and
he remembered not Ash's face alone but Major de Spain's
and Walter's and General Compson's too, and Ash's voice:
'Shoot? In course they'll shoot! Genl Cawmpson guv me
this un'—the buckshot—'right outen the same gun he kilt
that big buck with eight years ago. And this un'—it was
the rabbit shell: triumphantly—'is oldern thisyer boy!' And
that morning he loaded the gun himself, reversing the order:
the bird-shot, the rabbit, then the buck so that the buckshot would feed first into the chamber, and himself without a gun, he and Ash walked beside Major de Spain's
and Tennie's Jim's horses and the dogs (that was the snow)
until they cast and struck, the sweet strong cries ringing
away into the muffled falling air and gone almost immediately, as if the constant and unmurmuring flakes had already buried even the unformed echoes beneath their
myriad and weightless falling, Major de Spain and Tennie's Jim gone too, whooping on into the woods; and then
it was all right, he knew as plainly as if Ash had told him
that Ash had now hunted his deer and that even his tender
years had been forgiven for having killed one, and they
turned back toward home through the falling snow—that
is, Ash said, 'Now whut?' and he said, 'This way'—himself in front because, although they were less than a mile
from camp, he knew that Ash, who had spent two weeks
of his life in the camp each year for the last twenty, had no*

idea whatever where they were, until quite soon the manner in which Ash carried Boon's gun was making him a good deal more than just nervous and he made Ash walk in front, striding on, talking now, an old man's garrulous monologue beginning with where he was at the moment then of the woods and of camping in the woods and of eating in camps then of eating then of cooking it and of his wife's cooking then briefly of his old wife and almost at once and at length of a new light-colored woman who nursed next door to Major de Spain's and if she didn't watch out who she was switching her tail at he would show her how old was an old man or not if his wife just didn't watch him all the time, the two of them in a game trail through a dense brake of cane and brier which would bring them out within a quarter-mile of camp, approaching a big fallen tree-trunk lying athwart the path and just as Ash, still talking, was about to step over it the bear, the yearling, rose suddenly beyond the log, sitting up, its fore-arms against its chest and its wrists limply arrested as if it had been surprised in the act of covering its face to pray: and after a certain time Ash's gun yawed jerkily up and he said, 'You haven't got a shell in the barrel yet. Pump it:' but the gun already snicked and he said, 'Pump it. You haven't got a shell in the barrel yet:' and Ash pumped the action and in a certain time the gun steadied again and snicked and he said, 'Pump it:' and watched the buckshot shell jerk, spinning heavily, into the cane. This is the rabbit shot: he thought and the gun snicked and he thought: The next is bird-shot: and he didn't have to say Pump it; he cried, 'Dont shoot! Dont shoot!' but that was already too late too, the light dry vicious snick! before he could speak and the bear turned and dropped to all-fours and *then was gone and there was only the log, the cane, the velvet and constant snow and Ash said, 'Now whut?' and he said, 'This way. Come on:' and began to back away down the path and Ash said, 'I got to find my shells:' and he said, 'Goddamn it, goddamn it, come on:' but Ash leaned the gun against the log and returned and stooped and fumbled among the cane roots until he came back and stooped and found the shells and they rose and at that moment the gun, untouched, leaning against the log six feet away and for that while even forgotten by both of them, roared, bellowed and flamed, and ceased: and he carried it now, pumped out the last mummified shell and gave that one also to Ash and, the action still open, himself carried the gun until he stood it in the corner behind Boon's bed at the camp*

—; summer, and fall, and snow, and wet and saprife spring in their ordered immortal sequence, the deathless and immemorial phases of the mother who had shaped him if any had toward the man he almost was, mother and father both to the old man born of a Negro slave and a Chickasaw chief who had been his spirit's father if any had, whom he had revered and harkened to and loved and lost and grieved: and he would marry someday and they too would own for their brief while that brief unsubstanced glory which inherently of itself cannot last and hence why glory: and they would, might, carry even the remembrance of it into the time when flesh no longer talks to flesh because memory at least does last: but still the woods would be his mistress and his wife.

He was not going toward the Gum Tree. Actually he was getting farther from it. Time was and not so long ago either when he would not have been allowed here without

someone with him, and a little later, when he had begun
to learn how much he did not know, he would not have
dared be here without someone with him, and later still,
beginning to ascertain, even if only dimly, the limits of
what he did not know, he could have attempted and carried it through with a compass, not because of any increased belief in himself but because McCaslin and Major
de Spain and Walter and General Compson too had taught
him at last to believe the compass regardless of what it
seemed to state. Now he did not even use the compass but
merely the sun and that only subconsciously, yet he could
have taken a scaled map and plotted at any time to within
a hundred feet of where he actually was; and sure enough,
at almost the exact moment when he expected it, the earth
began to rise faintly, he passed one of the four concrete
markers set down by the lumber company's surveyor to
establish the four corners of the plot which Major de Spain
had reserved out of the sale, then he stood on the crest of
the knoll itself, the four corner-markers all visible now,
blanched still even beneath the winter's weathering, lifeless and shockingly alien in that place where dissolution itself was a seething turmoil of ejaculation tumescence con-
ception and birth, and death did not even exist. After two
winters' blanketings of leaves and the flood-waters of two
springs, there was no trace of the two graves anymore at
all. But those who would have come this far to find them
would not need headstones but would have found them
as Sam Fathers himself had taught him to find such: by
bearings on trees: and did, almost the first thrust of the
hunting knife finding (but only to see if it was still there)
the round tin box manufactured for axel-grease and con-

taining now Old Ben's dried mutilated paw, resting above Lion's bones.

He didn't disturb it. He didn't even look for the other grave where he and McCaslin and Major de Spain and Boon had laid Sam's body, along with his hunting horn and his knife and his tobacco-pipe, that Sunday morning two years ago; he didn't have to. He had stepped over it, perhaps on it. But that was all right. *He probably knew I was in the woods this morning long before I got here,* he thought, going on to the tree which had supported one end of the platform where Sam lay when McCaslin and Major de Spain found them—the tree, the other axel-grease tin nailed to the trunk, but weathered, rusted, alien too yet healed already into the wilderness' concordant generality, raising no tuneless note, and empty, long since empty of the food and tobacco he had put into it that day, as empty of that as it would presently be of this which he drew from his pocket—the twist of tobacco, the new bandanna handkerchief, the small paper sack of the peppermint candy which Sam had used to love; that gone too, almost before he had turned his back, not vanished but merely translated into the myriad life which printed the dark mold of these secret and sunless places with delicate fairy tracks, which, breathing and biding and immobile, watched him from beyond every twig and leaf until he moved, moving again, walking on; he had not stopped, he had only paused, quitting the knoll which was no abode of the dead because there was no death, not Lion and not Sam: not held fast in earth but free in earth and not in earth but of earth, myriad yet undiffused of every myriad part, leaf and twig and particle, air and sun and rain and dew and night, acorn oak and leaf and acorn again, dark and dawn and dark and dawn again in their immutable progression and, being myriad, one: and Old Ben too, Old Ben too; they would give him his paw back even, certainly they would give him his paw back: then the long challenge and the long chase, no heart to be driven and outraged, no flesh to be mauled and bled— Even as he froze himself, he seemed to hear Ash's parting admonition. He could even hear the voice as he froze, immobile, one foot just taking his weight, the toe of the other just lifted behind him, not breathing, feeling again and as always the sharp shocking inrush from when Isaac McCaslin long yet was not, and so it was fear all right but not fright as he looked down at it. It had not coiled yet and the buzzer had not sounded either, only one thick rapid contraction, one loop cast sideways as though merely for purchase from which the raised head might start slightly backward, not in fright either, not in threat quite yet, more than six feet of it, the head raised higher than his knee and less than his knee's length away, and old, the once-bright markings of its youth dulled now to a monotone concordant too with the wilderness it crawled and lurked: the old one, the ancient and accursed about the earth, fatal and solitary and he could smell it now: the thin sick smell of rotting cucumbers and something else which had no name, evocative of all knowledge and an old weariness and of pariah-hood and of death. At last it moved. Not the head. The elevation of the head did not change as it began to glide away from him, moving erect yet off the perpendicular as if the head and that elevated third were complete and all: an entity walking on two feet and free of all laws of mass and balance and should have been because even now he could not quite believe that all that shift and flow of shadow behind that walking

head could have been one snake: going and then gone;
he put the other foot down at last and didn't know it,
standing with one hand raised as Sam had stood that afternoon six years ago when Sam led him into the wilderness
and showed him and he ceased to be a child, speaking the
old tongue which Sam had spoken that day without pre-
meditation either: "Chief," he said: "Grandfather."

He couldn't tell when he first began to hear the sound,
because when he became aware of it, it seemed to him
that he had been already hearing it for several seconds—
a sound as though someone were hammering a gun-barrel
against a piece of railroad iron, a sound loud and heavy
and not rapid yet with something frenzied about it, as
the hammerer were not only a strong man and an earnest
one but a little hysterical too. Yet it couldn't be on the log-
line because, although the track lay in that direction, it was
at least two miles from him and this sound was not three
hundred yards away. But even as he thought that, he
realised where the sound must be coming from: whoever
the man was and whatever he was doing, he was somewhere near the edge of the clearing where the Gum Tree
was and where he was to meet Boon. So far, he had been
hunting as he advanced, moving slowly and quietly and
watching the ground and the trees both. Now he went on,
his gun unloaded and the barrel slanted up and back to
facilitate its passage through brier and undergrowth, approaching as it grew louder and louder that steady savage
somehow queerly hysterical beating of metal on metal,
emerging from the woods, into the old clearing, with the
solitary gum tree directly before him. At first glance the
tree seemed to be alive with frantic squirrels. There appeared to be forty or fifty of them leaping and darting from

branch to branch until the whole tree had become one green maelstrom of mad leaves, while from time to time, singly or in twos and threes, squirrels would dart down the trunk then whirl without stopping and rush back up again as though sucked violently back by the vacuum of their fellows' frenzied vortex. Then he saw Boon, sitting, his back against the trunk, his head bent, hammering furiously at something on his lap. What he hammered with was the barrel of his dismembered gun, what he hammered at was the breech of it. The rest of the gun lay scattered about him in a half-dozen pieces while he bent over the piece on his lap his scarlet and streaming walnut face, hammering the disjointed barrel against the gun-breech with the frantic abandon of a madman. He didn't even look up to see who it was. Still hammering, he merely shouted back at the boy in a hoarse strangled voice:

"Get out of here! Dont touch them! Dont touch a one of them! They're mine!"

Delta Autumn

Soon now they would enter the Delta. The sensation was familiar to him. It had been renewed like this each last week in November for more than fifty years—the last hill, at the foot of which the rich unbroken alluvial flatness began as the sea began at the base of its cliffs, dissolving away beneath the unhurried November rain as the sea itself would dissolve away.

At first they had come in wagons: the guns, the bedding, the dogs, the food, the whisky, the keen heart-lifting anticipation of hunting; the young men who could drive all night and all the following day in the cold rain and pitch a camp in the rain and sleep in the wet blankets and rise at daylight the next morning and hunt. There had been bear then. A man shot a doe or a fawn as quickly as he did a buck, and in the afternoons they shot wild turkey with pistols to test their stalking skill and marksmanship, feeding all but the breast to the dogs. But that time was gone now. Now they went in cars, driving faster and faster each year because the roads were better and they had farther and farther to drive, the territory in which game still existed drawing yearly inward as his life was drawing inward, until now he was the last of those who had once made the journey in wagons without feeling it and now those who accompanied him were the sons and even grandsons of the men who had ridden for twenty-four hours in the rain or sleet behind the steaming mules. They called him 'Uncle Ike' now, and he no longer told anyone how near eighty he actually was because he knew as well as they did that he no longer had any business making such expeditions, even by car.

In fact, each time now, on that first night in camp, lying aching and sleepless in the harsh blankets, his blood only faintly warmed by the single thin whisky-and-water which he allowed himself, he would tell himself that this would be his last. But he would stand that trip—he still shot almost as well as he ever had, still killed almost as much of the game he saw as he ever killed; he no longer even knew how many deer had fallen before his gun—and the fierce long heat of the next summer would renew him. Then November would come again, and again in the car with two of the sons of his old companions, whom he had taught not only how to distinguish between the prints left by a buck or a doe but between the sound they made in moving, he would look ahead past the jerking arc of the windshield wiper and see the land flatten suddenly and swoop, dissolving away beneath the rain as the sea itself would dissolve, and he would say, "Well, boys, there it is again."

This time though, he didn't have time to speak. The driver of the car stopped it, slamming it to a skidding halt on the greasy pavement without warning, actually flinging the two passengers forward until they caught themselves with their braced hands against the dash. "What the hell, Roth!" the man in the middle said. "Cant you whistle first when you do that? Hurt you, Uncle Ike?"

"No," the old man said. "What's the matter?" The driver didn't answer. Still leaning forward, the old man looked sharply past the face of the man between them, at the face of his kinsman. It was the youngest face of them all, aquiline, saturnine, a little ruthless, the face of his ancestor too, tempered a little, altered a little, staring sombrely through the streaming windshield across which the twin wipers flicked and flicked.

"I didn't intend to come back in here this time," he said suddenly and harshly.

"You said that back in Jefferson last week," the old man said. "Then you changed your mind. Have you changed it again? This aint a very good time to——"

"Oh, Roth's coming," the man in the middle said. His name was Legate. He seemed to be speaking to no one, as he was looking at neither of them. "If it was just a buck he was coming all this distance for, now. But he's got a doe in here. Of course a old man like Uncle Ike cant be interested in no doe, not one that walks on two legs— when she's standing up, that is. Pretty light-colored, too. The one he was after them nights last fall when he said he was coon-hunting, Uncle Ike. The one I figured maybe he was still running when he was gone all that month last January. But of course a old man like Uncle Ike aint got no interest in nothing like that." He chortled, still looking at no one, not completely jeering.

"What?" the old man said. "What's that?" But he had not even so much as glanced at Legate. He was still watching his kinsman's face. The eyes behind the spectacles were the blurred eyes of an old man, but they were quite sharp too; eyes which could still see a gun-barrel and what ran beyond it as well as any of them could. He was re-

membering himself now: how last year, during the final
stage by motor boat in to where they camped, a box of
food had been lost overboard and how on the next day
his kinsman had gone back to the nearest town for supplies and had been gone overnight. And when he did
return, something had happened to him. He would go into
the woods with his rifle each dawn when the others went,
but the old man, watching him, knew that he was not
hunting. "All right," he said. "Take me and Will on to
shelter where we can wait for the truck, and you can go on
back."

"I'm going in," the other said harshly. "Dont worry.
Because this will be the last of it."

"The last of deer hunting, or of doe hunting?" Legate
said. This time the old man paid no attention to him
even by speech. He still watched the young man's savage
and brooding face.

"Why?" he said.

"After Hitler gets through with it? Or Smith or Jones
or Roosevelt or Willkie or whatever he will call himself
in this country?"

"We'll stop him in this country," Legate said. "Even
if he calls himself George Washington."

"How?" Edmonds said. "By singing God bless America
in bars at midnight and wearing dime-store flags in our
lapels?"

"So that's what's worrying you," the old man said. "I
aint noticed this country being short of defenders yet, when
it needed them. You did some of it yourself twenty-odd
years ago, before you were a grown man even. This country is a little mite stronger than any one man or group of
men, outside of it or even inside of it either. I reckon,

when the time comes and some of you have done got tired
of hollering we are whipped if we dont go to war and
some more are hollering we are whipped if we do, it will
cope with one Austrian paper-hanger, no matter what he
will be calling himself. My pappy and some other better
men than any of them you named tried once to tear it in
two with a war, and they failed."

"And what have you got left?" the other said. "Half
the people without jobs and half the factories closed by
strikes. Half the people on public dole that wont work
and half that couldn't work even if they would. Too much
cotton and corn and hogs, and not enough for people to
eat and wear. The country full of people to tell a man how
he cant raise his own cotton whether he will or wont, and
Sally Rand with a sergeant's stripes and not even the fan
couldn't fill the army rolls. Too much not-butter and not
even the guns——"

"We got a deer camp—if we ever get to it," Legate said.
"Not to mention does."

"It's a good time to mention does," the old man said.
"Does and fawns both. The only fighting anywhere that
ever had anything of God's blessing on it has been when
men fought to protect does and fawns. If it's going to
come to fighting, that's a good thing to mention and remember too."

"Haven't you discovered in—how many years more than
seventy is it?—that women and children are one thing
there's never any scarcity of?" Edmonds said.

"Maybe that's why all I am worrying about right now
is that ten miles of river we still have got to run before we
can make camp," the old man said. "So let's get on."

They went on. Soon they were going fast again, as Ed-

monds always drove, consulting neither of them about the
speed just as he had given neither of them any warning
when he slammed the car to stop. The old man relaxed
again. He watched, as he did each recurrent November
while more than sixty of them passed, the land which he
had seen change. At first there had been only the old towns
along the River and the old towns along the hills, from
each of which the planters with their gangs of slaves and
then of hired laborers had wrested from the impenetrable
jungle of water-standing cane and cypress, gum and holly
and oak and ash, cotton patches which as the years passed
became fields and then plantations. The paths made by
deer and bear became roads and then highways, with towns
in turn springing up along them and along the rivers
Tallahatchie and Sunflower which joined and became the
Yazoo, the River of the Dead of the Choctaws—the thick,
slow, black, unsunned streams almost without current,
which once each year ceased to flow at all and then re-
versed, spreading, drowning the rich land and subsiding
again, leaving it still richer.

Most of that was gone now. Now a man drove two
hundred miles from Jefferson before he found wilderness
to hunt in. Now the land lay open from the cradling hills
on the East to the rampart of levee on the West, standing
horseman-tall with cotton for the world's looms—the rich
black land, imponderable and vast, fecund up to the very
doorsteps of the negroes who worked it and of the white
men who owned it; which exhausted the hunting life of a
dog in one year, the working life of a mule in five and of
a man in twenty—the land in which neon flashed past
them from the little countless towns and countless shining
this-year's automobiles sped past them on the broad plumb-

ruled highways, yet in which the only permanent mark of man's occupation seemed to be the tremendous gins, constructed in sections of sheet iron and in a week's time though they were, since no man, millionaire though he be, would build more than a roof and walls to shelter the camping equipment he lived from when he knew that once each ten years or so his house would be flooded to the second storey and all within it ruined;—the land across which there came now no scream of panther but instead the long hooting of locomotives: trains of incredible length and drawn by a single engine, since there was no gradient anywhere and no elevation save those raised by forgotten aboriginal hands as refuges from the yearly water and used by their Indian successors to sepulchre their fathers' bones, and all that remained of that old time were the Indian names on the little towns and usually pertaining to water— Aluschaskuna, Tillatoba, Homochitto, Yazoo.

By early afternoon, they were on water. At the last little Indian-named town at the end of pavement they waited until the other car and the two trucks—the one carrying the bedding and tents and food, the other the horses— overtook them. They left the concrete and, after another mile or so, the gravel too. In caravan they ground on through the ceaselessly dissolving afternoon, with skid-chains on the wheels now, lurching and splashing and sliding among the ruts, until presently it seemed to him that the retrograde of his remembering had gained an inverse velocity from their own slow progress, that the land had retreated not in minutes from the last spread of gravel but in years, decades, back toward what it had been when he first knew it: the road they now followed once more the ancient pathway of bear and deer, the diminishing fields they now passed once more scooped punily and terrifically by axe and saw and mule-drawn plow from the wilderness' flank, out of the brooding and immemorial tangle, in place of ruthless mile-wide parallelograms wrought by ditching the dyking machinery.

They reached the river landing and unloaded, the horses to go overland down stream to a point opposite the camp and swim the river, themselves and the bedding and food and dogs and guns in the motor launch. It was himself, though no horseman, no farmer, not even a countryman save by his distant birth and boyhood, who coaxed and soothed the two horses, drawing them by his own single frail hand until, backing, filling, trembling a little, they surged, halted, then sprang scrambling down from the truck, possessing no affinity for them as creatures, beasts, but being merely insulated by his years and time from the corruption of steel and oiled moving parts which tainted the others.

Then, his old hammer double gun which was only twelve years younger than he standing between his knees, he watched even the last puny marks of man—cabin, clearing, the small and irregular fields which a year ago were jungle and in which the skeleton stalks of this year's cotton stood almost as tall and rank as the old cane had stood, as if man had had to marry his planting to the wilderness in order to conquer it—fall away and vanish. The twin banks marched with wilderness as he remembered it—the tangle of brier and cane impenetrable even to sight twenty feet away, the tall tremendous soaring of oak and gum and ash and hickory which had rung to no axe save the hunter's, had echoed to no machinery save the beat of old-time steam boats traversing it or to the snarling of launches

like their own of people going into it to dwell for a week
or two weeks because it was still wilderness. There was
some of it left, although now it was two hundred miles from
Jefferson when once it had been thirty. He had watched it,
not being conquered, destroyed, so much as retreating since
its purpose was served now and its time an outmoded time,
retreating southward through this inverted-apex, this ▽-
shaped section of earth between hills and River until
what was left of it seemed now to be gathered and for the
time arrested in one tremendous density of brooding and
inscrutable impenetrability at the ultimate funnelling tip.

They reached the site of their last-year's camp with still
two hours left of light. "You go on over under that driest
tree and set down," Legate told him. "—if you can find it.
Me and these other young boys will do this." He did
neither. He was not tired yet. That would come later.
Maybe it wont come at all this time, he thought, as he had
thought at this point each November for the last five or six
of them. *Maybe I will go out on stand in the morning too;*
knowing that he would not, not even if he took the advice
and sat down under the driest shelter and did nothing until
camp was made and supper cooked. Because it would not
be the fatigue. It would be because he would not sleep tonight but would lie instead wakeful and peaceful on the
cot amid the tent-filling snoring and the rain's whisper as
he always did on the first night in camp; peaceful, without
regret or fretting, telling himself that was all right too, who
didn't have so many of them left as to waste one sleeping.

In his slicker he directed the unloading of the boat—the
tents, the stove, the bedding, the food for themselves and
the dogs until there should be meat in camp. He sent two
of the negroes to cut firewood; he had the cook-tent raised

and the stove up and a fire going and supper cooking while
the big tent was still being staked down. Then in the beginning of dusk he crossed in the boat to where the horses
waited, backing and snorting at the water. He took the lead-
ropes and with no more weight than that and his voice, he
drew them down into the water and held them beside the
boat with only their heads above the surface, as though
they actually were suspended from his frail and strengthless
old man's hands, while the boat recrossed and each horse
in turn lay prone in the shallows, panting and trembling,
its eyes rolling in the dusk, until the same weightless hand
and unraised voice gathered it surging upward, splashing
and thrashing up the bank.

Then the meal was ready. The last of light was gone now
save the thin stain of it snared somewhere between the
river's surface and the rain. He had the single glass of thin
whisky-and-water, then, standing in the churned mud beneath the stretched tarpaulin, he said grace over the fried
slabs of pork, the hot soft shapeless bread, the canned beans
and molasses and coffee in iron plates and cups,—the town
food, brought along with them—then covered himself
again, the others following. "Eat," he said. "Eat it all up.
I dont want a piece of town meat in camp after breakfast
tomorrow. Then you boys will hunt. You'll have to. When
I first started hunting in this bottom sixty years ago with
old General Compson and Major de Spain and Roth's
grandfather and Will Legate's too, Major de Spain wouldn't
allow but two pieces of foreign grub in his camp. That was
one side of pork and one ham of beef. And not to eat for
the first supper and breakfast neither. It was to save until
along toward the end of camp when everybody was so sick

'of bear meat and coon and venison that we couldn't even look at it."

"I thought Uncle Ike was going to say the pork and beef was for the dogs," Legate said, chewing. "But that's right; I remember. You just shot the dogs a mess of wild turkey every evening when they got tired of deer guts."

"Times are different now," another said. "There was game here then."

"Yes," the old man said quietly. "There was game here then."

"Besides, they shot does then too," Legate said. "As it is now, we aint got but one doe-hunter in———"

"And better men hunted it," Edmonds said. He stood at the end of the rough plank table, eating rapidly and steadily as the others ate. But again the old man looked sharply across at the sullen, handsome, brooding face which appeared now darker and more sullen still in the light of the smoky lantern. "Go on. Say it."

"I didn't say that," the old man said. "There are good men everywhere, at all times. Most men are. Some are just unlucky, because most men are a little better than their circumstances give them a chance to be. And I've known some that even the circumstances couldn't stop."

"Well, I wouldn't say——" Legate said.

"So you've lived almost eighty years," Edmonds said. "And that's what you finally learned about the other animals you lived among. I suppose the question to ask you is, where have you been all the time you were dead?"

There was a silence; for the instant even Legate's jaw stopped chewing while he gaped at Edmonds. "Well, by God, Roth——" the third speaker said. But it was the old man who spoke, his voice still peaceful and untroubled and merely grave:

"Maybe so," he said. "But if being what you call alive would have learned me any different, I reckon I'm satisfied, wherever it was I've been."

"Well, I wouldn't say that Roth——" Legate said.

The third speaker was still leaning forward a little over the table, looking at Edmonds. "Meaning that it's only because folks happen to be watching him that a man behaves at all," he said. "Is that it?"

"Yes," Edmonds said. "A man in a blue coat, with a badge on it watching him. Maybe just the badge."

"I deny that," the old man said. "I dont——"

The other two paid no attention to him. Even Legate was listening to them for the moment, his mouth still full of food and still open a little, his knife with another lump of something balanced on the tip of the blade arrested halfway to his mouth. "I'm glad I dont have your opinion of folks," the third speaker said. "I take it you include yourself."

"I see," Edmonds said. "You prefer Uncle Ike's opinion of circumstances. All right. Who makes the circumstances?"

"Luck," the third said. "Chance. Happen-so. I see what you are getting at. But that's just what Uncle Ike said: that now and then, maybe most of the time, man is a little better than the net result of his and his neighbors' doings, when he gets the chance to be."

This time Legate swallowed first. He was not to be stopped this time. "Well, I wouldn't say that Roth Edmonds can hunt one doe every day and night for two weeks and was a poor hunter or a unlucky one neither. A man that still have the same doe left to hunt on again next year——"

"Have some meat," the man next to him said.

"—aint no unlucky— What?" Legate said.

"Have some meat." The other offered the dish.

"I got some," Legate said.

"Have some more," the third speaker said. "You and Roth Edmonds both. Have a heap of it. Clapping your jaws together that way with nothing to break the shock." Someone chortled. Then they all laughed, with relief, the tension broken. But the old man was speaking, even into the laughter, in that peaceful and still untroubled voice:

"I still believe. I see proof everywhere. I grant that man made a heap of his circumstances, him and his living neighbors between them. He even inherited some of them already made, already almost ruined even. A while ago Henry Wyatt there said how there used to be more game here. There was. So much that we even killed does. I seem to remember Will Legate mentioning that too—" Someone laughed, a single guffaw, stillborn. It ceased and they all listened, gravely, looking down at their plates. Edmonds was drinking his coffee, sullen, brooding, inattentive.

"Some folks still kill does," Wyatt said. "There wont be just one buck hanging in this bottom tomorrow night without any head to fit it."

"I didn't say all men," the old man said. "I said most men. And not just because there is a man with a badge to watch us. We probably wont even see him unless maybe he will stop here about noon tomorrow and eat dinner with us and check our licenses ——"

"We dont kill does because if we did kill does in a few years there wouldn't even be any bucks left to kill, Uncle Ike," Wyatt said.

"According to Roth yonder, that's one thing we wont

never have to worry about," the old man said. "He said on the way here this morning that does and fawns—I believe he said women and children—are two things this world aint ever lacked. But that aint all of it," he said. "That's just the mind's reason a man has to give himself because the heart dont always have time to bother with thinking up words that fit together. God created man and He created the world for him to live in and I reckon He created the kind of world He would have wanted to live in if He had been a man—the ground to walk on, the big woods, the trees and the water, and the game to live in it. And maybe He didn't put the desire to hunt and kill game in man but I reckon He knew it was going to be there, that man was going to teach it to himself, since he wasn't quite God himself yet——"

"When will he be?" Wyatt said.

"I think that every man and woman, at the instant when it dont even matter whether they marry or not, I think that whether they marry then or afterward or dont never, at that instant the two of them together were God."

"Then there are some Gods in this world I wouldn't want to touch, and with a damn long stick," Edmonds said. He set his coffee cup down and looked at Wyatt. "And that includes myself, if that's what you want to know. I'm going to bed." He was gone. There was a general movement among the others. But it ceased and they stood again about the table, not looking at the old man, apparently held there yet by his quiet and peaceful voice as the heads of the swimming horses had been held above the water by his weightless hand. The three negroes—the cook and his helper and old Isham—were sitting quietly in the entrance of the kitchen tent, listening too, the three faces dark and motionless and musing.

"He put them both here: man, and the game he would follow and kill, foreknowing it. I believe He said, 'So be it.' I reckon He even foreknew the end. But He said, 'I will give him his chance. I will give him warning and fore-knowledge too, along with the desire to follow and the power to slay. The woods and fields he ravages and the game he devastates will be the consequence and signature of his crime and guilt, and his punishment.'—Bed time," he said. His voice and inflection did not change at all. "Breakfast at four oclock, Isham. We want meat on the ground by sunup time."

There was a good fire in the sheet-iron heater; the tent was warm and was beginning to dry out, except for the mud underfoot. Edmonds was already rolled into his blankets, motionless, his face to the wall. Isham had made up his bed too—the strong, battered iron cot, the stained mattress which was not quite soft enough, the worn, often-washed blankets which as the years passed were less and less warm enough. But the tent was warm; presently, when the kitchen was cleaned up and readied for breakfast, the young negro would come in to lie down before the heater, where he could be roused to put fresh wood into it from time to time. And then, he knew now he would not sleep tonight anyway; he no longer needed to tell himself that perhaps he would. But it was all right now. The day was ended now and night faced him, but alarmless, empty of fret. *Maybe I came for this*, he thought: *Not to hunt, but for this. I would come anyway, even if only to go back home tomorrow*. Wearing only his bagging woolen underwear, his spectacles folded away in the worn case beneath the

pillow where he could reach them readily and his lean body
fitted easily into the old worn groove of mattress and
blankets, he lay on his back, his hands crossed on his breast
and his eyes closed while the others undressed and went to
bed and the last of the sporadic talking died into snoring.
Then he opened his eyes and lay peaceful and quiet as a
child, looking up at the motionless belly of rain-murmured
canvas upon which the glow of the heater was dying slowly
away and would fade still further until the young negro,
lying on two planks before it, would sit up and stoke it and
lie back down again.

They had a house once. That was sixty years ago, when
the Big Bottom was only thirty miles from Jefferson and
old Major de Spain, who had been his father's cavalry commander in '61 and '2 and '3 and '4, and his cousin (his older
brother; his father too) had taken him into the woods for
the first time. Old Sam Fathers was alive then, born in
slavery, son of a Negro slave and a Chickasaw chief, who
had taught him how to shoot, not only when to shoot but
when not to; such a November dawn as tomorrow would be
and the old man led him straight to the great cypress and he
had known the buck would pass exactly there because
there was something running in Sam Fathers' veins which
ran in the veins of the buck too, and they stood there against
the tremendous trunk, the old man of seventy and the boy
of twelve, and there was nothing save the dawn until suddenly the buck was there, smoke-colored out of nothing,
magnificent with speed: and Sam Fathers said, 'Now. Shoot
quick and shoot slow:' and the gun levelled rapidly without haste and crashed and he walked to the buck lying still
intact and still in the shape of that magnificent speed and
bled it with Sam's knife and Sam dipped his hands into the

hot blood and marked his face forever while he stood trying not to tremble, humbly and with pride too though the boy of twelve had been unable to phrase it then: *I slew you; my bearing must not shame your quitting life. My conduct forever onward must become your death;* marking him for that and for more than that: that day and himself and McCaslin juxtaposed not against the wilderness but against the tamed land, the old wrong and shame itself, in repudiation and denial at least of the land and the wrong and shame even if he couldn't cure the wrong and eradicate the shame, who at fourteen when he learned of it had believed he could do both when he became competent and when at twenty-one he became competent he knew that he could do neither but at least he could repudiate the wrong and shame, at least in principle, and at least the land itself in fact, for his son at least: and did, thought he had: then (married then) in a rented cubicle in a back-street stock-traders' boarding-house, the first and last time he ever saw her naked body, himself and his wife juxtaposed in their turn against that same land, that same wrong and shame from whose regret and grief he would at least save and free his son and, saving and freeing his son, lost him. They had the house then. That roof, the two weeks of each November which they spent under it, had become his home. Although since that time they had lived during the two fall weeks in tents and not always in the same place two years in succession and now his companions were the sons and even the grandsons of them with whom he had lived in the house and for almost fifty years now the house itself had not even existed, the conviction, the sense and feeling of home, had been merely transferred into the canvas. He owned a house in Jefferson, a good house though small,

where he had had a wife and lived with her and lost her,
ay, lost her even though he had lost her in the rented cubicle before he and his old clever dipsomaniac partner had
finished the house for them to move into it: but lost her,
because she loved him. But women hope for so much. They
never live too long to still believe that anything within the
scope of their passionate wanting is likewise within the
range of their passionate hope: and it was still kept for him
by his dead wife's widowed niece and her children and he
was comfortable in it, his wants and needs and even the
small trying harmless crochets of an old man looked after
by blood at least related to the blood which he had elected
out of all the earth to cherish. But he spent the time within
those walls waiting for November, because even this tent
with its muddy floor and the bed which was not wide
enough nor soft enough nor even warm enough, was his
home and these men, some of whom he only saw during
these two November weeks and not one of whom even
bore any name he used to know—De Spain and Compson
and Ewell and Hogganbeck—were more his kin than any.
Because this was his land——

The shadow of the youngest negro loomed. It soared,
blotting the heater's dying glow from the ceiling, the wood
billets thumping into the iron maw until the glow, the
flame, leaped high and bright across the canvas. But the
negro's shadow still remained, by its length and breadth,
standing, since it covered most of the ceiling, until after
a moment he raised himself on one elbow to look. It was
not the negro, it was his kinsman; when he spoke the other
turned sharp against the red firelight the sullen and ruthless
profile.

"Nothing," Edmonds said. "Go on back to sleep."

"Since Will Legate mentioned it," McCaslin said, "I remember you had some trouble sleeping in here last fall too. Only you called it coon-hunting then. Or was it Will Legate called it that?" The other didn't answer. Then he turned and went back to his bed. McCaslin, still propped on his elbow, watched until the other's shadow sank down the wall and vanished, became one with the mass of sleeping shadows. "That's right," he said. "Try to get some sleep. We must have meat in camp tomorrow. You can do all the setting up you want to after that." He lay down again, his hands crossed again on his breast, watching the glow of the heater on the canvas ceiling. It was steady again now, the fresh wood accepted, being assimilated; soon it would begin to fade again, taking with it the last echo of that sudden upflare of a young man's passion and unrest. Let him lie awake for a little while, he thought; He will lie still some day for a long time without even dissatisfaction to disturb him. And lying awake here, in these surroundings, would soothe him if anything could, if anything could soothe a man just forty years old. Yes, he thought; Forty years old or thirty, or even the trembling and sleepless ardor of a boy; already the tent, the rain-murmured canvas globe, was once more filled with it. He lay on his back, his eyes closed, his breathing quiet and peaceful as a child's, listening to it—that silence which was never silence but was myriad. He could almost see it, tremendous, primeval, looming, musing downward upon this puny evanescent clutter of human sojourn which after a single brief week would vanish and in another week would be completely healed, traceless in the unmarked solitude. Because it was his land, although he had never owned a foot of it. He had never wanted to, not even after he saw plain its ultimate doom, watching it retreat year by year before the onslaught of axe and saw and log-lines and then dynamite and tractor plows, because it belonged to no man. It belonged to all; they had only to use it well, humbly and with pride. Then suddenly he knew why he had never wanted to own any of it, arrest at least that much of what people called progress, measure his longevity at least against that much of its ultimate fate. It was because there was just exactly enough of it. He seemed to see the two of them—himself and the wilderness—as coevals, his own span as a hunter, a woodsman, not contemporary with his first breath but transmitted to him, assumed by him gladly, humbly, with joy and pride, from that old Major de Spain and that old Sam Fathers who had taught him to hunt, the two spans running out together, not toward oblivion, nothingness, but into a dimension free of both time and space where once more the untreed land warped and wrung to mathematical squares of rank cotton for the frantic old-world people to turn into shells to shoot at one another, would find ample room for both—the names, the faces of the old men he had known and loved and for a little while outlived, moving again among the shades of tall unaxed trees and sightless brakes where the wild strong immortal game ran forever before the tireless belling immortal hounds, falling and rising phoenix-like to the soundless guns.

He had been asleep. The lantern was lighted now. Outside in the darkness the oldest negro, Isham, was beating a spoon against the bottom of a tin pan and crying, "Raise up and get yo foa clock coffy. Raise up and get yo foa clock coffy," and the tent was full of low talk and of men dressing, and Legate's voice, repeating: "Get out of here now and let Uncle Ike sleep. If you wake him up, he'll go out with us. And he aint got any business in the woods this morning."

So he didn't move. He lay with his eyes closed, his breathing gentle and peaceful, and heard them one by one leave the tent. He listened to the breakfast sounds from the table beneath the tarpaulin and heard them depart—the horses, the dogs, the last voice until it died away and there was only the sounds of the negroes clearing breakfast away. After a while he might possibly even hear the first faint clear cry of the first hound ring through the wet woods from where the buck had bedded, then he would go back to sleep again—The tent-flap swung in and fell. Something jarred sharply against the end of the cot and a hand grasped his knee through the blanket before he could open his eyes. It was Edmonds, carrying a shotgun in place of his rifle. He spoke in a harsh, rapid voice:

"Sorry to wake you. There will be a ——"

"I was awake," McCaslin said. "Are you going to shoot that shotgun today?"

"You just told me last night you want meat," Edmonds said. "There will be a ——"

"Since when did you start having trouble getting meat with your rifle?"

"All right," the other said, with that harsh, restrained, furious impatience. Then McCaslin saw in his hand a thick oblong: an envelope. "There will be a message here some time this morning, looking for me. Maybe it wont come. If it does, give the messenger this and tell h— say I said No."

"A what?" McCaslin said. "Tell who?" He half rose onto his elbow as Edmonds jerked the envelope onto the blanket, already turning toward the entrance, the envelope striking solid and heavy and without noise and already sliding from the bed until McCaslin caught it, divining by feel through the paper as instantaneously and conclusively as if he had opened the envelope and looked, the thick sheaf of banknotes. "Wait," he said. "Wait:"—more than the blood kinsman, more even than the senior in years, so that the other paused, the canvas lifted, looking back, and McCaslin saw that outside it was already day. "Tell her No," he said. "Tell her." They stared at one another—the old face, wan, sleep-raddled above the tumbled bed, the dark and sullen younger one at once furious and cold. "Will Legate was right. This is what you called coon-hunting. And now this." He didn't raise the envelope. He made no motion, no gesture to indicate it. "What did you promise her that you haven't the courage to face her and retract?"

"Nothing!" the other said. "Nothing! This is all of it. Tell her I said No." He was gone. The tent flap lifted on an in-waft of faint light and the constant murmur of rain, and fell again, leaving the old man still half-raised onto one elbow, the envelope clutched in the other shaking hand. Afterward it seemed to him that he had begun to hear the approaching boat almost immediately, before the other could have got out of sight even. It seemed to him that there had been no interval whatever: the tent flap falling on the same out-waft of faint and rain-filled light like the suspiration and expiration of the same breath and then in the next second lifted again—the mounting snarl of the outboard engine, increasing, nearer and nearer and louder and louder then cut short off, ceasing with the absolute instantaneity of a blown-out candle, into the lap and plop of water under the bows as the skiff slid in to the bank, the

youngest negro, the youth, raising the tent flap beyond
which for that instant he saw the boat—a small skiff with
a negro man sitting in the stern beside the up-slanted
motor—then the woman entering, in a man's hat and a
man's slicker and rubber boots, carrying the blanket-swad-
dled bundle on one arm and holding the edge of the unbuttoned raincoat over it with the other hand: and bringing something else, something intangible, an effluvium
which he knew he would recognise in a moment because
Isham had already told him, warned him, by sending the
young negro to the tent to announce the visitor instead of
coming himself, the flap falling at last on the young negro
and they were alone—the face indistinct and as yet only
young and with dark eyes, queerly colorless but not ill and
not that of a country woman despite the garments she wore,
looking down at him where he sat upright on the cot now,
clutching the envelope, the soiled undergarment bagging
about him and the twisted blankets huddled about his hips.

"Is that his?" he cried. "Dont lie to me!"

"Yes," she said. "He's gone."

"Yes. He's gone. You wont jump him here. Not this time.
I dont reckon even you expected that. He left you this.
Here." He fumbled at the envelope. It was not to pick it
up, because it was still in his hand; he had never put it
down. It was as if he had to fumble somehow to co-ordi-
nate physically his heretofore obedient hand with what
his brain was commanding of it, as if he had never performed such an action before, extending the envelope at
last, saying again, "Here. Take it. Take it:" until he became aware of her eyes, or not the eyes so much as the
look, the regard fixed now on his face with that immersed
contemplation, that bottomless and intent candor, of a child.

If she had ever seen either the envelope or his movement to extend it, she did not show it.

"You're Uncle Isaac," she said.

"Yes," he said. "But never mind that. Here. Take it. He said to tell you No." She looked at the envelope, then she took it. It was sealed and bore no superscription. Nevertheless, even after she glanced at the front of it, he watched her hold it in the one free hand and tear the corner off with her teeth and manage to rip it open and tilt the neat sheaf of bound notes onto the blanket without even glancing at them and look into the empty envelope and take the edge between her teeth and tear it completely open before she crumpled and dropped it.

"That's just money," she said.

"What did you expect? What else did you expect? You have known him long enough or at least often enough to have got that child, and you dont know him any better than that?"

"Not very often. Not very long. Just that week here last fall, and in January he sent for me and we went West, to New Mexico. We were there six weeks, where I could at least sleep in the same apartment where I cooked for him and looked after his clothes——"

"But not marriage," he said. "Not marriage. He didn't promise you that. Dont lie to me. He didn't have to."

"No. He didn't have to. I didn't ask him to. I knew what I was doing. I knew that to begin with, long before honor I imagine he called it told him the time had come to tell me in so many words what his code I suppose he would call it would forbid him forever to do. And we agreed. Then we agreed again before he left New Mexico, to make sure. That that would be all of it. I believed him. No, I

dont mean that; I mean I believed myself. I wasn't even
listening to him anymore by then because by that time it
had been a long time since he had had anything else to tell
me for me to have to hear. By then I wasn't even listening
enough to ask him to please stop talking. I was listening to
myself. And I believed it. I must have believed it. I dont
see how I could have helped but believe it, because he was
gone then as we had agreed and he didn't write as we had
agreed, just the money came to the bank in Vicksburg in
my name but coming from nobody as we had agreed. So I
must have believed it. I even wrote him last month to make
sure again and the letter came back unopened and I was
sure. So I left the hospital and rented myself a room to live
in until the deer season opened so I could make sure myself
and I was waiting beside the road yesterday when your car
passed and he saw me and so I was sure."

"Then what do you want?" he said. "What do you want?
What do you expect?"

"Yes," she said. And while he glared at her, his white
hair awry from the pillow and his eyes, lacking the spectacles to focus them, blurred and irisless and apparently
pupilless, he saw again that grave, intent, speculative and
detached fixity like a child watching him. "His great great
—Wait a minute.—great great *great* grandfather was your
grandfather. McCaslin. Only it got to be Edmonds. Only
it got to be more than that. Your cousin McCaslin was
there that day when your father and Uncle Buddy won
Tennie from Mr Beauchamp for the one that had no name
but Terrel so you called him Tomey's Terrel, to marry.
But after that it got to be Edmonds." She regarded him,
almost peacefully, with that unwinking and heatless fixity
—the dark wide bottomless eyes in the face's dead and tone-

less pallor which to the old man looked anything but dead, but young and incredibly and even ineradicably alive—as though she were not only not looking at anything, she was not even speaking to anyone but herself. "I would have made a man of him. He's not a man yet. You spoiled him. You, and Uncle Lucas and Aunt Mollie. But mostly you."

"Me?" he said. "Me?"

"Yes. When you gave to his grandfather that land which didn't belong to him, not even half of it by will or even law."

"And never mind that too," he said. "Never mind that too. You," he said. "You sound like you have been to college even. You sound almost like a Northerner even, not like the draggle-tailed women of these Delta peckerwoods. Yet you meet a man on the street one afternoon just because a box of groceries happened to fall out of a boat. And a month later you go off with him and live with him until he got a child on you: and then, by your own statement, you sat there while he took his hat and said goodbye and walked out. Even a Delta peckerwood would look after even a draggle-tail better than that. Haven't you got any folks at all?"

"Yes," she said. "I was living with one of them. My aunt, in Vicksburg. I came to live with her two years ago when my father died; we lived in Indianapolis then. But I got a job, teaching school here in Aluschaskuna, because my aunt was a widow, with a big family, taking in washing to sup——"

"Took in what?" he said. "Took in washing?" He sprang, still seated even, flinging himself backward onto one arm awry-haired, glaring. Now he understood what it was she had brought into the tent with her, what old Isham had already told him by sending the youth to bring her in to him—the pale lips, the skin pallid and dead-looking yet not ill, the dark and tragic and foreknowing eyes. *Maybe in a thousand or two thousand years in America,* he thought. *But not now! Not now!* He cried, not loud, in a voice of amazement, pity, and outrage: "You're a nigger!"

"Yes," she said. "James Beauchamp—you called him Tennie's Jim though he had a name—was my grandfather. I said you were Uncle Isaac."

"And he knows?"

"No," she said. "What good would that have done?"

"But you did," he cried. "But you did. Then what do you expect here?"

"Nothing."

"Then why did you come here? You said you were waiting in Aluschaskuna yesterday and he saw you. Why did you come this morning?"

"I'm going back North. Back home. My cousin brought me up the day before yesterday in his boat. He's going to take me on to Leland to get the train."

"Then go," he said. Then he cried again in that thin not loud and grieving voice: "Get out of here! I can do nothing for you! Cant nobody do nothing for you!" She moved; she was not looking at him again, toward the entrance. "Wait," he said. She paused again, obediently still, turning. He took up the sheaf of banknotes and laid it on the blanket at the foot of the cot and drew his hand back beneath the blanket. "There," he said.

Now she looked at the money, for the first time, one brief blank glance, then away again. "I dont need it. He gave me money last winter. Besides the money he sent to Vicksburg. Provided. Honor and code too. That was all arranged."

"Take it," he said. His voice began to rise again, but he stopped it. "Take it out of my tent." She came back to the cot and took up the money; whereupon once more he said, "Wait:" although she had not turned, still stooping, and he put out his hand. But, sitting, he could not complete the reach until she moved her hand, the single hand which held the money, until he touched it. He didn't grasp it, he merely touched it—the gnarled, bloodless, bone-light bone-dry old man's fingers touching for a second the smooth young flesh where the strong old blood ran after its long lost journey back to home. "Tennie's Jim," he said. "Tennie's Jim." He drew the hand back beneath the blanket again: he said harshly now: "It's a boy, I reckon. They usually are, except that one that was its own mother too."

"Yes," she said. "It's a boy." She stood for a moment longer, looking at him. Just for an instant her free hand moved as though she were about to lift the edge of the raincoat away from the child's face. But she did not. She turned again when once more he said Wait and moved beneath the blanket.

"Turn your back," he said. "I am going to get up. I aint got my pants on." Then he could not get up. He sat in the huddled blanket, shaking, while again she turned and looked down at him in dark interrogation. "There," he said harshly, in the thin and shaking old man's voice. "On the nail there. The tent-pole."

"What?" she said.

"The horn!" he said harshly. "The horn." She went and got it, thrust the money into the slicker's side pocket as if it were a rag, a soiled handkerchief, and lifted down the horn, the one which General Compson had left him in his will, covered with the unbroken skin from a buck's shank and bound with silver.

"What?" she said.

"It's his. Take it."

"Oh," she said. "Yes. Thank you."

"Yes," he said, harshly, rapidly, but not so harsh now and soon not harsh at all but just rapid, urgent, until he knew that his voice was running away with him and he had neither intended it nor could stop it: "That's right. Go back North. Marry: a man in your own race. That's the only salvation for you—for a while yet, maybe a long while yet. We will have to wait. Marry a black man. You are young, handsome, almost white; you could find a black man who would see in you what it was you saw in him, who would ask nothing of you and expect less and get even still less than that, if it's revenge you want. Then you will forget all this, forget it ever happened, that he ever existed —" until he could stop it at last and did, sitting there in his huddle of blankets during the instant when, without moving at all, she blazed silently down at him. Then that was gone too. She stood in the gleaming and still dripping slicker, looking quietly down at him from under the sodden hat.

"Old man," she said, "have you lived so long and forgotten so much that you dont remember anything you ever knew or felt or even heard about love?"

Then she was gone too. The waft of light and the murmur of the constant rain flowed into the tent and then out again as the flap fell. Lying back once more, trembling, panting, the blanket huddled to his chin and his hands crossed on his breast, he listened to the pop and snarl, the mounting then fading whine of the motor until it died away and once again the tent held only silence and the sound of rain. And cold too: he lay shaking faintly and steadily in it, rigid save for the shaking. This Delta, he thought: This Delta. *This land which man has deswamped and denuded and derivered in two generations so that white men can own plantations and commute every night to Memphis and black men own plantations and ride in jim crow cars to Chicago to live in millionaires' mansions on Lakeshore Drive, where white men rent farms and live like niggers and niggers crop on shares and live like animals, where cotton is planted and grows man-tall in the very cracks of the sidewalks, and usury and mortgage and bankruptcy and measureless wealth, Chinese and African and Aryan and Jew, all breed and spawn together until no man has time to say which one is which nor cares. . . .* No wonder the ruined woods I used to know dont cry for retribution! he thought: The people who have destroyed it will accomplish its revenge.

The tent flap jerked rapidly in and fell. He did not move save to turn his head and open his eyes. It was Legate. He went quickly to Edmonds' bed and stooped, rummaging hurriedly among the still-tumbled blankets.

"What is it?" he said.

"Looking for Roth's knife," Legate said. "I come back to get a horse. We got a deer on the ground." He rose, the knife in his hand, and hurried toward the entrance.

"Who killed it?" McCaslin said. "Was it Roth?"

"Yes," Legate said, raising the flap.

"Wait," McCaslin said. He moved, suddenly, onto his elbow. "What was it?" Legate paused for an instant beneath the lifted flap. He did not look back.

"Just a deer, Uncle Ike," he said impatiently. "Nothing

extra." He was gone; again the flap fell behind him, wafting out of the tent again the faint light and the constant and grieving rain. McCaslin lay back down, the blanket once more drawn to his chin, his crossed hands once more weightless on his breast in the empty tent.

"It was a doe," he said.

Go Down, Moses

I.

THE face was black, smooth, impenetrable; the eyes had seen too much. The negroid hair had been treated so that it covered the skull like a cap, in a single neat-ridged sweep, with the appearance of having been lacquered, the part trimmed out with a razor, so that the head resembled a bronze head, imperishable and enduring. He wore one of those sports costumes called ensembles in the men's shop advertisements, shirt and trousers matching and cut from the same fawn-colored flannel, and they had cost too much and were draped too much, with too many pleats; and he half lay on the steel cot in the steel cubicle just outside which an armed guard had stood for twenty hours now, smoking cigarettes and answering in a voice which was anything under the sun but a southern voice or even a negro voice, the questions of the spectacled young white man sitting with a broad census-taker's portfolio on the steel stool opposite:

"Samuel Worsham Beauchamp. Twenty-six. Born in the country near Jefferson, Mississippi. No family. No——"

"Wait." The census-taker wrote rapidly. "That's not the name you were sen—lived under in Chicago."

The other snapped the ash from the cigarette. "No. It was another guy killed the cop."

"All right. Occupation ——

"Getting rich too fast.

—none." The census-taker wrote rapidly. "Parents."

"Sure. Two. I dont remember them. My grandmother raised me."

"What's her name? Is she still living?"

"I dont know. Mollie Worsham Beauchamp. If she is, she's on Carothers Edmonds' farm seventeen miles from Jefferson, Mississippi. That all?"

The census-taker closed the portfolio and stood up. He was a year or two younger than the other. "If they dont know who you are here, how will they know—how do you expect to get home?"

The other snapped the ash from the cigarette, lying on the steel cot in the fine Hollywood clothes and a pair of shoes better than the census-taker would ever own. "What will that matter to me?" he said.

So the census-taker departed; the guard locked the steel door again. And the other lay on the steel cot smoking until after a while they came and slit the expensive trousers and shaved the expensive coiffure and led him out of the cell.

2.

On that same hot, bright July morning the same hot bright wind which shook the mulberry leaves just outside Gavin Stevens' window blew into the office too, contriving a semblance of coolness from what was merely motion. It fluttered among the county-attorney business on the desk and blew in the wild shock of prematurely white hair of the man who sat behind it—a thin, intelligent, unstable face, a rumpled linen suit from whose lapel a Phi Beta

Kappa key dangled on a watch chain—Gavin Stevens, Phi Beta Kappa, Harvard, Ph.D, Heidelberg, whose office was his hobby, although it made his living for him, and whose serious vocation was a twenty-two-year-old unfinished translation of the Old Testament back into classic Greek. Only his caller seemed impervious to it, though by appearance she should have owned in that breeze no more of weight and solidity than the intact ash of a scrap of burned paper —a little old negro woman with a shrunken, incredibly old face beneath a white headcloth and a black straw hat which would have fitted a child.

"Beauchamp?" Stevens said. "You live on Mr Carothers Edmonds' place."

"I done left," she said. "I come to find my boy." Then, sitting on the hard chair opposite him and without moving, she began to chant. "Roth Edmonds sold my Benjamin. Sold him in Egypt. Pharaoh got him——"

"Wait," Stevens said. "Wait, Aunty." Because memory, recollection, was about to mesh and click. "If you dont know where your grandson is, how do you know he's in trouble? Do you mean that Mr Edmonds has refused to help you find him?"

"It was Roth Edmonds sold him," she said. "Sold him in Egypt. I dont know whar he is. I just knows Pharaoh got him. And you the Law. I wants to find my boy."

"All right," Stevens said. "I'll try to find him. If you're not going back home, where will you stay in town? It may take some time, if you dont know where he went and you haven't heard from him in five years."

"I be staying with Hamp Worsham. He my brother."

"All right," Stevens said. He was not surprised. He had known Hamp Worsham all his life, though he had never seen the old Negress before. But even if he had, he still would not have been surprised. They were like that. You could know two of them for years; they might even have worked for you for years, bearing different names. Then suddenly you learn by pure chance that they are brothers or sisters.

He sat in the hot motion which was not breeze and listened to her toiling slowly down the steep outside stairs, remembering the grandson. The papers of that business had passed across his desk before going to the District Attorney five or six years ago—Butch Beauchamp, as the youth had been known during the single year he had spent in and out of the city jail: the old Negress' daughter's child, orphaned of his mother at birth and deserted by his father, whom the grandmother had taken and raised, or tried to. Because at nineteen he had quit the country and come to town and spent a year in and out of jail for gambling and fighting, to come at last under serious indictment for breaking and entering a store.

Caught red-handed, whereupon he had struck with a piece of iron pipe at the officer who surprised him and then lay on the ground where the officer had felled him with a pistol-butt, cursing through his broken mouth, his teeth fixed into something like furious laughter through the blood. Then two nights later he broke out of jail and was seen no more—a youth not yet twenty-one, with something in him from the father who begot and deserted him and who was now in the State Penitentiary for manslaughter—some seed not only violent but dangerous and bad.

And that's who I am to find, save, Stevens thought. Because he did not for one moment doubt the old Negress' instinct. If she had also been able to divine where the boy was and what his trouble was, he would not have been surprised, and it was only later that he thought to be surprised at how quickly he did find where the boy was and what was wrong.

His first thought was to telephone Carothers Edmonds, on whose farm the old Negress' husband had been a tenant for years. But then, according to her, Edmonds had already refused to have anything to do with it. Then he sat perfectly still while the hot wind blew in his wild white mane. Now he comprehended what the old Negress had meant. He remembered now that it was Edmonds who had actually sent the boy to Jefferson in the first place: he had caught the boy breaking into his commissary store and had ordered him off the place and had forbidden him ever to return. *And not the sheriff, the police,* he thought. *Something broader, quicker in scope.* . . . He rose and took his old fine worn panama and descended the outside stairs and crossed the empty square in the hot suspension of noon's beginning, to the office of the county newspaper. The editor was in—an older man but with hair less white than Stevens', in a black string tie and an old-fashioned boiled shirt and tremendously fat.

"An old nigger woman named Mollie Beauchamp," Stevens said. "She and her husband live on the Edmonds place. It's her grandson. You remember him—Butch Beauchamp, about five or six years ago, who spent a year in town, mostly in jail, until they finally caught him breaking into Rouncewell's store one night? Well, he's in worse trouble than that now. I dont doubt her at all. I just hope, for her sake as well as that of the great public whom I represent, that his present trouble is very bad and maybe final too——"

"Wait," the editor said. He didn't even need to leave his desk. He took the press association flimsy from its spike and handed it to Stevens. It was datelined from Joliet, Illinois, this morning:

> *Mississippi negro, on eve of execution for murder of Chicago policeman, exposes alias by completing census questionnaire. Samuel Worsham Beauchamp——*

Five minutes later Stevens was crossing again the empty square in which noon's hot suspension was that much nearer. He had thought that he was going home to his boarding house for the noon meal, but he found that he was not. *'Besides, I didn't lock my office door,'* he thought. Only, how under the sun she could have got to town from those seventeen miles. She may even have walked. "So it seems I didn't mean what I said I hoped," he said aloud, mounting the outside stairs again, out of the hazy and now windless sunglare, and entered his office. He stopped. Then he said,

"Good morning, Miss Worsham."

She was quite old too—thin, erect, with a neat, old-time piling of white hair beneath a faded hat of thirty years ago, in rusty black, with a frayed umbrella faded now until it was green instead of black. He had known her too all his life. She lived alone in the decaying house her father had left her, where she gave lessons in china-painting and, with the help of Hamp Worsham, descendant of one of her father's slaves, and his wife, raised chickens and vegetables for market.

"I came about Mollie," she said. "Mollie Beauchamp. She said that you——"

He told her while she watched him, erect on the hard chair where the old Negress had sat, the rusty umbrella leaning against her knee. On her lap, beneath her folded hands, lay an old-fashioned beaded reticule almost as big as a suitcase. "He is to be executed tonight."

"Can nothing be done? Mollie's and Hamp's parents belonged to my grandfather. Mollie and I were born in the same month. We grew up together as sisters would."

"I telephoned," Stevens said. "I talked to the Warden at Joliet, and to the District Attorney in Chicago. He had a fair trial, a good lawyer—of that sort. He had money. He was in a business called numbers, that people like him make money in." She watched him, erect and motionless. "He is a murderer, Miss Worsham. He shot that policeman in the back. A bad son of a bad father. He admitted, confessed it afterward."

"I know," she said. Then he realised that she was not looking at him, not seeing him at least. "It's terrible."

"So is murder terrible," Stevens said. "It's better this way." Then she was looking at him again.

"I wasn't thinking of him. I was thinking of Mollie. She mustn't know."

"Yes," Stevens said. "I have already talked with Mr Wilmoth at the paper. He has agreed not to print anything. I will telephone the Memphis paper, but it's probably too late for that. . . . If we could just persuade her to go on back home this afternoon, before the Memphis paper . . . Out there, where the only white person she ever sees is Mr Edmonds, and I will telephone him; and even if the other darkies should hear about it, I'm sure they wouldn't. And then maybe in about two or three months I could go out there and tell her he is dead and buried somewhere in the North. . . ." This time she was watching him with such an expression that he ceased talking; she sat there, erect on the hard chair, watching him until he had ceased.

"She will want to take him back home with her," she said.

"Him?" Stevens said. "The body?" She watched him. The expression was neither shocked nor disapproving. It merely embodied some old, timeless, female affinity for blood and grief. Stevens thought: *She has walked to town in this heat. Unless Hamp brought her in the buggy he peddles eggs and vegetables from.*

"He is the only child of her oldest daughter, her own dead first child. He must come home."

"He must come home," Stevens said as quietly. "I'll attend to it at once. I'll telephone at once."

"You are kind." For the first time she stirred, moved. He watched her hands draw the reticule toward her, clasping it. "I will defray the expenses. Can you give me some idea——?"

He looked her straight in the face. He told the lie without batting an eye, quickly and easily. "Ten or twelve dollars will cover it. They will furnish a box and there will be only the transportation."

"A box?" Again she was looking at him with that expression curious and detached, as though he were a child. "He is her grandson, Mr Stevens. When she took him to raise, she gave him my father's name—Samuel Worsham. Not just a box, Mr Stevens. I understand that can be done by paying so much a month."

"Not just a box," Stevens said. He said it in exactly the same tone in which he had said He must come home. "Mr Edmonds will want to help, I know. And I understand that old Luke Beauchamp has some money in the bank. And if you will permit me——"

"That will not be necessary," she said. He watched her open the reticule; he watched her count onto the desk twenty-five dollars in frayed bills and coins ranging down to nickels and dimes and pennies. "That will take care of the immediate expenses. I will tell her—You are sure there is no hope?"

"I am sure. He will die tonight."

"I will tell her this afternoon that he is dead then."

"Would you like for me to tell her?"

"I will tell her," she said.

"Would you like for me to come out and see her, then, talk to her?"

"It would be kind of you." Then she was gone, erect, her feet crisp and light, almost brisk, on the stairs, ceasing. He telephoned again, to the Illinois warden, then to an undertaker in Joliet. Then once more he crossed the hot, empty square. He had only to wait a short while for the editor to return from dinner.

"We're bringing him home," he said. "Miss Worsham and you and me and some others. It will cost——"

"Wait," the editor said. "What others?"

"I dont know yet. It will cost about two hundred. I'm not counting the telephones; I'll take care of them myself. I'll get something out of Carothers Edmonds the first time I catch him; I dont know how much, but something. And maybe fifty around the square. But the rest of it is you and me, because she insisted on leaving twenty-five with

me, which is just twice what I tried to persuade her it
would cost and just exactly four times what she can afford
to pay——"

"Wait," the editor said. "Wait."

"And he will come in on Number Four the day after tomorrow and we will meet it, Miss Worsham and his grandmother, the old nigger, in my car and you and me in yours.
Miss Worsham and the old woman will take him back
home, back where he was born. Or where the old woman
raised him. Or where she tried to. And the hearse out there
will be fifteen more, not counting the flowers——"

"Flowers?" the editor cried.

"Flowers," Stevens said. "Call the whole thing two hundred and twenty-five. And it will probably be mostly you
and me. All right?"

"No it aint all right," the editor said. "But it dont look
like I can help myself. By Jupiter," he said, "even if I
could help myself, the novelty will be almost worth it. It
will be the first time in my life I ever paid money for
copy I had already promised before hand I wont print."

"Have already promised before hand you will not print,"
Stevens said. And during the remainder of that hot and
now windless afternoon, while officials from the city hall,
and justices of the peace and bailiffs come fifteen and
twenty miles from the ends of the county, mounted the
stairs to the empty office and called his name and cooled
their heels a while and then went away and returned and
sat again, fuming, Stevens passed from store to store and
office to office about the square—merchant and clerk, proprietor and employee, doctor dentist lawyer and barber—
with his set and rapid speech: "It's to bring a dead nigger
home. It's for Miss Worsham. Never mind about a paper

to sign: just give me a dollar. Or a half a dollar then. Or a quarter then."

And that night after supper he walked through the breathless and star-filled darkness to Miss Worsham's house on the edge of town and knocked on the paintless front door. Hamp Worsham admitted him—an old man, belly-bloated from the vegetables on which he and his wife and Miss Worsham all three mostly lived, with blurred old eyes and a fringe of white hair about the head and face of a Roman general.

"She expecting you," he said. "She say to kindly step up to the chamber."

"Is that where Aunt Mollie is?" Stevens said.

"We all dar," Worsham said.

So Stevens crossed the lamplit hall (he knew that the entire house was still lighted with oil lamps and there was no running water in it) and preceded the Negro up the clean, paintless stairs beside the faded wallpaper, and followed the old Negro along the hall and into the clean, spare bedroom with its unmistakable faint odor of old maidens. They were all there, as Worsham had said—his wife, a tremendous light-colored woman in a bright turban leaning in the door, Miss Worsham erect again on a hard straight chair, the old Negress sitting in the only rocking chair beside the hearth on which even tonight a few ashes smoldered faintly.

She held a reed-stemmed clay pipe but she was not smoking it, the ash dead and white in the stained bowl; and actually looking at her for the first time, Stevens thought: *Good Lord, she's not as big as a ten-year-old child.* Then he sat too, so that the four of them—himself, Miss Worsham, the old Negress and her brother—made a circle about the brick hearth on which the ancient symbol of human coherence and solidarity smoldered.

"He'll be home the day after tomorrow, Aunt Mollie," he said. The old Negress didn't even look at him; she never had looked at him.

"He dead," she said. "Pharaoh got him."

"Oh yes, Lord," Worsham said. "Pharaoh got him."

"Done sold my Benjamin," the old Negress said. "Sold him in Egypt." She began to sway faintly back and forth in the chair.

"Oh yes, Lord," Worsham said.

"Hush," Miss Worsham said. "Hush, Hamp."

"I telephoned Mr Edmonds," Stevens said. "He will have everything ready when you get there."

"Roth Edmonds sold him," the old Negress said. She swayed back and forth in the chair. "Sold my Benjamin."

"Hush," Miss Worsham said. "Hush, Mollie. Hush now."

"No," Stevens said. "No he didn't, Aunt Mollie. It wasn't Mr Edmonds. Mr Edmonds didn't—" *But she cant hear me,* he thought. She was not even looking at him. She never had looked at him.

"Sold my Benjamin," she said. "Sold him in Egypt."

"Sold him in Egypt," Worsham said.

"Roth Edmonds sold my Benjamin."

"Sold him to Pharaoh."

"Sold him to Pharaoh and now he dead."

"I'd better go," Stevens said. He rose quickly. Miss Worsham rose too, but he did not wait for her to precede him. He went down the hall fast, almost running; he did not even know whether she was following him or not. *Soon I will be outside,* he thought. *Then there will be air, space, breath.* Then he could hear her behind him—the crisp, light, brisk yet unhurried feet as he had heard them descending the stairs from his office, and beyond them the voices:

"Sold my Benjamin. Sold him in Egypt."

"Sold him in Egypt. Oh yes, Lord."

He descended the stairs, almost running. It was not far now; now he could smell and feel it: the breathing and simple dark, and now he could manner himself to pause and wait, turning at the door, watching Miss Worsham as she followed him to the door—the high, white, erect, old-time head approaching through the old-time lamplight. Now he could hear the third voice, which would be that of Hamp's wife—a true constant soprano which ran without words beneath the strophe and antistrophe of the brother and sister:

"Sold him in Egypt and now he dead."

"Oh yes, Lord. Sold him in Egypt."

"Sold him in Egypt."

"And now he dead."

"Sold him to Pharaoh."

"And now he dead."

"I'm sorry," Stevens said. "I ask you to forgive me. I should have known. I shouldn't have come."

"It's all right," Miss Worsham said. "It's our grief."

And on the next bright hot day but one the hearse and the two cars were waiting when the southbound train came in. There were more than a dozen cars, but it was not until the train came in that Stevens and the editor began to notice the number of people, Negroes and whites both. Then, with the idle white men and youths and small boys and probably half a hundred Negroes, men and women

too, watching quietly, the Negro undertaker's men lifted
the gray-and-silver casket from the train and carried it to
the hearse and snatched the wreaths and floral symbols of
man's ultimate and inevitable end briskly out and slid the
casket in and flung the flowers back and clapped-to the
door.

Then, with Miss Worsham and the old Negress in
Stevens' car with the driver he had hired and himself and
the editor in the editor's, they followed the hearse as it
swung into the long hill up from the station, going fast
in a whining lower gear until it reached the crest, going
pretty fast still but with an unctuous, an almost bishoplike
purr until it slowed into the square, crossing it, circling the
Confederate monument and the courthouse while the mer-
chants and clerks and barbers and professional men who
had given Stevens the dollars and half-dollars and quarters
and the ones who had not, watched quietly from doors and
upstairs windows, swinging then into the street which at
the edge of town would become the country road leading
to the destination seventeen miles away, already picking
up speed again and followed still by the two cars containing the four people—the high-headed erect white woman,
the old Negress, the designated paladin of justice and truth
and right, the Heidelberg Ph.D.—in formal component
complement to the Negro murderer's catafalque: the slain
wolf.

When they reached the edge of town the hearse was
going quite fast. Now they flashed past the metal sign
which said Jefferson. Corporate Limit. and the pavement
vanished, slanting away into another long hill, becoming
gravel. Stevens reached over and cut the switch, so that
the editor's car coasted, slowing as he began to brake it,

the hearse and the other car drawing rapidly away now as though in flight, the light and unrained summer dust spurting from beneath the fleeing wheels; soon they were gone. The editor turned his car clumsily, grinding the gears, sawing and filling until it was back in the road facing town again. Then he sat for a moment, his foot on the clutch.

"Do you know what she asked me this morning, back there at the station?" he said.

"Probably not," Stevens said.

"She said, 'Is you gonter put hit in de paper?'"

"What?"

"That's what I said," the editor said. "And she said it again: 'Is you gonter put hit in de paper? I wants hit all in de paper. All of hit.' And I wanted to say, 'If I should happen to know how he really died, do you want that in too?' And by Jupiter, if I had and if she had known what we know even, I believe she would have said yes. But I didn't say it. I just said, 'Why, you couldn't read it, Aunty.' And she said, 'Miss Belle will show me whar to look and I can look at hit. You put hit in de paper. All of hit.'"

"Oh," Stevens said. *Yes,* he thought. *It doesn't matter to her now. Since it had to be and she couldn't stop it, and now that it's all over and done and finished, she doesn't care how he died. She just wanted him home, but she wanted him to come home right. She wanted that casket and those flowers and the hearse and she wanted to ride through town behind it in a car.* "Come on," he said. "Let's get back to town. I haven't seen my desk in two days."

WILLIAM FAULKNER, born New Albany, Mississippi, September 25, 1897—died July 6, 1962. Enlisted Royal Air Force, Canada, 1918. Attended University of Mississippi. Traveled in Europe 1925-1926. Resident of Oxford, Mississippi, where he held various jobs while trying to establish himself as a writer. First published novel, *Soldiers' Pay*, 1926. Writer in Residence at the University of Virginia 1957-1958. Awarded the Nobel Prize for Literature 1950.